MARKED BY THE MARQUESS

BOOK FOUR IN THE LORDS OF DISCIPLINE
SERIES

ALYSON CHASE

Cover image by Dar Albert.

Visit the author website: http://www.alysonchase.com

ISBN-13: 978-1-944802-06-6
ISBN-10: 1-944802-06-1

A Note from Alyson

This book is a work of fiction. While I am a big fan of history, and I did a not insubstantial amount of research for this book, I also made a lot of stuff up. There was a volcanic eruption in 1815 that led to 1816 being known as 'The Year Without Summer' but that is probably the limit of any historical veracity. (Oh, and Napoleon did have a troublesome brother. He is an interesting story in and of itself). If you see any inaccuracy in my book, I'll always appreciate a kindly email telling me the true story. Readers in this genre are impressively knowledgeable and I tip my hat to you.

Also, I feel the need to insert a word of caution. The characters in the book get up to some kinky good times. Sin and Winnifred definitely unleash their primal sides. There is light choking, biting, and slapping. Don't use this book as any sort of reference. Choking especially can be extremely dangerous. Please, have sex responsibly.

Chapter One

London, 1816

"Lord Stamworth is the most tight-fisted sot the ton has ever seen," John Chaucer, Earl of Summerset complained. The earl held a glass of suspiciously-pale wine up to the light. "I swear, he'd try to cheat the best lightskirt at The Black Rose, even if it meant he'd never get his Thomas wet again."

Sinclair Archer, Marquess of Dunkeld, had to agree. Stamworth's wine was little better than pink water. The man also threw the most tedious routs of anyone in London. Sin glared at the woman in the corner of the drawing room, plucking at the strings of a harp like they were the feathers from a chicken. A loud, dying chicken.

"Stamworth's wife is visiting her family in Bath." Sin picked up the dried-out bit of tongue on his plate and dropped it with disgust. "Perhaps that accounts for the poor hospitality." What he wouldn't give to be in Bath, be anywhere, rather than this dreary affair. If Liverpool hadn't requested his presence, he wouldn't have been caught dead in this bloody crush.

Another pair of chits sidled up to him and Summerset, trying to catch his friend's eye whilst avoiding his own. Only the bravest lass tried to turn the Scotsman's head. Despite his title, few set their caps at him. He was too large and untamed in appearance; his clothes, although made of the finest materials, always rumpled; his manner, too abrupt for the delicate English roses.

Which suited him fine. Whenever he settled down, it would be with a proud Scottish woman, one strong enough to hold her own.

A girl with lustrous brown hair swished her skirts and gazed back at his friend, her chin dipping seductively.

Sin grunted. Still. He did have the superior title over Summerset. These women were daft to not at least *try* to catch his eye.

Summerset arched an eyebrow, a perfect blond semi-circle. "I might forgive him the burnt seedcakes." He gave the chits next to him a wicked grin that sent them tittering behind their fans. "Even having no entertainment save the girl murdering the harp could have been excused. But I will not forgive serving this swill, not when Stamworth is reputed to have the best cellars in all of England. The greedy bastard doesn't want to share."

One of the girls pretended to swoon at the foul language.

Sin turned his back on her nonsense. If a girl spent her evening eavesdropping on men's conversations, she didn't have any right to object to its content. He grabbed his friend's elbow and dragged him into a deserted corner.

Summerset pulled a Pomona green pocket square from his jacket and brushed at the crease Sin's hand had left in the silk of his sleeve. "I know the sub-standard fare is aggravating, but that's no reason to assault an innocent, one-of-a-kind creation of Monsieur Jacques's."

"Don't be a halfwit." Sin shifted his weight. The girls were still eyeing his friend like a hunting dog did a fresh kill. Pampered, scheming coquettes, every last one. "Can we leave, or are there any other unsuitable women you wish to flirt with?"

"Every woman suits me." Summerset gave him a lazy smile that set Sin's teeth on edge. The hell of it was, his friend was right. Something about the sly fop had all the ladies raising their skirts. Luckily for the maters of the Beau

Monde, his friend tended not to turn his attentions on innocent maids.

"There's a game at Halliwell's tonight." Sin cracked his neck. "Our time would be better spent there."

Summerset cocked a shoulder against the wall and scanned the room. "And miss a meeting with our esteemed friend? Who knows what delightful little caper he'll send us on tonight. And stop tugging on your cravat. Not after my valet spent nearly an hour getting it just so."

Sin scowled but dropped his hands. "It was nary a minute I let your man fuss over me." And only because Summerset refused to leave his home unless Sin's 'travesty' of a knot was rectified. "Liverpool isn't showing. I'm done here. Let's go."

"One more drink." Summerset swirled the liquid in his glass and sniffed. "But it can't be this pig-swill."

"Fine." Sin squared his shoulders. "I'll get you some wine. The good stuff." Anything to escape this rout. And sneaking into their host's cellars was infinitely preferable to holding up the wall like a bluestocking.

Without waiting for his friend's response, Sin strode across the room, ignoring the raised hand of Lord Childers. The last thing he wanted was more stultifying talk on the merits of a Scottish referendum with a man who didn't know Hadrian's Wall from Stonehenge. The sounds of the ballroom disappeared as the door swung shut behind him. The hall was empty, and if Sin remembered the layout to this house correctly, the stairs down would be just around the corner. Without slowing, he plucked a taper from an elaborate silver candelabra sitting on a side table and trudged down the corridor.

He lightened his step, softening the sound of his boots as he made his way down past the kitchens and into the cellar. Old habits died hard, and entering unknown territory clomping as loudly as a shire horse was never optimal for survival.

He sighed. A mission right about now wouldn't have

gone amiss. Damn Liverpool for not showing. His mother's letters urging his return to Scotland were arriving more frequently, and if he didn't have a job soon to distract him, might become impossible to ignore.

The small wooden door to the wine cellar stood open, and a dim light flickered within.

Sin hesitated at the entrance but heard nothing. The steward might have left a candle burning if he needed to come down for more wine. If the cheap bastard Stamworth would let him.

He strolled down one corridor, bottles rising on either side. A slate sign at the top of each shelf listed the province and year of the wines across its dark surface.

Hmm, a '94 Bordeaux, an '02 Malaga, a.... Sin paused and lifted a bottle out of its slot. He blew dust from the brown glass. A 1783 hermitage from the Rhône valley. Sin pursed his lips. He preferred a good dram of whisky to grape juice, but even he knew he was holding a quality bottle of wine. And if their host ever watered down this vintage, Sin would bloody the man's nose himself.

"Drat," a soft voice muttered.

Sin whipped around but his aisle remained empty. He padded to the end of the row and peered around the corner. The unmistakable figure of a woman stood feet away, her back to Sin, the candle she held flickering precariously close to an escaped curl as she tugged at something by her leg.

"Release me, you infernal bit of metal," she muttered.

"Madam?" Sin glanced around the cellar, searching for a companion. The woman's gown wasn't the rich jewel tones common of married women at these types of functions, nor was it the washed-out pastels favored by the chits making calf-eyes at Summerset. Was she a miss? "Are you—"

She whipped around, eyes wide, and pressed a hand to her heart. The candle in her other hand tilted ever closer....

Sin leapt forward, snatching her wrist, and eliciting a muffled shriek.

Her chest heaved. "I assure you I carry no coin upon my person. If your intent is to rob me, you will be sorely disappointed."

Sin grimaced and dropped her hand. Summerset might jest that he looked a ruffian, but he was a marquess, damn it. He might refuse to wear the ballocks-hugging silk pantaloons and jewel-encrusted boots so many of the aristocracy favored, but he hardly looked a pauper.

"You were about to set your hair on fire." He slid his gaze down her figure. She was young, early twenties, he guessed. Her dress had a modest neckline, and lacked the ribbons, bows, and other whatnot he so detested. Her form was sturdy, and the top of her head reached his shoulder. A very tall woman, indeed. "Missus...?"

She held the candle further from her body. "Miss. Miss Winnifred Hannon. And I assure you, I was not. I am most careful when it comes to flammable materials."

"What are you doing down in Lord Stamworth's wine cellars?" He looked over his shoulder, but still no companion or liaison of hers appeared. "Are you a guest of his?"

"I am." She pressed her shoulders back. "My father is a friend of Lord Stamworth's. And you are, sir?" She hiccupped softly, and pressed her free hand to her mouth looking adorably abashed.

"Sinclair Archer, Marquess of Dunkeld, at your service." Lifting his own candle, he held it up to her eyes. They were a lovely light blue with deep, dark centers. He leaned towards her and sniffed. "Are you intoxicated?"

"I beg your pardon?" She glared up at him, her chin lifting in a manner that made him smile. "Why, I would never"—hiccup—"do something so disreputable."

Blowing out his candle, he lay it on a shelf. He leaned around her and plucked two bottles of wine from the top of the barrel behind her. One was uncorked, the other still retained its wax seal. He raised an eyebrow.

Cocking her head, she pursed her lips. "There is a

perfectly logical explanation for those."

"I was certain there must be." He widened his stance and settled in to hear it. Truly, he should have spent the whole of the rout in the wine cellar. It was certainly more entertaining.

"A colleague of my father's wanted to taste a vintage from 1810, preferable a Madeira, and was having trouble finding one on his home island." The lass narrowed her eyes, looking as put upon as a tutor whose student hadn't learned his tables. "Trade ships aren't sailing to Java every day, you know."

His lips twitched. "Of course not."

"So, knowing that Lord Stamworth keeps an excellent cellar, and also knowing my father was loath to ask him for a bottle...." She raised her hands as if the solution was obvious.

"You came down to take it." He nodded. He could appreciate such a direct resolution to a problem. "And the second, open bottle?"

She flushed. "Mr. Raguhram's theory concerning the influence of volcanic eruptions on agriculture was persuasive. I wanted to taste it for myself."

Sin blinked. Whatever he had expected to hear, that wasn't it. Was she in earnest, or spewing nonsense due to her half-sprung state? He raised the bottle to the candlelight. Half empty. "That was quite the taste."

Miss Hannon pressed her lips flat. "I only had a sip or two. The rest I spilled over there." She pointed over her shoulder. "Now, I really must be returning to my father." She took a step forward and was pulled up short. She sighed. "Once I free my skirts from a nail."

Sin returned the wine bottles to the top of the barrel. "Here, let me." Squatting down, he pushed her skirts aside, ignoring her sharp intake of breath, and found where she was snagged. The slippery fabric of her gown refused to slide back over the nail head. Sin pinched the skirt above the nail and pulled, a loud rent echoing in the cavernous cellar. "There." He stood. "You're free."

She thrust the candle into his hand and twisted her skirts, stooping to examine the muslin. She stared at the tear in the gown, glared at him and slowly straightened.

Sin cocked his shoulder against the nearest shelf, preparing for his tongue-lashing. Women and their clothes. She'd been stuck; now she was free. Really, there was no reason for her to complain.

But she surprised him. Dipping her chin, she said, "Thank you, Lord Dunkeld." She picked up the unopened wine and cradled it to her stomach. "Now, I really must be going."

He held out a hand. "Wait." He had too many unanswered questions for her to leave him now. "What is this Mr. Ragu..."

"Mr. Raguhram," she provided helpfully.

"Mr. Raguhram's theory? And why would tasting a bottle of wine help to prove it?"

"One cannot prove a hypothesis." She tapped the toe of her beaded slipper against the dusty floor in a rapid tattoo and peered over his shoulder. "Multiple tests with positive results may lead one to give the hypothesis a high level of probability, but replicated tests can only serve to disprove a theory."

"Is that right?" He should introduce this chit to Summerset. He was the chemist of their motley crew of spies and would find a woman with the same bent a delightful diversion. His gaze drifted down her well-built form. Then again, perhaps Summerset should stay well away from this one. She didn't seem the sort to tolerate his friend's easy virtue, and the earl might see her as a challenge. "You're very decided in your opinions for one so young."

He forgo adding 'and for a woman', although in England that was certainly true. He received nothing but weather reports from the Sassenach females of his acquaintance. One spouting about volcanoes and experiments was certainly novel.

All the color drained from her face.

Sin unfolded to his full height. "Are you al—"

"Fine." She plastered on an empty smile, one that he'd seen practiced by society ladies the world over. "I'm merely repeating my father's words on the subject. He is the man of science. If you have any questions about his or his colleagues' theories, you should direct them to him."

Voices echoed hollowly from behind them, growing louder and more distinct as the men attached to them neared the cellar's door.

"... and I insist," Summerset said.

"But it really isn't necessary for you to come down here yourself." A man, Lord Stamworth most like, sniffed. "My steward and I are perfectly capable of fetching more wine ourselves."

Sin whipped his head over his shoulder but couldn't see the entrance. Shelves of wine blocked his view. He looked back at Miss Hannon, who had frozen like a stag before a wildcat. He held a finger to his lips and motioned for her to go deeper into the cellar. If he could get Summerset and their host out of the basement without noticing her presence, all would be well.

Nodding, she spun. One long, loose curl of sandy-brown hair swung out and kissed the flame of his candle. The tendril lit up with a hiss.

"Confound it!" He dropped the candle, ignoring as it sputtered out, and reached for her. He clapped at the flame, his fingers catching in her hair.

She stumbled into him with a cry.

Wrapping his arm around her waist, he steadied her. "Are you all right?" Nothing around her glowed, so he assumed the flames had all been extinguished.

Her head scraped against his shoulder, but he couldn't tell if it was a nod or a shake.

Until the darkness lessened, and a light rose from the end of their corridor. Then he could see the horror etched on her face as Lord Stamworth called, "Winnifred? Is that you?"

Grimly, Sin set Miss Hannon away from his body and stepped between her and the men peering at them from down the aisle. Summerset's face matched Miss Hannon's in alarm. Lord Stamworth merely looked shocked.

Sin sighed, his shoulders sagging. He turned his back on his friend and faced Miss Hannon. "I'm sorry for this."

"I don't suppose if we logically explained the chain of events that led us here it would be of any use?" She set her bottle of wine down and tugged at the hem of her sleeve.

"I'm afraid not."

She nodded once, and a veil of dead calm dropped over her features. He never would have guessed that only moments ago she had been near panic. "Then no need to apologize," she said. "We can only accept life's challenges as they're presented."

A challenge? Acid burned in his gut. He supposed that was one way to look at it. A prison of societal expectations was another.

She smoothed her hands down the stomach of her gown and gave him a placid smile.

One he wished he could duplicate. His breath hitched. Who was this woman? She'd slipped on a mask as easily as a spy. Was she the lass who lectured about scientific process, the woman frightened of the future she'd just been thrown into, or the prim miss with an arsenal of false smiles?

His shoulders hardened to blocks. No matter. Whoever she was, she was about to become his wife.

Chapter Two

"We can figure a way out of this." Summerset stalked back and forth across the small vestry in St. Katherine's church. He raked a hand through his fair hair, mussing the artful locks.

Sin stared at his reflection in the full-length mirror. The swallowtail jacket and trousers were of simple black wool and his top hat was a sensible height, but still he felt a fool. Like a trussed-up dandy. It must be the shoes. Summerset had allowed him to forfeit breeches or pantaloons in favor of his trousers, but had put his stylish pump down at the boots Sin wanted to wear. "I think you're more upset over my upcoming nuptials than I am." He turned to the side. The plaid waistcoat was a trifle showy, but an appropriate nod to his heritage.

At least here in London he didn't have to wear a bloody kilt.

Summerset tossed his hat onto the chair by the door. "Why the sodding hell aren't you more upset? Getting leg-shackled just because you were caught alone with a chit. You didn't even take your pleasure from the crime of a seduction yet you still are enduring the punishment." He crossed his arms. "And what the hell kind of name is Winnifred? She's a bluestocking if ever I saw one. Definitely not someone you want to be your companion. For life." His friend made a moue of disgust with his lips, as though the very idea of a life-partner offended him.

Sin arched an eyebrow. If Miss Winnifred Hannon was how bluestockings were built nowadays, he had sought out liaisons in the wrong quarters. No, his betrothed wasn't some dainty little chit who barely came up to his chest, and he could definitely picture her surrounded by stacks of books, but her tall, sturdy form was pleasing to the eye. Her skin was clear and her eyes intelligent. And her wide hips and high bosom... well those definitely made an impression. What more could a man want?

"I find her handsome enough," he said mildly.

Summerset ignored that. "Winnifred. Do you suppose she goes by Winnie?" He huffed out a breath. "Good Gad, you'll be Sinnie and Winnie. How nauseating."

"No one will call us Sinnie and Winnie." He glared at his friend. "Not if he wants his tongue to remain in his mouth."

Summerset closed his eyes. "I'm sorry we didn't leave the rout when you wanted. None of this would have happened if I hadn't forced you to stay."

Sin snorted. His friend was tall, but Sin still had several inches on him and probably double the bulk. " *You* cannot force me to do anything I don't wish." He fingered the auburn tail of his queue. Perhaps he should have cut his hair to fashion for his wedding.

"Damn it, Sin. This isn't the time for jokes." Summerset kicked a chair, the emeralds on his heeled-boots glimmering in the sunlight slanting through the window. "Marriage is for life."

Sin went to his friend and laid a hand on his shoulder. "John, it had to happen sometime. Unlike some other poor sops, I don't need to marry for money. It might as well be to Miss Hannon. She seems as tolerable as anyone else." Tolerable, and puzzling. The two of them had only met once more before this rushed affair, in the presence of her disappointed father. The woman seemed to take the forced marriage in stride, giving no further hints of distress. No hints of any emotion. Perhaps she was as practical as he. A wedding would have been in her near future if she didn't want to be on the shelf.

His friend's shoulder was hard as a rock under his hand. "How do you know this wasn't a trap on her part. A marquess is quite the coup for the daughter of a botanist, even one who used to be under the tutelage of the Royal gardener and has befriended some of the ton. If she arranged her own disgrace, you cannot reward her with marriage."

Sin arched an eyebrow. "She was in the cellar before me. Do you think she ensconced herself among the wine bottles hoping someone with a title would wander down for a drink?"

"Perhaps she overheard us complaining of the wine...."

"And predicted that I would enter the cellar to pilfer my own bottle, racing ahead of me to get there first?" Sin shook his head. "Truly, your censure is unjustified. The woman is blameless in this. It was an unfortunate set of circumstances; one I must make the best of."

Summerset kicked a cabinet, his heel making a half-moon crescent in the soft wood. "She's dull, as tedious and flat as her dish-water hair. And she showed no emotion over this marriage whatsoever. She was disinterested. Cold. It will be like bedding a very large icicle."

"How would you know she's dull?"

"You forget, while you were making arrangements with her father, I sat with the girl. She didn't ask about her future husband or question me about Kenmore Castle. One would think a woman would be curious about her new home. She spoke only of her father's experiments and the practicalities of travel to Scotland."

Sin considered. She hadn't seemed dull in the cellar. A bit queer, perhaps, but he'd found her slightly inebriated discussion charming.

"I don't give a toss about a woman's hair color," he told Summerset. "And you know I prefer bigger women." And as for being bored in bed.... He grunted and pushed that disturbing thought away. He'd knock down that bridge if and when he came to it.

Summerset flapped his hand at him. "Yes, yes, you're scared of crushing a Pocket Venus, I know. But this is—"

"Enough. It's done." Sin turned back to the mirror and smoothed the end of his cravat under his waistcoat. "At least my mother will be happy. She's been trying to marry me off for years."

"She'll have your ballocks for marrying without her in attendance." Summerset heaved a sigh. "Perhaps you can yet delay the wedding. Say you want your family and friends to attend. We can figure something out."

"No delays."

A knock sounded at the door and a lined-faced topped with grey hair popped through the opening. "Gentlemen," Liverpool said as he slipped through and shut the door behind him. "This was truly the last place I expected to find you."

Summerset scowled. "Where the devil were you two weeks ago? If you'd met us at Stamworth's party, as you'd requested, none of this would have bloody happened."

The prime minister drew his bushy eyebrows together. "I had urgent business in Algiers." Only those close to him would hear the steel warning underlying his words. "Now I've returned." He nodded at Sin. "Are you going on a bridal tour?"

Sin shook his head. "No. I think it best to introduce my bride to her new home. We'll be traveling to my estate in Scotland directly after the breakfast."

Liverpool clapped his hands together. "Then my timing is perfect. There have been rumblings of discontent from our brothers in the North that are beginning to worry me. I'd like you to investigate, see if there is anything England needs to be concerned over."

Summerset planted his hands on his hips. "Bridal tour or no, he will be a newly married man. You cannot expect him to forgo his honeymoon."

Sin barely restrained his eyeroll. Even with such fervent objections to Sin's marriage, Summerset would still expect him to spend all of his time bedding his new wife.

Sin brushed a fleck of lint from his arm. "I'm sure your concerns are unjustified. The Scottish are always angry with our southern neighbors." And with good reason. Ever since the Treaty of Union a hundred years ago, the English had been treating their "brothers" with anything but brotherly love. Scotland's wealth and power seemed to flow south in a never-ending river of enforced tribute.

"I'd like you to look into it just the same. Determine if there is an organized power behind the disturbances." Liverpool tucked his thumb between two buttons on his waistcoat and scratched his rounded belly with his fingers. "We can't afford another rebellion. As one of only sixteen Scottish representatives in the House of Lords, one would hope you'd be interested in helping to maintain the peace between our two lands."

Sin inclined his head. According to the letters from his steward and his mother, his people *were* a bit tetchy. The crops were doing poorly this year and their discontent was to be expected. But if Liverpool wanted a report on each and every bellyache, he'd give it to him.

Any work for the Crown would be preferable to the drudgery of managing his estate.

Liverpool cocked his head and ran his gaze up and down Sin's form. "You know no one would fault you for not marrying some nameless chit, regardless of the circumstances in which you were found. Her disgrace wouldn't extend to you."

Summerset threw up his hands. "Exactly what I've been trying to tell him."

Sin snorted. The power that a name held for the English. If Miss Hannon had been Lady Hannon, how different their attitudes would be. "I was the cause of harm to Miss Hannon's reputation. She is no less deserving of the protection of marriage than any other lass."

"There have been odder alliances in your family's history." Liverpool shrugged. "I wish you well."

Sin narrowed his eyes, wondering to which alliance the prime minister was referring.

Liverpool paused at the door. "Let me know if the situation in Scotland requires more men. Bloodshed must be avoided at all costs." And he slipped out the door, his presence as fleeting as a ghost.

"Well." Sin tugged at his lapels. "Shall we get started?"

Summerset stopped him at the door with a hand on his sleeve. "I know you are determined in this marriage, but Montague, Rothchild, and Sutton would want to be here. Give our friends time to come in from their estates."

Sin rubbed his chest. All four of his closest friends *should* be here, not just Summerset. But it couldn't be helped. He turned for the door. "I'll throw a ball for everyone to meet my wife. That will have to do." His hand paused over the latch. *His wife.* That was a phrase he hadn't imagined himself uttering for a long while.

It rolled around his mind. In mere minutes, he would have a wife. Another person who was his responsibility. Under his care and protection.

The idea didn't fill his stomach with dread, not like the thought of the tenants and servants of his estate did. So many lives a marquess was responsible for. He'd felt nothing but an imposter since inheriting the title at age thirteen, knowing that regardless of how smart a decision he rendered, how sensible a policy he laid down, he was always just one misstep away from destroying everything his forefathers had built.

But the idea of attending to the wants and desires of one woman for the rest of his life was nothing short of intriguing. A challenge instead of a yoke around his neck.

He pushed through the door and strode to his spot by the altar, Summerset a step behind.

His wife. The words had a nice ring to them.

* * *

Winnifred's father stood at the small stained-glass

window, his hands clasped behind his back. Red-toned light filtered onto his face, deepening the appearance of the grooves that lined his forehead.

"What were you thinking?" he asked her for the hundredth time. "Why would you visit Stamworth's cellars alone?"

Winnifred stared at her reflection in the small mirror on the wall. She was pale, but that couldn't be helped. It matched how she felt. Faded. Detached. Once the initial terror of knowing her life had upended had passed, she'd felt nothing. Two weeks of impassively listening to her father's rebukes. Fifteen days of organizing her life in preparation for her move.

She knew little of her future husband, but she appreciated the speed with which he'd arranged for a common license, and the efficiency with which he'd organized the wedding. If he was as diligent in all things, they should have as good a chance of suiting as any other couple with an arranged marriage.

"You know why." She pinched her cheeks to no effect. "Mr. Raguhram asked us to find an 1810 vintage in his letter. I'll admit acceding to his request would only have sated his curiosity, not accomplished anything of significance to test his hypothesis. But after all the information he's been kind enough to exchange with us, I felt it was the least we could do."

"You should have brought the bottle to me immediately, not lingered in the cellar." He twisted his lips, as though he'd tasted something bitter.

"Yes, father." If she had, her own chances of tasting the wine to see if she could detect any notes of ash would have been next to nonexistent. And she'd been curious. Did a volcanic eruption on the other side of the world affect the flavor of grapes grown in Spain? Could an ash cloud travel so far?

Her heart squeezed. Such questions were no longer her concern. All her work was at an end. Even had the natural philosophers of her correspondence been willing to maintain their exchange of ideas with her without the pretext of being her father's secretary, no marchioness would be allowed such an eccentricity. There would be no more 'assisting' with her father's experiments. No further study into the effects of chemical agents on the local flora. The one bastion of pure rationality that she could subsume herself within was no longer available. All that remained was the management of household affairs that would be expected of her.

Hardly sufficient to keep her mind engaged.

She sucked in a sharp breath, battling back the nausea that burbled in her stomach. Alas, she did feel something, after all.

"At least you're marrying well. I've had nothing but congratulations from friends, and a slew of new people wishing to become my friend." Her father turned. "Having a marquess as my future son-in-law has made me popular."

Winnifred smoothed her hands down the bodice of her pale blue gown. That popularity hadn't extended to her. Until she was safely wed, she was still the girl who had been caught in a compromising position. She didn't blame the caution of her acquaintances, but when facing marriage to a stranger she realized it would have been nice had she cultivated true friendships. A woman to share her concerns with, perhaps someone already married who could give her some guidance.

The role her mother should have taken.

Her father frowned. "I'm only sorry he's a Scot."

"He doesn't sound Scottish." She'd wondered about that. He had the auburn hair and rougher appearance of their northern neighbors, but his accent was as cultured as any Eton-educated man.

"Well, hopefully he's been civilized." Her father stepped forward and took her hands. "You look lovely. I only wish your mother were here to see this."

The back of her eyes burned, and she dropped her

gaze. A knock at the door thankfully prevented them from traveling down that road any farther.

"It's time." She turned and tucked her hand into the crook of his arm. She led him out the door and down a corridor. The double doors to the nave stood open, and they paused between them.

The Marquess of Dunkeld stood at the altar, his stylish friend by his side. Her future husband was clean-shaven today, his hair neatly swept back into a low queue tied with a black ribbon. The tailoring of his jacket and green plaid waistcoat displayed a broad chest and thick arms. His thighs were as wide across as birch trunks, and he stood as though ready to take on an army of invaders. His size was intimidating, the set of his mouth stern.

Her belly quivered.

Dunkeld's eyes alit on her, and he gave her the smallest of nods, an acknowledgement that they were in this jumble together, and it settled some of her nerves. She pulled her shoulders back. It was, after all, only marriage. A condition that was the lot of the majority of women. Nothing to make a fuss over. She was observant and adaptable; she would analyze her husband to determine the proper actions that would make this union a success.

Winnifred took a deep breath and the first step towards her new life.

Her father patted her hand as they slowly paced down the aisle. "I always could count on you to face things sensibly," he whispered. "Just think. My daughter. A marchioness. And he's a member of the House of Lords, you know. You'll visit London often. But I will miss you."

She squeezed his arm. She hated to abandon him. When her mother had left, he hadn't risen from bed for a month. But he was as practical as she. They both knew the time had to come.

He leaned in to kiss her cheek before handing her off to the marquess. Dunkeld's hand swallowed her own, and he held hers gingerly, as though afraid she would break.

Looking up, she gave him her most reassuring smile. She would make this man a good wife. Care for him and their children, if they were so blessed. Be reserved and sensible in all things.

And he would never suspect the truth about her.

Chapter Three

"You don't mind that we left straight-away?" Sin eyed his wife as the carriage jostled her from side-to-side. She'd spoken hardly a word during their wedding breakfast. Made no complaints when he'd bustled her into his carriage to head for home straight after. Either the events of the day had left her in a mild state of shock or he'd married the most biddable woman in history.

She adjusted her cap. "Not at all. I'm eager to see my new home. How long until we reach Scotland?"

"We'll be on the road about twelve days." He quirked his lips. "Not the most comfortable way to begin a marriage."

"Oh?" She turned her wide blue eyes on him. They were a lovely light color; like the sky on a bright, sunny day. "I wasn't aware marriage was intended to be comfortable."

He snorted. She hadn't intended to be diverting, but he found her amusing all the same. No, he supposed there might be a reason comfort wasn't mentioned in the vows. Sin shifted on his seat, a damn spring poking into his arse. Something else that wasn't comfortable. He rarely rode in his carriage, preferring to travel on the back of a horse, and the contraption had become worn down. But he had a wife to consider now. It was time for the carriage to be refurbished or replaced.

"I intend to make you most comfortable." A particularly deep rut jolted the carriage, and Winnifred bounced. His gaze dropped to her bosom, his groin growing tight. He intended to make her content in many ways. A dutiful husband should see to all his wife's needs. He slapped his glove against his thigh. Damn family tradition. Twelve days was a long time to wait.

She looked out the window, giving him the profile of a most stubborn-looking chin. But her words were as bland as porridge. "And I you, husband."

"Sinclair. Or Sin, if you prefer."

She faced him. "Pardon?"

Sin leaned forward, resting his forearms on his knees. "I have yet to hear you use my Christian name."

"As you wish, Sinclair."

He shoved back, feeling disgruntled for no reason he could think of. It was every man's dream to have a woman so acquiescent as a wife. Picking up his hat, he turned it around in his hands. "You never did tell me about this theory of your father's. Something about this damned dark summer." The sun was being a coy bitch this season. When it should have been shining its strongest, making their crops grow tall, it played peekaboo through a haze that seemed to stretch endlessly.

Winnifred linked her gloved fingers together and placed her hands on her lap. "It was more a theory of one of my father's colleagues. Mr. Raguhram lives in Dutch East Indies. He believes a volcanic eruption in the southern hemisphere is the cause of our current weather."

"One volcano would disrupt the weather half a globe away?" He arched an eyebrow. That hardly seemed likely, but then, he'd never witnessed such an event. He had no conception of how powerful an eruption could be.

She raised one shoulder. "That was his theory. I have no opinion on the matter."

Did she have any opinions? She'd asked for no special concessions for their wedding, no preferences on the food served at their breakfast, no concern over which church Sin chose. Her agreeableness was highly irritating.

"And how did drinking half a bottle of wine help prove, excuse me, disprove, that theory?" A muscle in his right thigh cramped, and Sin stretched his leg out, his boot resting on the seat beside Winnifred.

She gave him a reproachful look. "Tasting the wine wouldn't in itself disprove anything. Mr. Raguhram asked to taste an 1810 vintage merely for anecdotal reasons."

Sin tilted his head. "Why 1810?"

"There was another eruption the year before. Not on the scale of this past year's one, but large enough in Mr. Raguhram's estimation to provide similar effects, that an episode half a world away could drop ash in Spain." She played with the lace cuff on her glove. "Environmental effects have been known to alter the flavor of wine. Grapes grown next to a lavender field will display elements of that flower. And grapes grown in an atmosphere of ash, should likewise develop its flavor. As I said, purely anecdotal evidence."

Sin pursed his lips. The idea was intriguing. He was more a scotch drinker, of course, but Summerset and Montague swore they could taste a myriad of flavors in a glass of wine that were undetectable to Sin. He tasted red or white.

"Your father and Mr. Raguhram weren't the ones who tasted the wine." Why he felt it necessary to poke at her, discover the woman behind the facade, he didn't know. But they were man and wife now. A married couple shouldn't be subject to artifice and polite pleasantries. He wouldn't go through life with only the barest acquaintanceship with the woman bound to him.

A slight stain pinkened her creamy complexion. "I was thirsty."

Sin huffed. "And? Did you detect traces of ash?"

She stared out the window again. "I wouldn't know. My familiarity with spirits and wine is limited."

"Hmph." Sin glanced out his own window and shifted position. Carriages weren't made for men his size.

Winnifred slid to the side of her seat. "If you'd like, you can stretch your other leg up on the bench."

Sin did so, his leg muscles singing with relief. "Aren't you accommodating."

She blinked. "Shouldn't I be so?"

"I don't know who you should be." He pinned her with a look. "I'm wondering who you are."

The lace edge of her glove crumpled under her fingers. "I don't understand. If I've displeased you, you only need tell me how you'd like me to behave."

What the...? Sin slammed his boots down to the floor. "I don't know how ye English ladies like to behave when wed, but in Scotland, we like our women to have minds of their own. I dunnae want to be telling you how to behave. You're my wife, not my dog."

"I see," she said faintly.

He doubted that. "You haven't asked me one question. Not about the home I'm taking you to, my family who lives there, your duties as marchioness. Aren't you curious?"

She fiddled with that damn lace, and Sin clenched his fists to keep from ripping the blasted frippery off her gloves.

"Yes," she finally said. "Yes, I am curious. Tell me about my future home. Please. Where is your estate located?"

Settling back into his seat, Sin crossed one boot over the opposite knee. "About one hundred miles north of the English border. We have roughly thirty thousand acres, and Castle Kenmore is about equal distant to Glasgow and Edinburgh. It's a damn drafty place in the winter but otherwise comfortable enough."

"Do you spend much time there?" She cocked her head. "Your accent hardly shows. Except when you're impassioned. It... it revealed itself a bit when you were yelling." She gave him a tentative smile, a true one this time, and the pressure in his chest eased.

"That wasn't yelling, wife." The edge of his lip curled up. "And I've spent most of my life in England. First in school, and now with my duties in the House of Lords. But never doubt that I'm a Scot, through and through."

She scooted forward in her seat. "Does it bother you having an English wife? I had a Scottish friend when I was younger, and he said his parents would have shunned him had he come home with a Sassenach."

He bit back a grin at her pronunciation of the Scottish word. "English, Scottish, French, it matters not. You're mine now." Something velvety slid through his veins at those words.

Her lips parted. The bottom one was full, plump, and the desire to scrape it between his teeth gripped him.

Winnifred cleared her throat. "What will my duties as marchioness be? Gentlewomen have been raised to be noblemen's wives, but I have not. I will need some time to learn."

Sin considered. Between his steward, butler, and his mother, the Dunkeld estate ran smoothly. With little interference on his part, as he liked. He didn't rightly know what his wife's duties would be. "We'll have to ask my mother."

She nodded. "What are your major crops and what are their yields? What type of irrigation system do you employ?"

"Trench irrigation, and the usual crops. Barley, wheat, potatoes, that sort of thing." Had they added the corn his steward had talked about last year? Sin couldn't remember.

"And your yield?"

He hardened his jaw. Perhaps having her ask questions hadn't been the best of ideas. He glared at his boots. His father would have known the answer to any question about Kenmore. Would have known which crop was their biggest producer, which tenants perhaps needed a little more help. Sin could help bring in the harvest with the best of them, but he would never have the acumen to run the estate like his father.

Which was why he preferred being a spy. Hunting down an enemy was straightforward. Stopping them as easy as a hammer pounding a nail.

Managing an estate of 30,000 acres, with over 600 people, servants, tenants, and their families, all depending upon him, was a wee bit outside of his ken.

Winnifred worried the lace. "I apologize. My father's work on botany has given me an especial interest in agriculture. I've learned a bit about it from him. But your business is your own."

"It's fine." Leaning forward, he captured her hand, stilling her agitated movements. The sleeve of her jacket rucked under his touch, and warm skin met his palm. Her pulse leapt beneath his fingers, and Sin realized this was the first time he'd actually touched her flesh.

He stroked her wrist with his thumb, that small patch of skin an enticing tease.

She sucked her bottom lip into her mouth and let it out with a pop. "You did wish me to ask questions."

"Aye. Be yourself with me, that's all I ask." Unlike the tenants and servants of Dunkeld. Always simpering, bowing, and scraping to their marquess, telling him how great his ideas were, how generous, even though he had nothing to do with them. Even his mother couldn't be counted on to tell him the truth. She refused to say what Sin had always known.

That he'd never be the marquess his father had been.

"I've never been married before, either," he said. "I am as ignorant as you as to the proper form of conduct between husband and wife. But if we're to make it a success, we'll need to be honest with each other. Tell each other our needs; help each other to flourish."

"A partnership?" She narrowed her eyes, and he could tell she didn't believe him. Didn't trust him although he'd given her no reason not to.

But they'd known each other all of fifteen days. Trust took time to develop. Trust and affection and, if they were fortunate, love.

He slid his fingertips from her skin, missing the contact instantly. Desire for his wife wouldn't be an issue, at least.

She inhaled, her bosom rising.

Sin averted his eyes. No, the only problem would be how to keep his hands off his wife until they reached Kenmore.

Damn traditions.

He pounded on the ceiling, and the carriage rocked to a halt.

"Why are we stopping?" She leaned towards the window, looking outside. "There's nothing here."

"I need to ride horseback." He pushed open the door and hopped down, avoiding the steps. "Call out if you need anything." He shut the door on his wife, cutting off the sight of her soft skin and the faintest scent of oranges that surrounded her.

It was going to be a blasted long twelve days.

Chapter Four

Winnifred took her husband's hand and stepped down from the carriage. She arched her back, hearing a pop, and sighed. After eight days of travel, she never wanted to pack a trunk again. And there were still four more nights before they reached Sinclair's home.

Her home.

He led her into the public house, a squat building at the intersection of two roads. Settling her at a table in the corner of the room, he left to make arrangements for their room and keep. As he had every night. And in that room, they'd sleep side-by-side, her under the covers and him atop, never touching.

She peeled off her gloves and dropped them on the table, her stomach a bundle of knots. While she had trepidations about the marital bed, the fact that her husband seemed to hold no interest in it was even more worrisome. She knew he'd felt honor-bound to marry her, but was she so unappealing that this would be a marriage in name only?

Sinclair returned, followed by a man and a woman bearing large platters of food and a jug of ale. Her husband sat across from her. "I hope you're hungry. This establishment actually has some decent food. Black pudding and eels." He rubbed his hands together. "I do miss good Scottish fare living in London."

The barkeep set plates of food down between them. "This close to the border you'll find many of the public houses serve Scottish food. And you can enjoy it here without risking yer neck in the northern troubles. But none as good as my Bertha makes." He beamed at the woman and took the platter from her hands.

"Troubles?" Winnifred poked her fork at the pudding, not liking the look of it.

"It's nothing, I'm sure," her husband said. "There have been reports of fighting breaking out in cities. Public property being destroyed. But with us having such a poor growing season, tempers will spike." Sinclair ripped the end off a loaf of bread and used it to hold a bit of eel in place as he speared it. He swallowed and tossed back a swig of ale. "Very passable. My compliments to the cook."

The woman pinked. "It's not often we have one as fine as yourself to cook for, Lord Dunkeld." She dropped into an inelegant curtsy. "A marquess and marchioness eating my food." She dropped another curtsy. "It's an honor, milord."

"Now, Bertha, let's let the happy couple eat in peace." The barkeep took her elbow. "Jus' holler if you need anything else, milord."

Sin nodded and tore off another hunk of bread.

Dust from the road dirtied his cravat and coat, and tendrils of hair had escaped his queue. Her husband looked rough, uncivilized, yet utterly confident and content, like a man who knew he could control every space and situation he found himself in. Every public house they entered, Sin bought the laborers a drink and sometimes joined them for a hearty laugh over some ribald jokes. Every evening he ate his meal with gusto, satisfaction making the edges of his lips curl up. Her husband was a man of large appetites.

Except, it appeared, for her.

He took another swallow of ale. "You're not eating. I can have them bring you something else, if you'd prefer."

Picking up her knife, she forced a smile. *Never appear upset. Never give cause for concern.* "This is fine. Besides, I'll have to become accustomed to Scottish food."

He stared at her, unblinking. "What's wrong?"

"Nothing." She placed a bite of the foreign sausage on

her tongue and smiled around it, like it was the most delicious thing in the world. Her throat rebelled but she forced herself to swallow. Dear Lord, she would never become accustomed to this.

"I thought we'd agreed to honesty." He pushed his plate away. "Tell me what's wrong."

She set her silverware down and clasped her hands on her lap. He seemed so sincere about wanting to hear her thoughts. But a woman who freely expressed herself was a dangerous thing. No matter how earnest her husband appeared, she could never let her guard down. Only bad things happened to those who did.

"Winnifred? I'm waiting." And he didn't sound patient about it.

"It's truly...." The word 'nothing' died on her lips under his withering glare. She sucked on her bottom lip. Would voicing this particular thought truly be so bad? This was a concern that most wives *would* probably raise with their husbands. She wouldn't be considered queer for mentioning it. She hoped.

She fisted her hands under the table. "It's only, we've been married for eight days now." Eight days and seven empty nights.

"I'm aware of that."

"And you haven't... we haven't..." She glanced around the room but no other patrons were within hearing distance. Still, she leaned forward and whispered, "Don't you wish to produce an heir?"

He pressed his lips flat. His eyes, a blue as deep as a sapphire, went as hard as that mineral. A small muscle ticked in his forehead.

Sweat gathered at the small of her back, dampening her gown. "Any wife would wonder. My question is perfectly common." *Never appear different from the crowd.*

"I didn't say it wasn't." He rubbed the back of his neck. "And I should have spoken of it before. But speaking of the act wouldn't help my situation." He shifted and cleared his throat. "There is a custom among the Archer family. Every Marquess of Dunkeld has bedded his wife for the first time in the ancestral bed." A delicate flush stained his cheeks. "Perhaps it seems foolish, but I don't want to be the first one to break that tradition."

"Oh." A tradition without a reason was as illogical as a superstition to Winnifred, but at least it answered her question. Her husband intended to have an intimate marriage.

Which left her with four more nights to fret over that particular marital duty. She wished it were over and done with. Lying next to her husband, wondering if he was going to touch her that night, dreading it yet always somehow disappointed when he didn't, was its own form of torture. He was a big man. A strong man. And one who didn't seem to care about the niceties. Yet he held her hand ever so gently. His contradictions intrigued her, and she couldn't help but wonder how he would behave when he took his husband's privilege.

Heat swept from her chest up to her cheeks. She needed to redirect her thoughts to something less impure. She landed on something he'd said. "What situation wouldn't it help?"

His gaze locked onto hers. "The one where I've thought about taking my wife every which way and can barely restrain myself from rutting into you every time we are alone together."

Her mouth went dry. That hadn't helped to purify her thoughts at all. But she'd asked. It wasn't Sinclair's fault she didn't know what to do with the answer.

Her husband seemed to have an idea. "Are you finished with your meal?"

She'd barely touched the dish, but was happy for any excuse not to finish it. "Yes."

Standing, Sinclair held out a hand and pulled her to her feet.

"Where are we going?"

He picked up her gloves and tucked them into his pocket. "Even though consummation must wait, I do believe it is time I took care of my neglected wife."

* * *

He pressed the door to their rented chambers shut and leaned against it.

Winnifred stood by the bed, clenching and unclenching her hands.

He was an idiot. Of course, she'd wonder why he hadn't touched her. Wonder and worry. And the delay in relations would only increase her nervousness of the act.

He unknotted his cravat and pulled it from his neck. Her nerves were something he could remedy.

Winnifred removed her spencer, folding it neatly. "I don't understand. If you wish to wait until we arrive at your home, what are we doing now? Do you wish to..." Her brow drew down, as though it took a physical effort to find the right word. "...cuddle?" By the slight wrinkle in her nose, it was apparent that word wasn't to her liking.

Well, he'd never been much for cuddling, either. But he would do that with her tonight. That, and more. "Aye." He tossed off his coat and started on his boots. "I'll hold you and make you feel good." An idea slipped into his head, one he should have thought of before. He was a large man. He wanted the first time he took his wife to be pleasant for her, not painful. Some preparation was due.

"Please don't feel that you need to simulate affection." She watched him carefully, drawing on her lower lip. "I am content to go on as before until we reach Kenmore."

He touched her cheek, marveling at the softness of her skin. Standing next to the bed, shifting on her boots, she seemed younger than her twenty-four years. He didn't know what their future held, but he didn't want his wife to feel insecure in his affections.

"I can't pretend to feel love for you this early in our acquaintance," he said. "But I promise to be true, and trust that affection will follow. And believe me, I will never simulate anything when it comes to our intimacies."

"You misunderstand me." The grin that spread across her face was crooked, like she had little practice smiling. A small muscle tugged behind his breastbone. "I am not speaking about anything so intangible as love. Indeed, I find the very idea of it unrealistic and naïve. I was merely stating that you don't need to try to appease any girlish feeling with such nonsense as holding me. Such an act would be pure sentimentality."

Sin paused. "You don't believe in love?" What a peculiar woman he'd married. He scratched his chest. He didn't know what to make of her. "That is unfortunate. I had hopes that our marriage would be one based on mutual affection."

"As do I." Winnifred clasped her hands together in front of her abdomen. "An affection borne from friendship and respect. That is the most one can hope for."

Sin narrowed his eyes. Such practicality should please him. He was fortunate not to have married a silly woman. So why did her attitude leave him feeling unsettled?

"You still wish to cuddle?" she asked, sounding as disinterested as a doxy at Sunday service.

"Yes." Sin pressed his lips together. Damn it, he would hold his wife. He would cuddle the hell out of her. Perhaps then she'd grow to have an appreciation of such sentimentalities.

She reached for the buttons of her gown, but he drew her hands away from the back of her neck. "Allow me." He pushed the delicate buttons through their holes. A smooth expanse of skin met his gaze, her shoulder blades pulled tight together over the top of her stays. He trailed a finger down the exposed spine.

He pushed her dress over her wide hips, and it slithered to the floor. The stays quickly followed suit. She turned then, stepping out of the puddle of fabric at her feet, and clutched the top of her chemise.

He pulled the pins from her hair, and the thick mass tumbled down her back. He hadn't yet decided if it was a light brown with golden highlights or a dark blond, but it was lovely all the same.

Running his fingers through it, he bent and pressed a soft kiss to the corner of her mouth. The side of her neck. The hollow at the base of her throat.

A fine tremor jerked her body.

"Would you feel more comfortable keeping your chemise on tonight?" His fingers itched to tear it from her body. The firelight made the thin linen translucent, her body a teasing shadow underneath. He clenched his fist, surprised at the intensity of his desire. She was his wife. He knew little about her except for the fact that she liked to hide. Hide her personality, her intelligence, her feelings. Anything that made her unique. But he had years to discover her. Decades for them to learn everything about one another until they became almost as one. His parents had had that type of relationship, his mother knowing what his father was going to say before he said it; his father understanding just when his mother needed a surprise bouquet of wildflowers to cheer her.

Sin wanted to have that meaningful of a relationship with his wife.

Possession hit him like a fist to the gut. *His. Wife.* His to care for, to make smile, to make moan.

His to fuck.

Carnal images rolled through his mind, each one more indecent than the picture before.

Sin rolled his shoulders. His thoughts bordered on uncivilized and were nothing an innocent should contend with. He shoved them down, deep into the part of him that he only let out when such primitive mindlessness would help him in a fight.

"You wouldn't mind my keeping it on?" she asked.

He stared at the chemise. It was short, falling to her upper thigh. The blasted undergarment was both an intoxicating tease and an infuriating border he wanted to breech. But leaving it on gave him something more to look forward to on their first night at Kenmore. Besides, tonight was about Winnifred.

He gave her a wicked grin. "It makes no difference to my purpose."

She nodded, pulled the covers back, and climbed onto the bed. Lying back against the pillows, she waited for him. The perfectly compliant wife.

Sin grunted. Something about her calm only riled him further. He pulled his shirt over his head and climbed beside her. His trousers he left on. She was enough of a temptation as she was.

She didn't resist when he pulled her into his arms, and that flicker of irritation grew brighter. Who was she to remain indifferent? Bed sport had long ago lost any significance to him, but she was an untouched woman. There should be some emotion when he drew his fingertip along her collarbone, when he pressed an open-mouthed kiss to her throat.

A sick feeling opened in his stomach. Unless she wasn't untouched.

If she were no longer a virgin, it should make no difference. One of his favorite pastimes was visiting The Black Rose, the pleasure house his friend Sutton now owned. Lord knew he wasn't pure.

But it did matter. Hypocrisy be damned, he wanted his wife to only be his.

Skimming his hand down her chemise, he caressed her thigh until her legs relaxed. He drew his hand up, bringing the linen with him, and danced his fingers along her upper thighs. Across the edges of her triangle of tight curls. Along the crease where thigh met hip.

She remained silent the entire time, her gaze locked with his, her expression undisturbed.

A mask.

He'd learned enough in his line of work to know when

someone hid their true face, and his lovely wife was a skilled practitioner of the art.

He couldn't wait to crack the facade.

"Spread your legs wider." His voice was a rough growl, one he almost didn't recognize. Christ, even with the lady-birds at The Black Rose he showed more charm. His wife deserved no less. But the thought of her spreading those legs for another man—

After a moment's hesitation, she complied, soothing his beast a fraction. "Should I be touching you?" A faint divot appeared between her eyebrows. "If there's something you'd like me to do, please tell me."

He grunted. Still so damned polite. Although the invitation wasn't unwelcome. He pushed images of her hands, her mouth, away. "Tonight is about you." He slid his index finger between her folds, finding her core and pressing his finger the slightest bit inside. He drew back and found her sweet little nub, tracing a circle around it.

Her throat rolled with her swallow.

Sin kissed her, keeping it gentle, undemanding. He nibbled on her lips, drawing on the plump flesh, until she parted her mouth on a soft exhale. He slid his tongue inside.

Muscle by muscle, her body relaxed under his. And when she tentatively met his tongue with her own, triumph coursed through him.

Her slit grew wet. He traced his finger along her seam, pressing inside her opening to his first knuckle. When he tried to add a second finger, her body resisted.

His heartbeat drummed in his chest. He sucked at a silky patch of skin on her throat. She was his. He didn't have to hurt anyone. Because one thing he knew was his wife's body was for his eyes only.

He circled his thumb around her clitoris, increasing the pressure and waiting for her breaths to quicken. He kissed his way down her throat, scoring her with his teeth for good measure. That faint citrusy scent he'd come to associate with her wafted off her heated skin, making his mouth water. Her breasts heaved beneath his face, and he accepted the invitation. He lapped at her nipple through the thin linen until the fabric became sheer and wetly clung to her skin.

His cock throbbed. Damnation, but he wanted her. The waiting would surely kill him. He rubbed his hard length against her thigh as he sucked that sweet berry of a nipple into his mouth, drawing hard.

A strangled gasp escaped his wife's mouth, and he pulled harder. He circled his thumb faster until her hips thrust up to meet his touch. Then, slowly, he eased his fingers into her narrow sheath.

Her body went stiff, and her legs closed around his hand. "Wait."

"Shh." He licked across her breast, hoping the rough scrape of wet fabric felt as good against her nipple as it did against his tongue. "A bit of pain now so there will be nothing but pleasure when we consummate our marriage." He dipped in father, kissing her eyelids when she squeezed them tightly shut. But she relaxed her legs. "That's it, *mo ghrâdh*. Open for me. I swear before the night is over, I'll make you feel such pleasure."

She clenched the sheet in her fists as a cry tore from her. That dark place inside, the one that was never civilized, roared in delight as he pushed through the resistance, breaking her maidenhead. She *was* his. Not only legally, but in body, as well. He'd never been possessive of his lovers before. But he'd never had a wife before, either. It changed things.

He flicked his thumb over her clit as he added a third finger. He watched as the fine muscles in her face loosened when her pain eased. Saw when they knitted back together as the first whispers of her crisis built.

Her cheeks were flushed, her bottom lip going red around the two white teeth she bit down into it. His wife truly was pretty. When they'd met, he'd found her pleasing to the eye. Handsome enough, but nothing remarkable.

He'd been wrong. Spread out before him, roused with her first taste of pleasure, she was lovely.

His nostrils flared, smelling her musk. More than lovely. She was delicious. She smelled of spice and oranges and honey, and his mouth watered.

"I... I think we're done now." She stared at a point on his throat, avoiding his eyes. "I believe you've accomplished your purpose tonight."

He snorted. "Not hardly. Have you ever brought yourself pleasure, wife?" He increased the pressure of his thumb. "Ever used your own fingers to rub this sweet little nub?"

Her gaze flew to his. "Of course not. That would be..."— her back arched—"... would be..."

"That would be beautiful to behold. But tonight, I get the pleasure." He kept his gaze fixed on her face as he sped his hand. His cock throbbed with every catch of her breath. Thrusting his hips in time with his fingers, he ground himself against her hip, the pressure not nearly enough to bring relief.

He wanted the torture to end. Wanted to break her control, see the woman beneath the mask. He wanted to hear her scream, watch her come undone.

Alas, a man didn't always get what he wanted.

Winnifred gave a muffled whimper and squeezed her eyes shut as her core pulsed around his fingers. He drew out her tremors as long as he could, but she made no further sounds. No cries of pleasure, no sighs of contentment.

Winnifred released her iron-grip on the sheets and opened her eyes. Aside from a wariness she couldn't hide, they were as placid as ever. "Thank you. That was nice."

Sin's gut clenched. Nice? Bloody nice? The first time she'd come to crisis and nice was how she described it? He'd just about spent in his trousers like a school boy from the experience, without one hand, mouth, or tongue touching his poor Thomas, and she acted as though the episode were on par with a pleasant afternoon tea.

His erection flagged and he rolled away from her, flopping onto his back. From the corner of his vision, he saw her tug her chemise down over her thighs.

Well, damn. He wasn't sure exactly how he'd wanted their first intimacies to end, but that hadn't been it. He felt unfulfilled, and not because he hadn't had his orgasm.

He climbed off the bed and trudged to the pitcher of water and bowl the maid had left for them. He dampened a small cloth to attend to his wife.

For the first time since the wedding, a trickle of unease slid down his spine.

Was Summerset right? Was a marriage between such different people doomed to fail?

Chapter Five

Sin stretched in his stirrups. The days in the saddle were taking their toll. Their arrival in Scotland couldn't come too soon, for his arse's sake if nothing else.

His driver, Gregor, pushed his cap back on his head. Although the driver's seat of the carriage was higher than Sin's horse, the smaller man's face was even with Sinclair's as he rode next to him. "We're getting close, milord. We might not 'ave crossed the border, but it feels like Scotland jus' the same."

Sin inhaled deeply. Yes. There was nothing distinctly different between the green hills of England or Scotland, but there was something in the air that he only noticed when he was home. Trees were few and far between along this road, and the landscape held a loneliness that continued to the rolling mountain range of the Southern Lowlands.

"Glad to be getting back home, are you?" Most of his London servants remained in England when he traveled to Kenmore, but a few were always eager to return north. Gregor and Dugald, Sin's valet, currently perched next to the coachman and gripping the brim of his hat, would kick up a fuss if Sin ever dared to leave them behind.

"Too right." The man tilted his head back and breathed deep.

Sin smirked. There really must be something in the air.

"I only wish summer were here to greet us instead of this constant winter." Sin rubbed his lower back. "I would like my bride to see the sun shining on her new home at some point." And for his farmers to be able to harvest their crops. But mother nature was one opponent he couldn't battle.

Dugald took off his hat and patted his face with a handkerchief. "Ach, we Scots can survive a bit of dark. We've survived worse before; we'll survive a bad growing season."

The carriage took a curve in the road, bending around a small hill. "If only the rest of Scotland believed the same," Sin muttered.

"Whoa." Gregor pulled back on the reins, bringing the horses to a sudden stop.

Sin walked his mount forward, examining the large oak tree that crossed the road, barring their path. Its branches reached in all directions, its trunk a solid two feet in diameter.

A light breeze rippled its leaves, and the horses leading the carriage pawed the earth.

The hairs on the back of Sin's neck rose.

"Why have we stopped?" Winnifred poked her head out the carriage window. "Is there a problem?"

"Get back inside," he yelled.

Irritation flickered across her face, so quickly he almost missed it, before she nodded and disappeared back into the coach's depths.

"Milord?" the driver asked.

Sin's horse danced sideways. "Can you turn the carriage about?" His gaze flew back to the trunk of the fallen tree, with its neat network of axe marks scoring the base.

The driver blew out his cheeks. "Cannae turn on this road. We'll have to unhitch the horses and back it up—"

"Ye can back it up after we've gone." A man with a kerchief around his nose and mouth stepped out from behind the hill, a similarly dressed highwayman at his side. Both men leveled pistols in their direction. "First, we'll have all yer blunt and gee-gaws."

"Gee-gaws?" Sin frowned. He refused to be robbed by an idiot.

"Yer buttons, yer pocketwatch." The thief narrowed his eyes above the white face covering. "Yer gee-gaws."

The second man elbowed his friend. "Would ye look at the crest on that carriage. We got ourselves some prime pickens' here."

Sin inhaled sharply. He grabbed the saddle's pommel and kicked his right foot out of its stirrup.

The first thief aimed the barrel of his pistol at him. "We didnae say ye could move."

Sin forced his expression to remain neutral, to keep the snarl from his voice. "If you want my coin, I'll have to dismount in order to retrieve it."

The second thief sidled over to the carriage, getting much too close to the door that lay between him and Winnifred.

Sin's knuckles went white around the reins.

The first thief nodded. "Slowly."

Sin assessed the men as he climbed down. Not much muscle on either of them. Probably been a while since their last meal. Easily defeated.

"You're bringing your trade a bit south, aren't you?" Sin rubbed his horse's nose, calming the animal.

"Better to relieve the English of their money." The man adjusted his handkerchief. "But a Scottish toff will do."

His driver and valet both eased to the edge of the seat. Sin met their gaze and gave a small nod. When he hired his servants, the ability to fight was a requirement, as well. He didn't have to worry about them. But one stray bullet near his wife—

Sin cut off that thought. Reaching into his saddle bag, slowly so the thief could see his movements, he drew out a large pouch of coins. The fight played out in his head. He'd toss the man the bag, wait till his greedy gaze focused on the flying pouch, and follow it in with a sound beating. Dugald would jump on the second man, and Gregor would follow to assist. They'd been in such situations before. It would be as choreographed as a play.

If only all the actors kept to the script.

"Who do we have in here?" the second thief asked.

Sin couldn't see him behind the carriage, but he heard well enough when the bounder pulled open the opposite door.

All thoughts of the normal plan of action were erased from his mind, pushed out by a blinding rage. Dropping the bag, he took the two steps to the carriage door on his side and yanked it open.

The thief blinked. His hand clutched Winnifred's skirts and the gun he held pointed carelessly at the ceiling.

Sin's gaze narrowed on the filthy hand touching his wife's gown. Heat exploded in his chest.

The man reached for Winnifred's arm as he dropped the pistol towards Sin.

With a roar, Sin reached through the cabin, grabbing the man by the wrist and the front of his shirt. Bones shifted, cracked under his grip, and the man screamed as Sin hauled him across the floor of the carriage, ripping his handkerchief off his face, and throwing him headfirst into the dirt.

A shot went off, and Sin didn't know if it was from his victim's pistol or the other thief's. He didn't care. He pounded his fist into the man's face, enjoying the spray of blood from his nose. He'd touched his wife. *Pound.* Held a weapon near her. *Pound, pound, pound, smash.* Dared to threaten something that was Sin's.

The man was limp in his grip, but still Sin hit him until the features on his face were unrecognizable.

Two gloved hands grabbed his arm, a tuft of lace at the hems blowing in the breeze.

It wasn't the strength in the hold that stopped him as there was barely any. It was the sight of that damned lace that brought him to his senses. His vision widened from its narrow focus on his victim. His driver stood over a kneeling highwayman, holding a short blunderbuss to his head. His valet scooped up his dropped bag of coin. All was under control.

Sin dropped the unconscious man and turned, chest heaving.

For once, Winnifred's face was completely readable. Her eyes were wide with shock, her mouth open in a perfect circle.

He gripped her shoulders, turning her about to look for injury. "Are you all right? Are you harmed?"

"Yes. No." She stumbled over the hand of the unconscious man.

Circling an arm around her waist, he lifted her away from the man's body and tucked her behind the carriage. "Which is it? Yes or no."

"Yes, I'm all right." She curled around him to peer back towards the carnage. "No, I'm not hurt. I can't believe what you did."

Sin swallowed. It wasn't something a woman should have to see. The violence he was capable of. A woman as measured as Winnifred wouldn't want a brute for a husband. But that's what she'd got. He was a blunt instrument. He wasn't patient like his friend Montague, thinking of a solution when force would do instead. Not sly like Summerset who preferred a surprise attack so his clothes wouldn't get ruffled. Sin used his fists. He beat threats into submission. He wasn't ashamed of his brutality, but it wasn't something he necessarily wanted to show off to his bride.

"He touched you." Sin pressed his fists to his sides. An ache made itself known in his right hand, but he ignored it. "They were trying to rob us."

"I know, but you picked him up and threw him like he weighed nothing." Her gaze slid up and down his body. "And you were in such a rage."

"Blood—" Sin reined in his irritation. "Of course, I was angry. He was a threat. You're my wife." How was she not understanding this?

"Still..." Her gaze turned wistful. "I suppose, as a man,

more is allowed."

He drew his eyebrows together. "What—"

"Milord?" The driver kicked the conscious thief, and the man fell forward onto his hands. "What should I do with this one?"

Dragging the man behind the hill and shooting him probably wasn't the best option, though it would be the easiest. "Have you anything to say for yourself?" Sin asked.

The man spit onto the dirt. "An empty belly causes a man to do many things he shouldn't. I dunnae have more to say than that."

Winnifred picked up Sin's bruised hand. She pulled a dainty lavender handkerchief from her sleeve and dabbed at his split knuckles.

He kept his eyes on his wife. "Tie him up. Tie them both up." Although he didn't think his man would need the restraints. He probably wouldn't be gaining consciousness for hours, if at all. "Put them by the side of the road. When we reach the next town we'll send a member of the watch back for them."

"We're going to leave them here?" Winnifred asked. "What if animals get to them?"

He could only hope. "They'll be fine."

"I dunnae know if we'll make the next town, milord." Dugald bent his legs, gripped a limb of the tree, and put his back into trying to move it. He failed. "We'll need more men to move this monster. And with all of these branches digging into the ground, I dunnae even think the horses could drag it off the road."

"My horses are strong. But if they cannae clear the road, we could turn back," Gregor said. He finished tying a knot in the leather he'd bound around the thief's wrists, an extra rein they carried in the supply chest. "The last town we passed was probably only ten miles ago."

Winnifred stepped around him, skirted the unconscious man, and stood next to his valet.

"We don't have a saw to cut off some of these

branches?"

"Not on this trip, milady," Dugald said.

Gregor stepped next to her. "I say my horses can do it."

"They're going to have to try." Sin removed his jacket and rolled up his sleeves.

Winnifred's gaze flicked to his chest, his arms, then dropped back to the tree. She opened her mouth, shut it.

"Something you wanted to say?" Sin asked.

She shook her head.

"Then perhaps you'd be more comfortable waiting in the carriage." He grabbed one of the tree's limbs and heaved. It didn't move an inch.

Winnifred remained where she was. "It's only...."

Sin planted his hands on his hips and glared at the tree. "Speak up, woman."

"Well, you see that tree?" She pointed at the fallen tree's twin, another large oak which rose across from the stump of its brethren. They had once stood as two proud and lonely sentinels on his drive home.

"The only tree left standing for ten miles along this road? Yes, I see it." Vexation curdled his stomach at the destruction wrought to lay a trap for travelers. He glared at the highwayman.

"Yes, well if we create a pulley system over it—you see where the trunk separates into two limbs?—the horses should have an easier time lifting the tree from the road. At least move it far enough to allow our carriage to pass." She clasped her hands together. "But it will require a fair bit of rope."

"Rope we have." Sin eyed his wife. "That might work."

"Aye, it could save us hours of back-breaking labor," Gregor agreed.

Winnifred drew a square in the dirt with the toe of her slipper. "My father did something similar once. The idea is not mine."

Sin harrumphed. He greatly doubted that. His wife was ever so eager to hide her intelligence. Did she think he was some milksop Sassenach, wanting a dull wife who did nothing more than smile and nod? That he wouldn't appreciate any advice to get them on their bloody way as soon as possible?

No matter. She'd learn. And he'd learn why she felt the need to hide. How she'd come to be so self-effacing. Last night he had felt defeated by her cool responses. Thought perhaps their temperaments were too different to form a happy union. But she was a challenge, and one he was determined to meet. He would strip her of her disguises and enjoy every moment of it.

"You heard the woman." He skimmed his palm down her arm, wanting the contact. "Let's collect every bit of rope we have. Gregor, help me unstrap the luggage. We'll use those bindings. And if it isn't enough, we'll throw in the reins."

Chapter Six

Winnifred peered out the carriage window when they turned from the rutted road onto a smoothly-groomed lane. A large lake lay to her left, its surface dark and impenetrable under the overcast skies. Across the water, a forest of Caledonian pine grew, dense and untamed. A valley thick with heather and thistle led to its near shore. This time of year, the purple of the heather should have been bright and vibrant, but the entire scene looked as faded as an old memory.

Perhaps that was only her mood.

The carriage rounded a curve, and Winnifred's jaw dropped. Kenmore Castle was like nothing she'd ever seen. It didn't have the grace of Windsor Castle nor the elegant lines of a Leeds, but it was impressive all the same. Built of a reddish-brown brick, the castle consisted of a core structure which towered into the sky, surrounded by three-story tall wings. The tops of the walls were crenelated, and she wondered if the battlements had ever been used by Dunkeld archers. Every corner of the castle was rounded into a bastion, and there were many corners. Whoever had designed the castle must have had an aversion to clean lines. The wings shot in every different direction from the central keep. The bastions were of unequal size, sometimes a sturdy outgrowth large enough to hold rooms and staircases, sometimes a dainty half-circle of brick only large enough for one window. Winnifred counted eleven turrets before the carriage rocked to a stop.

She pulled her head back in and clutched the edge of her

seat. The difference between her new home and the apartments she and her father had in London were as different as a thistle to the pines across the lake. Both in the plant family, but that was where any similarity ended. The difference in the sizes of the homes was, of course, most noticeable. But more than that, Winnifred already missed the orderly rectangle that was her old room. The sensible organization of London's architecture. Would the management of Kenmore be as chaotic as its outward appearance? How would she live here? Winnifred hated when her father moved her microscope just inches from its proper place.

A worry which no longer mattered. The back of her throat burned. She'd left her microscope with her father. Her microscope, the books on soil erosion and scientific processes that would be too shocking for a woman to own, her protective leather apron and gloves. Everything that made her happy but proved a danger. Normal women didn't share her interests, and her new family must never suspect.

The door swung open. Sinclair stood before her, stretching his hand out.

Winnifred took a deep breath and cleared her expression of any nerves. She slipped her palm against Sin's and climbed from the carriage. Her smile froze on her face. Every servant in a fifty-mile radius must have been arranged in a semicircle on the gravel drive in front of the castle's front door. Surely, they couldn't all belong to Kenmore.

"Welcome home," Sin said. He led her to an elderly man and woman at the head of the line. "This is my steward, Tavish McKinley, and his wife and our housekeeper, Sheona."

Tavish bowed and Sheona dropped a curtsy, both lowering their heads and showing similar white-grey hair.

"Welcome back, milord," Tavish said. "It will be nice to have ye aboot again."

Sin shook the man's hand. "Thank you. I present your marchioness, Lady Winnifred Archer, Marchioness of

Dunkeld."

Winnifred shook each of their hands in turn, careful of the paper-thin skin. "Good to meet you."

"And this is our butler, Niall Greer, and our head maid…." The introductions began to blur. Was Winnifred expected to remember all the names? Their positions? She could remember Ingenhousz' publication, *Experiments upon vegetables*, nearly word for word, but a houseful of forty-three, no forty-four servants was going to undo her.

"I'll introduce you to the grounds- and stablemen later." Sin patted her hand. He clapped a young boy on the back as they strolled towards the open door of the castle. "For now, I'd like to wash the dust of the road off of me."

"There's more?" she asked weakly. She blinked as her eyes adjusted to the dim entry. A figure to her right made her jump.

Sin chuckled, striding around her to rap his fist on the face plate of the standing suit of armor that had startled her. "All of these are empty. Souvenirs of our victory over the English at the Battle of Ancrum Moor. There are sixty-one more of these downstairs."

She ran her finger over the smooth metal chest plate. "You're well-prepared for battle, I see." Her words were only partially a jest.

"These are antiques." Sin planted his fists on his hips and arched his back in a stretch. "No, if trouble comes, our real defenses are downstairs, in the armory."

She cut him a sharp glance. "You're a member of the House of Lords. I thought you believed in the union. You do not truly believe you will need to defend yourself from England, do you?"

He crossed his arms. "I do believe in the union. We have had one of the longest periods of peace here in Scotland because of it. But I'm a member of the House to promote Scottish interests. Our two nations may have joined, but the partnership is not equal. Only sixteen of my fellow peers are allowed in the House. Our political power is limited. And peace is a fragile thing."

"Aye, and a costly one, too." A woman with Sinclair's auburn hair, only threaded through with silver, bustled across the tiled floor. She wore a green plaid dress in a finely-spun wool and a large sapphire pendant nestled above her bosom. "And it seems to be an account Scotland willnae ever finish paying." She planted herself in front of her son and crooked her finger.

Sinclair sighed, but bent and offered his cheek for his mother's kiss. He herded them out of the way as a line of footman bearing their trunks streamed past them and up the staircase. "Mother, let's not rehash old arguments. Now, greet your new daughter-in-law properly." He turned to Winnifred. "This is my mother, Deirdre, Dowager Marchioness of Dunkeld."

The woman clapped her hands together. "Well, let's have a good look at ye." She examined Winnifred from head to toe. "At least ye didn't bring home one of those sallow English lasses. She looks sturdy enough, and has ample hips for birthing Dunkeld young."

Winnifred sucked in a breath, swallowed her saliva down the wrong pipe, and started coughing.

"Mother!" Sinclair's cheeks went as red as his hair. The shock Winnifred felt at being discussed so faded away as amusement at her husband's discomfort took hold. It seemed hardly sensible that a man as hard and fierce as he'd shown himself to be should be embarrassed by mere words, but there it was.

Deirdre blinked familiar blue eyes up at her son. "What? Archer men dunnae produce small babes. That is a fact."

Winnifred pressed a hand to her abdomen. She looked at her husband from the corner of her eye. He *was* immense. Stood a solid eight inches above her own five-foot-nine height. When her mind had worried over the marriage bed, the consideration of how their consequent offspring would fit through her birth canal hadn't been one of her concerns.

It was now.

"Mother," Sin gritted out between clenched teeth. "Do not discuss such things with my wife. It is hardly proper."

"Well." Deirdre fisted her hands on her rounded hips, looking like a smaller, and feminine version of her son. "Does the proper English miss want a tour of Kenmore, or does she require a wee nap after her travels?"

The disregard in her mother-in-law's voice should have been cause for concern, but Winnifred's lips only twitched in response. No one at home spoke with such open contempt. Insults were treacherous, hidden things in England, a hole in the road one could unexpectedly fall into and twist an ankle. Such direct disfavor was refreshing.

"As a married woman I surely qualify as madam now, but I have no objection to answering to 'proper English miss'." Winnifred shrugged. "If you see no issue with prejudging a person based on the group characteristics of nationality, then who am I to disabuse you of such a notion. Many of my fellow Englishmen tend to do the same when speaking of the Scottish. It seems that we're all more alike than not."

Deirdre narrowed her eyes. "Are ye comparing me to the Sassenach?"

A pit opened in Winnifred's stomach, her amusement disappearing in an instant. That had been foolish. She'd let the woman's impropriety free her own tongue. She snuck a glance at her husband, preparing for his censure.

A raised eyebrow in her direction was his only response.

Winnifred's racing pulse slowed. Sinclair *had* said he wanted a free-thinking wife, and perhaps he was sincere. But it wasn't a theory she should test often. History had shown the results could be disastrous.

Sinclair draped an arm around her shoulders and squeezed. "I'm glad to know that I don't have to stand as a guard between you two. My wife is resolute enough to deal with you on her own, mother."

Winnifred peeked up at him, the last knot in her stomach unraveling. An ember of hope glowed to life behind her breast, but she quickly doused it. Her carelessness hadn't harmed her this time, but she needed to take better care in the future.

The steward and housekeeper came to stand before them. "Milord," Tavish said, "there is estate business I need to discuss with ye. Will ye have time to meet this afternoon?"

Sinclair's body tensed. "Of course."

Winnifred tilted her head. Perhaps the arrival at Kenmore was challenging for more than just her.

"Let's retire to my study." Sinclair turned. "Mother, will you give Winnifred that tour?"

"Of course." Deirdre lifted her skirts and turned, her back ramrod straight. "Come, daughter," she called over her shoulder. "I dunnae have all day for this."

Winnifred inclined her head to Sinclair and followed after her mother-in-law at a sedate pace.

The woman waited, foot tapping, in the next room. "First thing ye should learn, we move at a quicker pace here in Scotland."

Winnifred merely gave her a mild smile.

Deirdre huffed. "Now, here we have the great room. It's used for formal dinners if the guests number over fifty or—"

Deep barking interrupted the description. The sound of paws smacking onto the floor sounded behind Winnifred, and she spun, expecting to see an army of dogs descending. Instead, just two beasts caused all the commotion.

Two of the largest dogs she'd ever seen.

Charging straight at her.

She stepped back, but it was too late. The first set of thick paws struck her shoulders, and she went down in a tangle of fur and slobber and limbs. She opened her mouth to scream, and the second beast trailed its slimy tongue across her cheek.

She snapped her mouth shut in self-defense.

"Banquo. Horatio." Deirdre's voice was fond, but sharp. "Sit down."

With a whine, the slobbering kisser plopped his bottom next to Winnifred's head. The other demon dog stretched out across Winnifred's stomach and panted. She swore he grinned.

"Good boys," Deirdre cooed.

A dog's tail whacked Winnifred's face.

She pushed at the dog lying on her until he condescended to roll onto her thighs. She sat up, resting back on her hands. "What are these?"

"Scottish deerhounds." Deirdre bent and scratched the scruffy head of the dog pinning Winnifred to the floor. "The pedigree of these laddies goes back almost as far as the Archers."

"And here I thought they were a special breed of Scottish horses," Winnifred muttered. She pushed at the monster at her hips, and he rolled further down her legs until he exposed his belly. His four paws stood straight up in the air, waggling, and he looked at her hopefully.

"Move, Horatio." She tried to shift her legs out from under him. He howled.

"He wants ye to rub his belly. And that's Banquo." Deirdre lifted the watch pinned to her bodice and checked the time. "And I do have other things that require my attention."

Winnifred swallowed her response. Her new mother-in-law was most likely influential with Sinclair. Winnifred had to watch her tongue. She gave Banquo's belly three quick pats.

The animal whined, his large brown eyes glistening up at her.

Biting the inside of her cheek, she stroked his soft underside until he sighed with delight.

"Now will you release me?" she asked.

"Banquo. Up." Deirdre snapped her fingers.

The animal jumped to his feet and trotted over to Deirdre for a pat on the head.

Winnifred climbed to her feet and shook out her skirts. If it had been that easy to get the dog off of her, why hadn't Deirdre given the order sooner?

"Can we get on with it?" her mother-in-law asked, as if

the delay was all Winnifred's fault. "Lads, go find Sin."

One of the dogs, Horatio, she thought, howled again, and with a scrabble of claws on hardwood, the beasts took off and disappeared out of the room.

"Now, as I was saying, we also use this room for balls. I expect we'll be having one for ye in the near future." Deirdre walked as she talked, pointing out the gallery of portraits, a library, several drawing rooms, and the family dining room. They wended their way down a curved flight of stone steps, and Deirdre pointed to a room through a low doorway. "The armory."

Winnifred peered inside. "Armory? It looks more like a dungeon." Along with racks filled with axes, spears, crossbows, rifles, and other weapons she couldn't identify, manacles hung from the roughly-hewn walls, holding eerie suits of armor in their metal tentacles like phantom prisoners. "Why are you using the manacles in that manner?"

Deirdre shrugged. "It raises our spirits. Now," she said, turning and leading her up another staircase, "here are the kitchens. Our conservatory is through those doors, this floor's necessary is doon that hall, and my own personal parlor is that way." She pointed over Winnifred's shoulder. "Any questions so far?"

Winnifred shook her head. Aside from the dungeon, she was pleased to see that the rooms of Kenmore Castle were nicely appointed and appeared quite comfortable. It wasn't the drear and drafty castle of her imagination.

At the top of yet another staircase, Deirdre gestured to two sets of doors. "Those lead into the marchioness's bed chambers, and the other set belongs to the marquess. I must leave ye now, but I assume ye can explore your rooms without assistance?"

"Of course. I...." Winnifred spoke to a retreating back. She blew out her cheeks. "Thank you," she called down the stairs. With a sigh of relief, she opened the doors closest to her and entered the anteroom of her new chambers. Thick red carpet muffled her footfalls. She stepped into her bedroom. Tapestries of cream and pale reds and oranges covered the walls. A wan light filtered through the large, rectangular window. A door stood off to her right, and she pressed it open. A dressing room that was already filled with her belongings, and past that her husband's dressing room. She inched open the final door and peered into her husband's chamber.

Her jaw dropped and she stepped inside. Taking up a full quarter of the room was a bed. *The* bed. And Winnifred could understand how a family tradition came to be wrapped about it.

Made of a dark wood, the four thick posts had been carved in an octagonal shape. They rose almost to the ceiling, and delicate fleur-de-lis were etched at the top of each post. A wooden canopy topped the structure, the sides angling up into a vaulted peak. The backboard was covered with gold satin that was carried over into the coverlet and pillow cases.

The bed looked like a tiny medieval cathedral. A family of four could live in that bed.

And tonight, she and her husband would consummate their marriage upon it.

Drawing the door closed, she retreated to her own room. She sat on her much more modest bed and flopped onto her back. It wouldn't be so bad. Not if her husband made her feel as he had in the inn four nights before. Her body warmed, and she ran her hand down her stomach to graze the part of her that had given so much pleasure. His hands, his fingers had felt so good, she'd almost forgotten herself. Almost lost her restraint. She'd wanted to shout as the tremors had taken her; only her will and fear prevented it.

A man wouldn't want a wife to show such wantonness.

Tonight, she must take better care.

***

Sin tossed a treat to Banquo, then to Horatio when he whined. He kicked his boots up onto his desk. Bloody pampered animals. He'd missed them. Missed Kenmore. He hadn't, however, missed its numerous, and never-ending, problems.

"… only one-third of our wheat crops and the barley never sprouted more than a couple inches from the dirt." Tavish ran a hand over his head, a tuft of snowy hair sticking straight up in the back. "Tempers are running high, even among our tenants. People are getting hurt in these riots."

Sin pounded his fist into his thigh. "What do they think fighting with each other will do? It's the bloody weather. Only God can change it."

The older man shrugged. He'd been in the Dunkeld's service for three generations of marquesses. A young page with Sin's grandfather, head footman then steward under his father. He knew more about the management of the Dunkeld estate than Sin could learn in three lifetimes. There was no one whose judgment he trusted more.

"When ye have only a wee bit, your neighbor having even jus' a cupful more seems unfair." Tavish shook his head. "Unless the sun shows her face soon, it will only get worse."

Sin dropped his boots down to the floor. He was skilled at hunting enemies of the state, stopping plots, eliminating threats. But crop failures? Famine? There was fuck all he could do about that.

His impotence burned a hole in his gut.

Sin stared up at the portrait of his father that hung behind the desk. *He* would have known what to do.

"I can't make the sun shine, but I'll try to alleviate its effects on my people." He stood and paced the room. "Write to my man in London. Tell him to start sending shipments of grain to Kenmore. Apples. Whatever he can get his hands on that will survive the journey. I'll contact Montague. With his shipping company, he should be able to help." He rested his forearm on the top sill of the window and stared out onto Loch Munro.

His friend would help. Sin throwing blunt at the problem would provide a bit of relief, as well. And that was the extent of his power. He fisted his hand until it went white. "Tomorrow, I'll speak to the tenants. See what I can do to ease the tension."

A thread of panic wrapped around his chest and squeezed. He was the fourth Marquess of Dunkeld. He'd been given much: a thriving estate, enough wealth to keep an army of bankers happy, tenants who had formed a real community. What would he leave to his children? He was supposed to be the steward of his inheritance, and he didn't know the first thing about how to preserve it. Hundreds of people would suffer if he failed.

He knocked his fist against the wall and took a deep breath. It would help no one if he showed his fear. Even if he deferred his decisions to Tavish, Sin would at least have to appear to be in control. The people depending on him expected it. He might never be the marquess his father was, but he could damn well make it look as though he knew what he was doing even as the walls tumbled down.

If it wasn't for Winnifred, Sin would jump on his horse and manage the food shipments from London himself.

Winnifred. His mind filled with thoughts of her. Taking a wife was one duty he had managed to fulfill as a marquess.

There was another duty he had yet to undertake. His reflection in the window smiled back at him. That was a duty that was easily accomplished. One he had been looking forward to for eleven excruciating nights. This was one thing he could control, one part of being a marquess, being a man, that he understood. Satisfying a wife, making her round with his child.

It was the first responsibility he'd had as marquess that he not only felt fully competent to handle, but greedy to take on.

There was nothing more he could do for his tenants today.

But he sure as hell could fuck his wife.

Chapter Seven

He hunted her down in the kitchen.

Winnifred stood, bent over a large wooden table, and his gaze landed on her round bottom. She truly was a fine figure of a woman. Well-proportioned and large enough where he wasn't afraid of crushing her beneath him. His hand itched to palm that arse. And beneath that arse were two pale and plump thighs, and betwixt those thighs was the hottest—

"Milord!" The cook caught sight of him first and sketched a quick bow. "Welcome home."

Sin nodded to the man, but didn't take his eyes off of Winnifred.

She tucked a strand of honey-brown hair behind her ear. "Husband, I was just preparing a tray of food to be sent up to you. I didn't know how late you and your steward would be working."

"Most thoughtful of you." He stepped close to her and inhaled. Between the odors of raising bread and cooked meat, he scented her. Citrus and warm women. "I do have quite a hunger."

A light flush crawled up her neck, and she shifted her weight.

She was as hesitant as a young doe faced with a wolf for the first time. Not knowing if it were friend or foe. If she was protected... or prey.

His heartbeat thrummed through his body, echoing in his ears. That dark place in him, the one he'd worked hard to tame, blinked awake. God help him but he liked her this way. Nervous. Unsure. Waiting for him to pounce. He grinned, showing his teeth. He didn't want to disappoint her, so pounce he would.

Grabbing the tray of food with one hand and her elbow with the other, he drew her out of the kitchen and up the stairs to their bedchambers. He pushed the door to his room open with his boot and kicked it shut behind them.

Winnifred clasped her hands together, her knotted fingers hovering over the vee between her legs, and paced to the center of the room. She slowly twisted in a circle, examining her surroundings, before facing him, her face expressionless.

"Are you frightened?" Sin set the tray on the low table before the fireplace. He rolled up a thin slice of venison and popped it in his mouth. He watched her as an explosion of flavor burst upon his tongue.

She didn't pretend not to understand. "We are married. You need heirs. I am nothing if not practical about the necessity of procreation."

His abdomen pulled tight. "Practical? Yes, I'm sure practicality is a useful trait in a woman." He licked a bit of juice off his finger, and her gaze followed his movements. The tightness spread to the rest of his body, his muscles feeling too large for his skin. "But that doesn't mean you wouldn't feel some trepidation."

She gave a curt nod. "I'll admit I have the same apprehensions most women surely feel, but you don't need to worry about missish behavior on my part. I will perform my duties without complaint."

Duty. The word rolled through his head. He knew all about duty. He stalked forward, circling his wife. And conceiving an heir was surely one of his largest, but it didn't feel like an obligation. And he didn't want it to be one to her, either.

The knuckles of her fingers whitened, and her shoulders set, but otherwise she showed nothing as he prowled about her.

Surely, she was not like most women. The thought pleased him even as a compulsion gripped him to discover why she felt the need to hide her emotions.

Stopping behind her, he curled a loose lock of her hair around his finger. He tugged, and smiled when she sucked in a sharp breath. Fingering the top buttons of her gown, he leaned close and brushed his lips over the shell of her ear.

"This is a very serviceable travel gown." He sucked her lobe into his mouth. "Do you have any particular attachment to it?"

"To the dress?" Her voice was a breathy whisper. She cleared her throat. "Of course not."

Of course not. Not for his practical, impassive bride.

He gripped the neck above the top button and tore the back apart.

Winnifred clutched the sagging bodice before relaxing her arms so the gown could slip from her shoulders.

He shoved the fabric past her hips and to the floor. "Step out."

She complied.

Grabbing her about the waist, he turned and tossed her on the bed. She squawked as she bounced. Rolling to her side, she pushed her hair out of her eyes and glared at him.

Good. His bride could be roused, even if it was only with irritation.

He toed his boots off and shucked his outer garments until his shirt hung loose around his thighs. He padded towards her.

She looked everywhere but at him.

"Problem, lass?" He crawled onto the bed, the mattress sagging beneath his weight.

"Um." Her gaze fell to his face then shot to the top of the bed again. "You don't, you aren't wearing smallclothes?" Her tone rose at the end of the sentence, making it a question.

"They only get in the way. It's more efficient this way." He glided his finger up the stocking on her calf. She still wore too many underthings. Damn nuisances they were.

She swallowed. "And you like to be economical."

"I'm taking a cue from my practical wife." He circled her ankle with his fingers and tugged off her slipper. He pressed the sole of her foot to his thigh and raised her shift until the ribbon that held her stocking was exposed. "My father used to say it was best to start as you wish to go on. I don't think you want a sweet seduction that won't reflect our future marriage bed."

His cock twitched. He could do soft, but he didn't like it. And something about Winnifred made him want to be very, very hard.

He tugged the knot on the ribbon free and slid the stocking down her leg. He made quick work of the other stocking and slipper.

She fingered the top of her stays. "I don't suppose you wish me to leave my chemise on this time?"

He swung his head from side to side and pulled his shirt over his head.

Her gaze darted to his groin then to the bed's canopy, her cheeks flushing red. She swallowed. "All right then." She pulled on one end of the bow that held her short stays snug against her breasts. As undergarments went, her stays were the most practical, least frilly set Sin had ever laid eyes on. Yet he couldn't tear his gaze away as the ribbons loosened, as one of the straps slid down her shoulder. Winnifred let the garment drop to the bed. With her chin tilted up, she hooked her fingers under the hem of her shift. Slowly, she raised it, revealing, her bare flesh inch-by-luscious-inch.

Despite her disavowal of any finer feelings, he knew it was nerves that slowed her hands. And he was grateful for it; the unintentional stripping exhibition was erotic as hell.

Her thatch of brown curls dragged free from the linen, looking tantalizingly soft. The tiny button of her navel was exposed next. By the time her rosy nipples popped into view, Sin was as hard as a pike. He dug his fingers into his thighs. His palms itched to explore every inch of his wife. His mouth watered with the need to devour.

Finally, the shift was off her body. She tossed it to the floor and settled back upon the pillows, her expression measured.

Sin reached for her. He trailed his fingers over the skin covering her ribs, down over her wide hips. He pressed them harder into the soft flesh of her thighs. Pink lines followed after the tips of his fingers, fleeting marks that disappeared all too quickly for his liking.

He crawled over her, his knees bracketing her hips, his palms framing her face, and he examined what lay beneath him.

Beauty. His woman was beautiful. And completely his. Until they died, only her body would accept his flesh; only his cock would know her sex.

He rubbed his thumb over her nipple. Her areolas were a pretty pink, the color so faint as to be almost indistinguishable from the surrounding skin. A delicate contrast for such a sturdy woman.

Her nipple pebbled beneath his finger, and her breathing quickened. Sin lowered his head, needing to taste her. He sucked the nub into his mouth before nibbling around the soft underside of her breast.

Her skin was like velvet, her softness such a contrast to his own hardness. He kissed his way up to the pulse fluttering in her neck. "Open your legs for me."

She complied, but all of her muscles went rigid with the task.

"Relax." He flicked his tongue against her fluttering pulse, loving the feel of her blood racing just beneath her skin. "The painful bit is past."

And thank God for that. No need to ease his entry, hold himself back. He straightened his legs and pressed his erection into her belly, throbbing at the contact. Shifting his hips, he slid his cock between her folds, not trying to enter her, just letting her soft lips envelop him as he rocked against her.

Winnifred froze.

"Does that feel good?" He rolled his hips again, the gathering moisture easing his glide.

She clenched her jaw. "It's fine."

"Fine." The word tasted foul on his tongue. Her honey slicking his way revealed her lie. She could control her speech but not her body's response. He ground the base of his cock into her clit, and she smothered a moan. As long as her body didn't lie, he could forgive her words. For now.

He buried his hand under her scalp, pulling at the knot in her hair. "I'll see if I can improve upon fine."

He took her mouth as his hips set up a steady rhythm. He devoured her, hoping for a response with each thrust of his tongue, each nip of his teeth. Her skin grew damp beneath his, and she gripped his hip with one hand. To encourage him on or to try to control her reactions, Sin didn't know. It didn't matter. She might be afraid of her responses, but he craved them.

"Do you want me?" He drew back, the head of his cock prodding her slick entrance, before sliding back over her lips to nudge her clit.

Small tremors coursed her body. "Whatever you want, husband."

He gripped her chin, forced her to look at him. "Do you want my cock in your sweet little pussy?" His crown dipped the slightest bit inside her sheath, begging for full admittance. But he'd been a liar, too. He wanted her words, her confession of her own desire, as much as he needed her body's response.

She shuddered beneath him, no doubt unused to such uncivilized language in her practical little world. She'd learn. In his bed, there was no polish. No sophistication. In his bed, there was only raw animal lust.

"Yes," she said, her voice breaking.

His body expanded, his muscles swelling. He hid his triumphant grin by kissing her breathless. His wife wanted him, and by God she would have him.

He tugged her thigh wider and slammed into heaven.

* * *

Her breath fled her lungs. Winnifred threw her head back in shock. Had he said there'd be no pain? He'd been wrong.

He thrust again, driving deeper, and she couldn't contain the whimper that slipped past her lips.

Sinclair slapped his palms next to her head and raised his upper body. His eyelids were at half-mast, his mouth loose as he held himself pressed tight to her. "Fuck me. You feel better than I dreamed."

She exhaled a long breath, forcing her body to relax and accept the intrusion. The stretch of her body, the fullness, was as alien as his foul language. And as curious. It was inappropriate, speaking so in front of a woman. Taboo. A shiver trickled down her spine. Only a man could survive such a breach in propriety. Such freedom the male of their species had.

Sinclair gripped her skull, dropping his forehead to hers, as he eased out and thrust back in.

The pain was less this time, and the next foray brought a not unpleasant sensation to her core. Her legs widened on their own accord.

"That's it, *mo ghràdh*. Take all of me." Sinclair dragged his palm down her side and grabbed her bottom, digging his nails into her flesh. The bite of pain had her arching into his next slide. Skin slapped against skin, the sound obscene... and thrilling.

She'd never engaged in such a lewd act. Even married, it felt wicked. Ungoverned. And it was mandated by her position as his wife. As long as she didn't get too carried away. Didn't become too excitable, she could let herself enjoy this. A little.

Her sheath clutched at his length, heat spreading throughout her body. She fisted her hands, digging her own nails into her skin, fighting to control the rising tide of sensation. That feeling of breaking apart he'd given her two days ago had been lovely, but it shouldn't be replicated. It had left her too open when she needed her walls. She would take a measured enjoyment as her husband found his pleasure in her, and it would be enough.

Sinclair grunted and hooked his arm under her knee, pushing her leg high. The angle changed, his manhood stroking along a new set of nerves, and a moan tumbled past her lips.

"That's it." He held himself tight to her pelvis and ground his pubic bone against her sensitized bud. "Get there."

Shudders wracked her body. Turning her head, she pressed her cheek into the cool satin of the pillow. He'd have to finish soon. She only needed to hold out a little longer.

He growled. "Why are you fighting this? Fighting me?" He yanked on her hair, pulling her head up to his. He crushed his lips to hers, the kiss savage, stealing her breath. He drove faster, harder. Every time he bottomed out, she felt a pinch deep in her core, the little bite swirling with her pleasure until she couldn't decipher which was which. Her husband was relentless. A force of nature she struggled to resist.

Her body spiraled tighter and tighter until there was nothing left to fight. The orgasm bordered on pain the relief was so great. Pulses rocked her body, the pleasure spiraling outward until it reached her curled toes. She cried out as he bit down on the tendon where her neck met her shoulder. Heat flooded her core as he muttered profanities in her ear.

The pleasant haze around her brain lifted, the sounds of their ragged breathing intruding. His weight was heavy against her, his heat her only warmth as her body rapidly cooled. She released her hold on her husband, realizing that she was digging her nails into his back hard enough to draw blood.

Which he only deserved. Her body felt bruised from the inside out, bliss and soreness warring with each other for dominance. Her muscles were limp with fatigue from the pleasure he'd unwillingly wrung from her.

She'd lost control. Again. Tears burned the backs of her eyes. Was this how it started for her mother? The beginning of the end?

Sinclair pulled out of her body, the sensation strange. He rolled to sitting, planting his legs on the ground off the side of the bed. Looking over his shoulder, his dark blue gaze pinned her in place.

"Wife. We need to talk."

Chapter Eight

Winnifred tucked her cloak more tightly about her thighs, but the damp still crept through. The umbrella she held above her and Sinclair's head was next to useless when the very air was heavy with moisture.

"This mist might help the crops at least," she said, injecting cheer into her voice.

Sinclair grunted and slapped the reins onto the back of the cart horse soundly.

She smothered her sigh. He'd barely spoken all day. Ever since she'd answered his inquiries last night with bland placations. She'd been tempted, so very tempted, to tell him her fears. She knew her marriage didn't have a chance of being truly happy unless she was honest with her husband.

But an average marriage, where the husband and wife were merely civil companions, was far better than most alternatives.

Sinclair drove their cart down the next drive, a stone cottage rounding into view. The thatched roof was worn thin in a couple of spots and a bare-footed child chased chickens in the yard. The girl caught sight of the cart. "Mam! Da! Someuns comin'."

A middle-aged couple emerged from the cottage, both looking as faded as unpicked hay. The woman opened her eyes wide and she dropped a deep curtsy as they pulled to a stop. The man gave a brusque nod.

Sinclair jumped from the cart, landing heavily. He reached up and grasped her waist, swinging her down. "Farmer Beattie. How fare you?"

The man spit into the dirt, his saliva dark and thick, and Winnifred's stomach turned. "Aboot as well as ever'one else." He looked Sinclair up and down and turned his gaze on Winnifred. "Not as well-fed as some." The disgust in his look had Winnifred retreating a step.

So many of the tenants they'd visited today had shown the same anger. Nothing that could be classified as outright disrespect, but nothing polite in their manner, either.

Sinclair shifted his body partway between her and the farmer. "I'm sorry to hear that. This is my new bride, the Marchioness of Dunkeld."

Winnifred nodded to the couple, and the man, grudgingly, returned it.

Sinclair swept his hand out, indicating the cart. "I've ordered supplies to be sent up from London but until they arrive, my cart is full of food from Kenmore. Take what you need."

Beattie huffed. "From London, ye say. We dunnae want the help of the English."

His wife elbowed his side. "Hush. The marquess is bringing us food." She dipped another curtsy. "Thank'ee, milord. We're ever so grateful."

Her husband harrumphed, but followed Sinclair to the rear of the cart.

Sinclair flipped back the canvas covering the baskets and crates of goods they'd brought. The farmer's shoulders unbunched when he saw the array of foodstuffs in front of him. "Fresh bread? And meat pies?" He grabbed a crate. "Thanks," he said roughly.

Sinclair handed his wife a bag of oranges. "The fruit isn't fully ripe, but they can still be a good treat."

She clutched the bag to her chest. "They're perfect. Colleen," she called to the girl. "Look what the marquess and marchioness brought us." She gave the girl a small orange. "Say thank'ee."

"Thank'ee."

Sinclair ruffled her hair. "We'll let everyone know as

more food arrives. And if you need anything, you know where we are."

"Aye." Farmer Beattie dropped the crate by his front door. Face tight, he gave them a hard look. "That we do."

Winnifred shifted from boot to boot. That hadn't sounded friendly.

Apparently, Sinclair didn't think so, either. Jaw clenched, he turned and lifted Winnifred back into the cart. He hefted himself up beside her, bobbed his chin at Beattie, and slapped the reins against the horse's back.

They turned down the path and rode in silence for several minutes. Sinclair shifted on the bench, the wood creaking. "It didn't use to be like this."

She looked up at him. "How so?"

"The tenants. They didn't use to be so angry. Or disrespectful." He tugged the brim of his hat lower over his head. "We had good relationships with them. We worked together. There were summer festivals and games where the barrier between peer and tenant disappeared and we'd have a good time together."

"Some of the people we visited today were happy to see you."

He snorted. "Happy to see the food we brought."

The closely-built huts of a village drew into view, with some two-story structures sprinkled in between. More cottages were scattered off the main road, the gardens in the front yards brown and barren. A blacksmith looked up from his irons and watched them as they drove past.

Sinclair cleared his throat. "This is Inver, by the by. There's a draper and haberdasher's shop that some of my guests have said is well stocked. A hat shop that sells ribbons and the like that mother is quite fond of." He pointed to a glass-fronted building. "And that pastrycook there sells passable ices and tarts."

She nudged him with her elbow. "Passable? That's quite the ringing endorsement," she teased. Sinclair's spirits had lowered with each tenant they'd visited, and a melancholy husband wasn't to her liking. She didn't particularly favor him prodding and curious, either, but that at least didn't make her heart go heavy to see.

Her words had their desired effect. One side of his mouth twitched upwards. "It's a good village, full of hard-working and honest folk. I just—"

"Winnie!"

She jerked her head around, searching for the voice. No one had called her Winnie since—

"It is ye!" A young man trotted over to walk alongside the cart, his freckled face grinning up at her. "What on earth are ye doing in Inver? In Scotland, for that matter?"

"Donald." Her stomach squeezed at the sight of her old friend. "Is this your home? I always thought you were from Edinburgh."

Sinclair pulled the cart to a stop.

She turned to him. "This is an old friend of mine and my father's, Donald Innes MacConnell. Donald, this is my husband, the Marquess of Dunkeld."

"Winnie." Donald's shoulders drooped. He gave her a look of such disappointment that she couldn't help but blush, even without knowing its cause. "*Ye* married the marquess?"

* * *

What the bloody hell did that mean?

Sinclair draped his arm along the back seat of the cart, letting his palm settle against his wife's waist. "Yes, Mr. MacConnell. Luckily for me, I captured my prize."

Winnifred stiffened slightly, giving him a questioning look.

Sin's gut hardened at the blush that covered her cheeks. The blush *Donald* had inspired. She'd mentioned once a Scottish friend from childhood. At the time he'd paid it no mind. But now he wondered just how close the two of them had been.

"Congratulations." The boy bowed stiffly. His apricot

curls scraped against his starched collar. He had the sort of face women would consider pretty, Sin supposed. Delicate like a poet's. Extremely punchable. "Excuse the surprise. I didnae think my Winnie was the sort to run in the same circles as the likes of ye."

"My father is a friend of Lord Stamworth's," she said faintly. "We met at one of his routs."

"And ye caught the eye of the marquess." Was there disbelief in the man's voice? Sinclair tightened his grip on the reins, and on his wife. He didn't know if MacConnell was casting aspersions on him or Winnifred, but it was an insult to Sin either way.

"What can I say?" He gave MacConnell a hard look. "When I see something I want, I take it. And once I have it, I keep it."

"Yes," Winnifred said brightly. She smoothed a hand down her skirts. "It was all quite romantic. Now, tell me what brings you to Inver? And how have you been since we last met?" Her cheeks burned so bright, the blacksmith could have used her to heat his iron.

Sin turned his head to glare at her.

"I'm visiting friends in the area." MacConnell patted the cart horse's rump and rested his hand there. "As to how I've been"—he shrugged—"these are troubled times in Scotland. The working man has it rough." He slid a glance at Sinclair. "Fortunate for ye, you'll never have to experience our privations."

Like he didn't work? Sin tossed the reins down. All right, he'd had enough. The disrespect from his tenants he could tolerate. It was his responsibility to shelter and support them. But from this guttersnipe? Touching his horse, eyeing his wife, making her blush. A growl rumbled about in his chest. Like hell he'd sit here and suffer it.

Winnifred scooped the reins into her hand. "Well, it was lovely seeing you." She rested her palm on Sin's thigh and squeezed.

A warning? A plea? Whichever, it had its desired effect.

The irritation burbling behind his breastbone eased away. Sin sniffed. He'd wait to remove MacConnell's head from his neck until another time.

MacConnell wasn't as smart as his wife. Didn't know when it was best to escape Sin's presence. He put his hand over the reins that lay on the horse's back, preventing their departure. "Have ye heard aboot the fight that broke out at a coffeehouse in Glasgow? The guard was called in, killed two of our men. Just boys really. Students. I even heard the Earl of Abercairn got pushed around a wee bit. Nasty business."

Sin stilled. He hadn't heard about that incident yet. The paper from Glasgow lay folded on his desk, unread. But according to Tavish, fights were breaking out more and more across Scotland. Riots flaring and no one seemed to know the exact cause. "Yes, it is. But what business is it of yours?"

MacConnell shook his head, making annoying tutting sounds. "Just correcting myself from earlier. When I said the peerage willnae be affected by the troubles. With tempers running high, no one is safe." The man's freckled face didn't look so innocent as he gazed at Sin, a message hidden in his smirk.

The hairs on the back of Sin's neck stood on end.

MacConnell blinked, and the strange moment disappeared. He turned a sad smile on Winnifred. "I would hate for anything to happen to ye, Winnie. Be sure to take care."

"Rest assured," Sin said coldly, "I'd never allow harm to come to my wife. Anyone who attempts it, won't live to regret it."

MacConnell tipped his hat. "As ye say. Goodbye, Winnie." With one last pat to the horse's rump, he turned and strolled away, whistling a Scottish jig.

Sin took the reins and smacked them down, urging the horse into motion. As they rolled out of the village and towards the next farm, he said, "I don't think I like your friends, *Winnie*."

She worried the fraying hem of her gloves. At this rate, he'd need to buy her a new pair each week. "I haven't seen Donald in many years. He did seem changed."

He seemed like a snake, was what he seemed. And one who knew more than he was letting on.

Sin turned the cart down the drive of his next tenant. Something was afoot in his Scotland. Something bubbling just under the surface that he couldn't see. It was more than just hungry people becoming angry. Sin couldn't pin down his suspicions, but it was time he stopped ignoring the problem.

His tenant, a sheep herder named Clacher, raised a hand in greeting and trudged towards them.

In times of distress, his people used to pull together, not turn on each other. Was someone inflaming the mob as Liverpool suspected? To what end?

His home was tearing apart at the seams. He might not be able to feed all the hungry, but he did know how to investigate conspiracies. And put an end to them.

He squared his shoulders. His honeymoon was over.

It was time to go to work.

Chapter Nine

Winnifred hesitated, pen poised, before crossing an item off her list. The dowager marchioness seemed to enjoy ordering the meals for the day, and Winnifred didn't want to usurp all of her mother-in-law's duties. The woman barely tolerated her as it was.

She sighed, and looked out the window of her snug parlor. Finding her way as the new marchioness was proving difficult. It wasn't like one of her experiments. In her father's laboratory, she could test different hypotheses, observe the results, and move on to the next one if a theory was disproven. No judgment over an incorrect speculation. No consequences aside from lost time if her research proved faulty.

Here, one false move and social ostracism could result. Or worse. The servants seemed a friendly lot, but they reported to the steward, who would report any concerns to Sinclair. Or to Deirdre.

Banquo lifted his head from her feet. She bent down to scratch behind his ears. "If only relationships with people were as simple as they are with you." His tail thumped in agreement. Horatio blew out a breath from his bed on the settee, his upper lip flapping.

"Well, time to get to work." She picked up her list. Putting the pen back in its inkwell, she pulled a piece of lead from her desk and marched from the room, the dogs at her heels. The tour from Deirdre had been delivered at a brisk pace, and Winnifred hadn't been able to examine her new home as thoroughly as she'd wished. As its marchioness, she wanted a detailed accounting of it, and of any problems that might need remedying.

She would prove to her husband that she would be a useful and competent wife.

She started at the top of Kenmore, spending more time than was required on the ramparts and in the corner turrets. It struck her anew. She, unimportant Winnifred Hannon, now Archer, lived in a castle. She ran her hand along the rough stone inside one of the larger turrets. The space was empty, but the view from the window breathtaking. A family of red deer grazed near the outskirts of the woods. Two boys stood hip-deep in the loch, casting out nets in hopes of catching supper. If the sun had been shining brightly, it would have been a perfect summer day.

She wandered the space, pushed open a rotting wooden door that led to a small closet. If she had some shelves built inside, brought up a desk and some bookcases, the turret would make a grand laboratory.

Her heart twisted. Without her father, she had no excuse to run an experiment or correspond with fellow natural philosophers as his nominal assistant. Because she was useful, her father had accepted, even encouraged her endeavors. But she was a wife now, a marchioness, and that part of her life had ended.

She sighed. "Come on, boys." She wound down the staircase, the dogs at her heels, until she reached the battlements. One of the crenellations had crumbled, the stone looking as though it had eroded away. She scratched some notes on her paper. Repairing the castle's defenses was low on the list of priorities, the idea of an attack in this day and age absurd. But she didn't want her home to crumble down about her. "Time to explore the rest of the castle." She checked each room, looking for anything that might need to be repaired, cleaned, or replaced. Her list didn't grow overmuch. The marquess and his servants kept Kenmore in excellent shape. There was little that needed her attention. Little for her to do.

She found a door near the necessary on the lower floor and pulled it open, its hinges squawking. She made a note. Oil. She tapped her lead against her notebook and looked through the door. Complete darkness blanketed the entrance. Banquo lay down and whined.

"We only need a candle, silly. Nothing to be afraid of." Tucking her lead and notebook into a pocket in her skirt, she marched back to the nearest hall table and pulled a candle from an ornate five-pronged silver candelabra.

She looked back into the rectangle of black. Replacing the candle, she picked up the entire candelabra and strode forward.

The door led to a set of narrow steps, curving slightly and going down so deep she knew she must be under ground level. The air was dank, heavy, and the candles illuminated only a couple feet in front of her. She moved slowly, looking for any holes in her path, and thankful the two large dogs had followed her down. Marvelous creatures, dogs. Even when scared themselves, they remained stalwartly by her side.

About one hundred feet in, the dark began to lighten. A few steps more and she saw the exit to the tunnel she was in. The ground sloped up at a gentle angle, clumps of chickweed softening the path underfoot. Roots dangled from the ceiling, eventually giving way to glimpses of sky and broken beams as the roof of the tunnel rotted away. Winnifred quickened her step until she stood at the entrance.

One of the dogs leaned against her side.

"I know." She stroked his head. "A secret passage. How exciting. I wonder what it was used for and where it has led us." They must be close to Kenmore, but all she saw was a rocky hillside tufted with thistle underneath the dreary, grey sky.

Something shuffled behind her. Winnifred turned and held the candelabra up high but could see nothing but pitch. She stepped forward, peering. "Hullo?"

Her only answer was heavy breathing. Wood scraped against wood.

Winnifred froze. "It's I, the, uh, marchioness. Show yourself."

Horatio pressed against her legs, and she stumbled to the side. She patted his head. "It's probably nothing. Just—"

Something hissed, the sound slithering through the dark, wrapping around her, turning her feet to lead.

With a howl, Banquo reared onto his hind legs and charged – straight out of the tunnel. Horatio followed, hot on his heels, leaving Winnifred alone.

Traitorous beasts, dogs.

Something rushed towards her, the sound of feet pounding against the dirt growing louder. With a cry, she turned to flee, but the beast had grabbed her skirts.

"Get off! Get off!" She shrieked, kicking her feet out, and made glancing contact with the most dastardly badger she'd ever laid eyes upon.

It was about three feet in length, with a wide, squat body. Its dark eyes glared at her from its striped face and its tiny tail twitched in anger over her trespass. Fabric tore, the sound rending the air, and the beast staggered back, a jagged square of blue muslin in its teeth.

Seeing her chance, she picked up what was left of her skirts and ran as fast as her feet would carry her. Daylight was only feet away. She looked back, swore the animal's eyes glowed red with loathing, and ran headlong into an immovable object.

"Winnifred!" Sin grabbed her shoulders and pulled her away from the dropped candelabra. He stomped on the one wick that had remained alit. "I heard you scream. What is it?" He swung her around, peering down the tunnel, looking back over his shoulder, turning his head every which way.

She pointed a shaking finger back down the tunnel. "Badger!" Her chest heaved, and she dragged in shallow breaths.

He squinted, tilted his head. "I must have misheard. For a moment I though you said 'badger.'"

Grabbing his hand, she stepped back, pulling with all her might to drag him away from the danger. "Huge, possessed-by-the-devil badger. We'll have to get a new castle."

His lips twitched. "Because of a badger."

She peered back down the tunnel. Nothing. No hissing, no glowing eyes. The badger had gone back to wherever he'd holed up.

Her shoulders inched down her back, her tension easing. Only to be replaced by embarrassment. Heat crawled up her neck. Dropping his hand, she touched her hair, making sure it was all in its correct place. Tilting her chin up, she tried to give him a look a true marchioness would: haughty, imperious, controlled. "It was a large badger." She enunciated each word exactly. "And unusually aggressive. Most likely diseased. My reaction was only...."

She trailed off as Sin threw his head back laughing. His whole body shook with it, amusement dripping from every ounce of his being.

Winnifred blinked. She'd never seen a moment of such pure joy. He laughed freely, like a child without a care in the world.

All the emotions in her former home had been muted, faded. Mustn't get too excited. Mustn't let anyone see you're upset. Even when she and her father celebrated a scientific success, it was with a firm handshake and smiles that didn't quite reach their eyes. When her mother had been taken from the house, all the life had gone with her.

Sinclair's emotions acted like wine upon her. His joy seeped into her, warming her through. She hadn't realized how cold she'd felt until she stood next to his fire.

Sin dug his palm into his eye, his laughter tapering off. "I'll catch the wee, naughty badger for you. Dunnae fear."

Banquo slunk up to her and nudged her fingers with his snout. She rubbed behind his ear. "Do you realize that your brogue becomes more pronounced the more affected you are?" Like he wore his own mask, but powerful emotions knocked it down.

He sobered. "I hadn't noticed." Picking up a broken stick, he chucked it into the field, the dogs racing after it. Winnifred saw they were behind Kenmore. A small river that led to the lake was only a slight distance away. "Growing up in England, it seemed easier fitting in if I hid my accent. Made it easier to forget this place, and my duties to it." He gave her a deprecating smile. "Easier to fit in with the crowd, too."

She raised her eyebrows. Her husband stood a head above most men. Was as broad across as a bull, and his long, silky, auburn hair was unlike any other peer's. "A man like you could never fit in."

Heat sparked in his eyes, the deep, piercing blue so unlike her own faded periwinkle ones. "Aye, that is so." He stepped close, his body a shield against the breeze that lifted her hair. "Do ye like what you see, wife?"

Her cheeks heated, and she clasped her hands together in front of her. "Your form is pleasing." Complimenting her husband couldn't be taken amiss, could it?

He lifted his hand and cupped her cheek, brushing his thumb along her lower lip before sliding around to grip the nape of her neck. "Pleasing. I'm glad. I very much want to please you, *mo ghràdh.*" His lips hovered an inch from hers, his breath ghosting over her mouth.

Her nipples tingled, pulled tight, and her gaze flipped between his eyes. Was he speaking of their intimacies? Perhaps in the bedroom such talk wasn't improper, but in a field in the light of day, it seemed—*thrilling*—inappropriate.

If she leaned forward, pressed her aching body to his, what would the consequences be? Was this wantonness roiling through her inherited from her mother? Would it lead to the same result?

Her body cooled, and she stepped back.

Sin squeezed her neck once, his eyes narrowing, before

dropping his hand with a sigh.

He looked to the tunnel before bending and swiping the candelabra from the ground. "Someday, I'm going to understand you. You can allow yourself pleasure."

No, men could be free with their pleasures. Women had to take care.

She cleared her throat, needing to change the subject. "What is it you call me? *Mo* something?"

"*Mo ghrâdh.* My love."

Her back tensed. That hadn't changed the subject in the direction she'd wanted.

Horatio trotted up, the stick crookedly held in his mouth. Winnifred tugged it free and threw it as far as she could. "What is the tunnel for? Did your ancestors use if for smuggling? Or a tactic to sneak up on invaders?"

He arched one burnished brow. "Nothing so interesting. It was used to carry goods that were transported by the river into the castle. There was nothing secret about it."

"Oh." Her shoulders dropped.

Sinclair held out his arm, and she took it, turning with him to stroll around the castle to the front door. "It has gone forgotten for many a year now. But if there is a dangerous badger threatening Kenmore, I suppose it needs attention."

He was teasing, trying to lighten the mood. And she was grateful for it. But she had never learnt the art of play. She didn't know how to tease him back. "I have a list, a small one, of other improvements I believe Kenmore needs. If my saying so isn't too forward, that is."

He blew out a breath. "With you, nothing is too forward."

Chapter Ten

A scratch sounded at the door and both he and Winnifred looked up from their respective books. His, a treatise on Scottish history; hers, the King James bible, although her glance frequently drifted to *The Times* that he'd left on the settee beside her.

"Yes?"

A footman poked his head through. "Milord, Mr. Gavin Fraser is here to see ye."

Sin stood from his armchair. "Send him in, send him in." He hurried forward, arm outstretched to greet the man. "Gavin. It's good to see you."

"I was sorry to have missed ye when ye were making your rounds the other day." Gavin rolled up his cap and shoved it in the pocket of his jacket. "I was in Glasgow looking for a seed supplier."

"Gavin, may I introduce you to my wife. Winnifred, this is Gavin Fraser, a friend from childhood and one of the best farmers on the estate."

"Lady Dunkeld" Gavin inclined his head. He nodded at Sin, his eyes twinkling. "I'd heard that ye'd taken a bride, but I didnae believe it. But now that I see her, I can see why ye'd become leg-shackled to this lass."

"Yes." Sin eyed his wife, watched as her cheeks pinkened. "I was most fortunate in my circumstances." He could have been caught in a compromising situation with a truly boring woman. Not just one who pretended to be colorless. She was a puzzle waiting to be deciphered.

"Well, let us sit and I'll call for refreshments." Sin strode to the side of the room and pulled the bell for a footman.

Winnifred fiddled with the cuff of her gown. "Might I ask why you went to Glasgow for seed? Have you no local suppliers?"

"Gavin, here, is particularly fond of the Scotch whisky at the King's Boar in Glasgow." He dropped back into his chair and grimaced as its legs squeaked under his weight. "He takes any chance he can of riding to that fair city."

Gavin glared at him. "I didnae go there for scotch. Although the brew from that distillery is quite lovely," he told Winnifred. "The local seed supplier only sells Pole Rivet wheat, which is late to ripen. Add that to this confounded endless winter, and I'll ne'er harvest. I'm going to try another variety, the Losanna red. Mayhap that will put bread in our bellies."

A maid entered, pushing a serving cart. She placed a tray of berry tarts that Sin knew Winnifred was fond of in front of her mistress, but his wife didn't spare a glance at the pastries. She scooted to the edge of her seat. "And do you rotate your crops? Do you use any supplements to help aid growth?"

Gavin blinked. "Uh...."

Winnifred clenched her skirts before relaxing her hands and resting back on the settee, a tight smile on her face. "My apologies. I only ask because I'm sure it is something my father would be interested in."

Sin took the decanter the maid had brought and poured Gavin and himself a dram of whisky. "My new father-in-law is a botanist. Worked at the royal gardens for a time. My wife, I believe, was very involved in his research."

"I merely assisted him as best I could," she said.

Sin snorted, and garnered a reproachful look from Winnifred in return. Blast it, her interest went far beyond that of a note-taker for her father. Her mind was agile and curious and her father had struck him as neither. Sin wondered how productive Mr. Hannon would be now that his "assistant" was no longer in his service.

An ache grew behind his breastbone, and Sin rubbed his knuckle over it. It was no wonder Winnifred appeared listless at times. Kenmore must appear very dull to her without an occupation to engage her mind.

"There's naught much to tell at this point." Gavin rooted through a bowl of nuts until he found one to his liking. He popped it in his mouth. "Even the best seed cannae grow withoot the sun. My barley has barely peeked its head from the dirt." He sighed. "The worst of it is, in three years our barrels will be empty of good whisky. Might have to drink that swill coming from the Lowlands."

Winnifred fiddled her thumbs but remained silent.

"Wife, you were to write your father this afternoon, I believe. Why don't you ask Gavin the questions you think he would?" Sin sipped his whisky, eyeing her over the glass's rim. "Perhaps he'll even have a word of advice for the farmers up here."

"I'd listen to any ideas he has," Gavin agreed.

"Well...." Winnifred tipped her head to one side, her brow wrinkling slightly as though listening to an unheard voice. Or considering every option she could think of. Hell, his wife could have been running multiplication tables in her head for all he understood of her.

She nodded. "I do know my father is interested in crop management. Do you rotate your crops?"

"Of course. Four-field rotation." Gavin stared morosely into his glass. "I like to leave one of my fields to lie fallow, but I cannae do it this year. With how poor the harvest is, I need every square inch I can get."

"And do you spread manure on your fields?" Winnifred asked.

Gavin shot him an uncomfortable look, and Sin bit back a grin. It wasn't a typical conversation with a marchioness, but it was interesting.

"Aye. Fat lot of good it's doing," Gavin grumbled.

Winnifred pressed her lips tight, her right knee bobbing up and down.

Sin wondered how long she could keep it in, whatever it was she wanted to say. She looked near to bursting. But his wife swallowed her words down, her leg stilling, her fingers worrying her cuff again.

Sin pressed his lips flat. Well, if his wife needed prodding, he could do that. "What sort of experiments is your father running with soil supplements?"

"Well," she said hesitantly, "have you heard of Johann Fredrich Mayer?"

Gavin scratched his head. "Nae, milady. Cannae say that I have."

"Didn't he have some new ideas about crop rotation?" Sin asked.

Winnifred nodded. "Yes, but he also believed that gypsum should be used to fertilize the soil. He believed that it sped the growing time of crops."

"And does it?" Gavin paused, a nut halfway to his mouth.

"Well, no, not as far as our tests went, but his ideas have inspired many chemists to experiment in the same vein." She poured herself a cup of tea and tapped her thumb on the rim of the cup.

Sin waited until he could take it no more. "And? Any results that signified?"

"I'm afraid agriculture will always be a work in progress." She settled herself back in her seat, her ankles crossed neatly. "There have been promising studies. I— my father believes nitrogen may show the most promise. It is a chemical found in both water and the air, but not in significant enough quantities to increase current yields. A few natural philosophers believe it is also found in the roots of legumes, which is why crop rotation systems that include those plants tend to show better results. Mr. Fraser, if you aren't growing any legumes currently, I would encourage you to add them to your crops."

Sin leaned forward. Had his father known this? He didn't think Kenmore grew peas or beans in any significant quantity, but he'd have to discuss it with Tavish. "And this nitrogen, it travels from the roots into the soil?"

Winnifred nodded. "Just so. But we've been investigating whether it is also released when legume plant matter decays. Before our marriage, my father had been planning to experiment on this theory. I'd created a bin where I put chopped up peas and left it in the sun. I, we, were going to spread a thin layer of it over the soil while growing strawberries to see if it aided the process."

Peas and beans he could get. "Would that help this harvest?"

Winnifred raised her shoulders. "An experiment like this would take much trial and error. And there would need to be fields left as they are to appropriately measure the variables. It could take years to see any results."

Sin's shoulders slumped. So, still no answers. Nothing was bloody growing and no hope in sight for at least a year. His people didn't have a year.

He rubbed his forehead. "Gavin, were you in Glasgow when the riot broke out? The one where Lord Abercairn was injured?"

His friend blew out his cheeks. "I heard of the incident. I didnae witness it."

"And?" His friend wasn't stupid. He knew what Sin was asking.

Gavin shrugged. "Tempers are hot. Especially against the English, and anyone who supports them." He gave Sin a measuring look. "Ye need to step lightly, my friend. I know where your loyalties lie, but a member of the House of Lords, with a new English bride, would be a ripe target."

"Has it really become so bad?" Winnifred set her tea down and clasped her hands together. "Was Lord Abercairn attacked just because he was elected as a Scottish representative peer for the House of Lords?"

"You don't have to worry." Sin fisted his right hand, the knuckles cracking. "No harm will come to you."

She turned her sky-blue eyes on him. "It wasn't me I was

worried about."

There was a pregnant silence, until Gavin cleared his throat. "The talk is always there, but it's louder now. I almost believe it will happen this time."

"What will happen?" Winnifred asked.

"Rebellion," Sin said grimly. The dream of every Scot.

"Self-governance," Gavin moderated. "Since the English returned British Java to the Dutch, hope has been renewed. Mayhap the English bit off more than they could chew, trying to control the world."

"Self-governance won't put food in our bellies." Sin ground his jaw. In times of privation, it was necessary to enhance alliances, not break them asunder. The English had many faults, but in times of need they would support their northern brethren.

Unless the Scottish turned on them, inciting violence to the point where they cut off aid.

His mother breezed into the room. "Gavin! Dear, how are ye?"

Gavin and Sin stood, and his friend pressed a light kiss on his mother's upturned cheek. "Better, now that I've seen your bonnie face."

She slapped his shoulder. "Ye always were such a flirt, even as a wee laddie." She turned to Sin. "Did you ever tell your wife about the time the two of ye climbed through a bog to pick me some wildflowers. Ye came back covered in muck and smelling worse than the stables."

"We were eight, mother." But flowers weren't a bad idea. Perhaps a bit of wooing would encourage his wife to be more unreserved.

His mother pinched his cheek. "It still showed an unmatched level of devotion." She shot an undecipherable look at Winnifred. "The relationship between a child and his mam is one of the closest he'll ever have."

Gavin set his glass down. "Well, I must be getting back. My Maura will be missing me."

"Before ye leave, can ye take a look at my basil?" His

mother gave Gavin the smile that had wrapped his father right around her finger. "Ye are the best plant doctor around."

"Of course, milady." With a nod to Sin and a bow to Winnifred, Gavin followed the dowager marchioness out of the room, leaving Sin and Winnifred alone.

Sin sank back into his seat and picked up his glass. He took a sip, examining his wife over the rim. "You weren't expecting to face a rebellion upon your marriage, I expect."

"No." She shook her head ruefully. "I am sorry to say that my education in political events has been poor. My father rarely even looked at the papers. I didn't realize there was still such unrest."

"An unrest that is being encouraged, I fear." He drummed his fingers on his thigh. "Someone is inciting this. I can feel it."

Winnifred's mouth opened in a delightful little *O*. A knot formed in his gut. That look of surprise was the one she wore when she'd had her first orgasm. It was seductive as hell. He wanted those lips in indecent ways.

"Well, what can you do about it?" she asked.

He crossed one leg over the other. Yes, that was the question. He'd sent out inquiries to every contact he had in Scotland, but had heard nothing yet. And so he sat. And waited.

He hated waiting.

"I don't know." He rubbed his jaw. "Tell me what you think."

* * *

Tell me what you think. Five dangerous words.

Her husband's gaze landed on her, the weight of it making it hard for her to breathe. He made the question sound so simple. And so inviting. He made her want to believe she could trust him.

She pressed her hands into her thighs, digging her fingers into the fabric of her skirt. Her heart pounded.

Some small part of her knew it shouldn't be this frightening to speak openly. That the average person didn't become queasy at the thought of voicing an opinion.

But Sinclair wasn't just another person. He was her husband, with the full legal ramifications that position entailed. He held power over her of which she had to be wary. The power to send her away.

She swallowed, trying to bring moisture back to her mouth. But he had asked. Demanded, really. Could the consequences be so bad if she was following her husband's directive?

"I think," she said slowly, watching his expression, "that you cannot do anything about such intrigue if some element is subverting the masses. If you concentrate on alleviating the food shortages, the resentment and anger will dissipate, at least for your people here."

He stood. Pacing to the window, he clasped his hands behind his back and stared outside. "What you say is sensible, and with what I've ordered from London, my tenants will have a steady supply of food in their bellies soon enough. But I cannot feed all of Scotland."

No, nor the rest of the world. This dark summer was a global epidemic, with reports of crop failures coming in from as far away as the Americas.

Sinclair's shoulders were as tight as a drum, and she realized just how heavily his responsibilities weighed upon him.

Hesitantly, she stood and inched towards him. She rested her palm on his back, the action seeming somehow more intimate than their caresses in the marital bed. "There is nothing to be done about people's anger," she said quietly. "Nothing that has happened is your responsibility."

He spun and caught her wrist, setting her heart to pounding. He brought her hand up and pressed a kiss to her palm. "Thank you," he said, his voice a low rumble that shivered down her spine. "But there are steps I can take. And if these riots are being stirred up as a prelude for rebellion, indeed it is my duty to take action."

He stroked his thumb along the inner curve of her palm.

She stared at where their hands met. "Duty?"

He knitted his eyebrows together. "There is something I need to tell you, but it must be kept in the strictest confidence. Aside from a few trusted servants who work with me on occasion, no one else at Kenmore knows."

The tingles along her palm were starting to spread to other parts of her body. Her breath quickened. "Of course. I would never betray you."

He examined her face before nodding. "I am not only a member of the House of Lords, but I also aid the British government in another capacity. When threats against the Crown arise, I'm called upon to investigate and eliminate the risk. In short, I'm a spy."

Winnifred blinked. And blinked again. Of all the things she'd thought he might say, that hadn't been in her top one hundred imaginings.

"You understand why this can never be spoken of?"

She nodded. "Of course. I am at such a loss for words, I don't think I can speak of it."

Her husband was a spy.

It was indeed dangerous information to hold, and the fact he shared it with her sent a flutter to her belly. She licked her lips. But did it make her situation more dangerous or less? The information could be used as a bargaining chip, something to hold over his head in case he ever decided to be rid of her.

Or a reason to make locking her away more attractive. In Bedlam, no one would believe her ravings.

If only she knew whether she could trust him.

She pulled her hand from his and circled behind the settee, putting distance between them. "Even knowing this, I'm uncertain what can be done on your part to stop the riots. They seem to be happening all over Scotland. It's too widespread to be coordinated, surely."

"I disagree." The filtered sunlight limned his wide

shoulders. "One person or a small organization can coordinate a great deal, have tentacles in many places. If there is a power behind the mayhem, I intend to find him and put an end to it."

To him. She saw the violence in his eyes. The hard set of his jaw. If her husband caught this person, he would kill him. Had he killed before? Was that the job of a spy?

The knowledge of such brutality in Sinclair didn't shock her. She should be horrified, but she wasn't. He had a moral code. She hadn't mapped it fully yet, but she knew he wouldn't kill on a whim. That violence was carefully meted out on his part.

Others might not be so discriminating.

"You could get hurt," she blurted out. Dear Lord, her husband was a spy. Under constant threat of harm. A pit opened in her stomach. She might not have to worry about her husband controlling her. She could be a widow at any moment.

The thought should be comforting. A widow had the most freedom of any woman in society. She ran her gaze from the toes of his muddy boots to the wrinkle in his cravat where he'd tugged on it. No, not even to assure her own safety could she wish him harm.

"I'll be fine."

She huffed. "No man is invincible. Not even one as brawny as you."

Sin shot her a cocky grin. "Don't you worry, wife. Your husband hasn't been bested by any man yet. This soon married, you won't be getting rid of me so quickly."

Such arrogance. Everybody was subject to injury, illness, and decay. Burly highlanders were no exception. "That is a myopic opinion."

His smile faded. "Nevertheless, I've made the decision to investigate. The discussion is at an end."

Of course, it was. Her jaw went stiff from clenching it. He asked for her opinion but didn't truly wish to hear it. Why had she expected her husband to be any different?

"Of course, my lord." She inclined her head. "Anything you wish."

"Damn it!" He kicked the low table, the scones and sandwiches tumbling from their tray. "I didn't mean it like that. And you don't have to look at me like I just kicked a wee kitten. Even though I've made my decision, I don't want you buttoning yourself up, hiding yourself away. What is going on in that perverse head of yours?"

Perverse. That had been the kindest word said about her mother, and one of the earlier ones. They had quickly degraded. *Unsound,* she heard whispering through her mind. *Unbalanced. Barmy.*

Mad.

Her heart raced. "Nothing." She shook her head. "I'm not thinking anything."

He barked out a bitter laugh. "Did I marry a woman or a mindless poppet? Or worse, a coward?" He shook his head. "I won't live with a timid mouse. Speak up! Tell me what's wrong."

A lump rose in her throat, clogging it, until the words either had to burst out or she'd choke on them. "You said you wanted a partner in this marriage. That you wanted me to speak my mind. But it's a lie. You want me to agree with you, not make trouble, never be a cause for embarrassment. I know what happens when a woman dares express herself."

He stalked towards her and she backed away, trying to keep the settee between them. "What is it that happens, Winnifred? What has put it into your head that you have to hide your true self away?"

The back of her knees hit a corner table and buckled.

Sin leapt forward and grabbed her biceps, pulling her upright. He gave her a small shake. "Tell me what you're so afraid of?"

"That you'll send me away." Her voice broke. "Like my father did my mother."

A crease appeared in his forehead. "Your father said your mother died a decade ago."

"She did." Her pulse pounded in her ears, memories of the last time she'd seen her mother crashing through her brain. "In Bedlam."

Sinclair stilled. "Your mother was in an asylum? Why?"

Winnifred yanked from his grip. Tears burned behind her eyes, but she'd had years of practice never letting them fall. "Because she'd become an inconvenience to my father. She laughed too loudly, danced when there was no music, liked to throw feasts in the dead of night." She remembered those nights when her mother had come into her room. How she'd held her hands and spun and spun until they'd both fallen down. Even then, she'd known her mother hadn't been quite right; but had she been so bad as to deserve banishment and death?

"She was high-spirited. Lively." Until she wasn't. After days of laughter and cuddles and running through the streets without her shoes, her mother would cave in on herself, become a shadow who wouldn't leave her bed. The dramatic highs and lows had taught Winnifred the importance of controlling her spirits, of being measured in all things. She balled up her fist and pounded it onto her thigh. "She might have been unwell, but she didn't deserve to be sent away. I could have looked after her," she whispered.

Sin closed his eyes, his nostrils flaring. "Sweet mother of God." When he looked at her, pity was heavy in his eyes. "Your father should have told me."

It wasn't something her father liked to remember. He was riddled with his own doubts. He'd told Winnifred her mother would get better in an institution. Become fixed, as though she were one of his experiments he merely had to tweak to get the desired result.

Instead, she'd died of cholera after only a month.

Winnifred wrapped her arms around her middle, hiding her shaking hands, and raised her chin. "I'm not mad. You don't have to worry about our children."

"Christ." He thrust his hand through his hair, pulling

some of the locks from their ribbon. "It's not them I'm worried about." He strode to her and gripped her arms, running his hands up and down. "I don't believe you're mad, Winnifred. And I give you my word I would never send you away. But I'd like to get to know my wife. Who you truly are. Not who you want me to see."

He stepped closer, his chest brushing hers. "Trust is earned, I know this. Being your husband doesn't give me an inevitable right to it. I hope that soon enough, however, I'll have earned yours." He bent and pressed a butterfly-soft kiss on her forehead.

Something twisted, fluttered behind her breast. The feeling was strange, uncomfortable, and felt an awful lot like hope.

Instead of squelching the feeling immediately as she'd trained herself to do, she let it dig a tiny root into her heart.

Perhaps, with Sinclair, she'd found a safe place to call home.

Chapter Eleven

Winnifred adjusted the wick on her desk lamp. It was early afternoon but the shadows in her sitting room had taken a gloomy shape. Horatio and Banquo snored softly behind her, one stretched across her settee, the other on the rug before the fire.

Tapping her pen against her lips, she considered the letter before her. Mr. Raguhram had sent an introduction of her to a Scottish chemist at the University of Edinburgh, and his response to her query was promising. He'd even addressed her directly, although she'd signed her name as assistant to her father.

"Good afternoon, wife." Sin burst into the room, the space filling with the energy her husband seemed to carry about with him everywhere. He wore a jacket of black superfine and his cravat was loosely knotted, revealing his thick, bronze neck. Tan buckskin breeches stretched across hard thighs and snuggly cupped his—

Winnifred averted her gaze, her mouth going dry. "Good afternoon. What are your plans for the day?"

"*We* are going for a horseback ride." He plucked her pen from her hand and tossed it down. "Cook has prepared a picnic luncheon for us. I'd like to show you more of the estate."

She gave him an apologetic shrug. "I've never ridden a horse before."

"Never?"

"I've lived in London my whole life. I walked, or hired a hackney coach."

"Well, then, it's high time you learned." He clapped his hands together, and Horatio lifted his head from the rug and huffed at the disturbance.

Sinclair frowned. "Why are you letting Banquo lie on your settee?"

Winnifred stored her letters and rose. "You try moving him." Except for bribing them with treats, she had little recourse against animals that size. "Besides, he's not harming anything."

Banquo yawned widely, two long strings of drool stretching between his jaws and dripping onto the embroidered fabric, before dropping back down into slumber.

She blew out her cheeks. "Well, not much harm anyhow."

"Useless beasts," Sin grumbled. "Fatigued from a morning of running away in terror, no doubt."

Winnifred tilted her head, and a slight flush crawled up her husband's neck.

"I brought them with me to try to flush out your badger."

Her lips twitched. "And?"

He tugged at the bottom of his waistcoat. "We were unsuccessful. This time."

"I see." She would not laugh. She had decided to try to be freer with her husband, but finding amusement at his expense was still a step too far. She swept a hand down her wool morning dress. "Will this serve? I have no riding habit."

"Yes, you do." Sin turned for the door and she fell in step beside him. "I've had a complete new wardrobe made for you. It arrived this morning."

"New clothes?" Excitement quickened her words. Expensive frocks were unimportant, she told herself. A pointless expense when her plain gowns covered her as well.

And her feet still itched to fly to her rooms and see what

Sinclair had bought. She had thought as a marchioness an improved wardrobe would be one of the benefits. After coming to know her husband and how little he cared about appearance, however, her expectations had dwindled.

"Yes. The seamstress comes tomorrow to make any necessary alterations, but the riding habit should fit well enough for today."

"I'll go see, shall I?" She turned for the stairs, forced her legs to keep their sedate pace. Her measured steps didn't last. She took the stairs two at a time, ignoring the chuckle reverberating behind her.

Throwing open the door to her dressing room, she gasped. Gown after gown spilled from trunks and wardrobes. The door to her closet didn't close for the crush of silks and satins stuffed within. Evening gowns beaded with fine crystals, walking and carriage gowns of finely woven gabardine, and morning dresses made of the lushest silks and velvets. She caressed the sumptuous fabrics, inhaled the scent of the lavender flowers that had been packed with the clothing.

No, fine clothes didn't matter in the grand scheme of life.

But they didn't hurt.

She found the riding habit half-buried underneath a satin dinner dress. She called for her maid and within minutes, she was smoothing the hunter green corduroy skirts and jacket down her body.

"It needs a wee nipping in aboot the waist," Sheena, her abigail said, smoothing the velvet trim along the collar, "but otherwise 'tis a good fit."

"Yes." Winnifred angled her top hat to dip rakishly over one eye. "Very nice indeed."

She met her husband at the base of the staircase, and he tucked her hand in the crook of his arm as they strolled to the front door. Two horses stood, saddled and pawing at the gravel drive, a footman holding their reins.

Sinclair gave her a brief tutorial, showing her how to pull

on the rein, smirking as she tried to imitate his clucking sounds. Finally, they were ready.

"This is my mother's saddle. She never took to riding side-saddle so you'll have to ride astride. I'll order a woman's saddle for future rides if you like."

"This is fine." She hoped. Her position should be more stable riding astride, but what would she do with her skirts?

"Nevertheless, I suppose I should have some available for guests. Most of my friends are married now. You can test out both, see which you prefer. Until then...." Sinclair wrapped his hands around her waist and hefted her up. "Swing your leg over."

Gasping, she fumbled until she sat atop the beast, her face heating as she tugged her skirts out from under her, arranging them to cover her legs. The horse shifted, and she forgot her modesty to grip the thick mane.

Sin held her ankle and slid her boot into the stirrup. "Heather here is as gentle as she comes. You'll have no cause for concern on her back." He circled the animal and fitted her other boot into its stirrup. He patted the horse's neck and handed her the leather reins. Three knots held the ends together, and she squeezed them tightly.

"Easy." He pulled her hands forward so they were resting at the base of Heather's neck. "Unless you want to stop, don't pull back so. Heather has a sweet temper so she won't say anything, but you'll hurt her mouth if you keep pressure on the bit. With this type of horse, you want to be her friend, not her master."

Well, she definitely didn't want to be her enemy, not sitting so high up on a two-thousand-pound animal. "Indeed, friends it is." She relaxed her hands even further and eased her breathing. Millions of people rode horses every day. She could do this.

Sin took the reins for the other horse, lifted his foot to stirrup, and swung himself onto the saddle. He nudged his horse, directing him into a blessedly slow walk, and Heather turned to follow.

"I didn't tell her to turn." She eyed the reins in her hand suspiciously.

Sin grinned. "Like I said, she's an agreeable horse." He inhaled deeply, and raised his face to the sky. "Now, what do you say we move a bit faster?"

She didn't have much choice. When Sinclair's horse eased into an easy trot, her horse followed suit. Winnifred tightened her legs around the horse's middle and concentrated on not bouncing off the saddle.

"Do you see that stone wall, there?" Sin pointed into the distance, at a row of sandstone blocks that rose four feet high in points and crumbled down to the ground in others. "That's where my great-great-great-great-grandda held off the Sassenach invaders in 1575."

"That is a profusion of greats." Winnifred wondered at his knowledge of family history. She knew the names of her grandparents, had even met her paternal grandfather before his death, but that was the extent of her knowledge of her own people. There must be a feeling of security that came with such intelligence. Sinclair was but one link on a chain, one that he could see stretching back into history, with the next link waiting to be made.

With her. She would be a part of his chain now.

A breeze ruffled his hair, pinning a strand to his cheek. He pointed at a low ditch that ran to the east of them. "And that is where my great-uncle Ulric lost his head in the Forty-Five Rebellion." He leaned towards her, the leather of his saddle creaking, and whispered, "We had some Jacobites in our family. I hope your English sensibilities can countenance such a subversive history."

Winnifred rolled her eyes. Her husband could be as playful as a giant puppy. A quality that was quickly becoming endearing. She tapped her heels into Heather's flanks, and to her surprise, the horse moved forward. They continued the tour, crossing his land as Sin told stories of his ancestors, most of them bloody, all of them noble.

"I thought you said husbands and wives should be

honest with one another." She patted Heather's neck as they drew to a stop.

"I did. I am," he said, indignant.

"Surely there must have been some scoundrels in your family history." She gave him a small smile. "Not everyone could have been a heroic saint."

He grumbled. "Well, there might have been a bounder or two." He jerked his head to the left. "There's a nice valley over that hill where we can eat. Shall we try a gentle canter?"

She eyed Heather. The girl had been awfully well-tempered. Winnifred sat up straighter, a lightness filling her chest. "Let's." And digging her heels into the horse's flanks, she urged her into a smooth lope.

The desolate scenery streamed past in a muted blur. The craggy moors and rocky ravines were so different from the rolling green hills of an English landscape. There was a wildness to the land, a vulnerability that dug under her skin. Her new home was enchanting, untamed. It whispered to her, urging her to shed her inhibitions.

She clicked her tongue and slapped the reins, prodding Heather faster. Laughter tumbled from her lips as she bounced forwards. A wind whipped around her, and she shivered in delight.

"Easy," Sin shouted from behind.

Easy? Why should she go easy when it felt like she was flying? Riding a horse was marvelous. It was—

"Yowww!" Pain exploded in her groin and she nearly toppled from her saddle. She landed on the saddle again – and onto the knots in her reins that had slipped between her legs.

Sin pulled even with her just as she pulled the reins out from under her. "Winnifred, are you all right?" He gripped her elbow as both horses slowed to a stop.

"Yes." She bit back a wince.

"You yelled." He examined her from her head to her boots and back again. "What was the problem?"

"Nothing." She gave him a clenched smile, heat flooding her face. "Nothing's wrong." Good gad, but it burned. Bouncing up and down on a hard knot had been more painful that her wedding night, and with no redeeming aftereffects.

Not that she'd admit to such a humiliating injury.

He jumped off his horse then turned and pulled her down. "You are the most stubborn woman. If something ails you, tell me."

"It was nothing of consequence." She gazed over his shoulder, avoiding eye contact. "I merely landed wrong... on the knots of the reins."

"On your arse?"

Her cheeks flamed hotter.

From the corner of her eye she saw his lips stretch into a pirate grin. "Ah. On your cunny."

"Don't you dare laugh!"

He blew out his cheeks. His eyes sparkled with mirth, but to his credit he held back his laughter. "I wouldna dream of it. Wait here." After pulling the saddlebag from his horse, he patted his animal on the rump, sending him to graze further down in the valley. Heather followed placidly behind.

Sin pulled a wool blanket from the bag and spread it on the ground. He dropped down, legs crossed at the ankle, and patted the spot next to him. "Come down here with me."

She gave him a wary look, but eased down by his side.

"Lie back."

"Sin, truly I am fine."

He pulled off her hat and tossed it to the ground. "I like when you call me Sin. Now do as your husband bids. You have an injury and it is my duty to see to it."

"Nothing hurts anymore." Only her pride. But curiosity had her rolling to her back.

He lounged next to her, putting his weight on one elbow. His fingers drew up the hem of her skirts. "Now, tell me exactly where you hurt yourself?"

"Sin!" She twisted her head in every direction, looking for witnesses. "We can't do this out of doors." Yet she parted her legs an inch. Scotland was making her reckless. Reckless and foolish and—

"Oh!" she breathed.

He circled his palm over her mons, soothing away any lingering sting. "Feel better."

She gulped. "Yes, Sin."

"And do you wish me to stop merely because we are out of doors?"

She shook her head, her hair scraping free from its knot. "No, Sin."

The chilled air cooled her heated skin. She let herself relax into the sensation. This part of their marriage she was growing comfortable with. Her husband wanted to bring her pleasure; it would be churlish to refuse. Even those few moments when she lost control of her responses and her body flew apart weren't quite so frightening. Sin told her it was natural, and she wanted to believe it.

He scooted down and raised her skirts above her hips.

"Sinclair!" She pushed up onto her palms. Heather nickered from twenty feet away, but other than the horses, they were alone. But that circumstance could change.

His gaze was fixed at the vee of her legs. He inhaled deeply and sucked his bottom lip into his mouth. "You smell delicious." Placing his palms on her inner thighs, he spread them open.

Was there movement on that hill? Only a hare, searching for its meal. Still, she pushed at his shoulder. He had—

The first swipe of his tongue had her moaning in surrender. The second, and she fell back onto the blanket with a wail.

The sensations of his mouth upon her were amazing. Her legs turned to jelly and dropped open wide. He lapped at her opening, the tingles he created spreading to the very tips of her breasts. She stretched her arms overhead, arching her back, reveling in the building heat.

His caresses turned harder, his teeth tugging on her sensitive flesh, the roughness of his act as thrilling as it was taboo.

She stared at the sky, a queer dusky orange in the fading day. She tried to even her breaths, but she'd never felt anything so exciting in her entire life.

Sin dragged his tongue up her slit and sucked her nub into his mouth. Hard.

Her hips bucked. It was too much. Too intense. She grabbed Sin's hair, tried pulling him away.

He growled, the vibrations an added torment on her clitoris. Sliding his hands under her legs, he encircled her wrists and pinned them to the ground. His shoulders pressed into her inner thighs, holding them open.

She was completely defenseless. Easy prey for his taking.

Winnifred burst apart. His tongue and teeth worked her clit, never relenting, and another crisis overwhelmed her.

Sobs mingled with her moans. "Sin! Please. Enough."

He crawled up her body, his hair disarrayed, his eyes dark. He yanked at his falls, and a button popped off and stung her belly. "My wife has decided to make noise now, when we are outside for anyone to hear." His voice was low, rough, and held a note of approval. He swung his head from side to side. "Naughty girl."

She tried to hold onto one last shred of reason.

The head of his length bobbed against her clit, renewing the shudders in her body.

"Sin." She sucked in a breath and searched the empty land. "We can't. Not here—ohhhhh!"

He filled her with one thrust, the suddenness of the act shocking. His heavy breathing sounded almost as snarls, and the domination in his gaze nearly undid her. Her husband was as wild and single-minded an animal.

And she wanted more.

He set a bruising pace. She tried to swallow back her

moans. Her whimpers. Knew she mustn't alert anyone to their presence. To what they were doing. But her voice refused to be contained.

"You fucking love this, don't you?" Sin rose to his knees, pressing them snug to her bottom, He slammed into her. "My wife is a filthy little wanton."

Yes. So filthy. And completely his. But a small niggle of worry intruded. No matter how much her husband made wanton sound like praise, this behavior surely deserved censure. If anyone observed them, would Sin be embarrassed? Would he blame her?

Throw her away?

"Please." She wrapped her legs around his hips, taking him deeper. Sin needed to find his release, end this recklessness before they were caught out. "Please hurry. Someone might discover us."

He lowered his face until it was inches from her own. Color rode high on his cheekbones and sweat beaded his brow. He dragged his nose along her jaw, followed the path with his tongue. "I don't bloody care if the whole of Scotland sees how well I fuck my wife." He gripped her face between his hands. "But if you're concerned, *mo ghrâdh....*"

Sliding his hand across her cheek, he covered her mouth, muffling her cries. His lips brushed her ear. "Now you can scream as loudly as you want." He bit her lobe, the sharp prick of pain muddying her brain.

She moaned, with no thought of restraint. Whimpered and mewled as loudly as she wanted, made herself free for the first time ever. No one could hear the commotion she made. No one would judge.

The pressure on her mouth increased as her husband pistoned into her body. Her breath grew short, her abdominal muscles tensing. She inhaled as deeply as she could, but it wasn't enough. Her head grew light as her body wound tighter and tighter. She grabbed Sin's wrist, her fingers going numb with how tightly she squeezed him.

Black spots danced before her eyes. the rest of her body fading away until she was only the thin stream of air going in and out of her lungs and the pounding in her sex. And when she thought she couldn't take any more, she broke.

Everything in her clenched. Her cunny around his cock, milking him deeper. Her arms around his back, holding him tight. Her jaw, her eyes. Intense pleasure ripped through her from head to toe, and she knew. Her husband had just transformed her. Released something she would never recover.

After experiencing such a moment of pure abandonment, she didn't think she could cage her nature back up.

His curses, rumbling in her ear, revived her from her daze. Sin gripped her shoulders with both hands, pulling her into his hips with each thrust. Throwing his head back, he howled as he spent inside of her. The tendons in his neck bulged, his body jerking with his release.

Humans were animals, with the same needs to feed and procreate like any other. But she'd never understood just how close those primal forces lay under the veneer of civilization.

Her husband was a beast.

And she loved it.

He collapsed over her, bracing his weight on his bent arms, his breath hot on her cheek. "Fuck me, wife."

"I think I just did." Was that pride in her voice? If so, it felt well-deserved.

"You also nearly took a finger off." He raised his right hand and shook it, a wry smile creasing his face.

"What?" She grabbed his hand, looking for any broken skin. His index finger was reddened, with small indentations encircling it, but it was the scrapes on his wrist that stalled her heart.

A memory she'd long since forgotten flashed through her head. Images of bloody scratches on her father's face. Of her mother's red-tipped fingers, reaching for her.

Chills swamped her body. What had she done? A lifetime of good sense traded for a moment of pleasure. What if she'd drawn blood? Hurt him?

Wild things were put in cages.

"I'm sorry," she whispered, her throat going tight.

"Don't be. I like you high-spirited." He sat next to her and fastened three of the four buttons on his falls, ignoring the loose thread from the torn one. Grabbing the saddle bag, he pulled slices of Dunlop cheese wrapped in cloth, two rolls, and a bottle of wine out of it. "I didn't bring any glasses so we'll have to drink out of the bottle." He chattered on, oblivious to the torrent of shame and self-loathing that turned her stomach.

She took the bottle and swigged back some wine. It didn't help. Didn't let her forget how out of control she'd become. The type of woman she'd allowed herself to be. *Just like her mother.* She refused the cheese, ignoring the worried glances her husband sent her way.

It was fortunate she'd enjoyed her moment of abandon. Her heart thudded dully, her chest aching. Because it would be her last.

* * *

Castle Kenmore came into sight, and Sin blew out the breath he was holding. Had he worried that his wife was dispassionate? Nae, he should have been aggrieved that she was as variable as a changeling. In a wonderful frenzy one moment and as reserved as a nun the next.

He glanced at Winnifred from the corner of his eye. It was like constructing a wall out of sand when it came to building her trust. She had damned perverse ideas about how a woman should behave. Knowing the cause for her reticence did nothing to inform him on how to solve the problem.

Perhaps he shouldn't have rutted into her in an open field like a farm animal. She was shy enough in the bedroom, and that might be all she was ever comfortable with. But even as he thought it, the urge to fuck her in every room in his home, in his carriage, show her she belonged to him everywhere, gripped him low in the belly.

He tightened his grip on his reins. He'd never felt as undisciplined as he did when in her presence. He wasn't certain he liked the feeling. Not when it went unreciprocated.

A page raced up as they brought the horses to a stop at the front steps. The boy gripped his horse's bridle, gasping for breath. "Milord." *Pant, pant.* "Urgent message jus' came for ye. From the Duke of Montague."

Sin jumped down and reached for Winnifred.

She winced when her feet touched the ground and dug a knuckle into her lower back. "He's an acquaintance of yours, isn't he?"

He rubbed her back as he took the missive. "Yes. A good friend."

He handed the reins to the page and nodded towards the stables.

The boy tugged on his forelock and led the animals away.

Sin broke the seal and unfolded the letter. Another, smaller missive was tucked inside, and he recognized the prime minister's seal before turning to his friend's letter. His eyes flew over the scrawled words, his chest tightening as he read.

"What is it?" Winnifred placed a hand on his arm.

"There was an assassination attempt on the Duke of Beaumont. He was up from London to confer with the Board of Trustees. Though how the hell Montague learned of a shooting in Glasgow before I did, I don't know." He didn't need to read Liverpool's note. The stakes had just been raised and every level of government would now be turning a wary eye towards Scotland.

And that had never gone well for the Scots.

"Boy!" he shouted, and the page turned. "Have another horse saddled. A fast one." He shoved the notes into his jacket pocket and turned for the front door, Winnifred hurrying at his side.

"I must leave for Glasgow," he told her.

"Now?"

"At once." His boots clapped against the stone floor, echoing in the foyer.

Tavish poked his head from his office and nodded. "I'll have your trunk packed for ye at once, milord."

"I'm riding on ahead," Sin told him. "Have a carriage follow me."

"Of course." Tavish disappeared back into his room.

His mother emerged from her sitting room holding a vase of lilies in her hands. "There ye two are. I was hoping ye could—"

"Sorry, mother, but I'm leaving for Glasgow this very minute." He paused, looking at Winnifred. This would be the first time they'd be sleeping in different beds since their wedding. His stomach clenched. "Whatever it is will have to wait."

"Why ever would ye want to do that." His mother wrinkled her nose, her distaste for cities well-known.

"I've received bad news from a friend that I must attend to." He gave Winnifred a pointed look, but it wasn't necessary. She'd retreated into her guarded mode; no secrets would be slipping past her lips.

It should have made her the perfect wife for a spy.

He loathed it.

He'd seen a glimmer of the passionate woman beneath, and he craved more. Wanted to break her open and learn every part of her. Make her lose control over and over again.

He cupped her cheek, trying to rub the polite expression away with his thumb, to no avail. He sighed. Whatever he wanted to do to his wife would have to wait. Duty called.

He stepped back and pivoted away without a farewell. Without looking back, he strode out the entry and left

Kenmore.

Duty was a thankless bitch.

Chapter Twelve

Winnifred paced in front of the open door to her sitting room, keeping a look out for the butler with today's post. It had been a lonely three days without Sinclair, and her only connection to the world lay in letters and newspapers. She'd invited her mother-in-law to play cards after dinner, but had been denied every time. The meals themselves were silent, with Deirdre retreating to her own rooms as soon as the last bite was eaten. The woman even tried to steal the dogs away every chance she could.

She strode over to Horatio and scratched behind his ear, giving him a treat. Deirdre hadn't won today. A pocketful of cheese wedges ensured loyalty.

Hearing footsteps, she hurried to her door and met the butler. "The post has arrived, Mr. Greer?"

"Aye, milady." He handed her two envelopes.

She read the addresses, her heart falling. "No word from Dunkeld?"

"Nae, milady."

She gave him a tight smile. No matter. The letters from Mr. Raguhram and his colleague at the University of Glasgow, one Mr. Alasdair Holme, were enough to keep her occupied. And a more sensible way to spend her time rather than worrying about her husband. He was a strong, capable man. There was no need for concern.

"Thank you, Mr. Greer."

He inclined his head and shuffled away.

Winnifred strode to her desk. Eagerly, she took a blade to Mr. Holme's letter, breaking the seal, only to press her lips tight in frustration. The man's handwriting was a cramped, barely legible mess. It would take her an hour to decipher.

She wrapped her shawl more tightly about her shoulders and started the tedious work of interpretation.

A soft 'ahem' sounded behind her.

She turned to see the butler hovering at the door once more. "Yes?"

"Ye have a caller, milady." He sniffed. "A Mr. MacConnell. He says ye are previously acquainted."

Winnifred blinked. There was a time when she'd have thrown the door open and hurried to greet Donald herself, but their friendship hadn't ended to their mutual liking. She tapped her finger on her lips. Their parting hadn't been exactly unfriendly though, either. "Is the Dowager Lady Dunkeld in her rooms?"

"I believe she's in the garden, milady. Shall I ask her to join ye?"

She placed her letters in the top drawer of her desk. "Please. And please send up refreshments, as well."

She stood and smoothed her skirts. She'd forgone a fichu this morning and the bare skin above her bodice suddenly seemed too daring for a visit with an old friend, one who'd once hoped to be a little more than that. She pulled her shawl high over her shoulders and draped the ends down her chest. There. Perfectly respectable. She would never give her husband cause to doubt her faithfulness or respectability.

She eschewed the settee, not wanting to provide an opportunity for Donald to sit close, and settled herself on a sturdy chair, the one Sinclair always chose to hold his large frame when he joined her in her sitting room. The clock on the mantel ticked loudly as she waited. Finally, Deirdre swept in, carrying a pair of work gloves in her hands and a smudge of dirt on her chin.

Winnifred almost smiled. The bit of soil softened the woman, made her appear endearing.

Until Deirdre opened her mouth. "So, I'm here to chaperone ye and a former beau, is it? Ye do have a liking for Scottish men, I'll give ye that." She tossed her gloves on an end table. "Not that I can blame ye."

Winnifred's hands clenched before she forced them to relax. "You have dirt on your face. You might want to remove it before our guest arrives."

Deirdre scurried to the mirror over the fireplace, pulling out her handkerchief and scrubbing her chin. "Drat."

A footman stopped in the doorway. "Mr. McConnell," he announced, then stepped aside.

Donald strode into the room, his gaze lighting up when he caught sight of Winnifred. "Winnie. I'm glad ye could see me. I waited for what felt like ever so long." He took her hand, not shaking it, merely holding on tight as he looked down on her. "I thought, mayhap, that becoming a marchioness had made ye forget your old friends."

"Of course not." She slid her hand from his and pointed to the seat across from her.

Banquo and Horatio raised their heads at the stranger's entrance. Banquo lumbered to his feet and strolled to stand in front of Winnifred before circling twice and dropping down to curl on his side.

She winced and tugged her toes out from beneath him.

Horatio watched as Donald took his seat then rose to sit sentinel beside him. The dog's head was almost on level with Donald's.

Donald licked his lips. "Nice dogs."

Deirdre turned from the mirror, her face clear. "Yes, they are splendid creatures."

Craning his neck around, Donald jumped to his feet and gave a stiff bow to the dowager.

Deirdre circled around the settee and dropped heavily on the cushion. "The Dunkelds have always had Scottish deerhounds in our family," Deirdre continued. "The most loyal of animals. And trained to protect what belongs to us."

Winnifred pressed her lips together. She didn't know

which part of her mother-in-law's statement was most objectionable. The idea that she was a belonging, a possession of the Archer family that needed guarding, or the idea that Horatio and Banquo would protect her against anything larger than a fly.

"Of course." Donald sank to the edge of his seat and leaned on the opposite armrest from Horatio.

"Mother," Winnifred said, the word tasting bitter on her tongue, "this is a friend of mine and my father's, Mr. Donald MacConnell. Donald, the Dowager Marchioness of Dunkeld."

"Donald, is it?" Deirdre arched an eyebrow. "Ye must have been close friends to address each other such."

Donald chuckled. "I spent so much time in the Hannon's house, I should have had my own bedroom. I ran errands for her father, bought his supplies, helped him in his greenhouse. He was a wee bit barmy about his plants and dirt, but we kept him in line, didnae we, Winnie?" He winked at her, as though she were in on the joke.

Her stomach hardened. Jokes about a person's mental health were never amusing.

"I see." Deirdre's voice implied she saw much more than was proper, and Winnifred squirmed on her seat. Why had she thought having her mother-in-law present for the interview a good idea? This visit could hardly be more uncomfortable. *Because a woman must never give anyone cause to doubt her modesty.*

Winnifred exhaled loudly.

"Now, what can we do for ye?" Deirdre waved for a maid to enter, the girl pushing a rolling cart filled with refreshments.

Donald gave her the unassuming smile that Winnifred remembered well. She'd once considered the possibility of waking up to it every morning. "I'm leaving Inver tomorrow and wanted to say my farewells. The marchioness and I used to be good friends." He shook his head. "Marchioness. Not in a hundred years would I have thought

I'd be calling ye that. It is most strange."

"On that we agree." Deirdre poured a cup of tea and handed it to Donald. "What is it ye do, Mr. ...? I apologize. I've quite forgotten your name."

"MacConnell." Taking the cup, he leaned back in the chair. Horatio shuffled closer, his snout breaching the armrest. Donald leaned farther away. "And I do a lot of different things. A real jock-of-all-trades ye could say."

"Could one?" Deirdre curled her lip before taking a sip of tea.

Winnifred scooted forward and poured her own cup. "And how are your parents? You told me once your father had gout."

Donald sighed. "Aye, it ails him still, but what can ye expect when food is scarce and good Scotsmen work their fingers to the bone just to earn a few quid. Being subjugated by this *United* Kingdom as it's called, times are tough."

"Subject, don't you mean?" Winnifred didn't understand the animosity against the union. The English answered to the same laws and responsibilities. How was it unjust?

Banquo whined, and she slipped him a treat from her pocket.

Donald grinned. "You're Scottish now, Winnie. Time to put your loyalties to right. Who knows, ye might have come north at the right time. Ye might get to see a free Scotland."

Winnifred stilled, ignoring the nudges Banquo was giving her. "Do you advocate for rebellion?"

He scoffed. "Nae, that would be treason." His voice wasn't convincing. "But it's every true Scot's dream to live in a free and independent Scotland."

Deirdre nodded in agreement.

"And one never knows. England might be coming to her senses sooner than ye think." Horatio snorted, and Donald jerked his cup out of range. Some tea sloshed over the edge and landed on the armrest of his chair. Donald pulled out a handkerchief and swiped at the mess.

"I would hope," Winnifred said, carefully choosing her words, "that if and when the time comes for Scottish independence, it will have arrived through thoughtful discourse and mutual agreement rather than through fear and violence."

Her friend shook his head, shoving his handkerchief back in his pocket. "Ye always were naïve."

Winnifred flushed. He'd called her that once before, and like then, she paid the accusation no heed. She understood precisely how terrible human nature could be. She refused to apologize, however, for believing that people could, and should, behave in a proper and logical fashion. Donald had disappointed her once on that score; it seemed little had changed.

"How did ye come to be in Mr. Hannon's employ?" Deirdre set her cup down in its saucer, the china clinking harshly. "A good Scottish laddie like ye seems ill-placed in London."

"My family was evicted from our home during the Highland removals." Donald's nostrils flared. "My pa was desperate for work, so we moved to London. But he missed home too much and moved back with my mam only two years later. I stayed a couple more years, sending money back when I could."

Winnifred blinked. She hadn't known his family had been a part of the clearances. But then, she'd never asked. Banquo nosed her thigh, and she slipped him another wedge of cheese. He snapped it up without chewing. His body jerked, his head lurching forward and back, and the poor thing started wheezing.

"Oh dear." She rubbed his back, but the wheezing continued, adding a cough and a whistle as Banquo tried to suck air past the lodged bit of food.

Deirdre frowned and rose from her seat. "Come, Banquo. Let's take this outside." She grabbed him by the scruff and walked him to the door, calling for a footman.

Donald jumped to his feet, side-stepped past Horatio

and hurried to Winnifred.

She stood as well, meeting his gaze.

"I must be going soon." Donald stood closer than she liked. "I would hope with ye living in my country that we'd see more of each other, but I fear we no longer belong to the same spheres."

"No, I suspect I'll lead a quiet life here at Kenmore." She sidled backwards, and her legs hit the chair.

He inched forward, glancing over his shoulder.

Deirdre was still at the door waiting for a servant, poor Banquo still making enough noise to mask their conversation.

"I missed ye, Winnie." He lowered his head. "It seemed like one day we were as close as two peas in a pod and the next ye were never at home when I called."

She stared down at her feet. She had cut him out of her life, and thought she'd had good reason. But perhaps she'd overreacted. He had made her a proposition; she'd refused. Why couldn't they have gone on as before?

"I apologize," she said, meaning it. There had to have been a better way to end a friendship of two years. "Perhaps my decision was too hasty, but I did think it best at the time."

Donald rested his hand on her shoulder. "I know. That doesnae mean it didnae hurt."

"Sin!" Deirdre's voice sliced into their conversation. "It's good to have ye home."

Winnifred snapped her head to the door, eager for a glimpse of her husband as he strode past Banquo. He looked unharmed, thank heavens, and absolutely delicious, even though his clothes were dusty from the road and his shoulders were sloped with fatigue.

Until he caught sight of Donald's hand on her.

Slowly, like a bladder filling with water, Sin expanded until his shoulders seemed to take up the entire doorway.

Her stomach clenched, her excitement ripped away.

Caught standing improperly close to another man.

Women had been sent away for less.

Her husband's nostrils flared. "I see I've arrived just in time."

* * *

Without taking his gaze off the spot where MacConnell touched his wife, Sin told the footman behind him, "Take Banquo for some water."

Sin prowled around the settee, gratified to see the impudent sap skull take two hasty steps away from his wife.

Horatio padded up to him, wagging his tail, and Sin stroked his head, trying to rein in his temper. His arse was sore from the grueling ride back from Glasgow, his back ached, and he was grumpy as hell at the fuck all he'd learned about the assassination attempt. If MacConnell gave him one teeny tiny reason to toss his arse through the nearest window, Sin would be calling for the glazier come morning.

"Husband, have you eaten? Can I make you a plate?" Winnifred tangled her fingers in her lace cuff, her pleasant smile wearing a crack.

She'd damn well better remember who her husband was. A fire burned in his stomach. The urge to crush his mouth to hers in front of their visitor ran strong through his veins. Instead, he stepped up to her, placed his finger under her chin, and placed a soft kiss on her lips.

She didn't blink, her eyes ever watchful, but accepted the affection with alacrity.

The vise around his chest eased. "I ate on the road." Yet still his mouth watered for sustenance. It had been too long since he'd tasted his wife. He ran his thumb along her cheekbone. They both needed reminding of their attachment.

"Well, you came just as Donald was taking his leave." She gnawed on her bottom lip, and Sin's dislike of the man ratcheted higher. His wife needed to feel secure, and MacConnell's visit had accomplished anything but.

He swiveled his head and glared at the man. "Then let's not keep him."

MacConnell stepped back, knocking his knee into the low table. "Aye. Right." He nodded at Winnifred and bowed stiffly to his mother. "Be well, Winnie." He hurried for the door and pulled up short when Horatio flopped down on the threshold in front of him. MacConnell inched around the bottom end of the dog, hopping over his tail and scurrying out the door.

Deirdre pinched her lips together. "Ye didn't have to scare the wee lad so."

Yes, he had. Sin ran his pinkie finger along his wife's sleeve. "His feelings are not my concern." He locked gazes with Winnifred, her icicle-blue eyes warming to pale pools of interest. Her breath quickened, her bosom heaved.

Sin's body tightened. Three damn nights without feeling the velvet of her nipple against his tongue. Three nights without feeling her wet heat clench around him.

Too many hours without another small glimpse into her soul.

"As my presence as chaperone is no longer required, I'm returning to my garden." His mother patted her thigh. "Come, Horatio. Let's see how Banquo fares."

Sin heard the whisper of her skirts as she left them alone, the clicking of Horatio's nails fading down the hallway. All external sounds fading until he heard nothing but his wife's breath, swore he could just hear the hurried beating of her heart.

She clutched her hands together in front of her. "Sin, I want to assure—"

He didn't need to hear her explanations. It wasn't in words where she expressed herself best. Taking one step forward, he bent and tossed her over his shoulder, grinning at her muffled shriek.

Chapter Thirteen

His wife hissed in a breath. "I'm so sorry."

Sin turned for the door and palmed her arse to steady her. Mostly. "You have nothing to apologize for." A servant skittered around the corner of the hall, no doubt mortified at seeing his laird carrying away the marchioness. Sin didn't care. "This isn't a punishment. This is a man who's missed his wife's touch and is looking to rectify that situation."

She sagged, her body curving around his in apparent relief.

He gritted his teeth. He'd show her she had nothing to fear from him if it was the last thing he did.

Sweet words and tender touches would likely be the most effective way to earn his wife's trust.

He didn't do sweet. Nor tender. It wasn't something he was capable of, not when presented with his wife's flushed body, the heat rolling off her skin, her parted lips. All control seemed to desert him when she was in his arms.

He'd just have to show her he took care of what was his in his own way.

His feet ate up the floor, taking the stairs and the hallways to his chamber in record time. He pushed open the door to his bedroom and kicked it shut behind them. With a twitch of his shoulder, he sent his wife tumbling off and caught her about the waist. Slowly, he let her body slide down his until her feet hit the floor.

Strands of her honey hair drifted about her face, pulled loose from its knot. He couldn't wait to see it in a messy halo around her head on the pillow.

He tossed his jacket on the ground. "Remove your clothes."

He yanked off his shirt and kicked off his boots. He was down to his trousers by the time she'd just removed her shawl. "Too slow." Spinning her away, he ripped the row of buttons from their holes, tearing the gown from her body. Her stays and shift met a similar fate before littering the floor.

When she turned to face him, the skin above her chest was rosy, her nipples just beginning to peak. The pink buds begged for his teeth to nip them a shade darker.

A whisper of unease slipped between his shoulder blades. He liked it rough, but these feelings he was having towards Winnifred weren't normal. There was something, someone different lurking just below the surface, clawing to get out. Someone savage.

And, God help him, Sin wanted to let him free.

"It's been three nights without my cock in your cunny. Has it missed me?" He advanced until his bare chest pressed against hers, then kept walking until her back hit the wall. He slapped his palms on the wood by her head and leaned close, breathing her in.

"Tell me you missed me."

"I..." She swallowed. "Of course, I missed you, husband. What wife wouldn't?"

Like it was her damn duty to miss him. "Don't give me the words of a dutiful wife. Tell me." He cupped her mons, rubbing the heel of his hand into her clit. "Did Winnifred miss me?"

Her breath wavered, caught. She nodded, the knot of her hair scraping against the wall, loosing even more strands.

Gripping her shoulders, he turned her around and yanked the remaining pins free. Her hair tumbled past her shoulders, thick and heavy on his hands. He wrapped it around his palm and tugged her head back.

"I missed you, too." He ran his tongue along the top of

her shoulder. Jesus, she even tasted faintly of oranges. "The way your forehead creases when you think, the way you stretch in the morning then curl back into my side for five minutes more of slumber." He pressed his hips forward, nestling his hardening length against the crease of her arse. "The way you open to me so sweetly even as you fight your responses with every fiber of your being. And always lose."

Her resistance sent a deviant thrill through him. He hated the reason, that it came from a place of fear, but he couldn't deny he loved the battle to make her succumb. The feeling of power it gave him when she finally submitted to her base needs.

He might be a very disturbed man.

Winnifred pressed her palms flat against the wall. She curled her fingers, scraping her nails against the wood. "I'm glad I please you," she said evenly. As calmly as though asking him to pass the damn butter.

He narrowed his eyes. Pushing back, he replaced his cock with his hand, running it over her round arse, squeezing the meaty part of the flesh, before moving lower.

He found her slick, and the animal in him howled in relief. His need to push, dominate, had found a willing target. She could try to hide behind her words all she wanted, but her body didn't lie.

It liked his beast.

He yanked at his falls with his free hand, freeing his prick. "Spread your legs," he ordered. "Push that sweet arse out for me."

She took too long, her ideas of respectability getting in her way, no doubt, and Sin brought his hand smartly down on that arse he owned.

She whimpered and did as he said.

Sin stroked higher, circling her clit as he eyed his spoils. Winnifred was stretched out, her palms glued to the wall, her back arched, and her bum thrust back and up. Bending, he pressed his mouth to the base of her spine and licked his way up her backbone.

Her breath shuddered out of her lungs.

Sin's cock wept. He wrapped his hand around it and squeezed. "Shall I take you like this, *mo ghrâdh*? From behind, like a stag mounts his mate?"

She shuddered, and her head dropped forward to hang between her shoulders. "Whatever you wish."

He thrust his finger into her opening. "That's not what I want to hear. Give me something. Some damn reaction."

"You want a reaction?" She pushed away from the wall and spun. Her elbow flew back and smacked him in the chest. "Oh!" She clapped her hand over her mouth.

The blow barely stung, the show of spirit only managing to make him harder. He gave her a dark smile.

She shook her head. "I'm sorry. I didn't mean to strike you. But you keep pushing and pushing me."

"Like this...?" Gently, he prodded her back against the wall.

Her eyes flared wide. She stepped forward. "Don't do that."

He pushed her again, this time a little harder.

She clenched her fists tight, her body quivering. "Stop it, I say."

Crowding her against the wall, Sin put his mouth next to her ear. "Make me," he whispered.

The need to provoke, to tear down her walls, was a craving he couldn't resist. He gripped the base of her skull and twisted her head up. "In this bedroom, you can do whatever you want to me. Act however you will without consequences. So, tell me, love." He nipped at her bottom lip, tugging at it until the swollen flesh scraped through his teeth and popped free. "When I push you so, what do you want to do about it?"

* * *

What did she want to do?

The question burrowed deep, ringing in her ears. What she wanted and what she ought to do were two very different things. She *wanted* to feel like she had for that amazing moment in the valley. She clenched her hands, her nails biting into her palms. She *wanted* to push him back, exorcise all her fears and frustrations in a decadently perverse manner by lashing out. But was he in earnest about wanting that from her?

Her heart pounded so hard her chest ached. She pressed her slick palms into her thighs. It was reckless. Foolish. But there was only one way to ascertain if she could trust him. She'd run numerous experiments by a system of trial and error. It was time to test her husband.

Tilting her chin up, she reached over his shoulder and yanked the black ribbon from his hair. The dark red locks swung loose about his shoulders, making him appear even more rakish. She dug her fingers into his hair and pulled him down to her mouth.

There. See how he liked it.

The growl that vibrated his lips just before they crashed into hers told her he liked it very much indeed. His kiss pressed her head back against the wall, tore at her lips, and still she wanted more.

His need was so uninhibited. So raw. Her hands shook. He was everything she could only ever dream she could be.

And he wanted her to join him in the darkness.

She nipped at his lip, cautiously. waiting to gauge his reaction before pressing further.

He bit her back, twice as hard, and a shiver raced down her spine.

She pushed on his shoulders.

Sin slapped her thigh.

Wetness pooled at her core at her recklessness. At their combined ferocity. All those years when she'd never allowed herself to step an inch out of bounds. When she'd forced a smile and swallowed her bile.

Sin pressed his lips to hers, the pressure harsh and thrilling. She opened for him, scraping her teeth along his tongue. Her skin hummed as he deepened the kiss, pressed his body into hers until she felt every hard inch.

He tore his mouth from hers and sucked on her neck. He pressed his arm on the wall beside her, and she decided to push her luck a little further. See how much more wildness he'd allow.

She turned her head and sank her teeth into his biceps.

Sin hissed and yanked his arm free.

Banding an arm around her waist, he lifted and threw her face down on the bed. She pushed onto one arm, but his hard body hit her back, pressing her down.

He pinned her easily. He licked and sucked across her back and shoulders as her struggles grew weaker and weaker, her strength no match against his. He had free rein to score his teeth into her flesh, to pull on her hair, the sharp stings in her scalp a reminder she was his to enjoy. Carte blanche to take her any way he wanted.

And she melted.

He dominated her, fully, easily, his mastery over her so complete she had no qualms that he would truly hurt her. He knew just the right pressure to torment her without causing harm. And she knew no matter what she did, how she fought, she could never truly harm him. The blows that she landed, he allowed. Her attacks, he controlled.

Absolute freedom rushed through her veins. She could act out her most impetuous, irrational, wanton sensibilities, and he would absorb it all. Take every part of her.

He pushed her leg up until her knee was cocked up by her waist. The rough wool of his trousers scraped against her bottom and the inside of her thighs. Sin grabbed the back of her neck, pinning her in place, and notched the crown of his length at her entrance. He slid in on one hard stroke.

Winnifred moaned.

He slowly pulled from her, his cock dragging along her nerve endings, before pounding back in. An agonizingly unhurried retreat; a fierce and triumphant hammering home. She needed more, faster, but she couldn't raise her hips to meet him. She reached behind her, found the loose fabric of his falls, and tugged at him to pick up his speed.

Sin snarled and slapped her hand away.

Gripping her hip, he rutted into her. A steady stream of Gaelic tumbled from her husband's lips, the foreign words making him sound savage. Feral.

She'd brought Sinclair to this. Just as he drove her past her limits, she'd done the same to him. The realization made her feel powerful. Desired. *Accepted.*

Sin understood what she needed when she hadn't even known it herself.

The pads of his fingers dug into her neck, hard enough to leave bruises. Come morning, she'd be bruised all over.

His grunts filled the chamber. His thrusts shook even that huge bed. Winnifred held onto the coverlet, the muscles in her core coiling tighter. The friction against her sensitive flesh almost overwhelming.

Sin leaned down and licked a path across her shoulder blade. "I love how you taste." His voice was a growl. "How you smell. It's intoxicating. I could get drunk doing nothing but fucking this tight little pussy."

"Oh God." She clenched her eyes shut.

He chuckled softly. "I own this sweet pussy, don't I?"

"Yes." She gasped, her breath going short. Her channel clutched at his manhood, the beginnings of her crisis fluttering to life.

He yanked her head back. "Not yet. You don't get to finish until I say."

"Please." Tears filled her eyes, the need to release so great. "Please. I need..." Her voice trailed off as her lungs squeezed tight. There was no way she could fight this. She was moments from bliss and no demand of his would stop its arrival.

"All right." He pressed a kiss to her cheek. "Let go. Squeeze that pretty cunny all over my cock."

With a cry, she did.

Her body stiffened, her limbs shook. Wave after wave of

pleasure crashed through her, the release rivaling her flood of emotions.

She could bare herself, explore the darker emotions she'd always kept hidden. With Sin, she didn't have to hide.

Tears burned her eyes. She had never felt so undone in her life.

Sin ground into her, groaning. A spurt of warmth flooded her core before he pulled out. Wet heat splashed across her bottom and lower back.

Another mark.

Branding her as his.

He lowered his body, his chest brushing her shoulders. His breath came hot and quick against her ear. "Know this. Whatever you do. Whatever you say. I'm never letting you go."

Her body sagged into the mattress. And, for the first time ever, Winnifred let herself cry in front of another person.

Chapter Fourteen

Winnifred shifted the basket higher over her bent elbow and rapped on the cottage door. She smoothed her hand down her velvet skirts, hoping the fine fabric would help her to feel more like a marchioness. Her new position came with duties, and she wanted to perform them ably.

Wanted to make Sinclair proud.

A woman pulled the door open, a toddler resting on her hip. "Oh! Lady Dunkeld." She tried to dip into a curtsy, wobbled, clutched the babe tighter.

The child pulled his mother's hair, giggling.

Winnifred put out a steadying hand. "Good morning, Mrs. Fraser. How do you do?"

"Well enough. And please, call me Maura. Everyone aboot here does." She pulled the child's hands away from the basket handle. "That's not yours, child."

Winnifred laughed. "Actually, it is. Well, for your family. Another shipment of food has arrived at Kenmore, and Jock, the footman, and I are driving about the neighborhood making deliveries." She pointed behind her to the cart laden with goods and the young man standing beside it.

Footsteps sounded, and Maura was nudged aside by her husband, Gavin. "Milady." His broad face broke into a grin. "It's right lovely to see ye again. You're alone?"

"Yes, my husband is kept occupied on repairs to a canal wall." She rolled up onto her toes and bounced, a flush of excitement running through her body. She'd said the word 'husband' many times before. But this time it gave her an odd thrill.

The word made her feel settled. Safe.

Until last night, she'd never realized the freedom that came with marriage to the right man. He was stuck with her for the next fifty years or so, through good or bad. As long as— She bit her lip. She didn't think her husband was the kind of man to abuse his power over her. Who'd send her away even if she began acting erratically. She was truly beginning to believe she could trust him, and for that, he'd forever have her gratitude.

"Aye, well it was good of ye to come alone." Gavin caressed his son's bald head and stepped outside. "I'm glad you're here. I've been meaning to talk to ye. Dunkeld sent me a cart full of peas, beans, and even some clover. Told me to try this nitrogen idea of yours. I dug a trench out back where the plants are rotting away as we speak."

A moment of breathlessness rocked her. "You want my advice?"

"Aye. Your husband thought ye wouldn't mind guiding me in this. Besides, it's your idea." He smiled. "I figure you'll deserve a share of the blame if all I get is a field that stinks to high heaven."

Winnifred pressed a hand to her chest, her heart feeling full to bursting. Sinclair had set this in motion? He couldn't know that not having her experiments was a constant ache of loss. Couldn't know how happy he'd just made her. She tipped up her chin. "As long as I get some of the credit when your barley grows taller than you."

Gavin chuckled. "That ye will, milady." He turned to his wife. "Maura, can ye see what we need from the cart and direct the footman where to put it?"

"Of course." Hefting the child higher, she bustled to the cart.

"Milady, the rotting vegetables are this way." He shook his head. "I still cannae believe we're letting good food go to waste. Bless Dunkeld for having the means to make this happen, and for feeding the lot of us while we wait for the sun."

Winnifred followed him behind a small shed. "I know it's difficult, but experiments such as these can lead to providing more food to people than we ever have before." She waited impatiently as Gavin pulled wood boards off a long, narrow trench in the earth that ran the length of the shed.

Gavin rested the make-shift lids on the wall behind him. He spread his hand, indicating the mess in the trench. "Well? Am I doing this right? When do I take this muck oot to spread on the soil?"

She knelt and scooped up a handful of the vegetation. "I'd give it another day or two. Mr. Fraser, would you be willing to run a true experiment? One where we control for variables?"

He scratched his head. "I'll do anything that may help. What do ye mean?"

Winnifred watched the plant material sprinkle through her fingers back down into the trench. She stood, brushing her hands together. "It would be most helpful if you could divide each field into three parts. The first part, plant and sow your seeds as you normally would, using manure as your supplement. The second section, use these legumes instead of the manure. And the third, use both. I think we'll be best able to observe whether the legumes actually do release nitrogen into the soil from a topical application if we test it in this manner."

"Manure. Rotting vegetables. Manure and rotting vegetables." Gavin raised a finger with each phrase. "That I can do."

"Splendid." She clasped her hands together, her basket pressed against her side. "And you won't mind if I return periodically to observe the results?"

"Nae, you're welcome any time. And bring that husband of yours. He doesnae come around near enough." He replaced the planks over the trench and they turned for the cottage.

"I will tell him so." Winnifred paused on the drive and gazed over the open fields. "For everyone's sake, I hope we derive some benefit from this experiment. It's a risk not spreading manure on some of the land."

"My da used to say t'was better to risk a little if the reward was large." He took her basket and placed it on the seat of the cart.

"Oh, there's strawberries and cream in that basket for your family." She reached for it, but Gavin stilled her hands.

"Keep if for the next family. Maura and I are getting by."

If only everyone were so sensible and generous. Winnifred nodded, and let the footman help her up onto the seat. She lifted a hand to Maura who waved from the doorway of the house.

"On to the next home, milady?" Jock slapped the reins on the horse, prodding the animal into a trot.

"Yes." Winnifred unfolded the woolen blanket next to her and draped it over her lap. "Last one for today."

They bumped over the country lanes. Raised voices met them as they neared the drive to the next house.

She laid her hand on Jock's arm. "Wait." They stopped at the end of the rutted lane, and she peered towards the cottage's front door. Four figures stood in front of it, and one she recognized well.

Donald leaned into the huddle of men, waving his hands about, his voice an indistinguishable buzz.

One of the other men, a tenant from a neighboring home, gave an angry shout. Donald clapped his shoulder and leaned closer.

Her stomach sank. The group looked angry. Disgruntled.

And Donald was right in the thick of it.

As if feeling her presence, he raised his head, their gazes catching. A look she didn't recognize crossed his face.

Her shoulders sagged, as though weighted. Years previous, she'd been shocked to learn that her friend hadn't known her, not truly. He wouldn't have made his disgraceful proposition if he had.

But she'd been as guilty. Looking at him now, she realized she saw a stranger. Their sympathies had never been aligned.

The other men followed the path of his gaze. Red flushes stained their faces. One burly farmer clenched his hands.

"Shall we drive on doon?" Jock asked.

"No." Winnifred sat back and looked down the road. Away from the angry glares. "Let's go home."

* * *

His wife was finally back. The left rear wheel on her cart squeaked as it revolved, a handy way to keep track of her return, and one more damn thing he needed to fix.

Sin threw his gloves down on the dirt in disgust. Was there one thing that worked properly at Kenmore? Anything that would show he wasn't a piss poor excuse for a marquess?

Loud hissing mocked him as he stalked out of the tunnel, and Sin's shoulders clenched into boulders. Two hours. Two damn hours he'd try to catch that blasted badger, and all he had to answer for it was an aching knee and some nasty scratches on his hand.

He couldn't even keep Kenmore free of vermin. Pathetic.

The sunlight, so pale this summer, burned achingly bright as he emerged from the dark. He circled to Kenmore's front entrance, blinking as his eyes adjusted. The cart stood before the door, and the footman was just reaching up his hand to help Winnifred down.

"Ho, there!" he called, lengthening his stride.

Winnifred looked up and waved in greeting. She waited for Sin to nudge the footman out of the way.

Gripping her about the waist, he lifted her from the seat and into his body, slowly sliding her to the ground. "Good afternoon, wife." The softest parts of her were pressed against his body. He tipped the brim of her bonnet back to see her face, and his chest tightened at the small, secret smile that stretched her lips. Everything else might be going to hell around him, but his marriage was turning into a glowing success. Winnifred was the only thing right with his world.

She tugged off her glove and ran her finger along his cheek. She held her hand up, revealing a smudge of mud on her finger. "What have you been up to?"

He grunted and tucked her into his side before turning for the front door. "Nothing. Tried to kill the badger." Slippery, scheming little bastard.

"Glad to know I'm not the only one he's bested."

"The animal is trickier than I credited," Sin grudgingly admitted. "But why do you think it's a lad? With the scratches it left on me, I thought she was more likely to be a female."

Winnifred's cheeks went pink, and she stumbled.

Sin smiled smugly, and tucked her closer. Pulling his shirt over his head this morning had been a tender business with the scratches she'd left him, but he loved each ache. "Careful, now. I have plans for my wife tonight. I need her unharmed."

Winnifred cleared her throat, not meeting his gaze. "Yes. Well." She removed her cloak and bonnet, handing them to the butler. She patted her hair. "I guess we'll see about that."

Sin brushed a curl off her cheek. Indeed, they would.

"I saw Donald today. He seemed to be engaged in a very impassioned conversation with several of your tenants."

The back of Sin's neck prickled. "Did you?" He stretched out his arm and led her to his study. "And what did he have to say? I'd thought he was leaving the area."

"He said nothing to me." Winnifred wrapped one arm around her middle, holding her opposite one. "I didn't stop. He was at the Magee house. It was to be my last visit to distribute food, but I told Jock to keep driving."

"You were visiting our tenants?" He should have accompanied her. It was his duty, damn it, to help their people. He was pleased she was settling into her own duties so easily, but that didn't remove the responsibility from his shoulders.

"Yes, and I need to thank you." She dug her teeth into her lower lip. "I don't think you realize the kindness you showed me by sending Mr. Fraser the legumes. Asking him to try my... father's idea." She stared down at the carpet. "It means a great deal to me."

"I'm glad." Sin closed the study door and leaned back against it. "Although I had mercenary reasons for my actions, as well. If your experiment works, it will be a boon to my tenants." Though it had mostly been to make her happy. Keeping Winnifred in good spirits was quickly becoming one of the most important parts of his life.

She strolled about the room, dragging her hands over the back of the settee, flipping through the pages of a book. "I will have to write my father. Keep him apprised of—"

"Stop." He pushed off the door. "Let us put an end to this bluff. You weren't merely your father's assistant, were you? And this idea does not belong to him." He waited, impatient, willing her to tell him the truth.

Her back was to him as she spun a globe that sat on the edge of his desk, and he saw her shoulders tense. "I did become interested in the natural world while assisting my father." She turned, her expression blank. "But I am your wife now, and a marchioness. Such interests can no longer be indulged." She blinked, and looked away. "Can they?" she asked, her voice small.

"I don't bloody see why not." Sin fisted his hands on his hips. Bloody society and their asinine, bloody rules. If poking around in dirt like any other natural philosopher made her happy, she could do whatever she wanted. "As long as you still attend to your duties as marchioness, why not study soil? I have a second job, too."

Her face lit up before being displaced by that adorable frown she wore when she was thinking too hard. She shook her head. "It isn't tenable. I can run my experiments here, and I thank you for that, but so much of research depends upon corresponding with other scholars. They replied to me when I wrote in my father's stead, signing my name as his assistant. When it becomes widely known that I am married and no longer living with him, I will no longer be able to use that pretext."

Sin stomped to the fireplace and grabbed the poker. He stabbed at a log. "Sign your own damn name."

"They won't respond."

His fist tightened on the metal rod, his muscles flexing, wanting to bend the iron to his will. "They will respond to my marchioness." Or face consequences. He had friends the world over. Friends who had retired their scruples long ago. One letter, and he could make anyone's life most unpleasant.

She chuckled, and Sin's body jerked. It was the first time he'd heard her laugh, and it was his threat that had uncovered it. Strange, lovely woman. "Thank you," she said. "Your encouragement means more than you can know."

Because that father of hers never gave her one ounce of it. Miserly, terrified mouse of a man. Scared of his wife's illness, so he sent her to her death. Scared of impropriety, so he let his daughter do his work yet took the credit. Sin poked the log again, and it fell apart into a cascade of embers.

Winnifred's skirts brushed his leg, and she squeezed his hand. Her skin was warm, and even that small bit of contact soothed his anger. "Especially now when you and the rest of the peerage in Scotland are under such scrutiny, it's best if I don't behave out of turn. And any woman, much less a marchioness, running experiments, trying to get published, would attract a lot of attention. None of it good."

He harrumphed. All right, it would be odd as hell. But

not unheard of. Lady Mary Montagu introduced smallpox inoculations to England. And Caroline Herschel kept discovering new comets every damn week it seemed. Frankly, he didn't give his left ballock about appearances. Perhaps it was the Scottish in him, not wanting to bow to English sensibilities. Or the fact he detested Society. If he were snubbed for having an unusual wife, that only meant more time home alone with her.

He rubbed the back of his neck. All the times he'd pictured his future wife, knowing that at some point a man in his position had to start looking, Sin had pictured a sweet, biddable woman. Scottish of course. In his mind, she had been an accessory. Someone to provide an heir and help his life run smoothly.

He cupped Winnifred's cheek. Never in his drunkest imaginings would he have pictured Winnifred.

Thank God she'd been fool enough to be compromised with him in a wine cellar.

"It isn't your job to worry about the safety of Kenmore, or me. You live how you wish and leave any angry tenants for me to handle." People could glare at Sin all they wanted; but if anyone said or did one thing to insult Winnifred, they would soon be understanding just how feudal their laird could be. "Besides, if your research succeeds, I don't think anyone will care who helped the crops grow as long as they have food in their bellies."

She rolled up onto her toes and kissed his cheek. "I don't know how I was so fortunate to gain you as a husband. You are the best friend a woman could want."

His thoughts froze. Friend?

"I am your husband." He pinched her chin. "I hope we are more than mere friends."

She patted his chest. "Friends and paramours. A wonderfully sensible combination for a solid marriage."

She tugged his head down, brought their mouths together, ending whatever objection Sin was about to say.

And he had much to say.

He slid his hands down her back and squeezed her arse.

Later. He'd speak to her later.

Finally, she was giving him her body, no hesitations, holding nothing back.

It wasn't enough. Sin was a greedy bastard. He might have unleashed her sensual nature, but he wanted more. None of this *friends* nonsense. He wanted, needed, her soul to belong to him, too, not just her body. Needed it like a fish needed water.

And he would use every weapon in his armory in order to get it.

Chapter Fifteen

A servant scratched at the drawing room's door, and Winnifred glanced up.

"Pardon me, milady," he said. "The Earl of Summerset and the Baron of Sutton are here to see the marquess."

She laid her needlepoint on the seat next to her and took a deep breath. Sin's close friends. She could only hope the baron would be more accepting of her marriage than Summerset had been. He'd given her the evil eye all through the ceremony and wedding breakfast.

"Please, send them in along with refreshments." She shook out her skirts and adjusted her fichu. "I believe my husband is in the rear pasture this morning. Send for him at once, please."

He bowed and backed out of the room.

Her palms grew damp, and she pressed them against her thighs, the silk crinkling beneath her hands. She was wearing one of her new dresses. Beautiful but a bit frivolous. Ostentatious really. She wished she were in one of her sensible gowns. Much less suited to her station, but she felt more confident in their practicality. And she wouldn't look as though she were spending her husband's money freely, that she hadn't married him for his wealth and position, one of Summerset's suspicions about her she was sure.

As the footman led the men in, she rose to her feet. The earl was as wickedly good looking as she remembered. His cream-colored jacket and pantaloons gave no indication of his recent journey and not one lock of hair was out of place.

The other man showed the wear of travel, his dark brown trousers wrinkled at the knees and the knot of his cravat askew. Though not as big as her husband, he was a large man, standing a couple of inches taller than Summerset, with untamed black hair and a bushy beard.

She inclined her head to the earl. "Lord Summerset. And you must be the Baron of Sutton." She gave the other man a smile. "Welcome to Kenmore. My husband speaks highly of you. Well, of all his friends."

"As well he should." Summerset examined her like a bug under the microscope. "We've watched his back for nigh over a decade. We protect our own against any threats, physical, financial, or otherwise." The look he gave her was pointed; the brow he arched, insolent.

Unbidden, heat rose to her face. "Yes, well." She cleared her throat. "Please have a seat." Two maids entered carrying trays of refreshments. They set them down on the low table between the settee and two armchairs. Winnifred sank to the edge of her seat and picked up the teapot. "Tea?"

Sutton brushed past Summerset, knocking him with his shoulder and sending him stumbling, before sitting opposite Winnifred. "Thank you, Lady Dunkeld. The ride from London was long and tiring."

Summerset glared at his friend. He dropped into the other chair and draped his leg over the armrest. "Tea won't warm you up. How about offering us a real drink? I know Dunkeld has a twenty-year scotch around here somewhere."

"Yes, and it's reserved for deserving men, not bounders like yourself." Sin strode into the parlor, and Winnifred's shoulders sank an inch down her back. Just with his presence, the room seemed brighter. Warmer. Safer.

The men stood and shook Sin's hand, clapping him on the back. "It's good to see you," Sutton said. "And felicitations on your marriage. Colleen and I were sorry we couldn't attend."

Sin twisted his lips, and he arched an eyebrow in her

direction. "It was a rather rushed affair."

"Too rushed," Summerset muttered.

"John." Sin's voice was a warning. "I have a very nice fifteen-year-old scotch, but you have to play nice to get it."

Summerset shrugged and draped himself back over the chair. "If that's the best you have."

The tension was thick as Sin poured three glasses of whisky. Winnifred's voice grated against the silence, doing nothing to relieve the tension. "Mutton pie?" She held a plate of small pastries in Summerset's direction.

He curled his lip.

"I'll take one." Sutton leaned forward and grabbed a pastry. He tore off a large bite. "The food in the public houses was rubbish," he mumbled around his mouthful.

"We're in Scotland." Summerset buffed his nails on his satin, primrose waistcoat. "Don't expect it to get any better."

Sin kicked his chair, making it almost tip over, before crossing to sit next to Winnifred on the settee.

She pulled her needlepoint away before he sat on it. "Is there a reason behind your visit?" Her mouth went dry when she realized how impertinent her words were. She tried to make amends. "I mean, it's lovely the two of you made the time to travel to Scotland. I was only wondering if this was a social call or did you have some business here?" She pressed her fingertips into the brocade of the settee. That hadn't sounded much better. She wasn't practiced at receiving callers of such superior quality. What sort of drivel was she supposed to say to them? "I meant...."

Sin laid his hand over hers and squeezed.

Summerset tossed back his dram of whisky. "No need to apologize. It is rude to just drop in on a newly-wedded couple, but it's not as though yours was a love-match. The impertinence didn't seem so great."

The mantle clock ticked loudly in the silence. Sutton stopped chewing to narrow his eyes at his friend. Sin stiffened beside her.

Winnifred rolled the hem of her cuff into a tight coil.

"What?" Summerset widened his cobalt eyes innocently. "Is it impolite to state a fact?"

Winnifred squared her shoulders. She could handle Sin's friend not liking her. And he was right about their marriage. It hadn't been a love match. She and Sin had decided to make the best of a compromising situation, and she was fortunate to have married a man as sensible as she was. "The reasons for our marriage are well-known and not something of which I am ashamed. There is no reason you shouldn't speak plainly."

"Lovely." Summerset bobbed his foot, the emeralds on his boot winking in the light. "Now, let us get to know your plain-spoken new wife." He plucked a strawberry from a tray and held it up to the light. "Who are your parents, dear? From where do you hail?"

He already knew the answers. Winnifred could see the knowledge in his gaze. But she wouldn't embarrass her husband. She took a small sip of tea. "My mother passed when I was but eight years old. My father is a Mr. Hannon, a botanist. I was born and raised in Ludgate."

"Ludgate?" Summerset bit the bottom of the berry and watched her as he chewed. "I don't believe I'm familiar with the neighborhood."

No, an earl wouldn't be.

Sutton combed his fingers through his beard. "Yes, you are. That pub we like is in Ludgate. The one with the good mackerel."

"It doesn't matter where my wife used to live." Sin's voice was icy, the look he shot Summerset glacial. "It only matter where she lives now."

"Of course." The earl nodded to her needlepoint. "I suppose you exceed at needle work and drawing, and play the pianoforte exceeding well."

Winnifred frowned. An insult lurked within those words, but she couldn't decipher where it lay. Was he intimating that a woman of a lower class wouldn't be a competent practitioner of those feminine arts or mocking those endeavors as common? Unable to figure his angle, she went with honesty.

"My needlepoint is quite good, I draw very ill, and we never had a pianoforte to practice upon." She glanced over her shoulder. "My hearing is also quite good. I believe Horatio and Banquo are asking to be let in." She stood. "If you gentlemen will excuse me for a moment."

They rose with her, even Summerset plopped his leg down and pushed to his feet. He obviously knew better that to engage in outright rudeness, not with Sin in the room. Although, with the way her husband clenched his hand, the earl's covert rudeness might not go unpunished, either.

She practiced gliding from the room. Turning out of view, she slouched her shoulders and tromped down the hall.

She followed the sound of barking to a side door on the lower level. She pushed it open and stepped out to the east garden.

Deirdre held a stick above her head, both dogs jumping for it, a wide smile on her face. She chucked the stick and laughed when the dogs tripped over each other to retrieve it.

Winnifred raised a hand, shielding her eyes from the sunlight. Playing with the dogs, Deirdre seemed almost agreeable. Warm even.

Then she caught sight of Winnifred. Her smile dropped and her back stiffened. Horatio bounded back up to her, stick in his mouth, but she ignored him. "Spying now, are we? Or is there something ye needed?"

Winnifred sighed. She should hold her tongue. Deirdre was Sin's mother, and he loved and respected her.

Banquo bounded up to her for a chest rub, and Winnifred obliged.

"I came to see what the commotion was about." She folded her arms under her chest. "And now I'd like to discuss your animosity. I don't need us to be friends, but I'd like for us to at least be companionable, for Sin's sake, if not for our own comfort living together. Is there something I can do, besides change the nationality of my birth, that will aid in that endeavor?"

Deirdre mimicked her pose. "'Aid in that endeavor'?" she repeated in perfect Queen's English. "I know ye Sassenachs cannae help but talk doon to us Scots, but perhaps if ye tried, it might help us be 'companionable,' as ye say."

Winnifred blinked. "Talk down to you?" She shook her head. "You're the Dowager Marchioness of Dunkeld. You occupy one of the highest positions in the land. And you think *I* look down on *you*?"

"Don't ye?" She took the stick Horatio dropped at her feet and threw it again. "Ye dunnae come down to the kitchens to order the day's meals, ye dunnae help in the garden, do nothing that will get your hands dirty."

"I thought you enjoyed your kitchen duties and your garden." Winnifred pressed her lips together in exasperation. "I was trying to be considerate, letting you retain some of your previous tasks as marchioness. You'd earned that consideration due to your position."

Deirdre glanced away. "My position wasnae any better than yours. Sin's father didnae find himself a titled man's daughter to wed, either. He found me. I worked in my da's dairy but Dunkeld didn't care. He saw what he wanted and didnae care what society would say." She sniffed. "Like father like son. In that respect at least," she muttered.

Winnifred cocked her head. And here she'd thought she had to live up to the reputation of a true lady of the manor. "Sin doesn't speak much of his father. What was he like?"

Deirdre's shoulders rounded. "He was a good man. Too soft for this world, but good."

Too soft? Winnifred had seen his portrait. Like every other Dunkeld, the third marquess looked anything but soft. "W—"

"So, are ye saying you'd like to help me in the garden?

141

My son has indicated that ye have some knowledge when it comes to agriculture." Deirdre settled her hands on her hips as she gazed over her stunted plants. "That might come in useful."

An olive branch if she ever saw one, and Winnifred gratefully grabbed ahold of it. "I'd love to. Just not right this moment."

At her mother-in-law's arched eyebrow, she hurried on. "My husband has two friends visiting. I left them in my sitting room. The Earl of Summerset and the Baron of Sutton."

Deirdre's face lit up. "John and Max are here! How lovely. Give me a moment to clean up, and I'll join ye."

Winnifred nodded. She tried a tentative smile in the woman's direction. It was ignored. Oh well. She turned and slid through the door, closing it before Banquo could enter with his dirty paws. She'd made a small bit of progress today. It would have to be enough for now.

Loud voices slowed her steps as she approached the drawing room. Something smashed into the wall, and she froze outside the door.

"And I'll tell ye for the last bloody time, she didn't trap me." Sin's voice was as hot as a volcanic eruption. "Saying such insults her honor. And insulting her honor, insults mine. I willnae give ye another warning."

Winnifred swallowed. She didn't want to be the cause of a rift between Sin and his friends. Never wanted to give him reason to regret their marriage. She leaned forward, pressing her ear to the crack of the door.

"Everyone, calm down," Sutton said. "We have matters more important to discuss than the circumstances of Dunkeld's marriage. No offense." There were some soft thuds, like furniture being moved. "Besides, Summerset only has a bee in his smallclothes because he's the only bachelor left in our group. He feels abandoned."

"I bloody do not!" Summerset shouted over Sin's "None taken."

"Liverpool asked us to come to Scotland to help you investigate," Sutton said. "There are more and more rumblings in parliament about possible rebellion. He'd like us to find evidence to discredit the movement."

"Or concoct some," Summerset said, his voice a cynical drawl.

"I understand the prime minister's concerns, but I won't be a party to slandering a good Scot."

Winnifred pressed closer. Sin sounded tired, and she wondered about this job of his. Was it one he found fulfilling, or was it only a duty? He had so many already. His shoulders were broad, but not wide enough to hold the burdens of the world.

She only had a moment's warning. The sound of his nails was muffled on the long rug running down the hallway. His excited huff had her spinning a moment before his paws knocked into her chest, sending her back through the sitting room doors.

She tumbled through with a cry, hitting the thin carpet hard. Banquo stood over her, panting happily and woofing at the three men, like he'd just retrieved the biggest stick in the world.

* * *

Sin rushed forward and pulled the dog off his wife. "Are you hurt?" he asked, helping her to her feet.

Winnifred rubbed her bum. "Only my... back."

His lips twitched. He could take care of her *back* later. When he showed her how naughty wives who lurked outside doors were punished.

He turned to Banquo. "Bad dog. What have I said about jumping on people?"

The deerhound whined and dropped to the floor, tucking his grey head under his paw.

Summerset flicked his pocket square from his jacket and waved it at Winnifred. "You have a little mud on you. Just there."

Winnifred looked down and flushed beet red. She snatched the handkerchief and spun, giving Summerset and Sutton her back as she tried to brush the two brown paw prints from her breasts.

Sutton smothered a chuckle, and even Summerset looked genuinely amused. Which meant they had both been looking at his wife's breasts.

Sin narrowed his eyes and stepped between his wife and his friends. Dirty, rotten, buggers, all of them.

She turned back around and sighed. "Are you leaving again?"

'Why do you ask?" With the back of his knuckle, he swept a last bit of dirt from her bodice. If it was his choice, he'd never leave her again. But that wasn't the way of life.

"Don't you need to go investigate with your friends. If Liverpool sent them, the situation must be serious."

"She does have good hearing." Summerset righted his chair which had been lying on its side. He flicked the tails of his coat out and took a seat. "Pray tell, Lady Dunkeld, what else did you hear us say?"

Sin's body tensed. "She already knew my business."

"My, my," Summerset said. "Our inner circle does keep expanding. Pretty soon all of England will know we're spies."

"I'll never speak of it to anyone." Winnifred stood next to Sin, the back of her hand brushing his. "You have my promise."

"Good enough for me." Sutton smiled at her and grabbed another mutton pie. "Besides, it's just not practicable to keep such secrets from one's wife. You'll understand when you marry, John."

"Oh, I'm not concerned." Summerset pulled a monocle from his waistcoat pocket and buffed it against his sleeve. The gold chain attaching it to his buttonhole clinked softly. "After all, a woman who's worked so hard to attain her position wouldn't be foolhardy enough to risk it by exposing her husband."

Sin was going to toss him through the window. It didn't matter that the windows in this room were only a foot wide; he'd shove him through without his skin if necessary.

Winnifred's hand clutching the back of his jacket was the only thing that restrained him. "Summerset, a word outside please." Where Winnifred didn't have to see him pound his friend black and blue. John had gone too far with his insinuations. They were friends. The best of friends. But that didn't mean Sin wouldn't still enjoy bloodying his damn nose.

"Not when I've just arrived." His mother swept into the room, Horatio at her heels. "John. Max. Let me look at ye boys." She kissed both men's cheeks, earning a blush from Sutton and a dramatic hand clutched to his chest from Summerset. "It's been too long since any of Sin's friends came to visit."

"Not long enough," Sin gritted out.

Sutton gave Sin an appraising look. "Summerset, why don't you take the dowager to our carriage and show her the gift you brought?"

"A present?" His mother's eyes lit up. "For me?" Like such a thing was unheard of.

Sin gritted his teeth. "I buy you gifts all the time, mother."

She wagged her finger at him. "It's not the same. It's your duty to be kind to your mother."

Summerset crooked his arm, and she slipped her hand into the hollow. "A woman such as you should be inundated with presents. Positively buried with them. It's every man's duty to see to that."

Sin watched them leave, torn between smiling at the ass his friend could be and still wanting to rip his head off. Which was about how he normally felt around Summerset.

Sutton rubbed the back of his neck. "Well, now that the annoyance has left the room, perhaps you'll answer your wife's question. Will you leave for Glasgow with us?"

Sin blew out a breath and nodded. "Not immediately,"

he said to Winnifred. "I'm waiting to hear back from a couple of contacts." He hesitated. He'd already heard back from some, and one of them had an interesting account. "Winnifred, did you know MacConnell used to write a column in *The Messenger* when he lived in London?"

A small divot puckered the skin between her eyebrows. "No, he never mentioned it. Why?"

"That paper was a revolutionary one. All his columns were about Scottish independence."

She lifted one shoulder. "Donald never hid that he wished Scotland to be an independent nation. As every other Scotsman does, as well." She gave him a pointed look.

Sutton coughed back a laugh. "She's not wrong. If the Crown picked up everyone who wrote a column for Scottish sovereignty, the prisons would be full."

"The prisons are full," Sin grated out. He rested his hands upon Winnifred's shoulders and gave her as soft a look as he knew how. From Winnifred's frown, he had to assume he wasn't successful. "You do not object if I investigate your acquaintance?" He couldn't call MacConnell her friend. The word for such an intimate relationship refused to leave his lips.

"No objections whatsoever." She stepped back and made another quick examination in the mirror. She brushed at a spot on her collar. "Although I think you'll find he is no rebel leader. If he is causing trouble, it is unwittingly. Donald is high-spirited and loves his country. That is all."

Sin inclined his head, neither agreeing nor disagreeing.

Winnifred clasped her hands in front of her and took a deep breath. "The dowager has invited me to help tend the gardens. I believe I'll run my own soil experiments on them. If you gentlemen will excuse me, I have research to do."

Sutton turned to him after she'd left. "Soil experiments?"

Heat spread through Sin's chest, and a satisfied smile curled his lips. "Yes. My wife is a woman of science."

Sutton blinked. "Oh. That's... interesting?"

Sin dropped onto his seat, crossing one leg over the other. The interesting part wasn't that Winnifred was a natural philosopher.

The interesting bit was that she'd finally admitted to it. In public.

"I may be in some trouble," Sin told his friend.

"How's that?"

Sin looked to the empty door. He would build Winnifred a workshop, someplace to hold all the microscopes and chemicals she'd need for her work. "I have become fascinated with my wife."

Obsessed more like. He needed to know what she was thinking, what she was doing, her opinions and desires. He felt impelled to know everything about her.

The back of his throat ached. Except her heart. He didn't know if he was prepared to know that organ. Because chances were this obsession was all on one side. His.

And that wasn't an option he was ready to face.

Chapter Sixteen

Winnifred pressed the stamp down to seal her letter. She examined the impression in the red wax. A robust letter *D* with two swords crossing behind it. The seal for the house of Dunkeld was definitely more impressive than what she'd used for her previous correspondence. As was the weight of the cream paper and the quality of the ink. She turned to the next letter. Such a correspondence would be difficult to ignore. Should she sign her name to it? After all, she'd written to these men before. They were hardly likely to turn her post away if she didn't scribble *written at my father's behest* at the bottom beneath her signature.

Sighing, she signed the next one using her customary language. The research was more important than her ego.

She felt him before she heard him. His presence held a certain weight, like that of a predator stalking into the forest. Everything hushed. The roaring fire dimmed to a soft mutter, the mantle clock stilled, her own breath stuck in her lungs.

Sin reached over her shoulder, picking up her letter, and the scents of cedar and musk drifted over her. Her eyelids sank as heat pooled low in her belly.

Just his nearness did that to her. Not one touch was required. She couldn't imagine all married women were so fortunate in their partners. The world would be a much happier place if that was so.

He placed the letter back in front of her, and she sealed it, placing it on the stack of four other correspondences.

"Did you sign in your father's stead on all of them?"

Winnifred twisted in her chair, surprised at the anger lying in wait beneath his words.

"Yes." She cocked her head. "Of course. Although I won't be able to do so for much longer. It might be believed that I would help my father for a short while after I've married until he finds another secretary but not for much longer."

His nostrils flared. "There's nothing 'of course' about it. I had thought," he said carefully, "that when you announced to my friend that you had an experiment to run, that had meant that you were no longer hiding your true nature."

She looked down, his scuffed boots filling her vision. His valet despaired of them. No matter how brightly the man buffed them to a shine in the morning, Sin always managed to bring them back scraped and dirty. He never hid behind polish.

"Perhaps I shouldn't have done so." She traced a line on the print of her gown. "I hope I didn't shame you in front of your friend."

He gripped her chin and tilted her head up. "You could never shame me, Winnifred. Though I must admit to being disappointed you continue this pretense of being your father's assistant. Did he do any of his own research anymore, or had you taken over completely?"

She opened her mouth. Shut it. "My father is a very learned man. His research was his own and will continue without me." Probably. In the last few years she had become the driving force behind most of their experiments.

He leaned down, his eyes darkening to sapphire chips. "*Mo ghràdh*, I can tell when you dissemble. Just as you study soil, I've made a study of you."

She worried her bottom lip. Her entire life had been lived in pretense; she would have thought she'd be more accomplished at it.

"Why did you tell Sutton the truth?" he demanded.

"Because it seemed safe to do so." She drew her shoulders back. "I learned confidences about you and your friends that you don't wish me to speak of. It's only reasonable they won't speak out of turn about my own secrets."

Sin barked out a laugh. "A bit of blackmail, is it?" He arched an eyebrow. "If anyone spills your secret, you inform on us?"

Her pulse fluttered. When he said it that way, she sounded awful. "I didn't... I..."

He pressed a finger to her lips. "Hush." One side of his mouth curved up. "I like it when you fight dirty." He leaned closer, his breath caressing her cheek. "I like it when you fight. Full stop."

The hunger in his gaze made something deep within her unfurl. This man could consume her, strip her restraint as easily as he did her dress. Part of her thrilled at the abandon he evoked. He'd taught her how to enjoy a bit of wildness. But another part, the one she'd listened to all her life, still wanted to flee in terror.

"Come with me," he said. "I wish to show you something."

"All right." She put away her pen and paper and stacked her correspondence in the corner of her escritoire. After ensuring everything was in its place, she stood and took her husband's outstretched hand.

He led her out of her rooms and down a winding corridor before climbing to the third floor of the castle. He pushed open the door to an unused bedchamber and tugged her inside. "I, uh, thought perhaps you might like this."

His palm grew damp against hers, and she wondered at his nervousness until she stepped around him and saw what was in the room.

Her jaw dropped. The chamber had been cleared of any bed or wardrobe. Instead, a row of flat wooden desks lined the walls. On one, thick glass bottles of chemicals stood—Winnifred bent to peer at the labels—in alphabetical order. On another, a pair of thick leather gloves and a leather apron. And on a third....

"Ohh," she breathed. She ran a finger along the smooth mahogany case before lifting the lid. A three-stage brass and ivory contraption rose with the lid, mechanically erecting until it locked in its tower formation. "A Withering Botanical microscope!" She pulled out and replaced the scalpel, dissecting needle, and stage forceps that came in the velvet-lined case.

Sin cleared his throat. "If you don't like it, or want another model, you have only to ask. I asked Tavish to furnish a laboratory for a natural philosopher who studies agriculture, but I think he knows as little as I about your needs."

She ran her thumb along the edge of the top lens. "You understand my needs quite well." A laboratory of her own. Hers to arrange and manage as she liked. Her hands tingled, itching to dive in. She turned to face him. "I don't know how to thank you."

One edge of his mouth slanted up. "I'm sure we can think of a way."

Winnifred blushed. Yes. There were several ways to thank a husband. And he deserved every naughty idea she could conceive. "Are you certain you are comfortable with your wife having a lab? Everyone will think—"

"I don't care." He cocked his shoulder against the door jamb and crossed his arms. "Are you happy?"

"Yes." She'd never felt such happiness. Winnifred turned in a circle, spying new toys her first examination of the chamber had missed. Never was a woman so fortunate in her husband. He might not understand the science, but he understood her love for it. That was more than enough. "Why did you choose this room?"

"It's in the corner, with windows on two sides." He shrugged. "I thought the light would be useful. Why? Do you not like it?"

"No, it's quite serviceable."

"But?"

She scraped her teeth across her lip. "Would you mind terribly if I had the equipment moved to the room in the center turret? When I was up there before I had thought that it was an excellent space."

Sin pushed off the wall and prowled towards her. He rested his palms on her shoulders, brushing his thumbs along her collarbone.

A shiver danced just under her skin.

"Then it shall be yours." He bent and placed a soft kiss on her lips.

Her breath quickened. Never could she have imagined being so forward, but something about her husband gave her courage. She took his hand and pulled him to the door. "I have a letter I want to place in Mr. Greer's hands to post but after that there is something of yours I'd like to place in my hand." She glanced over her shoulder as she hurried down the staircase. "If you have no other engagements, that is."

Sin huffed. "There isn't an engagement in the world that would keep me from your plans."

Good. She bustled into her sitting room, eager to complete her errand and get her husband in bed. Her belly tightened at the thought.

She pushed a stack of letters she'd received to the side and reached for her outgoing correspondence. One of the letters addressed to her fell to the floor.

Sin plucked it up, moving to hand it to her before sucking in a sharp breath. He held the letter up to his face and read the return address, his jaw clenching.

"You said you hadn't spoken since he called." He flicked his wrist, and the paper snapped open.

Her stomach clenched, this time not with desire, and she gripped the edge of her desk, resisting the urge to snap her letter from his hands. He had no right to read her correspondence.

A husband held all the rights in a marriage.

"We haven't spoken," she said, proud that her voice

sounded so even. "That is a letter I received just today. And as you can see, contains nothing but banal pleasantries and well-wishes for the future."

"Have you received other communications from him?"

"A few." Letters laced with regrets and fond memories of their time together in London. Winnifred had contemplated tossing the correspondence. His remembrances were tainted with his last proposition. But it seemed disrespectful to someone she had once cared for.

Sin held out his hand, palm up. "I will take those now."

Her back stiffened. "I didn't realize my correspondence were subject to inspection."

He held the back of her chair, his knuckles going white. "When my wife is receiving letters from a former beau, and a suspect in treason, everything is subject to inspection."

She clenched her hands. "He was never a beau."

"The letters." He held his palm up.

Hand trembling, she yanked open the top drawer of her desk and found the two missives from Donald. She threw them at her husband's chest. Rationally, she knew his actions shouldn't anger her so. He was open with his correspondence, told her of his business and expected the same in return.

Yet still it stung.

He read them quickly, his face darkening. "What does he mean? He wishes that circumstances were different and implies you made an incorrect decision. Did he ask you to marry him?"

Was that outrage or disbelief in his voice? It didn't matter. Her husband had certain rights, and knowing the history of his wife wasn't remarkable. She would remain calm.

"No." She was proud of how steady she sounded. Her dispassion was familiar territory. A refuge that was second-nature.

A defense that numbed her to her soul. "He would never have considered marrying a woman who wasn't

Scottish."

"Hmm." He tossed the letters on the desk. "Still closer to you than I like. It's fortunate for me that you aren't the sort of woman to embolden a man's advances."

Heat crawled up her face. No, she wasn't a beauty eligible bachelors had vied for. Nor the sort to flirt or engage men with her wit. And definitely not the sort of woman to make a fuss over an insult from her husband.

She turned, her heart beating quicker. Oh, but how she wanted to be. The insult landed harder coming on the heels of his sweet gesture giving her a lab. Just moments ago she had been thinking how compatible they were, how the two of them were so well-matched.

But Sin would have bestowed tender kindnesses on any wife. And the attentions he paid her in the marital bed, the heat in his eyes, those would have been roused for any other woman he had wed, as well. He was a lusty man. There was nothing special about her. "No, Donald didn't ask for my hand in marriage. He asked me to be his mistress."

The shocked silence gave her a grim sense of satisfaction. When Donald had asked her that in her father's laboratory those years' ago, she had been shocked, too. He had made his affection clear, his desire for more, and as a woman of science, she knew what it was he wanted. She'd thought his desire would lead to a marriage proposal, however. That he couldn't think her so reckless as to accept his lesser offer.

"Donald also didn't think I was the type of woman who would receive many proposals." Her pulse raced beneath her skin. "That I would be grateful to accept the alternative." And she'd thanked him. *Thanked. Him.* Before politely refusing. She hadn't let herself become agitated. Couldn't show her distress because bad things happened to those who did.

Two points of color rode high on his cheeks. "Repeat that," he growled.

"What?" She flexed her hands but the itch, the tremble in them remained. "That you were correct, your wife is so completely lacking in attractions to the opposite sex that you were my first marriage proposal?" She shoved at his chest.

He blinked, but didn't move otherwise.

"That all a woman like me is entitled to is an offer to tup in the back of her father's shed?" She put all her weight into it, pushing against him as hard as she could, needing to be able to move him. Nothing. She hit him instead, pounding her fists into his unflinching body. "Yes, you are fortunate indeed that you need never worry that your wife will dally with another, as no man will have her. Her appearance won't *embolden* anyone into impropriety." She'd always been too tall, too sturdy, too charmless to make an impression on men, and it had never mattered to her. Being plain had been a blessing in her need to fade out of sight, not bring attention to herself and make herself a target.

But she had hoped her husband would look at her differently, thought that he had, that he'd found her appearance pleasing. Pleasing enough to ravish every night.

Her wrist stung with her last blow, but she didn't care. It felt too good to pour out all her anger, her frustrations. Her wildness in the bedroom had been but playacting compared to this, this frenzy of emotion.

She was interchangeable to Sin. He would behave such with any wife.

Jealousy stole her breath. The fact her husband didn't find her especially attractive shouldn't matter. But it did.

Sin grabbed her wrists, pinning them to his chest. "Don't be daft. That wasn't what I meant. Obviously I meant you aren't the sort of woman to encourage improper advances."

Winnifred struggled against him. Now she was daft as well as unappealing? "Release me," she hissed. She leaned away, her body straining, but he easily held her to him. "You can't invade my privacy, insult me, and then hold me captive."

A muscle ticked in his jaw. "It appears that I can. You are *my* wife. Mine. And I won't let you forget it."

She shrieked in anger. Her struggles were ineffectual, her arguments falling on deaf ears. Reason deserted her and her body's instinct took over. Leaning forward, she bit a hand that held her. Hard.

He jerked, and shook the sting from the abused hand whilst maintaining his grip with the other. His eyes blazed as he glared down at her, and Winnifred knew she should be afraid. She was provoking a very large animal, but a perverse part of her wanted to poke him harder. Force him to join her in this depraved state.

All the fear she'd buried deep, the terror that she might be sent away burbled to the surface. The anger. The disgust that more hadn't been done to help her mother. It overflowed, like storm water over a dam.

The pressure grew until it had nowhere left to go. Her emotions burst.

She yanked one hand free. Her fingers tore at his flesh, wanting to claw their way inside. Her hands slapped at his chest, his abdomen, anywhere they could reach. Any sense of propriety, of measure, was lost. There was only a primal need to mark, to possess, to be possessed.

He took her blows, grunting softly when they landed, but allowing her assault.

Her body warmed.

She kicked at his shins, tore at his shirt. Her breasts scraped against his chest, and her nipples ached. Power raced through her veins. Fearless abandon. A needy pulse beat in her sex, her thighs growing slick as she struggled. The rational part of her that would be disgusted with such licentiousness was beaten back, the gaoler becoming the prisoner.

Sin neatly swept her legs and took her to the thick Turkish rug. He gripped her wrists in one of his hands and slammed them to the ground above her head. "You spoiling for a fight, *mo chridhe*?" His voice was a threat, a silken caress. "Give me your best shot."

Chapter Seventeen

She snapped at him. Out and out bared her teeth and snapped. A small part of Winnifred worried at her willfulness, but she had no more damns to give.

Sin lowered his body over hers, holding her writhing form pinned beneath him.

She bucked harder, knowing she could push and claw all she wanted and it wouldn't matter. She could slice through all the strings that tied her to respectability, strangling her, because Sin would be there to hold her together when she let it all go.

She wedged her leg out from his body and hooked it up around his hip. His hard length pressed against her belly, and heat radiated through her chest. She'd done that to him. She wasn't alone in her need.

Sin pressed his hand to her throat before sliding it down to her chest. He tore away her lace fichu, eyes flaring as he eyed the tops of her heaving bosom. He released her hand and gripped her bodice. Shoulders flexing, he pulled it down, fabric ripping as the seams at her sleeves split, her stays and shift rending. Cool air met her puckered nipples a moment before his mouth descended.

He scored his teeth along the side of her breast, bit into the soft underside before licking the sting away. He ground his hips into the vee of her thighs, spiking her temperature, making her toes curl.

She shoved her hands under his coat, dug her fingernails into his shirt, pulling him into her. He was delightfully heavy against her, solid in a way she'd never known. Tough enough to take any of her assaults. Rough enough to break down her barriers. Sin touched her as though her body were merely an extension of his own.

His bristled jaw rubbed her delicate skin raw. He sucked her nipple into her mouth, drawing so hard she arched her back. The nip of pain made her skin feel alive, put an end to any thought in her brain until all it measured was sensation.

She shoved at the lapels of his jacket, shoving it down his shoulders.

He reared up and threw it off.

She yanked his cravat, earning a growl as she garroted him.

He beat her to his shirt, reaching behind his head and tearing if off in one go.

The sweat on his skin glistened. A damp thatch of hair, a darker auburn than his head, dusted his chest. She traced the tantalizing trail arrowing down his stomach until she hooked her finger into the waist of his trousers.

He was beautiful, her beast. Beautiful, and wild, and hers, no matter his regard. She might not be handsome or witty enough to have earned a marriage proposal from him without being caught in a compromising situation, but the end result was the same. He was her husband. She was his wife. And she wouldn't let him forget it.

Using his pants as leverage, she pulled herself up to suck at his throat, his collarbone. She licked the beads of sweat from his shoulders, loving the earthy taste of him.

A shudder rippled through his body, and a grin stretched her lips. She'd done that. She lifted her pelvis to rub against his. She'd made him tremble.

He looked down on her, his hair falling from its queue to brush his shoulders.

She reached for his face, but he intercepted her hand, gripping her wrist and hip and flipping her to her stomach. One side of her face pressed into the carpet.

His breath was hot on her temple. "Don't make one

damn sound. I don't want to hear one more word about how you think you're unappealing, or how misunderstood *Donald* is, or why it's only sensible that you hide behind your father's name."

He scraped his fingers up her legs, pulling her skirts with him until they bunched at her waist. "I might be the Dunkeld who let's Kenmore crumble into the ground, but I damn sure won't allow you to diminish yourself. You're a fierce, cunning, carnal little creature, and thank God for it. I worship your wildness, even as I need to control it." He sucked her earlobe into his hot mouth, pulling. "So, you're going to stay quiet as I fuck this pussy, *my* pussy, so hard you won't be able to climb from bed on the morrow."

The hair on the nape of her neck stood on end. Tingles started at the base of her spine and spread through her body. Dear Lord, they were going to have intercourse in her sitting room in broad daylight. She would need to remain silent, if nothing else, so as not to draw anyone's attention.

The decadence of the situation thrilled her.

Sin grabbed the knot that held her hair and tugged her head back. "Nod if you understand."

Chest heaving, she bobbed her head, her hair pulling at the roots he held.

Sin released her and dug his fingers into her hips. He jerked her back onto her knees, tilting her bottom up.

She sagged into the rug, the rough wool abrading her cheek and nipples. Her body went limp, surrendering to his superior strength.

He slapped her arse, and she whimpered at the sting.

Sin's crown bumped her entrance, notching inside her channel.

His command was all-consuming, surrounding her, enveloping her until she no longer knew where her reality ended and his began.

He impaled her with his length, their union complete.

* * *

A dark mist clouded his brain. Deliberate thought was but a distant memory. His blood pounded beneath his skin, a storm raging just below the surface.

He stared at the woman stretched out beneath him. His woman. Her hands lay limp by her head. Her mouth was soft, her eyes closed, her hair a knotted nest. Sin drew his finger down the creamy skin of her spine, feeling each bump of her vertebrae until he reached the cleft of her arse. The lingering pink handprint made his cock twitch inside her.

He pushed deeper into her, taking that last two inches until he was pressed flush against her bottom. Her sheath was liquid heat around him, sucking wetly at his prick as he pulled out until only his head remained. He pounded back home, his trousers slipping an inch down his hips.

Mine. The one word reverberated through his consciousness. The infuriating, marvelous woman before him, surrounding him, was his and his alone. And if any man tried to write sentimental words to her again, Sin would rip his fingers off, one by one.

It wasn't rational. Wasn't civilized.

He didn't care.

Sin slid his hands higher, adjusted his grip on her waist. Small round circles pinkened her flesh where his fingertips had been.

A growl rumbled low in his throat. His marks looked good on her. He raised a hand and brought it down on her plump arse, watching the red print bloom.

Jesus fucking Christ, he was mad. His desire for his wife went beyond what was normal. He wanted under her skin, inside her head, his imprint covering every inch of her.

He fucked her slow and hard, his gaze transfixed as his purpling cock disappeared and reappeared from her body.

Winnifred sighed and arched her back, raising her hips to his thrusts.

Something rumbled deep in his chest.

He loved it when she fought him like a wild thing.

He loved it more when she submitted to his power, when she realized she'd been caught and that her capture would bring them both the greatest pleasure.

Whatever the future of their marriage held, whatever feelings Winnifred may or may not develop, he knew at least in this one aspect there would be no complaints.

He pulled out, his cock weeping at the separation. He pulled her cheeks apart and rubbed his crown against her arsehole. "Can't wait to fuck you here. Can't wait to fuck you everywhere." Her arse, her mouth, her breasts. Her body was a veritable feast for his hungry prick.

He slid back inside her hot sheath, the skin at the base of his spine tingling.

The compulsion to plant his seed deep inside her, brand her in the truest way he knew how sank its teeth into him. He wanted to fill her with his child, link her to him in a way no man could break.

He thrust deep, his cock begging for relief.

A whimper escaped her lips and she pressed her mouth tight.

Sin gripped the back of her neck with one hand, held onto her hip with the other, pulling her to him to meet his drives. He fucked her harder. Faster.

Winnifred bit her lower lip, her shoulders tensing.

Leaning over her, he whispered, "Is there something you need to say, *mo chridhe*?" He skimmed the hand at her hip down to graze her pouting clit.

Her mouth opened on a silent gasp, her hips jerking back on him in her desperate spiral.

He licked the tendon straining in her neck before biting down.

Her whimper only spurred him on. She wouldn't be thinking about MacConnell or her life before Sin. Not now. "I want to hear you scream my name. You have permission for that."

She wailed, her dewy skin flushing pink all over, "Siiiin." His name was a tortured groan. A plea. The best goddamn sound he'd ever heard.

Planting one foot by her side, he fucked his wife for all he was worth. The ride was wilder than any runaway horse, any country race.

The slap and squelch of their bodies melded with his grunts. With her moans every time he hit bottom. Lightning raced along his cock and fire pooled low in his ballocks. They pulled up tight just as Winnifred's shoulder muscles hardened to stone.

The need for release was overwhelming. He shouted as he spilled into her, pulse after pulse of his seed filling his woman, and he ground his finger against her clit. Her core clamped hard around him as she cried out, and he circled her nub, trying to drag out the excruciating moment for as long as possible.

It wasn't long enough. It would never be enough. He collapsed on top of her, pinning her frame, keeping her from ever escaping.

A log in the fireplace popped, and the skin of his back cooled. Finding her hands, he interlaced their fingers together and rolled to his side, wrapping their hands around her middle.

When he'd gained a wife, he'd felt the lure of possession. As Winnifred revealed her soul bit by bit, like a sultry little dance of seven scarves, his feelings had bordered on obsession.

Now, something else took root under his breast.

He buried his nose in her hair and kissed the back of her head.

Something that felt an awful lot like love.

Chapter Eighteen

Everything ached. The muscles in her shoulders and legs. The bruises on her hips. The soreness between her thighs.

Winnifred shifted with a groan. Sin had been right. She didn't want to rise from bed this morn.

Rolling onto her back, she stared at the cathedral ceiling of the bed and reveled in the luxury of the silk sheets. They were good aches, she decided. The fatigue one felt after a long and successful day of running experiments. Twinges that would remind her of the day before with every move she made.

She'd let Sin strip her of all control. Reduce her to her basest self. Striking him. Loosing all of her anger upon him.

She waited for the flood of panic to crush her. It never came.

Sin had seen her at her worst. Her wildest. She'd behaved in ways her mother would have blushed at.

And he'd accepted it. Taken pleasure in it. Shown her how to discover her own bliss in the storm of passion in return. Her cheeks heated. And shown her that she might have been the tiniest bit foolish to believe he found her unappealing. No man could fake such ardor.

Her husband had shown her so much, and she would forever be grateful. Expanded her constrained world and allowed her to explore her limits. Her frenzies when alone with Sin were their own private moments. They didn't reflect the entirety of her behavior. She could control her emotions during the day, saving her curative passions for her times alone with Sin.

She pressed a hand to her heart, tears stinging the backs of her eyes. She wasn't her mother. She wasn't broken. Madness didn't master her; she mastered it. She lay silently for a moment, enjoying the relief that filled her. She'd lived in fear for too long.

Her stomach growled, and she rubbed a hand over her abdomen. She could wait for the maid to bring her breakfast, but there were guests in the house and the thought of entertaining them wasn't as dreadful as it was the day before. Throwing her covers off, she swung her legs over the side of the bed and dropped to her feet. She winced at her first step but by the time she rang for her maid, her steps were even.

Sheena breezed into the chamber. "'Morning, milady." Her abigail flung open the door to the dressing room, chattering like a magpie. "Going doon to break your fast this morn? I dunnae blame ye. Have ye seen the Earl of Summerset?" The girl held up a blue-stripped satin gown, and Winnifred nodded approval. "Of course, ye've seen him. He's the laird's friend, but cor, is he handsome."

Winnifred put her stays on herself while her maid talked, but there was nothing for it but to bare her back for the girl to help her with her dress. Her cheeks burned. Would Sheena notice the bruises and scratches from Sin? The bite marks? How could she not? Would she understand just how Winnifred had earned them?

She lifted her chin. What did it matter? Her abigail would have to become used to them. She didn't foresee her and Sin's manner of intercourse changing, and, truly, it was no one's concern but theirs.

If Sheena noticed them, she didn't comment, instead prattling on about Summerset's hair, and wondering how long it took him each morning to get the curls just so.

"Thank you, Sheena." Winnifred gave her own hair one last adjustment, cutting the girl off mid-sentence. She turned for the door, not knowing how much more gossip before her morning tea she could take.

Sheena dipped a curtsy and skipped from the room.

Winnifred followed more sedately She gripped the bannister tightly as she eased down the stairs. She stood in the door of the breakfast room, an odd flutter that had nothing to do with hunger tickling her stomach at the thought of seeing her husband. Which was foolish. She and Sin had come to an agreement of sorts, albeit a nonverbal one. They would allow themselves to act in a frenzy when it came to their bed sport and maintain their friendly companionship through the rest of their marriage. A harmonious union. Nothing that should cause any flutters. She fiddled with her fichu before pushing through the double doors.

Into an empty room.

"Hm." She twisted her lips. She knew Sin wasn't still abed. Her stomach twisted. He wouldn't have left for Glasgow without saying goodbye. Would he?

A footman entered carrying a tray of cold meats. He bowed to her before setting the dish on the end table, exchanging it for an empty tray.

"Do you know where the marquess and his guests are?" she asked.

"Aye, milady. I believe Laird Dunkeld and the others are in the west tunnel."

Her shoulders drooped with relief. Still at Kenmore. And making another attempt at badger-removal.

Her stomach growled again, and she quickly loaded up a plate. As no one was around to see her, she ate quickly, licking grease from her lips. She'd heard that most fine houses had abandoned the tradition of serving a substantial breakfast, instead only having light breads and cakes for the morning meal. She popped another bit of beef into her mouth. Thankfully, Sin still served a good country breakfast.

Gulping down the last of her tea, she rose to search for her husband. Not wanting to walk through the dark corridor again, she exited a side door and wrapped around to the mouth of the tunnel.

No sounds emerged. No flash of a lamp. But she felt its presence, knew its beady eyes were staring at her.

A shiver rolled down her spine and she stepped back. She walked around the castle, waving at Jock as he helped a young boy carry a bale of hay. Voices rose from the shed next to the stables, and Winnifred followed them to stand at the open door.

Sin stood with his back to her, his jacket nowhere in sight, his back a quivering line of tension.

"Are we ready to go back in?" Sutton's voice sounded exhausted, resigned. He shifted on his legs, the only part of him Winnifred could see around her husband's body.

"Yes." Sin swung a length of lead pipe. The back and forth made an ominous swishing sound in the air. "I'm going to beat its bloody head in this time. He won't slip past me again."

Summerset stepped into view. The coiled locks that Sheena had sighed over were sticking up in all directions, and a small trickle of blood ran down the side of his neck. He held up a burlap sack. "Or we can capture it in this sack," he said, his voice a lazy drawl.

"And then I'll beat its head in." *Swish, swish.* Sin nodded. "Thereby containing the blood spatter to the sack. Smart plan."

Summerset blinked. "This badger has really gotten under your skin."

"Kill it. Capture it. Who cares?" Sutton's hands stretched into view over Sin's head. "I'm just tired of rolling about with it."

"Agreed." Summerset plucked a shovel from its spot on the wall. "I have other things I could be doing, like rolling about between a woman's thighs. Is Widow MacGregor unmarried yet? She was always an eager one."

Heat bloomed on her cheeks. Winnifred cleared her throat. "Good morning, gentlemen." She couldn't quite meet her husband's eyes when he turned. Her belly quivered at memories of the rolling about between *her* thighs he'd done. "I see the badger hunt has begun anon."

"We almost had him earlier." Sin clenched the pipe. "Brought Banquo in on a lead to help flush him out."

She examined the dirt streaking the front of his shirt and trousers. Sweat had dampened the linen across his chest and stomach, making the fabric cling to his muscles. "What happened?"

Summerset snorted. "The mongrel snapped his lead in two in his eagerness to escape." He shook his head. "Really, Dunkeld, I thought you said those dogs would fly into battle beside the family."

Winnifred finally looked into Sin's face. His eyes were focused on her, cataloguing her face, her breasts and hips. His gaze was possessive, knowing, like every wanton act they'd ever performed was running through his mind, as well. "Their ancestors did. Something went wrong with this litter."

She licked her lips, attempted to slow her breathing. Now was not the time for these improper thoughts. "Might I speak with you, husband?"

He tossed the pipe to Summerset who snatched it from the air an inch before it struck his nose. "That wasn't called for," he hollered at Sin's retreating back.

Winnifred followed him outside and they strolled past the stables to a large oak tree. She ran her palm along the rough bark of the trunk, feeling each prickle and scratch. "Do you know yet when you leave for Glasgow?"

"On the morrow." He ran the pad of his finger along her cheekbone, over the bridge of her nose. It was though he were trying to memorize her features, imprint them in his brain.

"I would like to come with you."

His hand stilled. "As I and my friends investigate a rebellion? Out of the question."

She squared her shoulders. "Surely, not every moment

will be spent engaging in fisticuffs. You will stay in nice accommodations, socialize with your fellow peers? I'm not asking to accompany you when you go out on your investigations, only to travel with you as many wives do with their husbands."

"Why?" He stilled her hands, and she frowned, not realizing that she worried her lace cuff until he stopped her.

She tilted her chin up. "There is a scholar there, at the University of Glasgow. We've communicated via post several times, but I'd like to discuss his insights into nitrates in person."

"This is important to you?"

She hesitated. It was. Discussing research in person was nearly always more efficient than through the back and forth of letters. She'd attended a hundred salons her father had held in his home with fellow natural philosophers. Listening, lurking, never speaking of course, but they were edifying all the same.

Sin's response to her request was even more important. He'd stated that he wanted her to acknowledge her work. When faced with that reality, how would he react?

"Yes." Her pulse thrummed beneath her skin. "Most important."

"Very well," Sin said. "It will be nice to show you Glasgow anyhow. It is a beautiful city."

She clapped her hands together. "Thank you!" She hopped onto her toes and kissed his cheek.

Sin's arm curved around her back, keeping her close.

"Are we going to rid your castle of vermin or are we stopping for a romantic interlude?" Summerset leaned against the wall of the shed, one leg carelessly crossed over the other.

Sutton stood next to him. "It is coming up on nuncheon."

Sin draped his arm over her shoulder as they strolled towards his friends. "The badger can live. For now."

"Marvelous." The earl's eyes tracked every point of

contact between Sin and Winnifred, narrowing slightly. A small furrow creased his forehead when he looked up into his friend's face.

"There has been a slight change in plans." Sin squeezed her shoulder. "Winnifred has business to attend to in Glasgow. She will be accompanying us."

Sutton pursed his lips. "What business—" He cut himself off.

Could a woman possibly have? A woman like her? Winnifred swallowed. "It's with a man of science, a professor at the university there."

"A colleague of Winnifred's," Sin added.

"Of my father's." The words were a reflex, and she felt Sin's glare burning the side of her face. "But I've communicated with him, as well," she amended.

Sin bobbed his chin at Summerset. "What? No snide commentary from you?"

The man shrugged. "It will help with appearances, having your new wife along. Much of our work will involve dinner parties and the like, and it would be only natural for you to want to introduce her to Scottish society." He flicked a leaf from his shoulder. "In fact, I'm surprised you haven't had a ball here in her honor, yet."

"With neighbors going hungry, a ball hardly seems proper." Sin blew out a breath.

Summerset straightened and gave them a bright smile. "Of course, that's the reason. I never once thought it was because you weren't proud to show off your wife."

Sin's arm turned to an iron band around her shoulders.

"And how about you, love." Summerset ran his fingers through his hair, a move that, instead of further ruffling his locks, seemed to spring them back into place. "Are you excited to finally meet the Polite Society that you married into? Don't be concerned that you don't look the part. Most of us quite respect the intelligence it takes to climb into our ranks."

Sin released her so quickly that she stumbled. He was a

blur as he sprang forward. Red highlights glinted in his queue as it flew behind him. A tear in his shirt near the elbow gaped wide as he drew his arm back. The sickening sound of bone cracking against bone followed.

Summerset's body seemed to move before the blow landed, rolling with the punch. His head jerked back from the impact, and he stumbled against the shed, nearly sliding to the ground before Sutton grabbed his shoulder.

The baron stood between his two friends. "Enough." He swiveled his head to glare at both men. "Enough nonsense out of you," he said, shaking Summerset, "and you, save it for the men we seek. We have enemies enough without you two turning on each other."

Winnifred fell a step back, the surprise of the attack shocking her. The violence of their intercourse was nothing compared to the brutality her husband kept pent up inside. She'd known he was rough; she hadn't realized how much he'd held back from her.

Sin spun away from his friends, clenching and unclenching his hands, eyes burning with anger. They landed on Winnifred, and narrowed even further.

A spiral of lust swirled in her belly. Her nipples tightened under her stays, an involuntary response to his ferocity. She took another step back. Brutality shouldn't affect her such. This evidence of her husband's violence.

But it did. Because she knew he would use that violence to protect what was his. Protect her. And he knew how to hone that violent edge to bring her to the peaks of pleasure.

His Adam's apple bobbed as the distance between them grew. Emptiness pushed out the anger in his gaze.

Her heart stumbled. She raised a hand to stop him, tell him she wasn't scared of him, but he'd already turned his back to stomp away. "I'm going after the badger," he shouted over his shoulder. "Enjoy your nuncheon."

She lifted her skirts to chase after him, but Sutton stopped her. "You'd best let him calm himself. Your husband tends to hit first, think later, but he'll come out right in the end."

She frowned. She didn't need lectures about her husband. She spun on Summerset. "Why did you goad him so? I thought you were supposed to be his friend."

Summerset pressed his fingers to his cheek. A lovely bruise would develop, and one very well deserved, too.

He gazed at her, his expression thoughtful. "In anger, true emotions are revealed. Now I know his mind. It isn't just a duty to defend his wife. He actually has feelings for you."

Sutton threw up his hands and muttered 'idiot.'

The earl ignored him. Cocking his head, he gave her an appraising look. "I now understand Sin. All that's left to understand is you."

Chapter Nineteen

Winnifred examined the row of forks beside her plate and grimaced. What a foolish conceit the members of the Quality had when it came to such things. And more fool her to think that she would fit into such company, even wearing the beautiful new emerald-green gown her husband had given her.

She darted a glance down the Earl of Abercairn's long dining table, wishing custom hadn't separated her from her husband by several chairs. The whirlwind of new names and faces made her feel as turned about as a shell tumbling in the surf. She didn't know how she was expected to keep track of all the new acquaintances. She longed for the support of someone familiar. She'd even have wished for Summerset to be seated next to her at this interminable dinner party. At least his hostility was open and honest. The vipers at this table hid their malice behind coy smiles and double-edged words.

"My dear girl, it is so brave of you to attempt that fashion." Lady Abercairn, the viper with the sharpest bite, cooed to the guest across from Winnifred. Lady Abercairn's voice held only the barest hint of a brogue, and Winnifred could only assume years spent in London with her husband had smoothed over the harsher burr of her people.

Lady Margaret Masson, daughter to the Earl of Brandon, flushed brick red. She fingered the military-style braiding on her bodice, her long à la mameluke sleeves swamping her hands.

Lady Abercairn buttered a roll and poked her knife in her victim's direction. "A real triumph of spirit over caution."

Winnifred stiffened as her hostess turned to her. "Lady Dunkeld, you have yet to say how you find our fair city. This is your first visit to Glasgow, is it not?"

"Yes, although I cannot yet give you much of an opinion." Winnifred nodded to the footman to refill her wineglass. "We only arrived just this afternoon. But from what I saw on the ride from our lodgings to your home, it does appear quite lovely." It would have been lovelier still if she had remained at their apartments as Sutton had. She knew as Sin's wife she needed to embrace society, but after a day of travel, she didn't know if her fortitude would last the night.

"I hope ye go to St. Mungo's." Dr. Neil Masson, the earl's younger son, leaned forward. He sat next to his sister, and the fact that they were allowed to sit together while she and Sin were separated grated against Winnifred's sensibilities. "The cathedral is necessary for every visitor to see."

"Yes, the Lady Newton said the very same thing when she visited with me last summer." Lady Abercairn lifted her wineglass and examined Winnifred over the rim. "Are you acquainted with Viscount Newton's wife, Lady Dunkeld? She holds the best soirees in all of London."

Winnifred pushed at a turnip on her plate. "No, I'm afraid I don't have the fortune of her acquaintance."

"No, I suppose you wouldn't." Lady Abercairn sipped her wine. "But I believe your husband knows her." She raised her voice. "Isn't that right, Dunkeld? That you were once a particular friend to Lady Newton?"

Silence descended on the table. Winnifred clenched the napkin on her lap, refusing to look at Sin. Of course, he'd lived a full life before her, had many women, but she didn't need to see such knowledge in his eyes.

"I made her acquaintance briefly when she was yet Lady

Featherstone," Sin replied, his voice low. "I have not seen her since she remarried."

"That's not surprising." The Duke of Beaumont waved away a footman with a platter of roast meat. "I so rarely see you in society in London, Dunkeld, that it is more astonishing you know anyone at all."

Summerset chuckled. "You have his character well. It is all I can do to drag him out into the world so as not to molder away in his home. Though I suppose that task now falls to Lady Dunkeld."

Sin shifted, his chair creaking. "And what about you, Duke? I was surprised to see you here tonight. I would have thought after the attempt on your life that you would avoid society for a time. Or at least until you return to London."

"I return tomorrow." Beaumont leaned back in his seat. "The case has been made that my position as trustee would be one better fulfilled by a Scotsman. Someone who is more familiar with the economy of Scotland. I am inclined to agree."

Winnifred caught Sin's glance. Did the duke agree before or after the assassination attempt? If it was so easy to scare away the English, this rebellion had a good chance of succeeding.

"We're sorry to see ye go," Lord Abercairn said. "We need more level heads around here."

Beaumont raised his glass in their host's direction. "With men like you and Dunkeld, I leave Scotland in good hands."

Lord Abercairn sighed. "With emotions running so high, even the best of men will be hard-pressed to maintain control. Next session of parliament there will have to be a discussion about how to handle this. Perhaps some more concessions to appease the populace of Scotland."

Summerset swirled his wine in his glass. "And what concessions will you offer when a man is actually killed? Appeasement is the coward's way; you may delay the consequences but you will still have to face them in the end."

Abercairn turned red. "How—"

His wife interrupted. "Perhaps the duke could carry a message back to London for you." Lady Abercairn smiled at Winnifred, an attempt to relieve the tension, no doubt, but the expression left Winnifred cold. It was like watching a lion smile before going in for the kill. "I'm sure your family is anxious to hear news from you."

Winnifred shook her head. "I correspond regularly with my father. No additional messages need be taken to him."

"And your mother?" Lady Abercairn tilted her head. "Does she not like to hear from her daughter?"

Winnifred's lungs squeezed. It was a common inquiry, nothing that should cause her instinct to flee to spring to life.

But it did.

"My wife's mother is no longer with us," Sin said.

"Oh, that's right. Lady Newton mentioned as much in her last correspondence." Lady Abercairn turned back to her plate.

"Lady Newton wrote to you about me?" Winnifred dug through her memories but she was certain she had never met the woman.

"The daughter of a gardener marrying a marquess was the most interesting thing to happen this season." Lady Abercairn shrugged. "There has been much discussion of you. And she did mention your mother." A delicate frown turned her lips down. "I can't recall what she wrote, however."

Winnifred pushed her plate away. Of course, there would be gossip. By marrying her, Sin might have nipped the scandal in the bud, but the circumstances would still be discussed. Chewed over like Banquo did on a bone.

"Her father is a botanist," Sin said stiffly.

Lady Abercairn ignored him and turned to Lady Margaret. "Did you hear the dreadful news about poor Mrs. Milligan's mother? Gone quite mad, the dear thing. And now Charlotte is worried for her children, and herself, of course."

A headache began to pound behind Winnifred's right eye.

Lady Margaret made a noncommittal sound.

"You study medicine, don't you, Mr. Masson?" Lady Abercairn's words sounded as though from a tunnel. They echoed around Winnifred's mind, becoming fainter and fainter.

Dr. Masson's response was but a low buzz. "I've been a physician for three years now, so aye, I'd say so."

"Does dear Mrs. Milligan have cause for concern?" Lady Abercairn asked. "Madness is passed from parent to child, is it not?"

Winnifred wanted to stand, to leave the room, but her legs wouldn't cooperate. The sounds of the dinner would hush, and then burst into a loud crescendo, every clank of a fork a piercing shout, every sip of wine like nails on her brain. Her stomach twisted, and she pressed a hand to her mouth.

"It can be, aye." Dr. Masson's mouth kept moving, but his words became as muffled as Winnifred's thoughts.

"So sad." Lady Abercairn's voice, however, refused to be muted. "And— Oh!" She set her knife and fork down. "I've just remembered what Lady Newton wrote." She reached over to Winnifred and patted her hand. "Of course, just because *your* mother went insane is no reason to fear that you will suffer the same malady."

The room fell silent again, and Winnifred knew it wasn't only in her head. Had Lady Abercairn written a play, she couldn't have come up with a more dramatic statement.

Sin threw his napkin on the table and made to stand.

Winnifred caught his eye and shook her head. No need to cause an even greater scene. Showing weakness would only make people wonder more.

"I have no such fears." If there was a slight wobble to her voice, Winnifred could forgive it. "My mother and I are two different people. But I thank you for your concern."

After a few moments of silence, Lady Margaret leaned forward. "I'm certain you're right." The girl gave Winnifred a timid smile. "We all must make the best of the circumstances we are born into. Isnae that right, Neil?"

Dr. Masson fiddled with his knife. "Aye, sister." But his expression remained watchful. As though expecting Winnifred to leap over the table to attack at any moment.

She sipped her wine, tasting nothing. Well, the worst was over. Her secret was out. If Sinclair could forgive her this embarrassment, then the humiliation to herself made no matter. She'd fallen as low as she could go, and would survive.

There was always lower.

She could always be dragged from home, kicking and shrieking as her mother had been, put away in a little box.

The back of her throat ached, and she sipped more wine. Sin wouldn't let that happen. She trusted that the protection he offered was absolute. Well, as absolute as any one man could offer.

Picking up her knife and fork, she cut her venison into square, even bites.

She darted a glance at her hostess. A woman best avoided. Someone who enjoyed stirring up trouble. And until she left Glasgow, Winnifred would tread as carefully as she ever had.

Chapter Twenty

"I hate waiting." Sin shifted, his arse growing numb on the hard gig seat.

Sutton sighed. "It's not an activity I particularly enjoy either. Especially as the newspaper's office is next door to a charming-looking coffeehouse I'd much rather be sitting in."

"I don't think you can call an illicit weekly pamphlet a newspaper." Liverpool suspected MacConnell of being the anonymous author of several columns in the Glasgow rag, *Le Nouveau Monde*. Columns rallying for independence. Calling for rebellion. It would make sense. The boy didn't have the ballocks to proclaim his alliance so openly.

Sutton grunted and tucked his head down to his chest, stretching his legs as best he could in this small contraption.

Sin examined his friend. He looked well, even with that damn beard regrown. Content like he never had before.

"Why are you here?" Sin asked.

Sutton gave him a look from the corner of his eye. "Because if I held the position in the coffeehouse and Summerset was in here with you, I don't believe both of you would emerge from this gig alive. He only means to protect you, you know."

Sin ignored that. "I meant why are you here in Scotland. I thought you'd given up the espionage business. Told Liverpool he could stuff it. A quiet life with Colleen out in the country. Wasn't that what you said to me at your wedding?" And one Max and his wife vastly deserved after the troubles at his club.

Sutton tugged his beard. "I have retired. For the most part. But when Summerset comes to me saying there's a nasty business up in your neck of the woods, of course I'll come. All of us will. You have damned amazing friends."

Sin grunted. "Yes."

"Even Summerset."

Sin focused on the door to the paper's office. The typesetter and editor were the only employees inside. "Are we certain the pamphlets are printed in there? I'd hate to be sitting here with our thumbs up our arses for no good reason."

"Sinclair."

He forced his gaze to meet his friends. "Yes, I know. Even that dandied-up fool, Summerset." The blow to his friend's jaw hadn't been nearly as satisfying as Sin had hoped. Partly because he'd pulled his power, and partly because the sneaky bounder knew how to roll with a punch.

Mostly because he knew Summerset's interference was well meant. Summerset could be a cold, calculating devil when it came to the rest of the world, but with his friends.... Well, he was still an arsehole, but one who meant well. He'd lay down his life for each and every one of them and there was no one Sin trusted more to watch his back.

"Of course, if he doesn't buy us some meat pies, I'll bruise his other cheek." Sutton slumped back into the seat. He tracked a boy who stopped in front of the offices only to tip a pebble out of his boot and move on.

Sin cracked each knuckle on his right hand. "We could just go in and ask for the information."

Sutton dipped his chin. "This is supposed to be a reconnaissance mission only."

"Hmph." Maybe Sutton had the right end of it in retiring. This business used to be exciting. Now more often than not information was gathered at tea parties rather than at the end of a knife. What was the point of being so large if he didn't get to smash something now and then?

"He's leaving." Sutton picked up the reins as their

quarry hailed a hackney cab. He slapped the horse's back, and they took off at a slow roll. "Do you think Summerset will be able to search the offices? It's broad daylight."

Sin twisted his lips. "He'll have that typesetter out on some pretense in under two minutes. No one denies a request from the Earl of Summerset." Equal parts charm and cunning, except when he was irritating his friends. "The real question is whether any incriminating evidence is kept there. It is supposed to be the offices of a lady's journal. Evidence of printing a pro-independence rag won't just be lying around."

The cab let the editor off at the corner of two busy streets. Sutton fought to find a space along the sidewalk to pull the gig into. "Have I mentioned how much I dislike crowds?"

"Many times." Their target pulled open a door to a tavern, holding it for an elderly gentleman to leave, then strolled inside. Sin looked at Sutton. "Feel like a spot to eat?"

"Always." He set the brake. Both men jumped down and strode to the tavern. The scents of ham and boiled cabbage greeted them as they made their way inside and found a table.

The editor tucked a napkin into the top of his collar as he gave his order to a server. Their quarry threw his head back and laughed at something the man said before the server moved on. A frequent customer it seemed.

"It doesn't look like he's waiting for company," Sutton said in a low voice.

"No." Sin straightened his cravat. "I think now would be the perfect time for a conversation."

"Reconnaissance, remember? See who he associates with, where he goes, that sort of thing."

"That will take entirely too long." And more patience than Sin was born with.

Sighing, Sutton nodded. "You're right. I don't want to be away from home any longer than I need to be." He waved the server over.

"You'd better order me some food, too." Sin glowered at his friend as he stood. "And don't eat it before I return."

Sutton shooed him away.

Sin stomped to the other table and pulled out the chair across from the editor. "You're Rory Fairbairn, editor of the lady's journal, *Women's World*." He didn't phrase it as a question. Best to make your target assume you knew as much as possible.

"Aye." The man sat back and rubbed a circle on his paunch. "And ye'd be?"

"The Marquess of Dunkeld," he said, and waited for the inevitable disbelief. Not only had most newspaper editors never met a marquess, Sin knew he wasn't what most people pictured when they thought of the peerage.

Fairbairn didn't disappoint. His jaw dropped as his eyes zig-zagged over Sin's bulky form and rumpled clothes. "Milord!" The man half-stood, his hip knocking into the table, and gave an awkward bow. "What can I do for ye? How do ye know who I am? Why would ye—"

Sin held up his hand. "Perhaps if I tell you what I want, our conversation will progress more quickly."

The server returned, placing a plate of haggis in front of Fairbairn, and Sin's stomach grumbled. He shot a glance at Sutton, who held a meat pie in each hand. He took a bite from one and raised the other in greeting, a string of cheese sliding into his beard.

"Do ye want something, milord?" Fairbairn and the waiter looked at him expectantly.

"No, thank you, I've already eaten." He nodded at the server, who turned and scurried back to the kitchen. "I come to you with a proposition."

Fairbairn held his fork, but made no move towards his meal. "For me? What business could a marquess have with the likes o' me?"

Crossing one leg over the other, Sin leaned back in his chair and tugged at the hem of his waistcoat. "Donald

MacConnell told me I should speak with you about investing in your paper."

"*Women's World?*" He stabbed at his haggis. "That's owned by Mr. Campbell. You'll have to speak with him."

"Not that paper." Sin leaned forward, into the other man's space. "Your other pamphlet. The one you print after-hours. MacConnell is quite proud to write for it."

Fairbairn's ruddy face flushed a shade darker. "Bloody, pompous writers," he muttered. "Cannae stand not having a byline." He shot Sin an accusatory glare. "He wasnae supposed to tell anybody."

Sin shrugged. "That's not my problem." God, espionage was easy when people were idiots. The man was so easily manipulated Sin almost felt bad. But he now had confirmation of the identity of two of the principals.

Fairbairn pushed his food around on his plate. "Why would a toff like ye want to be supporting the cause. The union has been verra good for your family."

Sin slowly eased straight. "I had hoped that as a member of the House of Lords I would have been able to work within the system to help our country. Alas, it now seems impossible that diplomacy will accomplish that end." He planted his index finger on the table. "I am, and have always been, a patriot first." He brushed a bit of dust from his sleeve. "Also, due to the changing political climate, I think the investment could be profitable."

Fairbairn huffed. "How quickly the ideals of freedom turn to money."

"Does it matter if I make a little blunt while Scotland works its way towards independence?"

Fairbairn dropped his gaze under the heat of Sin's. "Nae." He pushed his plate away. "But it isnae money we need. It doesnae cost much to run a weekly pamphlet. It's nerve. We've become complacent under English rule. Soft. If ye could rally the other Scottish peers to the cause, that would be a worthy contribution."

"People aren't so soft now," Sin said in a low voice.

"Riots in the streets, assassination attempts. The populace is showing its teeth."

Fairbairn slumped into his seat. "Those incidents were awful. That's not what the movement is about."

"No? Rebellion is rarely accomplished using peaceful means."

"I'm not naïve. I ken there might have to be some battles." Fairbairn pressed his palms to the table and sat up straight. "But shooting at someone on the street is the act o' a coward. Starting fights that can get innocent women and bairns hurt is nae better. There has to be a better way."

Sin pursed his lips. That hadn't been the attitude he'd been expecting. The man's sincerity almost made Sin want to invest in earnest.

But the editor was just one man. Others in the movement might feel differently about tactics. "Since your pamphlet doesn't need investors, can you think of anyone else connected to the cause who might? I want to help my country in any way I can."

Fairbairn rubbed his cheeks and blew out a long breath. "Nae. Your MacConnell brings me columns to print, some written by him, some by his friends. But he doesnae tell me names, to protect those involved." He snorted. "At least, he didnae use to."

Sin stood. He removed a card from his inside pocket and tossed it on the table. "If you need anything, show this and you'll be allowed into any of my homes." He hoped Fairbairn didn't get caught up in any arrests. He seemed like a decent man, one who loved Scotland and only wanted what was best for it. Who was to say that Sin's vision for his country was any better than Fairbairn's?

With a final nod, he turned on his heel and strode from the tavern. He climbed into the gig knowing Sutton would follow.

The conveyance creaked as Sutton climbed aboard, licking his fingers.

Sin glowered at him. "You couldn't save me one?"

"You could have eaten with Fairbairn." Sutton picked up the reins and urged the horse into motion. "What did he say?"

Slouching back onto the seat, Sin watched Glasgow roll by. The tall obelisk of Nelson's monument turned into view. "He confirmed MacConnell is involved, but says he doesn't know any other names. He also doesn't know anything about the populace being stirred up, at least not more so than his pamphlet would induce. That sin rests squarely on MacConnell's shoulders, I'll wager."

"You want him to be responsible."

Sin couldn't deny that.

"The rioting could still be happening naturally, with no direction behind it." Sutton pushed his hat back on the crown of his head. "Perhaps we're chasing ghosts."

"No." Instinct told Sin otherwise. The attacks were too directed. Too purposeful. "MacConnell could be another unwitting lackwit," Sin conceded.

They reached an intersection. "Where to now?"

Pulling out his pocket watch, Sin pointed left. "To the university. Winnifred should be finished speaking with her professor soon." She had a landau at her disposal, but Sin wanted to see her. At Kenmore, he knew with a 40,000 square foot accuracy where she was. He felt unsettled with her roaming all of Glasgow without him by her side.

"If instigators are being used, someone has to pay them." Sutton rubbed his jaw.

"And if this comes to civil war, someone has to arm them," Sin finished grimly. Operations like this took money.

The gig turned on High Street and pulled even with the university's clocktower. Sin hopped down. The landau he'd hired for Winnifred idled across the street. "If you'd like to return to our apartments, I'll drive back with my wife."

Sutton set the brake and climbed down. "I'll wait with you. Besides, last time I was here there was a lovely little pastrycook shop just around the corner. I might pop in to see what sort of tarts they have today."

"You just ate!" Sin's stomach grumbled. "And you ate my meat pie, too, you gluttonous bastard."

Sutton stretched, his back cracking. "Now, now, be nice or I won't give you your surprise."

Sin's gaze homed in on the tall figure emerging from the pavilion. Winnifred's sandy brown hair and shapely form clad in a lavender gown made her easy to distinguish among the black-robed students.

He lifted a hand to steal her attention. "What surprise would that be?"

The smile that spread across his wife's face as she moved towards him made it easy to ignore the arsehole who knocked into his side.

"The surprise is that I didn't order two meat pies. I ordered three." Sutton reached into his inner pocket. "But if you're going to be a right pain in the arse, I'm not inclined to share."

Heated voices rose behind them, and an elbow stabbed into Sin's back. He looked over his shoulder and growled. Bloody students. All wandering about with their heads down reading some leaflet, not looking where they were going.

"There he is!" someone shouted. The crowd turned like a flock of birds in flight, all focused on the man in a professor's gown who strolled a couple steps behind Winnifred.

"Now what?" Sin muttered. He threaded his way through the crowd towards his wife.

"Oy!" Sutton called. He pulled a paper-wrapped object from his coat. "Don't you want—" A projectile smashed into the pie, meat and cheese exploding out onto Sutton's shirt and cravat. "What the...?"

The rest of Sutton's words were drowned out by the crowd's dull roar. It surged forward, across the lawn.

Towards Winnifred.

The professor's face went slack with shock. A student

shoved a pamphlet at him, screaming in his face.

Sin couldn't distinguish the words, but he saw the rage. The inchoate violence that took hold of the student's face. The faces of everyone in the crowd. The mob mentality stripped away their individuality, their ability to reason.

Another stone was thrown, striking the professor in the stomach. The man clutched his satchel to his chest and spun, his eyes going wide. He darted through a hole in the crowd, knocking into Winnifred.

Winnifred stumbled forward, throwing her hands out as another body hit hers, and disappeared from sight.

His heart clogged his throat, his gaze never moving from the spot she disappeared. Sin powered his way through the mob, tossing students aside as they got in his way. "Winnifred!" Something stung his ear. "Winnifred!"

The professor's scream was just background noise to Sin. Whatever the man had done to earn the wroth of Glasgow's finest, Sin didn't know. Didn't care. Only his wife mattered.

He reached the spot where she'd disappeared and searched the ground. Two students tussled, getting in his way, and he grabbed them by the backs of their necks and tossed them aside. Where the hell was she? She'd fallen right—

"Sin!"

He jerked his head to the left. There, rising from the ground, Summerset stood, Winnifred in his arms.

She had her hands wrapped around his friend's neck, her face buried in his chest, and rage flooded Sin's veins at the sight of his sensible, stoic wife in fear.

He shouldered his way to his wife and friend. Placing his fingertips under her jaw, he turned her head to face him. Relief weakened his knees when her pale blue eyes met his. She looked a bit rattled, but her gaze was steady and she appeared unharmed. He took her from Summerset's arms and clutched her to him, burying his face in her hair.

Safe.

Someone pushed into his back, and Summerset grabbed his arm to steady him.

For now.

He looked at his friend. "We have to get out of this."

Summerset clenched his jaw and nodded. "Where's Sutton?" he shouted.

Sin shook his head.

Summerset side-stepped another pair of fighting students, sweeping the leg of one of the boys and grabbing the shoulders of the other, yanking him backwards to the ground. The students blinked up at them, stunned, and the earl gave a satisfied nod. "Come on." He turned and threaded his way through the riot.

A flash of wild hair, a dark beard. Sin swung his head to his right. He knocked Summerset's shoulder. "Over there. Trying to protect the professor."

Sutton threw another punch, curled his back to toss the arsehole jumping on it over his shoulder.

Summerset changed course. "Get her out of here," he called over his shoulder. "I'll help Sutton."

Sin hesitated. He didn't like leaving a fight. Didn't want to abandon his friends when the odds were about fifty to two.

A rock struck Winnifred's leg, and she bit back a cry.

Sin growled, his eyes searching for the assailant even as his feet carried him and his wife out of the storm and into the sheltered nook of a nearby bookstore.

"Are you all right?" He hefted her higher in his arms. "Tell me you're unharmed."

Winnifred dug her hand into his cravat, her fingertips brushing over his racing heart. "My injuries are all minor. I turned my ankle and fell. There were people everywhere, stepping on me. I tried to crawl away...." She shuddered.

Sin turned, pressing her closer into the corner, trying to put as much of himself as he could between her and the violence.

She took a deep breath. "Then your friend was there.

Pulling me away from getting trampled upon." The smile she gave him was shaky, but genuine. "He has more than made up for his previous rudeness."

She was safe. His pulse slowed. Safe and in his arms. Pressing his lips to her temple, he inhaled her scents of oranges and woman. "If anything had happened to you...." His heart stuttered at the thought. If anything had happened to her, he wouldn't survive it. Somehow, in their short marriage, his life had become inextricably linked with hers.

He pressed his forehead to hers, his chest aching. "I love you, Winnifred."

Her body went stiff, and Sin pulled back, frowning.

A curtain fell across her eyes, another damn wall when he'd thought he'd knocked them all down.

Nausea swirled in his stomach. "Winnie?" Blood pounded in his ears and he told himself to hold his tongue. That no good would come from this.

But he needed to know. "Don't you love me?"

* * *

Her chest went tight. Why did Sin have to spoil a relationship that had been running so smoothly? She knew he was a passionate man, but she'd thought their feelings were similar when it came to such fancies as love.

She stared at the stick pin in his cravat. It was nothing extravagant, no flashing jewels like in his friend, Summerset's, only a plain silver pin. Elemental and simple, just like her husband. She believed the truth in his words, because he never tried to hide behind artifice or pride, not with her. The yearning in his voice caused something within her to ache.

She couldn't hurt this man who'd given her so much. She didn't know how to explain that love was beyond her. Even when she'd hoped for Donald's marriage proposal, she'd never thought herself in love with the man. Never felt that emotion for any man. She didn't quite understand it and never felt the need to. Friendship was much more sensible. A practical and harmonious life with a man was all she ever hoped for.

Running her finger over the pin, she bit her lip. She'd never felt diminished by her lack of womanly feeling. Until now. She would give anything to be normal. To be the wife her husband deserved.

She licked her lips and tried to force a smile across her face.

By the cloud of pain that darkened his eyes, she knew she was unsuccessful.

"Sin, I—"

"Don't." His voice was a hoarse rasp. "Don't say something you don't feel."

The hollowness in his eyes slayed her. She dropped her forehead to his chest.

"I care for you greatly." Why had he done this? Why would he ruin the balance of their marriage by developing such an irrational attachment?

He barked out a harsh laugh. "Well, at least that's something."

"Isn't it enough that we enjoy a satisfying physical relationship and have a wonderful friendship?" She clenched his lapel. "I am most content." Why wasn't he?

"I don't want you content." He shook her in his arms. "I want you as mad as I am."

She had no response to that so they fell silent. She would rather have been back in the riot than face his crushing disappointment. "I believe the crowd is dispersing. You can set me down now."

He turned, but kept her in his arms. They waited in their nook until Sutton and Summerset found them.

The baron's hair was sticking on end, his shirt torn, his lip bloody.

The earl flicked a speck of dirt from his otherwise pristine tan velvet tailcoat. Aside from the bruise Sin had left on him days before, Summerset appeared completely unharmed. "Nasty business." He pulled a crumpled piece of paper from his pocket. "This is what stirred them up. Some rubbish about that professor teaching lies about the history of England." He jerked his head back towards the school. "We left him barricaded in his office where he'll remain until the mob disperses."

"He was a history professor?" Winnifred chewed the inside of her cheek. "Just teaching about a subject was enough to rouse this amount of anger?" She gazed at the square. One man lay propped on an elbow, a friend holding a handkerchief to his bloody brow. The ground was littered with papers and torn gowns. An eerie silence lay heavily in the riot's wake.

"He wasn't teaching it the correct way, apparently." Sutton fingered a tooth, gently testing its hold. "Too favorably towards England, according to one of the students."

"This is what happens when mobs gather." Her husband's nostrils flared. "There is no reason to the violence. Regardless of intent, innocent people get hurt." He glared down at her. "This is what your friend has wrought, and I fear he intends to do much worse."

He turned to Summerset. "Call for my carriage, would you? I'm taking Winnifred back to our apartments."

The earl nodded and turned.

Sin called him back. "And Summerset...." He dug his fingers into her waist. "Thank you. For saving my wife. However did you get here? We thought we'd left you at the paper's office."

"You did. But before I could encourage the typesetter to leave so I could search it, he tore out of there like the devil was after him." Summerset raised his hands, palm up. "I was curious and followed. He came directly here, checking his watch every five minutes as though there was someone he didn't want to miss."

"Or something."

A shiver coursed through her at Sin's dark tone. Why would men wish to wreak such mayhem? And how was it even accomplished? Printing and distributing the leaflets was easy enough, but inciting people to pick up stones was another story.

Her stomach cramped. All the gratification of her meeting with Mr. Holme vanished. His ideas on soil enrichment had inspired new ones of her own. Ideas that now seemed small and unimportant.

She was finally understanding how terribly wrong the situation was in her new home.

Both in Scotland, and with her husband.

She peeked at his square jaw as he strode to the waiting landau.

Could their relationship ever return to normal after his declaration?

He settled her inside and climbed in after her.

Sutton shut the door and cocked his elbow on top of it. "We'll see you back at the house." He jerked his chin at Winnifred. "Do you require a doctor?"

"No," she said the same time Sin said, "Yes."

He grumbled and slouched back on the seat, crossing his arms.

The carriage rocked into motion, and Sutton stepped back with a wave. They turned off High Street, the silence growing until she could no longer stand it. She hated leaving things unsettled. She needed structure, a plan moving forward, even in her relationships. Especially there. "Where do we go from here?"

He chose to ignore her meaning. "You return to Kenmore. It's not safe in Glasgow." He cracked his neck. "I'm staying until I discover who is behind this."

Which could take a very long time. Winnifred turned on her hip, away from her husband. Rebellion could be a convenient thing. It didn't escape her attention that while Sin investigated, he was able to avoid her company, as well.

A separation of sorts. One that could only bode ill for their future.

Chapter Twenty-One

Sin hefted the sledgehammer and slammed it down onto the post. Stay in Glasgow until he'd discovered the traitors? Bah. He swung the hammer again, the vibration in his hands at the contact a soothing balm. His resolution hadn't lasted five minutes. The urgent letter from his mother requesting his return had seen to that. A wall breach and a flooded field. He hefted, and pounded out his frustration. A field they could ill afford to lose, not when crops were already failing.

So, he stood in the mud and swung a hammer, something any simpleton could do. He had no solutions except brute force. No inventive plans to save Kenmore. *Thwack.* A marquess? Nae. *Thwack, thwack.* He was a bloody imposter. Not good enough to be laird of Kenmore. Not nearly good enough to be Winnifred's husband. And now unable to complete his investigations.

At least Sutton and Summerset remained in Glasgow. They wouldn't leave that city until they'd uncovered the plot.

A shout rose, and Sin spun to see the section of canal wall he and his men had been rebuilding for the past four hours collapse into rubble. He scrambled back from the splintering beams and the cloud of dirt, only to dart in when he saw the lad, Jock, half-buried beneath debris.

"Dig in!" he shouted to the others. "Let's get him out." The rocky soil sliced into his fingers as he hand-shoveled the earth off of the footman. The boy's exposed face was a grimace of pain.

Other hands joined in, pushing dirt off and uncovering Jock's limbs. Thank God the temporary dams they'd built to hold the water back while they rebuilt still held. If they breached, the boy could drown. In a matter of moments, Jock was pulled from the scree and lifted out of the trench. Dozens of hands carried him to safety and laid him on the ground.

Sin climbed out of the pit and knelt by Jock. "What hurts?" He ran his gaze over the lad's body but saw no obvious broken bones or abrasions.

"Besides it feeling like Ole Man Seamus sat on my chest, only my knee, milord." Jock pushed up onto his hands. "I'll be all right."

The crush of men gathered about him laughed. Most of Kenmore's tenants had come out to help with repairs. The canal was the life blood of all their fields. The bit of sport at the ponderous crofter's expense acted like a pin to a blister, popping the tension and relieving the pressure.

Sin blew out a breath. Only the knee. The boy sounded just like his wife, who also insisted she was unharmed even as she hobbled about her rooms, wincing with each step.

He'd told her to stay abed, but did the obstinate woman listen? Of course not. And now every pained step she took was a reminder of his failure to keep her safe.

He helped Jock stand and waved to another to bring his horse.

"I can stay and work more." Jock straightened and tried to put weight on his left leg. He winced. "Nae need to send me back."

"You'll return to Kenmore and rest." Sin's voice brooked no objection.

Another failure. His tenants, his servants, his wife. It was his duty to care for them. Protect them. And he was failing on every front. "And if your knee isn't better by tomorrow, we'll send for the doctor. Now up with you." He and two other men lifted Jock into the saddle.

Sin jerked his head at Gregor, and the coachman

gathered the horse's reins and led him away towards the castle.

Gavin stood at the edge of the trench, hands on hips, looking down at the mess in disgust. "What now?"

Sin joined him. The posts they'd used to anchor the wall hadn't been deep enough, he could see that now. The weight of the canal required stronger bracing. More hours of back-breaking work. All for a bit of water that wouldn't make a fuck lot of difference if the sun didn't shine.

He forced optimism into his voice and clapped his friend on his shoulder. "Now we get back to work."

A general round of grumbling met this announcement.

Sin jumped back into the trench and found his sledgehammer. "Quit your glumping, princesses. You aren't going to let a toff show you up out in the fields, are you?" A strand of hair clung to his cheek, and he brushed it away with the back of his wrist. "I wager you that I'll dig two holes for every one you lazy sots do, or a cask of ten-year-old scotch is on me."

He grinned as the men pushed each other, jumping back in the hole and picking up their tools.

"I think you're going to lose a lot of fine whisky," Gavin said.

Sin slammed the handle of his sledgehammer into the loose soil, marking the spot he would dig. "Your lack of faith pains me. Why would you think that?" Not that Sin hadn't been planning on giving all these men a reward for their labors, but it took a rare man to best him in any physical competition.

Gavin jerked his head towards Kenmore. "Because you're going to be too busy jawing instead of digging."

Sin looked where he indicated and saw the lone figure coming towards them on horseback. His mother's bright red hair was the only spot of color on the bleak moor.

"Hmph." He slammed the hammer into the earth. As he climbed from the trench, his friend laughed behind him. "Come on, men. We have him at an advantage, ye ken?

Let's use every minute of it."

Sin strode to his mother, wishing it were another woman coming to see him.

She waited until he took the horse's bridle before swinging her legs from the stirrups and hopping to the ground. "Hello, *mo ghràdh*."

Wished it were another woman telling him she loved him.

"Mother. Come to check on our progress?" He gritted his teeth. "As you can see, there's very little. I didn't have the men dig the posts deep enough and our first attempt failed."

She pressed her lips together. "Well, blaming yourself willnae help anything. It looks like repairs are going well now."

Sin bit back a snort. Only a mother's eyes would think that anything on this whole bloody estate was going well. He shook his head, giving her a fond smile. "It's kind of you to say so, but I don't require humoring. We both know Kenmore is a right mess, and I've done little to improve it."

The stone and wood wall of the canal ran the length of the pasture. It had stood for over two hundred years, held together by every previous laird. "I am... sorry that I'm not the marquess the house of Dunkeld deserves. I only wish I'd had more time to learn from father before he died."

He'd been sent to school in England when he was eight. His education was useful for his life in London, but had never taught him the art of managing his own estate. Tavish and Sin's mother had held the reins until Sin had come of age, and even then, he'd allowed them to make the decisions with but the barest interference on his part. His tasks from the crown had always been of more importance, his duties in the House of Lords a higher calling.

He looked over his shoulder at the men working together, heedless of his presence. "I thank you for notifying me of the canal's collapse, but as soon as it is repaired, I'm returning to Glasgow."

She gave him a shrewd look. "Just Glasgow?"

He turned away, not wanting to see her disappointment. "Then London. It is where I belong."

"And your wife?" Her tone was flat, showing neither disgust nor the disappointment Sin knew she must feel.

"If Winnifred wishes to accompany me, she may." She wouldn't. He knew that now. Whatever passion he'd seen in her had been nothing but animal heat, not an indication of any feeling on her part. The extra slices of ham she liked to put on his plate at breakfast no more than friendly regard. "I think her new laboratory will keep her occupied here, however."

His mother crossed her arms and sighed. "'Tis a shame that I raised such a daft son. It must have been all that book learning. Forced the common sense straight oot of your head."

He stared down at her. "Pardon?"

"Ye heard me." She poked his arm. "I know ye think that you're being noble, blaming yourself for every problem in Scotland, but there are many things that are outside your control. It does nae one, least of all your tenants, any good to believe that ye are king o' the world."

"I know I don't control everything," he gritted out. If he did, he would have heard four little words yesterday, *I love you, too*. "But keeping Kenmore in good condition is my job. Essentially the only job of a marquess. Father would have—"

"He would have done nothing but sit back with a large dram while Tavish took care of the canal." She blew out her cheeks. "Lord knows I loved the man, but he wasnae the sort to get his hands dirty with his own people. I'm glad ye remember your father as a wise and powerful laird, but the truth is more tangled than that."

He turned fully to face her. "What are you saying?"

"I'm saying that your father was an able enough marquess who never had to prove himself." She rested a hand on his arm. "It was easy for him to keep things running smoothly because he never faced difficult times. He was a fortunate man, and easy in his fortune. The biggest problem he ever had to face was when the Beattie family wouldnae stop poaching on our lands. Dunnae measure yourself by him; I fear the comparison would show him in a poor light."

She planted her hands on her hips. "I'll never repeat this, not to my dying day, but ye are a better man than my husband was. I see it with every burden ye willingly shoulder, every tenant ye climb down into the dirt to help. It's time ye stopped your whining and started acting like the marquess I know ye can be."

Sin gaped at her. It was absurd. His normally sensible mother was uttering nonsense. "You can't mean—"

"I mean every word." She sniffed and turned her back to watch the men laboring. "You're old enough to put away your childish fancies aboot your father and see him for the man he was, flaws and all. And stop using his memory as an excuse to run away."

Sin gripped the back of his neck and squeezed. That nonsense about being better than his father he couldn't credit, but his mother was right about one thing. Sin had used his fear of not living up to his father's memory as an excuse to avoid Kenmore.

Shame burned in his gut. He'd never wanted to be a man who avoided his duty, but there it was. That was what he'd become.

"Now, aboot that wife of yours—"

"No." Sin raised his hand, palm out. "I've let you prattle on about father, but my wife is off limits."

His mother slowly arched her eyebrow, a look Sin recognized. One he utilized with utmost efficiency to make his opponent feel a quiver of dread.

"Prattle on?" she repeated.

Sin leaned back before catching himself. He would not be intimidated by a five-foot four-inch woman. He would not.

"Just because ye may not like what a woman has to say doesnae mean she is prattling." She slashed her finger in the air between them. "And if I have something to say about your wife, I shall say it. Understood?"

He sighed and nodded in resignation.

"It's clear ye have feelings for the Sassenach, which is fortunate, since you're bound to her for life. So why would ye abandon her here while ye traipse about the world?" She crossed her arms over her chest. "And I willnae get any grandbairns if ye two aren't together."

A strange pang squeezed his heart. Babes with Winnifred's solemn eyes and his wild hair. It would be a perfect combination.

Their children would be even more perfect if they were conceived in the love of both parents.

"I want her to be happy."

His mother nodded. "That's a fine goal. Why wouldnae she be happier with ye?"

A roar of laughter emerged from the trench, and Sin's feet twitched, eager to take him away from this awkward conversation and go join his men. "You've guessed my feelings, mother. But Winnifred doesn't feel the same."

"Not yet." She held out her hands. "She's English; ye have to take that into account."

"What do you mean?"

"We Scottish are more hot-blooded. Your father only had to look at me the right way and I was his for life." She shook her head. "The English use their minds instead of their hearts. Ye'll have to work for it, but that's nae reason to give up. And leaving her here at Kenmore while ye traipse about is a special form of surrender."

He rubbed his jaw. Could his mother be right? Did Winnifred just need more time? They'd been married for barely a month. He did have several decades to conquer her heart. "Winnifred's a logical, practical sort of woman. Do you really think someone like her could love me?"

"She is a queer one, your wife," his mother said. "But

she's intelligent. And an intelligent woman couldnae help but fall in love with ye."

He grinned and kissed her cheek. "Thanks, mam." She was biased, of course. But her words made his body feel lighter. Sin had always considered himself a fighter, and it was time he fought for what was most important to him. His wife and his home.

"Ye cannae just sit on your rump," she added. "Ye have to put in some effort to win her heart. And that requires—"

"Living together." He rolled his eyes. "I heard you the first five times."

She patted his cheek, a little harder than the situation called for. "Good. Then my work here is done." She strode to her horse and swung easily into the saddle. "I'll see ye at supper." And with a toss of her fiery hair, she was off.

Sin strolled to the canal, ignoring the jibes from the men about the scotch he owed them. His mind was on his mother's words.

He'd always faced life head on. If there was a plot afoot, he ended it. A problem, he fixed it. He only needed to look at his wife as a problem to solve. She didn't love him. Yet.

He picked up his sledgehammer, found his post, and swung.

But he could be a determined man. And he was determined not to be the only one in his marriage suffering from this horrible, wonderful feeling called love. He'd broken through her reserve in the bedroom. He could break through the wall surrounding her heart.

Gavin clapped him on the back and hooted. "Still only half way on your first post and the rest of us have planted all the rest." He tutted. "A sad day for the reputation of the Archer family."

Sin grumbled good-naturedly, his spirits too high to mind his trouncing.

He gazed at the smiling and dirty faces of his people.

Finally, he knew his place. Where he belonged, and where his duty lay.

And he was determined to have the heart of the woman who stood beside him. He wouldn't settle for anything less.

Chapter Twenty-Two

"A ball?" Winnifred blinked. Had close proximity to the fumes wafting from the rotting legumes affected the man's mind? "What on earth are you talking about?"

Gavin blew out his cheeks, his face going red. "Confound it. Mayhap it was supposed to be a secret."

Or perhaps her husband simply hadn't wanted to tell her. Ever since Glasgow, conversation between the two of them had been strained.

She forced a smile. "I won't tell him I know, not if it is to be a surprise." It couldn't have been meant as one, not with all the preparations that a house party and ball necessitated. Another sign of the wedge in her marriage, all because she couldn't say those three little words. Couldn't feel them. The largest wedge was the expanse of mattress that lay between them each night, neither of them making any move to cross it.

The back of her throat ached, and she swallowed past the lump. Thank goodness she at least had her work to distract her. "Now, how fares our experiment?" she asked. "Do your crops show any variance between the supplements?"

"Come see for yourself." He led her down a narrow dirt path between fields where tiny green shoots were just beginning to show their heads. "I dunnae see any differences, but then it's only been a little over a week." He scratched his jaw. "Perhaps that section there is a wee bit higher than the others."

Winnifred pulled a small glass jar from her satchel. "It *is* early yet. Visible results were too much to hope for." Kneeling in the first row of barley sprouts, she scraped a small amount of soil into the jar. She made a notation in her notepad. Working her way down the sections of field Gavin indicated, she took soil samples for each type of supplement on each crop.

She rubbed her back as she stood. The jars in her satchel clinked together as she shifted the bag higher up her arm. "There. I'll examine these to see if the soil tells us anything."

"Ye talk to dirt a lot, do ye?" Gavin's mouth twisted up on one end as he plucked a stone from the ground. He tossed it into a field of corn.

Winnifred's heart sank as she watched the rock disappear into a row of stunted stalks. "It won't matter." She shook her head. "Regardless what we discover here, it won't affect the estate's crops this year, except for the small portion of your field we're testing. Perhaps not even next year's either."

Gavin planted his hands on his hips and surveyed his land. "We dunnae know how long the sun will hide. Whichever year help arrives, it will be appreciated." He nudged her with his shoulder. "We'll make it through. We Scotch always manage to survive. A bit like weeds we are."

She turned to smile up at him, then paused as a lone figure riding a donkey plodded down the drive in their direction.

Her shoulders stiffened. Donald.

He tipped his cap to Winnifred and nodded to Gavin when he drew even with them. "Good afternoon. I wasnae expecting to find ye here, Winnie."

He looked between her and Gavin, but she didn't bother to explain her presence. "Nor I, you," she said coolly. "You've said before, several times now, that you were not long for Inver. I expected you to be back in Glasgow."

He shrugged. "The distance is not so great to keep me

in one place. Not when there is work to be done."

"And what work is that?" Gavin asked. He tucked his thumbs in his braces and widened his stance.

"Yes." Winnifred frowned. In all their conversations, Donald had never said what he did now. "What is your occupation?"

Donald drew his shoulders back. "I do a little of this, some o' that. Important men trust me to see to their affairs."

"You never went into business with your father?" she asked. "Didn't he want you to become a cobbler, as well?"

"My da turned to shoemaking only after we were evicted from our farm." Donald gripped his reins tightly, and the donkey shifted uneasily beneath him. "He never made enough to support himself, much less a family. I dunnae know why I should follow the same shabby path as that witless idler."

"It's an honest trade." Winnifred tilted her head. Had he always looked down on his father so? She couldn't remember.

"Honest?" Donald snorted. "Aye. My da is an honest serf, bowing and scraping and content to always serve others. We're tired of obliging others; we want to serve ourselves."

"We?" Gavin asked.

Donald didn't respond.

Winnifred worked through his words, weighing each one. "You used to speak plainly. Did that quality disappear the same time as your respect for your father?"

A brick red flush stained his cheeks. "I came to speak with Mr. Fraser. Perhaps I'll come back another day when his time isnae otherwise occupied."

"I'm always busy." Gavin stepped forward and stroked the donkey's nose. "Tell me what ye've come to say and be done with it."

Donald raised his chin. "I've come with a warning for all right-minded Scots. Times are changing, and ye'd best get right with your fellow man. Memories are long in these parts. Ye want to be remembered well, don't ye, Mr. Fraser?"

Gavin inhaled sharply.

"That sounds like a threat." Winnifred shaded her eyes as she looked up at the man she'd once thought might be her husband. "You used to speak kindly, too. What has happened to the boy I knew?"

The donkey tossed his head and took a step back. Donald loosened his grip on the reins. "As I said, times are changing, and I with them."

"I'm quite familiar with your changes." Winnifred gripped the handle of her satchel. "I was nearly killed in one of them – a riot at the University of Glasgow." Her blasted ankle still ached. Only Sheena's skill in wrapping a bandage tightly about it prevented her from limping. "Is that what you want for your country? Mob rule over reasoned debate? Sparring with stones instead of words? Anger instead of cooperation? Surely what I saw in Glasgow is not what you want for your beloved Scotland."

His hands jerked, and the animal beneath him whined.

"You're hurting the mouth of that poor cuddie." Gavin pressed his lips together. "Besides, she dunnae seem large enough to be carrying a full-grown man. Why don't ye climb down off your ass?"

Winnifred snorted, the burst of laughter escaping her before she covered her mouth with her hand. It might be childish, but the phrasing of Gavin's words struck her as funny. An ass for an ass. Fitting.

"Not everyone can afford a fine piece of horseflesh. The working man must make do." Donald peered down his nose at Winnifred. "I'm saddened that ye were caught up in any high feelings of the crowd. And that violence is ever necessary. But as the French say, ye can't make an omelet without breaking some eggs." He sniffed. "Besides, it's a husband's job to protect his wife. Perhaps Dunkeld should attend to his duties and not allow his wife to traipse about when emotions are running high."

Every inch of Winnifred's spine snapped to attention. If she could have reduced Donald to ashes with the heat of her glare, she would have. "Pardon me? Are you insinuating that it is my husband's job to proscribe my movements? That I am in need of being contained?" Good Lord, how could she have contemplated marriage to this pompous sap skull for one moment?

She shifted her satchel to her other arm, the bag feeling unbearably heavy. Her entire body felt heavy. Donald was right; most husbands did control their wives. Winnifred was one of the fortunate ones. She'd moved from the house of a permissive father to that of her husband's, a man who showed no interest in being her manager, her gaoler. All Sin wanted was for her to speak her mind.

And for her to love him.

Her heart clenched. He'd given her so much. Not only a wild kind of freedom that tolerated no restraints when they were alone together, but a freedom in her daily life most wives could only dream of.

Why couldn't she love such a man?

Donald huffed out a laugh. "If the cap fits...." His lips curved into a brittle smile. "And with a woman like ye in particular, well, let's just say your father should have married ye to a man with a stronger sense of right and wrong."

Fury propelled Winnifred forward, but Gavin slid between her and the ass. "It's time ye were on your way," he said to Donald. "Your sly tongue isnae welcome here."

Winnifred scuttled to one side of Gavin's body only to meet his outstretched arm. She circled to the other, and he side-stepped in front of her. Well, really. Poking her face over Gavin's shoulder, she glared at Donald. "You right sot. I remember when you were but a pimple-faced nuisance. When you cried like a babe after tripping over my father's stepstool. Don't try to act commanding now you... you... cretin! I know the truth. And if you were even half the man my husband is, you would be fortunate indeed."

Face red, Donald leaned forward in the saddle, his glare never leaving her face. "It seems my mam was right about Sassenach women. Ye should be careful with that tongue of yours. In times of old, the penalty for insulting a man would be cutting it out."

"Show me a man to insult," she sneered.

Donald grabbed the donkey's mane, kicking his feet from the stirrups.

Gavin raised his hand. "Dunnae be a fool, lad. She is a marquess's wife. Now, run along. Spread your poison in another neighborhood."

Donald's narrow shoulders heaved, but he settled back in the saddle. "This willnae be forgotten."

Winnifred didn't know if he meant her insults or Gavin's dismissal. It didn't matter. The pathetic worm was unjustly arrogant. He only imagined power, wielding none of his own.

Digging his heels into the donkey's sides, he turned the animal and trotted away.

"Ye've made yourself an enemy, milady." Gavin watched Donald until the donkey carried him off his property. He turned to Winnifred with a rueful smile. "I suppose you're in good company."

She tugged at the hem of her spencer, boxing her anger back into its proper place. She took a deep breath. "Men like Donald don't worry me."

And yet she remained unsettled. As she took her leave and climbed into her cart next to the footman, she wondered why. She waved one last time to Gavin, everything about her appearance exuding calm.

But inside, her stomach was twisting and flopping like a fish out of water.

She didn't fear a little weasel like Donald, but the men he could inflame?

Well, that was an entirely different story.

* * *

"Ye just missed your wife." Gavin greeted him with a hearty handshake and backslap as Sin climbed down from his mount. "She left here not ten minutes ago."

Sin dropped his horse's reins, knowing the animal wouldn't wander far. "She must have returned by way of Inver. I didn't pass her. How fares your experiment?"

"It's too early to tell, but I have nae doubt that your wife will get the right end of it." He shook his head. "She's a clever one."

Sin pulled in a deep breath. That she was.

If only— Sin cut off that ungrateful thought. Her lack of love was just something he'd have to work on.

Gavin shifted. "She also might be a wee bit upset that you didnae tell her about your ball." He stared down at his boots. "I might have made mention of it to her."

Sin sighed. "It wasn't a secret; I just hadn't gotten around to telling her." They had been politely avoiding each other since his declaration of love. An awkwardness descending over their marriage that he didn't know how to escape.

His friend's expression clouded. "Did ye also not pass that friend of hers, MacConnell? He was here, too."

The hair on the back of Sin's neck stood on end. He narrowed his gaze on his friend, trying to read it. "And? What did he have to say for himself?"

Gavin shrugged and plucked a hoe from the ground. "His usual nonsense." But he hesitated, and Sin's hackles raised further.

"There's more." Sin gripped his hips. "What is it? Do you think he is finding success rousing my tenants to rebellion?"

"Nae." Gavin ran his hand up the back of his head, ruffling his hair. "I mean, there has been some talk, but I think for the most part your people are loyal to ye, and therefore the union betwixt the countries. But that wasnae what worries me."

Sin was losing his patience. "Well, what does?"

"The way he was looking at Lady Dunkeld."

Sin flexed his fingers, his knuckles cracking. "How did he look at my wife?" His voice was low. Deadly. It matched the way he felt. If that little shit bucket had done anything to insult his wife, his life was forfeit.

Gavin flushed. "Well, Lady Dunkeld had some choice words of her own which MacConnell didnae take kindly to. He made some mention that women like her used to have their tongues cut out and— bugger, where are ye going?" He leaned on the handle of his tool. "Ye only just arrived."

Sin swung into his saddle, any thoughts of sharing a mug of ale with his friend evaporating. "In which direction did he go?"

"Now, Dunkeld, there's nae need to go rushing—"

"Which. Direction?"

Gavin pointed west down the lane. "He's most like at Farmer Beattie's house. He seems to have a route he likes to travel while proselytizing for independence."

Nodding at his friend, Sin kicked his heels into his mount. He tore down the drive, his blood thundering in his veins. He leaned forward in his saddle, anticipation nipping at his heels.

This. This was what he needed. Something, or someone, to beat his feelings out upon. And the man who threatened his wife made the ideal vessel on which to vent his spleen.

He didn't find MacConnell at the Beattie cottage, nor at the Clacher's. But the sway-back stride of the man's donkey greeted him past the MacGregor home.

Coming even with him, Sin reached down, grabbed the man by the back of his starched collar, and flung him to the ground. He jumped off his horse, his boots landing inches from MacConnell's fingers.

"What the bloody hell are ye on about?" MacConnell pressed to his hands and knees, and Sin assisted him by planting the top of his boot under his collar bone and flipping him to his back.

"Haven't you heard it isn't polite to curse in front of your betters?" He stalked in a circle around his prey.

The bounder's face grew blotchy with rage. He spat into the dirt. "An English title doesnae make ye my better. Ye should hang your head in shame that your family sold their pride to the Sassenach for a powerless marquessate." He climbed to his feet, and Sin allowed it. "Ye think the English respect their Scottish peers? You're a laughingstock to them. Nothing more than a useful poppet. And ye betray us every time ye cooperate with the invaders."

Sin shot his hand out and gripped the pup's neck. So slender. So easy to snap. "Strip me of my title and I am still your better in every conceivable way. But my *cooperation* with the English, as you call it, is not why you're to receive a pummeling. Did you truly think you could threaten my wife without consequences?" He shook the man, satisfaction curling through him as the color drained from the arsehole's face.

"I meant nothing." He clawed at Sin's fingers. "I could never hurt Winnie."

Sin growled. "Lady Dunkeld to you."

"I meant nothing." MacConnell gasped, his eyes wide, imploring, and Sin tossed him away in disgust. The broken bones and bloodied face he'd envisioned weren't to be. Beating such a pathetic excuse for a man went against all that Sin believed.

Clenching his hand, he slammed his fist into the man's stomach, and MacConnell dropped like a sack of potatoes.

Sin cracked his neck. He couldn't let the sot get off completely free, however. "Get up." He toed the man's thigh. He'd pulled his punch to half power, and the blow had done nothing to alleviate the itch between his shoulder blades.

MacConnell coughed, spittle hanging from his mouth.

"Good Lord." Sin planted his hands on his hips. "And you expect to lead the rebellion? One punch and you're mewling like a wee kitten." Crouching by the fallen man, he grabbed his chin and forced MacConnell to look at him. "You have no idea what battle looks like. You rouse our people into fights and riots, and you skulk in the shadows, with naught but a stiff prick to contribute. Does the sight of other people's blood excite you?" Sin dropped his chin and wiped his hand on his trouser leg. "You deserve a sound thrashing. To feel the pain of a true beating. Perhaps then you'd understand the harm you've caused."

MacConnell swiped his sleeve under his nose. "You're wrong. The people of Scotland will revere my name. There are only a few of us brave enough to finally break our chains of servitude. We'll be remembered."

Sin stilled. "Names."

MacConnell pushed up to rest on his palms. "What?"

"What are the names of these few patriots?" When MacConnell pressed his lips tightly together, Sin said, "I will have them. I'm done being polite. You will give me the names of your fellow conspirators or...."

"Or what?" MacConnell tilted his chin up, trying, and failing, to look brave.

Sin lifted one shoulder. "There really is no 'or'. With enough pain, every man can be brought to the point where he'd spill all his secrets." He looked MacConnell up and down. "Sadly, I don't think your point will take all that long to reach."

He grabbed the man's shirt with his left hand, pulled his right one back.

MacConnell threw his arms up in front of his face. "Abercairn!"

"What?" Sin dropped his hand, disappointment making him frown. He would hold the most cowardly Scot to ever live in his grips when his need for violence was running high. He pushed MacConnell's chest away in disgust and stood.

"Lord Abercairn asked for my help in getting the public to lay their grievances at the feet of the English." He scuttled backwards, out of the range of Sin's boots. "He gave me the blunt to pass around to a couple well-placed blokes to start the first fights. People need to be angry in order to act. I was only lighting the match."

"And hiding when the powder keg blew." Sin shook his head. "Why would Abercairn want rebellion? He's always supported the union in parliament. Hell, he and the Duke of Beaumont are friends. He wouldn't try to have him killed."

"I dunnae know anything about the assassination attempt." Warily, MacConnell struggled to his feet. The way his gaze slid to the left led Sin to disbelieve his statement. "Perhaps Abercairn isnae as comfortable with the yoke of ownership as the rest of ye lot appear to be. Perhaps he never intended Beaumont to actually get hurt. I cannae tell you his reason." He smirked. "I can tell ye there's nothing ye can do to stop us. The stone is already rolling down the hill and ye'd best stay out of its way or else—" He clapped his hands together.

Sin snorted. "Spare me your attempts at intimidation. They only make me feel bad for you." He glared at the man. "What is your next task? Raising another mob to beat each other black and blue? Inciting my tenants to storm the castle?"

MacConnell scowled. "I am to do nothing more than talk to my people, make them realize that our current system does nothing but enrich England. And its toad-eaters," he added with a pointed look at him.

Sin considered. If he were running such an operation, he wouldn't divulge to his lackies any more information than was necessary to perform their immediate duties. MacConnell most likely knew little more. And once Sin informed Liverpool of this latest bit of intelligence, the prime minister would ensure that MacConnell had told them everything. Liverpool was thorough.

"I pity Winnifred." MacConnell's thin chest heaved. "Forced to marry such a man. She's too good for ye."

Sin's fingers twitched at his wife's name on the man's

tongue. He reconsidered his leniency, remembering the indecent offer the man had once made to her. The idea of MacConnell touching Winnifred made Sin want to relocate the man's front teeth to the back of his throat.

But in this one instance, Donald was right. Winnifred was too good for him.

"If I catch you on my land again, I'll have you detained. Either with the local constabulary, or in my dungeon. There will be no more allowances; no further warnings." He stomped to his horse and swung into the saddle. "I'll give you an hour to vacate my property. You'll need forty-five minutes of it to hunt down your ride."

MacConnell whipped his head from left to right, and sucked in a gasp when he caught sight of his donkey a quarter of a mile distant. He took off running, waving his arms wildly and baying like a stuck pig for the animal to stand in place.

Sin turned his horse and prodded him into a canter. Thank all that was holy his sensible wife hadn't seen fit to form an attachment to such an unworthy fool. If he'd met her later, on that lout's arm, by any other man's side—

He kicked his horse into a gallop.

The thought was intolerable. She might think only their marriage vows bound them, but he knew better. Every bone in her body, every inch of her flesh, belonged to him. His possession far surpassed archaic legalities. Dove deeper even than love. Their connection was primitive. Elementary.

And if he had to play every card in his hand to convince her of that simple fact, he would.

He might not deserve her, but he had Winnifred all the same.

And he would use that privilege to press every advantage available.

Chapter Twenty-Three

Winnifred held the piece of paper to the window of her bedchamber and peered at it through her magnifying glass. Why did Mr. Raguhram's friend have to write in such illegible, disjointed script? Mr. Johnson's poor penmanship couldn't even be attributed to unfamiliarity with her native tongue. He was a British émigré, a man who'd decided to study the flora and fauna of the unknown world. There was no excuse for his scribbling.

She squinted. Was that an especially large E or an F? She blew out a breath. Neither made sense in the context.

The door to her sitting room swung open, the bottom frame swishing over the rug. Her husband's heavy tread met her ears.

She angled the letter into more direct light. "Perhaps you can make this out," she said to Sin. "It has taken me nearly twenty minutes to decipher only—"

Her husband swept her into his arms, and her words ended with a squeak.

He didn't speak, gave her no explanations, as he strode through the double doors into their dressing room, kicked open the doors to his bedroom, and slammed them behind them.

A shiver started at the base of her skull and ticked down her spine. Sin's face was hard, his hair wind-blown, the arms that encircled her unyielding as iron. His manner and silence should have frightened her. Sin was rarely quiet.

But the thrill she felt had nothing to do with fear.

"Is something the matter?" she asked. "Has something

happened?"

In response, he tossed her on the bed and ripped off his jacket.

Her core clenched.

"Strip." His voice was a brusque demand.

Winnifred arched an eyebrow, following his movements as he unknotted his cravat and peeled out of his waistcoat. Had he decided to return to the usual pattern of their marriage? Enjoy their physical compatibility and forget that love nonsense?

Her breath hitched. It would be for the best. So why was she disappointed?

He gripped the hem of his shirt and ripped it over his head. His hands were twice the size of hers, rough and strong. They had the power to break men, and bring her the sweetest pleasure. He yanked off his boots and stockings and stood before her in just his trousers, his chest heaving.

Winnifred bit her bottom lip, her nipples tingling.

He glared down at her. "You wish to deny me? Today of all days?"

She could never deny him. Not when she only felt truly alive when his hands were upon her, but she wouldn't ignore his odd behavior, either. "What has made today of note?"

He stepped to the bed and gripped her skirts in response. A great rent tore through the air. Cool air kissed her thighs as Sin ripped her gown in two.

"Sin!" She grabbed his wrists. "The modiste only just finished this dress." The speed with which she went through her gowns was becoming embarrassing. "Stop acting like an animal and tell me what is the matter."

"An animal?" He flipped her to her stomach and another tear met her ears. "Aye, I suppose I am nothing but a beast." His fingernails scraped against her flesh as he disrobed her until she was bare but for her slippers and stockings. He rolled her onto her back, and in reflex she pressed an arm to cover her breasts as she bounced. "Tell me now if you wish me to stop."

Winnifred opened her mouth, shut it. She'd missed being in his arms the last few nights. Missed the release she felt when she embraced her wildness, when she gave herself the luxury to kick and fight and lose control.

Missed the comfort she felt when Sin subdued her into surrender. He was her anchor while she stormed.

But the solace shouldn't be all on one side. He was her closest friend, and something obviously disturbed his mind.

Sin pulled her arm away from her chest and pressed it into the velvet coverlet. His eyes flared wide as he stared at her heaving chest. "I am nothing but a beast when I'm with you, and I make no apologies for it." He lowered his head and bit the soft underside of her breast.

The nip of pain made her gasp. She pushed at his shoulder with her free hand even as her back arched into his mouth. "Stop. We should..." He pressed his knee between her legs, spreading her thighs, and she prayed he couldn't feel the wetness that gathered there through his trousers. "... we should discuss what ails you."

He raised his head, his eyes narrowed, his lips reddened. "You held silent when I asked if you wanted me to stop. You forfeited your right to object, and I'm done talking. I'm taking what is mine."

The utter possession in his eyes made every hair on her body stand on end. Her breaths grew shallow. She rolled her hips against his leg. It wasn't right. It wasn't fair that he could own her responses. But it was a fact.

Fine. If he didn't want to talk, she would oblige.

Digging her nails into his biceps, she pushed at him with all her might.

He didn't budge an inch. She'd known he wouldn't, but it didn't stop the struggle from thrilling her.

She pounded on his shoulder with the heel of her palm, the exertion flushing her with a sense of exhilaration.

Sin grabbed her wrists, holding them above her head.

He swiveled his hips, his wool covered length pressing into her most intimate parts. "No?" He nipped at her jaw and scraped his teeth down her throat. "When you're soaking my trousers straight through with your desire? When your heart, soul, and body belong to me, and I belong to you?" He pressed his lips to the hollow where neck met throat, and pulled hard.

Another mark left on her body. Another bond between them.

They did belong to each other. The sense of security that came with those marriage vows was absolute.

"Yes," she hissed. She raised her head to snap at him, but he jerked away and her teeth closed on air. "Yes, I want you. And I'll have you." She shook her head. "But it won't come easy." And so saying, she bucked with all her might.

Sin's eyes widened in surprise as he slid partially off of her.

Warmth spread through her body at her minor success. She tore one hand from his grip and scraped her nails across his chest, three pink scratches a memento he wouldn't soon forget.

He growled, a slow smile spreading across his face, and Winnifred knew the skirmish had just begun.

Wrapping a leg around his thigh, she bucked once more.

Sin rolled to his back, and she straddled his waist. He must have let her. There was no way she would be able to move his body without his consent. She dropped a quick kiss on his lips before laughing in triumph.

Beyond the physical pleasure, such bed sport was *fun*. She hadn't realized intercourse could be diverting as well as passionate. And she meant to take full advantage of that knowledge.

Sin stared up at her, his gaze half-lidded, assessing.

She picked up one end of the black ribbon which held his hair back, easing the bow free. She dug her fingers into the mane and tugged. "I've found having my hair pulled to be a surprisingly sensuous experience." She yanked harder, pulling his head back. "How about you?"

He remained silent, only watching. Ever watching.

She slapped his cheek, the sting in her palm shocking. Sitting up straight, she bit down on her lip. Had she gone too far?

Her mother's fists were a blur of movement, striking her father's face. Blood trickled from his nose as he stared at her in horror.

Winnifred shook the memory away. The situations were different. *She* was different. And her husband wasn't looking at her in revulsion. That secret smile still ghosted about his lips.

"Well?" She smacked his chest, and he silently allowed the abuse. "Confound it, say something!" *Do something.*

His grin only widened.

She would wipe that smug look off of him. She pulled back, and he shot his hand out, grabbing her wrist. He rubbed his thumb around her pulse point. "Ah, *mo chridhe.* My heart. I love you so."

Winnifred sat back on her haunches, frowning. That wasn't what she wanted to hear, not at that moment.

Not ever.

Scooting back, she worked at the buttons to his falls, the task made difficult with the use of only one hand. Reaching inside, she grasped his heat and ran her grip up and down. His skin was so soft to her touch and so hard beneath, a delightful contradiction.

He groaned, and brought her palm to his mouth, pressing a kiss to her flesh. "You are the best thing to ever happen to me. My life would be incomplete without you, my love."

Now he wanted to bandy words? And nonsense ones at that. Why couldn't they simply fuck.

The profanity skipped through her mind, as heady as the taste of Scotch whisky. She thought it again. Fuck.

Leaning down, she pressed her teeth to the point where

his pectoral muscle met his side, and bit down.

Sin bellowed and tossed her to her back. He shoved out of his trousers then grabbed her ankle, reeling her into him. "You wish not to hear my feelings? Fine. I've always been better communicating with my hands anyhow."

He smoothed his palm up her calf and along the inside of her thigh. His tongue followed.

She sagged back into the mattress. Yes. This was what she needed.

A mewl of frustration escaped her lips as his mouth avoided where she ached. He kissed her lower abdomen, swirled his tongue around her navel before nibbling his way higher. He trailed the pads of his fingers along her collarbone, circled her pouting nipples, before gliding down her ribs.

She clutched the coverlet. His gentleness was disquieting. Each stroke of his fingers laden with meaning.

He swallowed, his Adam's apple bobbing, and the adoration in his eyes made her heart burn.

She turned her face away. She couldn't see it. His heart was exposed, bleeding in front of her, and the intensity of his emotions was something she couldn't reciprocate. Didn't think she was even capable of feeling.

She spread her legs and tried to guide him inside.

He pinned her hands by her head and continued his soft assault with his lips, his tongue. No inch of her was left untouched by his tenderness.

She arched her hips, desperate to have him inside, but managing only to rub her clit against the underside of his cock.

"Damn you." She struggled against his hold. "Why can't you leave me be? I've given you my body, my loyalty, my friendship." Her voice caught. "I have nothing left to give."

He squeezed her wrists until her fingers went nerveless. "I won't stop until I have everything."

She saw the truth of those words in his eyes. Their blue was as dark as the midnight sky. His resolve was writ in every line of his face.

She had nothing to say in response. No way to express her frustration and despair except with her body. She writhed beneath him, kicking him with her heels. Her lips and her teeth became weapons. The sweat on his skin tempted her tongue. The pulse in his throat a taunt for her bite.

He allowed her to fight until her breath grew short and her strength waned. Let her spill all of her raging emotions out onto his body. She could imagine no other man incensing her so, or being so adept at assuaging her ire. She lay panting beneath him, her energy spent, her need unmet.

Sin slid her hands above her head, holding them in one of his own. He dropped his lower body to cover hers, his cock nestling between her lower lips. His breath skittered across her ear lobe. "My turn," he whispered.

Reaching under her head, he threaded his fingers in her hair and jerked her head back so he could crush his mouth to hers.

All traces of that unsettling softness were gone.

His lips were a bruising force, a battle she could engage in. He plundered her mouth, brutal, dominating, everything she needed.

Sliding down her body, he applied the same wicked brutality to her throat, her breasts, the soft skin under her arms.

Sin lifted his torso. Lips red, he stared down at her, rocking his hips, making her quake.

"I love you, Winnifred Archer. And I believe you have feelings for me, too." He traced a finger down her throat. "After all, what is love but friendship and devotion and yearning all knotted together?"

She snarled at him, pulling at her hands and bucking with all her might.

All she managed was to coil her need tighter, higher.

"Damn it, get off me if you wish to speak so." Her legs wrapped around him, hugging him to her, her body clearly disagreeing with her brain.

He arched an eyebrow and tutted. "Such language. Most unbecoming of a marchioness." He slapped her breast.

The sharp sting reverberated through her body. She watched as he raised his hand and brought it down again, this time over her aching nipple.

"Don't you understand yet?" He lowered his head and wrapped his lips around the throbbing bud. The strong pulls shot pleasure straight to her core, as though the two parts of her were connected by a string. "My body." He squeezed her breast just to the point of pain. "My breasts. My wife." His eyes burned. "No one else will ever see you as you are. I'd dig the eyes out of any man that dared. You're mine to love."

A whimper tumbled from her lips. His to love. If only some of his feeling could be shared with her, that she could reflect it back. He deserved to be loved and she—

She closed her eyes. Love was more than just friendship and passion. It had to be. Her parents hadn't been friends, barely even companions. Yet even through the fits and frenzies, her mother had loved her father. Perhaps too much. When her father showed more interest and excitement in his work than in her, it had broken her mother's heart, and her mind.

Love. She shook her head. That way madness lie.

She couldn't watch him as they came together, see the reverence that she was unable to feel. Couldn't let his gaze pore into her and discover her ultimate inadequacy.

With the last of her strength, she leveraged off of him, driving her heel into his thigh and pushing herself up the bed. She flipped to her stomach and raised her bottom. An offering her husband was quick to accept.

Sin gripped her hips, raised her higher. He fitted his crown at her opening and slid into her on one stroke.

She moaned, the pleasure too great.

He began slowly, filling her at his own pace. He gripped the nape of her neck with one hand, holding her steady as he pistoned in and out.

The steady rhythm, the dominance of his hold, it all worked on her as a sedative. Every muscle in her body relaxed. Her worries about hurting Sin, over losing her mind like her mother had, all drifted away. The moment was only about seeking bliss. She clenched around his shaft, increasing the friction.

Sin cursed. He pounded into her harder, his tempo erratic.

The sounds their bodies created were obscene. Exquisite. She slid her hand under her belly and found her clitoris. She circled it as Sin drove into her, her sheath holding him tighter and tighter.

Her lungs seized, black spots danced before her eyes.

Her heart beat once, twice, and she exploded. Her toes curled, her back arched as wave after wave of pleasure consumed her.

Sin held himself flush to her bottom. His cock twitched, and he spent deep within her with a bellow. He shuddered, his fingers digging into her nape and hip, as her core clutched his length once more, milking his seed.

He collapsed next to her, breathing heavily. "Winnie," he whispered.

She turned on her side, facing away, and stared at the door to the dressing room. This wasn't a calamity. No matter what words were spoken or remained unsaid, they still found pleasure in each other. Their marriage could still be a successful one, filled with joys and achievements, even though she would always remain a bit of a disappointment to him.

He ran his fingers along the line of her shoulder and arm, and her skin tingled. Physical satisfaction would go a long way into making her husband content. She would keep him so well-satiated that he would barely notice their feelings did not match.

It would have to be enough.

Sin hooked his arm over her waist and pulled her back

into his warmth.

It was all they had.

Chapter Twenty-Four

Winnifred pressed a hand to her stomach and blew out a slow breath. The queasiness refused to dissipate.

"Something the matter?" Deirdre asked.

They were in the garden, cutting flowers, Banquo and Horatio lazing in the sun nearby. Deirdre wanted to line the hallways with vases full of color. The guests would start arriving that afternoon for the ball and Highland gathering set for a week's time. Since Sin hadn't given her any details, Winnifred had pestered Tavish to learn what would be expected of her as marchioness.

Thankfully, blessedly little.

Aside from welcoming guests and acting as hostess at dinners and afternoon teas, the bulk of the festivities would proceed apace without her leadership. At the Highland gathering, a festival of Scottish games as Winnifred understood it, she only had to enjoy herself as a spectator, the steward had said. Observation. Finally, a task as marchioness for which she felt qualified.

Her stomach grumbled as she bent to snip a small bud from a rose bush.

"Winnifred?" Deirdre's shadow fell upon her. "I asked if ye were well."

"Quite well, I thank you." She added her flower to her mother-in-law's basket and forced a smile. "Just a minor stomach-ache."

Deirdre's eyes brightened. "Do ye think ye are increasing already?"

Winnifred paused. She hadn't considered the

possibility, but she should have. She laid a hand over her abdomen. Lord knew she and Sin had spent enough time in bed.

A flutter of excitement whispered through her veins, quickly extinguished. She swallowed. Would she be as unsuccessful a parent as her mother had been? Or as distracted as her father? She hadn't been raised with good examples from whom she could observe and learn proper parenting techniques.

"I don't know, but I wouldn't raise your hopes just yet." Winnifred shrugged casually. "It could also be the bit of beef tongue I ate to break my fast this morn."

Deirdre sniffed. "Fine Scottish food does a bairn good. I'll ask Cook to prepare special meals for ye, just in case."

Winnifred's shoulders slumped. She'd never feel well again, not on a diet of haggis. She wiped her palms on her apron and shook the cotton out. "I think I'll go check on the preparations for our guests. You don't need my help here, do you?"

Deirdre sighed as she surveyed her garden. "Nae. There's hardly enough blooms to fill the ballroom, much less the guest rooms and hall tables. Kenmore will make a poor show of it this year."

Clasping the woman's shoulder, Winnifred squeezed. "Everyone knows of the troubled growing season. No one will expect a castle full of bouquets."

"I suppose." Deirdre sounded so forlorn that Banquo rolled to his feet and leaned into her thigh. She rubbed his head.

"Instead of flowers from your garden, how about I collect flora more native to Scotland? The thistle and gorse are blooming on every hillside."

Deirdre wrinkled her nose. "They're naught but weeds."

"Quite lovely purple and yellow weeds, if you ask me." Winnifred tapped a finger against her lips. Why was it that the plants that held little value seemed to thrive even in the worst conditions? She might have to investigate the growing cycle of these native plants, see if there was anything she could learn that would help the crops.

She shook off the urge to disappear into her laboratory. It was not the time. "I believe we can fashion some lovely bouquets with them."

Deirdre shifted her basket higher on her hip. "Well, if ye think so."

"I'll collect some samples and meet you in the day room. We can experiment with differing arrangements."

A smile broke over Deirdre's face, small but genuine. "Thank ye, dear. I believe we'll be able to make this work, after all."

Stomach-ache forgotten, Winnifred hopped down the path and out of the garden. She headed around the castle, heading in the direction of the loch. A thick hedge full of the velvety, yellow blossoms caught her eye, and she bent to cut a thin branch from a gorse bush.

A watery shadow fell across her path.

"Did you decide to help me gather the flowers?" Winnifred notched the branch into the crook of her arm. She should have brought her own basket along with her.

"Nae," an angry voice said.

Winnifred spun, lost her balance, and landed on her rear in the dirt. She looked up, and her pulse evened out when she recognized Donald's form limned in the afternoon light. "You gave me a start." She climbed to her feet and shook the dirt from her skirts. "What are you doing at Kenmore? You must know that my husband won't welcome you here." She raised her gaze and got her first good look at him. His bottom lip was swollen, red and purple bruises covered his face, and a ragged cut etched its way from his eye across his cheek.

"Aye, I know it well." He swept the fallen gorse from the ground and shoved it at her. "He threatened my life just days ago."

Winnifred waved the branch in the air in front of his face. "He did that to you?" She pressed her lips together.

She wasn't quite sure how to feel about that. Not that Donald didn't deserve it but the beating seemed severe. She strode to another clump of gorse. "Then why are you here? If my husband doesn't want you on his land then you need to leave."

"The independent, unconventional Miss Hannon has yielded to the duty to obey her husband's wishes." He picked up a stick and tossed it away. "Ye disappoint me."

"Is it obeying my husband when my judgment aligns with his on this matter?" She cut another flowering branch with her pocket clippers. "You have become a nuisance, and I cannot condone the trouble you've caused."

He grabbed her elbow and swung her to face him. His nostrils flared. "Trouble *I've* caused? I told my comrades, men I considered friends, that your husband suspected me, and because of this I was set upon. They tried to kill me to keep me silent."

She slapped her clippers into her palm. "So my husband wasn't responsible for that patchwork of bruises." His coconspirators must be desperate men to turn so on Donald. "Perhaps their betrayal shows you've chosen the wrong side. Come back to Kenmore with me. Tell Dunkeld everything you know. Stop this madness before it gets out of hand."

He clenched his fists. "The only madness is allowing the English to remain as our masters. Cannae you see that? I willnae let some turncoat marquess stop me from my purpose."

"Your purpose?" She chose to ignore the insult to her husband. Sin loved his country and didn't require defending.

"To overturn the union."

A burst of laughter escaped her lips. "You? You think you will be responsible for ending the union? Single-handedly, as you are now cut adrift from your motley crew of rogues?"

His face purpled. "Ye've never had vision. Even with all

the books ye've read, ye never learned the power of devotion to an ideal. Of being willing to do anything necessary to achieve it." He grabbed her arm and started walking, dragging her away from the castle.

Winnifred dug in her heels, but still she was propelled inexorably forward. "What the devil do you mean by this?" She smacked the back of his head with the gorse, yellow blossoms exploding over his hat and collar. "Release me at once!"

"Not until I get what I want." Donald's hat tumbled to the ground under her blows, but he ignored it. "The Marquess of Dunkeld might be a traitor to his own people, but I've seen the way he looks at ye. He'll do as I say when I have his marchioness stashed away. Ye'll be all the protection I need."

Irritation tore through her breast. She wouldn't let herself be scared, not of Donald.

His donkey was tied to a bush down the lane, and the beast pawed her hoof when she saw them coming.

"Oh, for goodness sake." Winnifred tried to jab him with her clippers, but the hand she held them with Donald clasped too tightly. "You don't intend to carry me away on that poor animal, do you? It will barely hold you, much less the both of us."

He adjusted his grip. "She'll hold us."

Hell and damnation. She couldn't allow herself to be taken from her home. She let her knees buckle, made her body drop to the earth, halting their progress. She dug her free hand into the loose earth and flung a fistful of dirt into his face when he turned.

Dropping her arm, Donald let loose with a torrent of curses and pawed at his eyes.

Winnifred crab-crawled away from him then jumped to her feet. "If you are the best Scotland has on offer then I pity your chances to gain independence."

Slowly, he scraped a path of soil from his eyes, revealing an iron-tipped glare.

She took a step back.

He followed.

Perhaps she shouldn't have been so hasty with her insults. "Now, Donald, we've known each—eep!"

He lunged, and Winnifred twisted away. She threw the clippers at him, and they bounced harmlessly off his chest. Lovely. Lifting her skirts, she tore back down the path, heading for safety. For Sin. Rounding the low hill, she waved her hands at the footmen in the distance.

Donald's fingers slid off her shoulder.

Winnifred changed direction and heard him stumble behind her. She put on a burst of speed. She'd never make it to the castle before he caught her. The broken beams of the rear tunnel rose from the ground just a hundred feet away. There, in the dark, she could evade her former friend.

"Stop! I won't hurt ye." Donald's words ended on a gasp.

She pressed her lips tighter together and quickened her step. She would have thought a man riding about the countryside stirring up trouble would have been in better form. Her slipper skidded on a stone at the tunnel's entrance, and the ankle she'd twisted the week earlier flared with pain. Limping into the dark, she cursed the man behind her. She threw herself against the earthen wall and tried to hold her breath.

The air shifted as he rushed past. "Winnie! Be reasonable." Something scuffed against wood, and she sidled back towards the entrance, her lungs burning.

"After the revolution, I can protect ye," Donald called. "The wife of a member of the English House of Lords willnae survive over long, but if ye cooperate, I'll make sure to keep ye safe."

She edged closer to the light. He couldn't be so simple as to think that he could protect her better than Sin. Even surrounded by an angry mob with her neck heading for the gallows, she'd still feel safer standing beside her husband than hiding next to this craven fool.

"There ye are." He heaved a sigh. "I'm glad ye saw reason."

Winnifred paused. Donald's voice was at least fifteen feet distant, nowhere near her position. What—

An unholy shriek filled the tunnel, followed by familiar hissing.

Her eyes widened, but still she saw nothing. She knew that sound. Knew what unearthly beast could produce such fear in man. Forgetting stealth, she turned for the entrance and ran headlong away from the badger.

She grasped the beam at the end of the tunnel and clutched her stomach as she sucked in air. The high-pitched squeal grew louder, and Donald's panicked face broke into the light. He raced past, hands covering his bum, a large section of torn fabric flapping from the seat of his trousers with every step.

Donald spared her no glance as he fled to safety behind a large oak tree. He clung to the trunk, peering around its width, eyes wide.

The badger waddled into the open, a strip of black wool impaled on a lower tooth. He gave her a sidelong warning look before retreating back into the tunnel.

"For someone who thinks himself Scotland's savior, that was a poor display of manliness," she shouted. She tucked a loose bit of hair back into its pin.

Donald raked a hand through his hair. "That... thing..."

"Yes?" She rested her palm on the wall and winced. She held her hand to the light. An angry-looking scrape ran its length.

He adjusted his neckcloth and tugged on the hem of his jacket. The effort to look respectable failed miserably. "Ye will regret your decision here."

She snorted. "I think not." A carriage rolled down the drive in the distance. The first of their guests was arriving, and Sin would be wondering where she was. "You'd best leave now. My husband will be coming, and I don't want him to hurt you."

Donald blinked. "Ye still care for me?"

"Not in the least." She ran her gaze over her girlhood friend. He still looked the child. Never maturing; never thinking beyond his own immediate desires. "I care about what happens to my husband. I don't want to see him tried for your murder."

He pressed his lips into a white slash. "Ye've condemned yourself to your own fate. May God have mercy on your soul."

She flapped her hand at him. "Worry about your own. I have guests to attend. It's time for you to leave."

With a curt nod, he turned and did just that. He trotted over to his donkey, climbed into the saddle, and disappeared down the path, away from the castle's entrance.

Winnifred smoothed the stomach of her gown. She couldn't face their guests, or Sin, not looking like this. And the only way into Kenmore without garnering attention was directly behind her.

Squaring her shoulders, she turned to face the darkness. "Badger, I promise not to molest you if you give me the same consideration. A compact of mutual cohabitation. What say you?"

Only silence answered her, the lack of hissing she took as a good sign. And with halting, sightless steps, she limped her way home.

Chapter Twenty-Five

Sin found Winnifred in her dressing room, her maid buttoning her gown. He waved her abigail off and took over the task. "Lord and Lady Abercairn have arrived. I'm hoping you can keep the women well-occupied tonight after dinner so I can speak with him." He hated this part of investigations, when he couldn't use his best tool: his fists. Abercairn had too many friends, and the word of one fuckwit against him wasn't enough to justify violent methods.

Winnifred kicked her morning gown under a settee, and the maid balled it up and scurried from the chamber.

Sin frowned. "Was that mud on your—"

"Is Lord Abercairn the man Donald named as the brains behind the rebellion?" Winnifred smiled over her shoulder. "I do hope his wife isn't privy to her husband's misdeeds or this could make for an awkward house party. I don't know how talented I am at deception."

"Something for which I am glad." He slid the last button into place. "I can hardly credit MacConnell's accusation. Abercairn has been one of my most sensible colleagues in the House of Lords. We are in agreement on most bills. I can't believe he would behave so recklessly."

She turned to face him. "Can't, or don't want to believe?"

Sin twisted his lips. "The latter." He paced across the small chamber. His world was spinning topsy-turvy, and there seemed to be little he could do to right it. Another of his tenants had moved, informing him the Highlands couldn't provide for him and his family. Except for his four friends, Sin no longer knew who he could trust in the House of Lords. And Winnifred....

He gripped the back of his neck. He'd spoken no more of love to his wife, not even while he was buried ballocks deep inside her. He knew she preferred it that way, but something had to change. It wasn't right to hold that sentiment in.

Wasn't right that he was the only one to feel it.

Stepping forward he clasped her hands.

She grimaced, and Sin released her at once. "What is wrong?"

"Nothing."

He narrowed his eyes and took her wrists, flipping her hands over. The palm and fingers of her right one bore deep red scratches. "What happened? This isn't from gardening with my mother, is it?"

She tugged at her hand, but he held it firm. "No, this isn't from gardening. It was a minor incident, that is all."

He ground his back teeth. "The more you dance around the cause, the more I am determined to know it."

She bit her lip. "If I tell you, I need your promise you will do nothing about it. Especially at this critical time for Scotland. You cannot be losing your temper over such a minor injury."

Heat rose up his body to his face. Whatever she had to say, he knew he wouldn't like it. He also didn't appreciate the attempts to moderate his behavior.

"I want the truth, and no restrictions on my actions."

She shrugged. "You can't have both. I won't be responsible for you landing in prison."

He arched an eyebrow. "I am a marquess. The third richest man in Scotland. Whatever you have to say, I can assure you, will not result in my imprisonment."

"Oh." She shook her head, as though to clear it. "Sometimes I forget how different you are. Peers are a different species than the rest of us."

He scowled. She was now a member of the damned peerage, as well. He refused to allow her to raise another division between them. Or allow for her to evade his question. "How did your hand become injured?"

She lifted one shoulder. "Donald attempted to remove me from Kenmore. What you see is merely the result of my flinging dirt and pebbles into his eyes."

Sin blinked, but the white dots refused to disappear from his vision. He nodded once. Right. That was that. The man had signed his death warrant with his actions. And after Sin had shown him such kindness in not beating him to a pulp earlier. He turned and strode for his bedchamber's door.

Winnifred darted around him and spread her arms wide, a feeble attempt to block his exit. "You promised not to act foolishly."

He picked her up under the arms and moved her out of his way. "I promised no such thing."

She skittered around him to block his path before he reached the hall door. "Consider what is at stake. You have been tasked to stop a rebellion. Murdering Donald can only impede achieving that objective. We have a house full of guests, one of whom might be a traitor. Think about vengeance later."

Perhaps if he tied her to the bed she'd stop flinging herself in his way. "Does his life matter so much to you?" Not even to make her happy did he think he could refrain from his duty. And it would be a duty as much as it was a pleasure. Any man who laid hands on his wife deserved to die. Slowly. Painfully.

"It is not his life I am concerned about." She poked his chest. "Although I confess I would rather he were alive and away from our notice than dead. Not all my memories of him when we were younger are unpleasant." She placed her hand on his arm and squeezed. "You cannot let your emotions override your common sense. Donald is but a small cog in a much larger wheel. You need to remain focused on your goal."

Sin growled. Her and her blasted sense. How could she remain so level-headed after an assault when he wanted to rage loud enough to raise every selkie from the ocean?

She pressed both her palms flat against his chest, and heat from her hands seeped through his waistcoat. That itching feeling, like ants crawling beneath his skin, eased to a mere tickle and his pulse slowed from its race.

She had him better trained than the damned dogs were.

"All right," he grumbled. Picking up her injured hand, he pressed a soft kiss to the reddened skin. "For the moment, I won't act." He did have much to do with the houseguests upon them. Horse rides to lead and secrets to uncover. And later, when his time was his own again, he wouldn't need to inform his wife of any irksome little tasks he might undertake. Like murder.

"Splendid." Winnifred patted his chest. "Now, tell me what I need to know about our guests. I imagine all your friends will be curious about your common wife and watching for my every misstep. I'd like to give them as little to gossip about as possible."

Sin grimaced. "Unless Summerset, Sutton, Montague, or Rothchild show, our guests are not my friends. But they are the cream of Scottish society, and the introduction of my new marchioness to them would be expected. It was a fortuitous coincidence that my investigation coincided with the necessity of a ball."

"Even more reason I need to be as well armed as possible." She straightened the knot on his cravat and slid her arm in his before turning for the door. "Growing up on the outskirts of society as I did, I always imagined functions like this as akin to a lion's den, something to be avoided. Now I am the head lioness. I'd like to be as deadly as the next woman."

A chuckle burst from his lips. He opened the door and led her out. "For once, I believe your sensible mind is being overly dramatic. Just keep the women as occupied as possible so I'll have time to investigate the men, and you'll be fine. The ladies here are just like every other. You have absolutely nothing to be concerned about."

* * *

Nothing to be concerned about? What a load of tosh. That first dinner was everything and more of what Winnifred had dreaded. It was silly to fret about the proper silverware etiquette, or whether the fashionable Lady Teodora Eirlie found her diverting, not when their neighbors were hungry. But aside from that disastrous dinner at the Abercairn's, this was her first public performance as marchioness. Nerves got the better of her regardless of the stern lectures she delivered to herself.

She glanced mournfully at the door to the drawing room. The ladies of the party were gathered after dinner, sipping their drinks and sighing with boredom. Only three parties had arrived that day, and Winnifred eagerly anticipated more guests on the morrow. A larger party would surely take the burden off her as guests would converse easier amongst themselves. If it weren't for Deidre now, there would be no discussion at all.

Clearly, the art of conversation was a skill she needed to practice. Winnifred tapped her finger against her glass and searched her mind for an interesting topic to broach. Travel to Kenmore (*tedious and dreary*), the weather this summer (*infernally bad*), the price of lace (*too high*), all this had already been discussed.

Deirdre stepped into the breach once more. "The neckline on your gown is most becoming, Lady Abercairn. Is that the latest fashion in London?"

The countess kept her gaze on the ceiling. "Paris. We were there just last month. London is becoming a positive backwoods." She arched a delicate brow and looked down her nose at Deirdre. "Though I guess by comparison it would seem an Eden to you."

Winnifred's shoulders tensed. "I take it Glasgow isn't to

your liking then? How fortunate that a girl from the Lowlands was able to find herself a diplomat as a husband. The travel his position affords must be gratifying."

While Sin had been next to useless in imparting the *on dit* about their guests, her mother-in-law had been more helpful. Lady Abercairn had been born the youngest daughter of an obscure baronet. While nothing to scoff at, the position was nothing to the pretentions the woman now held. And after insulting Deirdre, she needed reminding that she wasn't born with the proverbial silver spoon in her mouth.

Lady Abercairn's cheeks flushed pink, and Winnifred felt a stab of satisfaction. It felt good to bare her own fangs. Whilst she didn't want to become a lion herself, perhaps she could succeed at being a lion tamer.

Lady Eirlie snorted delicately. "*I* find Scotland to be a beautiful country, and Glasgow as cosmopolitan as Madrid." The woman's lyrical accent made the words sound sweet, even while her glance at Lady Abercairn was cutting. According to Deirdre, these two were rivals to be the grand dame of Scottish society. Even though Lady Eirlie was of Spanish origin and had only lately arrived in Scotland with her new husband, the Viscount Eirlie, she seemed to be the preferred style-leader. She turned to Winnifred. "Have you seen much of your new homeland? Do you not think it lovely?"

"Indeed." Striking, harsh, and wild, but lovely all the same. "And while Glasgow is beautiful, my Eden is here in the country." She shot her mother-in-law a small smile. "There's much more space for plants to grow."

"Oh, are ye a botanist like the dowager marchioness?" Lady Margaret asked. The Earl of Brandon and his two children had been the third party to arrive that day, and while the son, Dr. Masson left Winnifred with a gnawing pit in her stomach whenever they met, Lady Margaret was nothing but sweet and friendly. She scooted to the edge of her seat. "Her gardens are always so beautiful. At least in the years where there is sunlight."

Deirdre gave the girl a wide smile. "Thank ye, dear. This summer has been hard on my garden, but that is nothing to what our farmers are facing. Fortunately for us, the new marchioness is a bit of a natural philosopher with an interest in agriculture. We are hopeful that her new ideas will help our crops."

Lady Abercairn lowered her wineglass. "A natural philosopher?" She tittered. "Why, Dunkeld is just full of surprises with his new bride. And we thought his marrying a Sassenach was scandalous enough."

Winnifred forced her hand to relax its grip on her skirts. "I'd have thought, being as worldly as you are, that an English wife wouldn't have been shocking to you or your husband. It was my understanding that Lord Abercairn is a supporter of the union. Surely that would extend to more intimate unions, as well." She observed the woman acutely. Was Lord Abercairn as open with his wife concerning his affairs as Sin was with her? If Abercairn was trying to stir up a rebellion, surely his wife would have some inklings.

Lady Abercairn drew her shoulders back. "Despite our worldliness, my husband is a patriot." She tilted her nose at Lady Eirlie. "*We* were both born and raised here, and Scotland will always be our first love." She swallowed the last of her wine. "Abercairn was most surprised when he heard of Lord Dunkeld's marriage to an Englishwoman, but the rushed nature of the wedding explained his decision. A Scotsman is nothing if not honorable."

Deirdre sucked in a breath, and Winnifred's cheeks burned. Her shame made no logical sense. She knew her and Sin's behavior in that cellar had been innocent. What cared she for what others thought? She swallowed. Illogical or not, embarrassment had her staring at the floor nonetheless.

"A common license was sought." Deirdre set her glass down and gripped her hands together, looking as though she'd rather be wringing the other woman's neck. "There was naught improper or rushed about it."

Lady Eirlie swung her head from Deirdre back to Lady Abercairn, like a spectator in a tennis match. Lady Margaret stared at her skirts, looking like she wanted to be anywhere else but in that room.

Winnifred knew the feeling.

"And I didn't mean to imply anything improper, I'm certain." Lady Abercairn's smile was smug. "I'm sure our new marchioness would never have been caught alone with a man, especially one such as Dunkeld. It would have been too unseemly."

Winnifred narrowed her eyes, any insult to herself forgotten. "And what do you mean by that? If I was to be found with any man, why wouldn't it have been with Dunkeld?" There was nothing unseemly about Sin. Just because he dressed rougher than a marquess should, didn't have a sweet tongue ready to compliment, by no means reflected a flaw in his character. "My husband is the best of men. I consider myself fortunate that I was caught in a cellar with him."

Lady Eirlie smothered a laugh with her handkerchief, and Winnifred realized her error. "Not that I intended to be caught with any man." She cleared her throat. "It was an unintended event."

Deirdre sighed. "Ye are only making it worse, dear. Perhaps we should change the subject."

"Oh, but I find the topic of how to capture a marquess fascinating." Lady Abercairn dipped her index finger in the remains of her drink and sucked on the tip. "Finally, a woman who admits her cunning in landing a titled man. It was an impressive capture on your part, Lady Dunkeld. A marked step up in your circumstances, as I understand it. And it only cost you your reputation."

Winnifred gritted her teeth. She wouldn't let this woman provoke her. She. Would. Not.

"If I recall, your marriage was won under similar circumstances." Lady Eirlie settled back in her chair and crossed her ankles. "Wasn't there talk of your father running Lord Abercairn through if he refused to wed you?"

Lady Abercairn shrugged. "Not nearly as impressive a feat. Abercairn could hardly dishonor the daughter of a baronet who used to be his clan's chieftain. But I was proud of my efforts."

"That sounds so mercenary," Lady Margaret said, her voice shocked. "What about marrying for love?"

The countess and viscountess caught each other's eyes and chuckled. "Only an unmarried woman could indulge such fancies." Lady Abercairn flicked open her fan and cooled her face. "Your father will marry you off to the man most useful to his purpose. That is the way of the world. And if you want to reserve any part of it for yourself, you need to think strategically."

"Here, here." Lady Eirlie tapped her ring against her empty glass.

Winnifred rose and refilled everyone's wine. "Surely affection plays some part. After all, you and your husband seem to be in remarkable sympathy, Lady Abercairn. You are a vocal supporter of his proposals in parliament, are you not? I believe you were quoted in *Women's World* as saying that his latest bill, bolstering trade regulations, would serve to strengthen the United Kingdom."

She licked wine from her lips. "I support my husband whatever his position, as all smart wives do. His position is that a strong United Kingdom results in a strong Scotland. He wants only what is best for our country."

Winnifred set the decanter of sherry down on the table. Yes, everyone wanted what was best for Scotland. It was defining what was best that was the issue. And how far people were willing to go to attain it.

"And does your husband believe an independent Scotland is the future?" Winnifred settled back in her seat and picked up her wine. Everyone was on their third glass while she yet nursed her first. She hadn't realized how important that drink was. It had played a part in her marriage, and, she hoped, would loosen lips enough to play a part in uncovering a treasonous plot. Sin might be focused on obtaining information from the men, but he shouldn't ignore the knowledge of wives.

"An independent Scotland is all our futures, according to my husband," Lady Eirlie said. "We can only hope that when revolution comes, it doesn't follow the path of the French." She placed her hand on her throat. "The citizens have been behaving like louts lately. A firm hand is needed to settle them down."

"The people are hungry," Deirdre said. "Empty stomachs can rouse men to anger. If we support our people, they'll support us."

Lady Margaret scooted forward. "My father says the same thing. The poor growing season is hard on all of Scotland. But he says our fighting spirit will see us through. If we focus on the good, the bad loses some of its power."

"How quaint." Lady Abercairn rolled her eyes over the rim of her glass.

Deirdre ignored her. "I agree with your father, dear. To that end, all Kenmore tenants are invited to the Highland gathering the day of the ball. Dunkeld believes it just the thing to raise everyone's spirits."

Lady Abercairn arched an eyebrow. "We're to consort with the tenants? How egalitarian."

"Better they fling logs about than chop off heads." Lady Eirlie smiled wickedly. "Besides, there's nothing wrong with a group of Highland lads running about in kilts."

That gave Winnifred pause. Would Sin wear a kilt? She leaned back on her chair and took a long sip of wine. The idea held merit.

Lady Eirlie sighed. "A Highland gathering or not, I think the people will not be easily appeased. With these latest riots, I fear none of us will live to enjoy Scotland's freedom."

Lady Abercairn buried her face in her glass and said nothing. But a hint of a smile played around her lips, one that Winnifred didn't like the look of.

Like Lady Abercairn, at least, knew something that would ensure her survival.

Chapter Twenty-Six

Sin drummed his fingers on the tablecloth and tried to pay attention to the discussion next to him. Why did men cease saying anything of interest when they sat at a dinner table? Six long nights of stultifying conversations. Of uninformative, tedious talk where he learned nothing but where the best brandy could be procured in Edinburgh and the latest racing rule formulated by the Jockey Club.

He eyed Winnifred seated at the opposite end of the long, wooden table. She wore a polite smile on her face, but the edges looked frayed. He wanted nothing more than to secrete her away and make that smile genuine.

The man next to him chortled at his own joke, and Sin ground his back teeth. Thank the heavens the guests would be leaving in two days' time. He was not meant for small talk and suffering simpering fools.

He sighed and pushed his turnips about with his fork.

"Then ye agree with me, Dunkeld?" Lord Brandon peered at him from under bushy brows. "That latest prison reform bill was made in jest, surely. Only meant to appease the masses."

Sin molded his features, trying to approximate interest. "Yes. But then all bills are attempts to appease the people. Very few politicians truly care if their policies succeed, and won't until the masses have more political power. As long as the goose remains fat in their own kitchens is all that matters to parliamentarians."

"How positively anti-monarchist of ye." Lord Abercairn swirled the wine in his goblet. "I didnae realize that you had such democratic leanings, Dunkeld. You rarely speak in the House."

Sin grunted. Speaking was overrated. "Do you disagree?"

The man puckered his lips. "Only with your conclusion. Placating the masses is often for their own good. Not everything needs a Machiavellian reason behind it."

Sin narrowed his eyes. No, but more often than not, the people he met didn't operate with the common good in mind. He opened his mouth to respond, but two figures at the dining room doors drew his attention.

A genuine grin stretched Sin's cheeks. He stood and strode for his friends. "Montague! Rothchild! How are you?" He shook their hands. "I didn't think you two would be able to make it."

The Duke of Montague raised his eyebrows. "And miss the chance to meet your new wife? I hardly think so. I'm only sorry Elizabeth couldn't come. She was most interested to meet the woman who would be a match for you, but I dropped her off at Rothchild's estate. You know her sister is increasing with their first child."

The Earl of Rothchild frowned, small worry lines radiating out from the corners of his eyes. "And it has been a difficult couple of months for my wife. If it hadn't been for Elizabeth's presence, I wouldn't have left her."

Montague coughed into his fist.

Rothchild grimaced. "Fine, I didn't have much choice in the matter," he bit out.

"Amanda packed your trunks herself." Montague chuckled. "She couldn't wait to see the tail end of you. Something about your incessant hovering."

"I do not hover." Rothchild's nostrils flared. "I was merely showing the appropriate level of concern."

Montague slapped him on the back. "The first child is always the hardest." He eyed Dunkeld. "You've been married about a month now. Any such concerns on your part?"

Sin stepped to the side as footmen carried past two more chairs to the dining table. He ignored the sinking feeling in his stomach. He wanted a child with Winnifred, couldn't wait to see her round with his bairn, but couldn't deny that the idea of a baby coming from a union where only one parent loved was like a punch to the gut.

Which was nonsense. Most marriages weren't love matches, and the children that resulted from them suffered no ill-effects. "Perhaps you should at least meet my wife before seeing her pregnant." He searched out her gaze and nodded, beckoning to her with his fingers.

Winnifred popped to her feet and circled the table, looking relieved to be free of her conversation.

Her skirt brushed his boot as she stood close. "Husband. Judging by your reaction, might I presume these are friends of yours?"

He placed his hand on her lower back. "Indeed. I present the Duke of Montague and the Earl of Rothchild, two of the veriest blackguards I've ever known."

She pressed her lips together, but the edges curled up. She turned to his friends. "I feel like it should be my duty to apologize for my husband, but since you've known him longer than I have, I presume you are accustomed to his unique manner of speech. Welcome to Kenmore." She gave a short curtsy as Montague and Rothchild bowed. "Your wives have not accompanied you?"

"They wished to, but were unable at this time," Montague said. "You and Dunkeld will have to visit us on your next trip south."

"Speaking of," Rothchild said in a low voice, "we bear an important message. Can you escape your dinner party for a few minutes?"

Silverware clattered against porcelain. Winnifred glanced over her shoulder and back at his friends. "I'm afraid dinner has just ended. The gentlemen are retiring to the east drawing room." She sighed. "And I suppose I must lead the women to the parlor."

Sin squeezed her hip. Winnifred wanted their home as empty of guests as he did. He bowed his head to whisper in her ear. "Almost over. We just have to get through the games and the ball tomorrow, and then Kenmore will be our own again."

She smiled up at him. "I can't wait." To his friends: "I'm glad to have finally met you. I hope we can speak more when the gentlemen join us in the parlor." Turning, she squared her shoulders and marched off, like a general to a battle.

"She was not what I was expecting," Rothchild said. "Much more forthright than is conventional. I like her."

Sin drew his gaze from her retreating hips. "I'm well pleased with my circumstances." The men filtered out of the dining room, and Sin's shoulders rounded. Duty called. "Shall we adjourn for some whisky or do you want to eat first and meet me in the drawing room later? I can have the kitchen send up more plates."

Montague nodded at Lord Brandon as he passed through the doors. "We had a basket in the carriage. Let's go play nice with the other gentlemen and we can have our private conversation later."

Sin led them to the drawing room, his muscles tensing when he spied Abercairn seated in his favorite chair. The only one in the room sturdy enough to not make him feel like he was about to topple over. He gritted his teeth as he trudged to the sideboard and poured himself and his friends a drink.

"What's the lay of the land?" Rothchild leaned against the wall and swirled his whisky. He looked the epitome of bored elegance, but his eyes were hard as they flitted from face to face.

Sin raised his glass to cover his mouth. "Abercairn has been implicated in the recent riots but is as cagey as a sodding sneak." He gritted his teeth. "I've learned nothing from him this past week. He never struck me as a Jacobite, but due to conversations with his wife, Winnifred suspects it is so." Thank heavens she had more luck loosening tongues or else this house party would have been a complete waste of time. "I want to know the reasons behind his involvement. And put a stop to it, of course."

"Of course." Montague cracked his neck. "Liverpool asked us to give you whatever aid you needed."

Sin squeezed his friend's shoulder. "And it is most appreciated. Although you have already provided the best aid possible. Your shipments of grain and produce have been life-savers to my people. It is something I can never repay."

"And as my friend, you never have to." Montague raised an eyebrow. "Besides, what is the point of being the duke who sullies himself in trade if not to help those I care about?"

"Charming as this show of amiability is," Rothchild said dryly, "it gets us no closer to a solution. How do you propose to investigate Abercairn? As a member of parliament, we can't just accuse the man."

"I'm trying to make him think I'm supportive of independence." Sin pursed his lips. "Which I am, but I want it done in the proper fashion and time."

Montague's lips twitched. "*You* are attempting a ruse?" He shared a look with Rothchild. "I think we've come at the right time."

Sin pushed away from the wall. "I might be the bruiser of the group, but I can be stealthy when required."

Rothchild smothered a snort. "Have you searched his rooms yet?"

"Of course." Sin glared at Abercairn as the man threw his head back and laughed as though he hadn't a care in the world. "My man, Dugald, found nothing." He turned his back on the room and huddled closer to his friends. "Summerset was to search his Glasgow residence in his absence, but I have yet to receive any report."

"So, it is up to us to feel him out." Rothchild jerked his chin towards Abercairn. "Shall we have a go at it?"

Sin nodded and stomped to an unoccupied sofa near the earl. He plopped down and tried to think of another angle of attack. It seemed he and Abercairn had spoken of everything and nothing over the past six days. Aside from threats of physical force, he was at a loss of how to proceed.

Rothchild sat next to him and crossed one silk-clad leg over the other. "Where are Sutton and Summerset? I thought they were yet in Scotland?"

Lord Abercairn turned in their direction and leaned forward in his chair. Sin's chair. "Last I'd heard, Sutton was causing trouble in Glasgow. Something about a fight in a distillery. Several casks of whisky were destroyed apparently."

Damn. Sin hadn't heard about that yet. Which raised the question— "Where did you hear that? I've seen no such report, and if Sutton or Summerset found trouble in Scotland, I do think I'd be the first they'd write."

"Would ye?" The man licked the tip of his index finger and ran it along his eyebrow. "Perhaps ye aren't as informed as ye think of your friends' activities, or who directs them."

An uneasy silence descended. Montague, standing next to the sofa, stiffened. Rothchild grew deeply interested in a scuff on his boot.

"I'm sure there is much of my friends' lives that I'm unaware of." Sin examined Abercairn's words from every direction. Did he know Sutton and Summerset worked for the crown as spies? Did he suspect the rest of them? "My friends don't go about starting fights." Not unless it was necessary. Or diverting. "And in these times of unrest in Scotland, I'm sure they'd know not to rouse unnecessary anger."

Abercairn shrugged. "The line between necessary and unnecessary grows slimmer every day." He glared up at Brandon as the earl stepped too close and jostled Abercairn's drink arm. "Careful. Save the physical sport for the games tomorrow."

"You intend to participate in the games?" Montague asked.

"Of course." Abercairn finished his whisky and waved to a footman to refill his glass. "A Highland gathering is a way for real men to demonstrate their skills, and an uplifting display for our downtrodden countrymen." He raised his glass Sin's way. "I commend ye for holding them before your ball." He looked at Montague and arched an eyebrow. "But dunnae worry, your grace. No Englishmen would be expected to muddy his boots in them."

"I quite like muddying my boots." Rothchild gave the man a smile as false as a dockside harlot's. "Besides, as you say, these are difficult times. I think it would be a good show if the English and Scottish were to join together."

Abercairn raised his hand, palm up, and shrugged. "I look forward to meeting ye on the field of play tomorrow. Perhaps a gentleman's wager would be in order?"

Sin tuned the voices out, having no interest in the prick-wagging contest. He and his friends had been agents of the crown for over ten years now. He supposed it was only to be expected that their activities would be uncovered with time. Since their marriages, Montague, Rothchild, and Sutton had cut back on the jobs they'd taken. As the thought of leaving Winnifred for any extended period of time made Sin's skin itch, he'd likely curb his activities, as well. But if word was getting out, they'd all be forced into early retirement.

Summerset would be seriously displeased.

There was a lull in the conversation, and Sin lifted his head. Montague raised an eyebrow at him, expectant.

Sin grunted. Right. Host duties. This was why he never held balls or parties. He stood. "Shall we join the ladies?" Not caring if anyone objected, he turned and strode for the door. A footman swung it open just before he reached it.

The evenings with his guests were interminable, but at least Winnifred would soon be by his side. He could survive anything with her next to him. Even another night of mindless gossip and failed attempts at espionage.

Chapter Twenty-Seven

Winnifred tugged at the bit of plaid fabric that hemmed her new kid gloves. New bits and bobs seemed to appear in her wardrobe almost daily, and almost all with the Dunkeld tartan on them. Another way to identify her as Sin's, she supposed. Another way to make her feel as though she belonged.

"Lovely day for a festival." Lady Margaret pulled a hamper towards her and rooted through the wicker. She, Winnifred, Deirdre, and Lady Abercairn sat on a wide blanket spread on a hill overlooking the loch. The rocky shore was to be the central grounds for the games, and it seemed as though everyone in the whole county had come out to watch or participate.

Horatio inched towards Lady Margaret on his belly, sniffing the air. "Do ye know I've never actually seen any of these games," she said. "Unless ye count the summer my brother and his friends decided to attempt a caber toss on their own. It didnae go well." She bit into an apple.

Lady Abercairn wrinkled her nose. "If you consider freezing on this hill a nice day then I don't wonder what you consider a bad one. And please, use a knife. You look like a horse eating an apple in that manner." Banquo flopped down next to her and rolled to his back, offering his belly up for a hopeful rub. Lady Abercairn pulled her cloak more tightly about her.

Lady Margaret paused, apple poised at her lips, then slowly lowered the fruit to her lap, looking downcast.

Winnifred exchanged a look with Deirdre. Her mother-in-law rolled her eyes before picking out her own apple and taking a large, noisy bite.

Winnifred turned towards the loch, pressing her lips together to hide her smile. She leaned back on her palms and surveyed the mass of burly men thronging the beach. The Dunkeld colors encircled the waist of most men, but some reds and blues dotted the field of play, the guests from other clans. Winnifred had never seen so many bare knees and hairy thighs before in her life.

She scooched forward on the blanket, searching for a familiar pair of knees. Sin had dressed and left Kenmore before she'd awoken, and the thought of seeing her own burly Scot in a kilt did something queer to her insides.

Two familiar faces strolled towards their blanket. Unfortunately, Montague and Rothchild wore trousers, the duke in a pair of fine, black wool breeches and the earl in a worn pair of buckskins.

Winnifred wasn't the only woman disappointed. "Had our host no kilts to lend you gentlemen?" Lady Abercairn asked. She looked the men up and down. "Even though neither of you are Scottish, I'm certain no one would object to wearing our uniform while you play in the games."

Banquo hopped to his feet and bounded up to the newcomers. He raised on to his back legs, poised to jump, when Montague held up a hand and stared down at the dog. Caught mid-leap, Banquo whined and flopped to the side, stumbling. With a grumble, he lowered to his belly and stared up at the duke, watchful.

Montague knelt and gave the dog quiet words of praise. Rubbing the animal's back, he said to the women, "I am not participating in the games."

A chorus of protestations erupted from their blanket.

The handsome duke gave them a small smile. "Rothchild is, however." He cocked his head at his friend. "Yes, why are you not wearing the appropriate uniform for the games?"

"I'm not showing my knees like a schoolboy!" The earl's

nostrils flared. "I borrowed these clothes from my groom, and they will serve me well enough."

"Good luck to you," Winnifred said. If Sin didn't win everything, it would be nice to see England represented as a champion.

Montague rose and held out his hand. "Yes, don't let our northern neighbors pummel you too badly."

Rothchild merely glared at the offered hand and, with a nod to the women, stomped away.

Montague chuckled. "Might I watch the games with you ladies?"

"Of course." Winnifred spread her hand over the wide blanket. "Anywhere you can find a spot." She caught the gaze of Lady Eirlie seated several blankets away and nodded a greeting. The lady wore an elaborate turban, a peacock feather jauntily sprouting from its depths. She was surrounded by a group of similarly fashionable women who were laughing heartily at some antic or another. The women seemed to be without a care in the world, and for a moment Winnifred wished that she could join them.

Banquo popped to his feet and trotted over to her. He flopped across her legs, stretching out to his full length and pinning her to the ground.

Winnifred gently tapped the dog's head. "This isn't a spot."

The dog sighed, and settled deeper, and Winnifred couldn't help but scratch behind his ears.

Montague gracefully lowered himself on a patch of blanket slightly behind her and to her left. "You shouldn't allow the animals to countermand your authority. If you'd like, I can show you some training techniques that will help to keep them in order."

Banquo twitched an eyebrow and gave her an appraising look. She patted his side. "It's all right, your grace. I don't mind a bit of disorder now and then. Besides, they're good dogs."

Banquo huffed out a breath before closing his eyes for a

nap.

"Filthy, flea-ridden creatures." Lady Abercairn took a small bowl of strawberries Lady Margaret handed to her and picked out the largest berry. "I don't understand why anyone keeps them." She bit into the red flesh, just below the stem, her white teeth flashing.

Horatio crept towards the new food source, keeping his eyes pinned on the bowl of fruit. His paw left a bit of dirt on Lady Abercairn's skirts.

Deirdre patted the ground beside her hip. "Horatio, come here. Ye wouldnae like what she has to offer."

Winnifred didn't know if Deirdre meant the strawberries or the woman herself. Both were accurate, she supposed.

Montague stretched out his legs. "What am I to expect? Dunkeld said that in the past his clan has met with others for a gathering that included games, but didn't mention much else."

Winnifred stroked Banquo's ear. "I'm not certain. I believe there is a log toss—"

"Caber toss," Deirdre corrected.

"And the men throw rocks—"

"A stone put." Deirdre sighed. "Truly, I'd hoped my son would have taught ye some of our customs."

Winnifred shrugged. "I will learn about your gatherings by observing today. Besides, he has taught me much of your history."

"Has he?" Lady Abercairn adjusted the brim of her bonnet. "I wonder. Which version of history have you learned?"

Winnifred drew her brows together. "There is only one version. History is a set of facts, immutable."

The woman chuckled. "In your history books, I assume the Jacobites were merely a group of traitors, hung for treason."

Winnifred slowly nodded. According to the Treaty of Union, in point of fact they were traitors. The Scottish leaders had signed an accord to form the United Kingdom, and it would take another treaty to sever that union.

"To your new family, the Jacobites were martyrs to the cause. Freedom fighters." Lady Abercairn leaned forward, her gaze so intense it made Winnifred recoil. "That is the version that we live and breathe by. Your husband has spent too much time with the English if he teaches you any different."

Had Winnifred wondered if Lady Abercairn held the convictions to assist her husband with a rebellion? The answer to that question seemed to be a resounding affirmative.

"The cause of freedom is indeed a worthy fight." Montague rolled back to his elbows. His posture was relaxed, his voice easy, but Winnifred wasn't deceived. The duke paid close attention to the words of Lady Abercairn. "But the manner of fighting is always in question. The past fifty years are proof enough that more is gained through negotiation than battles between two peoples who should be as brothers."

Lady Abercairn laughed, a light tinkle. "My husband would agree with you. I am most proud of the influence he's wielded in your House of Lords, and how he has served our country. I trust his influence will continue long into the future."

A cheerful wail sounded through the air, and everyone turned to look where a young man stood in the middle of the beach, bagpipes under one arm, calling the games to a start. Winnifred bobbed her foot to the melody. The crowd's excitement was a palpable thing. Every crofter, farmer, and baker felt it just as Winnifred did. Pride warmed her heart. Sin's decision to hold the festival was the right one. Everyone needed this diversion to uplift their spirits from such a hard summer.

"What a skirl." Lady Abercairn shook her head. "Who is killing that poor goat a second time?"

Deirdre clenched her fist in the blanket, her knuckles

going white. "Young Hamish, our assistant gamekeeper, plays our pipes. He plays for services every Sunday, too, and a verra fine job he does of it."

Winnifred nodded. Truly, Lady Abercairn's tongue was poison-dipped, and she was growing tired of it. She opened her mouth, preparing a set-down, when a flash of auburn hair tied back in a neat queue caught her eye. Her gaze dropped to the broad back crossed with a strip of green-and-blue checked wool that exposed as much as it covered. The fabric continued down to wrap about narrow hips and drape over a muscular arse.

She snapped her jaw shut, her lower belly tingling. Even in an unfamiliar kilt, she knew that arse. She'd bitten it just the other night.

Sin turned, his eyes locking with hers. His nostrils flared as though he scented the air. There was no chance he could smell her soap, not through the throngs of sweaty men, but her nipples drew tight and tingled just the same. The crowd grew muted, the edges of their bodies indistinct until only she and Sin remained.

He possessed her. Made her feel when for her whole life she'd locked her emotions away. He'd brought her joy and pleasure, smiles and moans.

He loved her.

And she.... Her chest constricted. Why couldn't she love him back? Was she so broken that love was lost to her forever? She'd always believed her sensibility to be a strength. A protection against her mother's madness. She'd never thought of all that she was missing by excising those emotions.

A man slapped Sin on the shoulder, and her husband turned to speak with him. The connection snapped, like a worn thread. She stared at her hands, breathing deeply and fighting against the burn in her eyes. Now wasn't the time for such maudlin thoughts. It would hardly do for the marchioness and hostess of the gathering to be sniffling into her handkerchief at what was supposed to be a joyous festival.

When she raised her head, her smile was back in place. "What is the first event?" she asked Deirdre.

"A foot race." Her mother-in-law waved at a young boy selling chestnuts and gave him a shilling for a small bag of them. "I believe Sin has designated that old oak tree on the far side of the loch as the turnaround point."

A foot race seemed ordinary. Winnifred had expected something a bit more exotic. She tried not to let her disappointment show. She clapped her hands along with the rest as around thirty men lined up along the shore. Bare shoulders jostled. Booted feet scuffed the earth as they dug in.

The thin crack of a gunshot sounded, and the men were off.

And Winnifred realized that this foot race wasn't at all ordinary.

The first blow occurred before the leaders even reached the near curve of the lake. A young man with a shock of pitch-black hair threw his elbow into the jaw of the runner next to him. He leapt over his victim when the man stumbled to the ground.

A man old enough to know better stuck his leg in front of the runner next to him, shouting in triumph when the racer went down.

"What on earth...?" Winnifred gaped at the spectacle.

"Ye didnae think Scotsmen would merely run peaceably around a loch, did ye?" Deirdre smirked. "Our men want to win and will do most anything to accomplish that."

The first men reached the oak tree. There was a blur of arms and swinging kilts and a man was heaved into the lake with a large splash.

Montague shifted. "My decision to remain a spectator looks better and better."

Lady Abercairn tilted her head. "You don't appreciate physical exertion then, your grace?"

Winnifred couldn't determine if the silky threads in her

voice were meant as a seduction or an insult. With Lady Abercairn, those were most likely one and the same.

Whichever bait the lady dangled, Montague didn't rise to it. "Not of this type," he said mildly. He winced, and Winnifred turned to follow his gaze. The one man wearing trousers tumbled forward as he was pushed from behind.

Rothchild took his forward momentum and made a neat roll before rising to his feet and charging back towards the finish line. He closed the distance between his assailant and himself and with a quick turn of his hand, pulled the man to the ground by his hair.

"I do believe the earl might win." Deirdre held a hand to her forehead, shading her eyes. The leaders were pounding around the final curve of the lake, rounding on their target. Sin was back near the middle of the pack. He wasn't built for speed, but there was nothing wrong with how he looked while running. Leg muscles bunching and flexing. Arms bulging as he pistoned them back and forth. Sweat dampening his chest....

Well, Winnifred couldn't actually see that last bit, but she could envision it. She dug her teeth into her lower lip. Her mouth watered with the desire to lick every last bead of sweat from his body.

Montague sighed. "Rothchild will be unbearable with this win."

A victorious grin stretched Rothchild's face. He glanced back over his left shoulder... and missed the swinging hammer fist that struck his jaw from the right. He staggered, off-balance, and a young man wearing the Dunkeld tartan flew past him to cross the finish line.

Montague rubbed his hands together. "These games are delightful. You really should hold them every summer."

Winnifred blew out her cheeks. Entertaining this much every year would kill them. If it hadn't been for Sin's investigation, she might have holed up in her room this past week pleading illness. Although seeing Sin in a kilt every year would be a fair recompense.

She sighed. Truly, she made a poor marchioness. But she clapped along with everyone else as the winner was handed a small casket of whisky and a new dirk as his reward.

The games progressed, each one less violent than the race but showcasing the men's brawn to better effect. Sin came in second for the stone put, losing only to the village blacksmith, and Winnifred suspected he might have intentionally let the other man win. He sat out what looked like a seated tug-of-war to Winnifred but which Deirdre said was called *Maide-leisg*. Aside from Sin, none of the other noblemen had the brawn to compete with men who worked with their hands all day long.

The log for the caber toss was carried to the center of the field by two men. Lord Abercairn called out. "Forfeiting this game, as well, Dunkeld? Starting to feel the ache in your bones that age brings?"

The exposed skin on her husband's shoulders pulled taut, and he turned to his fellow peer. His eyebrow's knitted, but otherwise he appeared calm. "I thought to leave the fun to the other men." He slapped one of his tenants on the back.

Abercairn barked in laughter. "Oh, don't let womanly fears get in the way of a spirited competition. But mayhap ye've been in England for so long the virility has been sapped out of ye."

Winnifred couldn't hear what her husband said, but she saw his response. His spine slowly straightened, his shoulders hardened to boulders, and the look he shot Abercairn.... Only in the most technical sense could it be considered a smile. Many teeth were exposed and his lips were twisted up, but friendliness had no part in it.

A delicious shiver rolled over her skin at the ferociousness in his expression.

Abercairn didn't have the same pleasant response. He took a hasty step back, away from the threat. But his purpose was accomplished.

Sin joined the line of men waiting to participate.

"Oh good." Lady Abercairn clapped her gloved hands together. "All the lairds are going to join in the last game. Even your father," she said to Lady Margaret.

"Aye." A worried frown crossed the young woman's face.

Winnifred pushed Banquo off of her lap. Ignoring the pins and needles in her legs, she scooted to the edge of the blanket. The first man, their stablemaster if she wasn't mistaken, stepped forward. A group of men helped him position the log against his shoulder and neck. With a nod from the competitor, the other men stepped back and the stablemaster crouched, sliding his hands down the wood until he could dig his fingers underneath the base. He screwed his face in concentration then stood, cupping the caber in his hands.

He swayed, the massive log weaving in the air. The other competitors roared with laughter as they hopped out of its path. But before it could fall, the man took two running steps and heaved the pole, the tendons on his neck bulging with the effort. The other end of the caber hit the ground and the whole thing crashed into stillness.

A disappointed groan swept over the spectators.

"What was he supposed to do with it?" Winnifred asked Deirdre.

"Toss it head over tail so the end he was holding falls pointing away from him. If the field were a clock, the caber should be landing at the twelve 'o clock position."

Winnifred blinked. "That tree trunk must be at least twenty feet long."

"Close to," Deirdre agreed.

"Depending on the density of the wood, it could weigh two hundred pounds or more!"

"Aye, so not too bad." Deirdre smiled.

"Not so bad...." Winnifred shook her head.

The next man stepped forward, a look of grim determination on his face.

Winnifred glanced at Lady Margaret, wincing. Her father had to be in his fifties and although he still sported a fine figure, he had nowhere near the muscle mass of the younger men.

Lady Abercairn picked another strawberry from the bowl. "If it were easy, anyone could do it. Even the English."

The caber crashed before Lord Brandon could even stand upright. He kicked the dirt in disgust and moved on for the next man to give it a try.

Man after man squatted and heaved, faces growing red, faint Gaelic words that could only be curses drifting up the hill to the spectators.

Lord Abercairn made a decent throw. The caber didn't revolve fully but fell at about a three o'clock position to the earl. Rothchild's throw was next, and there was much debate about whether his caber was nearer to the 2:30 position than Abercairn's or not. The consensus fell to Rothchild's toss being superior, and the crowd groaned good-naturedly at the Sassenach's victory. Until a good Scottish farmer beat him by tossing his log at a solid two o'clock position.

Sin stepped to the caber. Montague made a comment, but his voice was merely the buzz of a fly for all the attention Winnifred paid him. A bruise darkened her husband's cheekbone and his right eye was red and swollen. His green and blue plaid flapped in the breeze, exposing the bottom of his thick thighs. He unwrapped the portion of his tartan that crossed his chest and tossed it aside.

Her breath caught. No barriers between Sin and his goal. Winnifred recognized the focus in his face. The determination. She'd seen it directed at her often enough.

Her shoulders relaxed. Sin wanted to win this competition and so he would. He didn't know how to do anything less.

The log was nestled into a hollow he carved in his shoulder and neck. He squatted low, grasped the base of the caber, and smoothly stood upright. The other end of the caber wavered an inch before Sin brought it under control. He took three running steps and flung the pole into the air.

A hush fell over the crowd as the head of the pole hit the ground. The tail end rolled after it, the caber looking like a metronome as it fell directly away from Sin. He planted his hands on his kilt covered hips, his wide chest heaving and gave a decisive nod.

A roar went up. Men crowded Sin, slapping him on the back.

"Is that it?" Winnifred rolled to her knees, wanting a better look at her husband. He stood a head taller than everyone else and Winnifred was thankful for his massive size. She would never lose him in a crowd. "Did he win?"

"That he did." Deirdre gave a triumphant tilt of her chin to Lady Abercairn, and Winnifred couldn't help the burst of laughter that escaped her lips. She clapped and hooted along with everyone else.

Montague offered her a hand and pulled her to standing. "Is it safe to say you enjoy the Scottish traditions then?"

"Very much so." She turned to the crofter's wife and accepted her congratulations. "Living with my father in Ludgate, I could never have imagined such a life, and now I can't imagine how I could go without. The Scottish are free."

The duke strolled with her down to the playing fields. "That is an unusual sentiment, what with their gripes about the Union. In what way?"

"Free with their expression, with their excitement, with their lo—laughter." Her throat tightened but she cleared that dark emotion away. She wouldn't allow her deficiencies to ruin the moment. "I never realized how constricted the English are, always trying to conform to society's expectations, until I came here."

Montague turned soft grey eyes on her. "I am glad for

my friend that you are content. Glad for you. It amazes me that some of the best matches come about in such surprising ways."

Her cheeks heated at the reminder of her marriage's origin. At how fortunate she was that Sin was the sort of man who let honor guide his actions. That he was the sort of man who strove to make her life as good as possible. Her heart burned. If that wasn't deserving of love, nothing was. So why couldn't she feel it?

Lady Abercairn also wasn't feeling the love. She and her husband stood by the shore of the loch, her finger poking into his chest, her heated words bringing angry or shamed blotches of red to her husband's face.

"Lady Abercairn doesn't appear content with her husband's performance at the games," Montague said mildly.

Winnifred cocked her head. By the ugly twist to the lady's lips, that seemed a great understatement. Winnifred chewed on the inside of her cheek. Why did her husband merely stand there and take the abuse? How much control did Lady Abercairn have over the earl? Winnifred had thought the woman passionate enough of the cause for Scottish independence to support her husband in treason. But perhaps there was more to it.

Lady Abercairn grabbed her husband's elbow and pulled him away, stalking back towards the castle.

Perhaps Lady Abercairn was the ringleader.

* * *

Sin strode into Rothchild's room, Montague a step behind him. Rothchild lay spread-eagle on top of his bed, a soft snore puffing from his lips.

Sin cuffed his friend's boot. "Get up. Good lord, it's only five in the afternoon. Are you getting to the age where you need to nap?"

Rothchild jerked awake. He rubbed his mouth with the back of his hand. "I was only resting my eyes." He stretched, groaning. "And other parts of my body."

Montague straddled the bench at the foot of the bed. "In future, perhaps you should remember that Scottish games aren't for you."

Rothchild raised his head and turned his narrow-eyed glare on the duke. "I only needed some preparation. I've never thrown a bloody log before or run a foot race that involved deadly assaults. Next time Dunkeld holds these games, I'll be ready and I'll win one of them."

"Next time I hold a Highland gathering, you and I will be in our dotage." He pulled a crumpled letter from his pocket. "A courier just arrived. This letter is dated three days past. I don't know why it took so long to arrive from Glasgow, but judging by the stains, it has had a difficult journey." He tossed the missive on Rothchild's stomach and paced the room.

Rothchild sat up, his gaze flicking over the page. "Is Summerset certain? If this were to take place—"

"Then the British economy would collapse." Montague gripped the back of his neck. "A disruption of this size on our currency at a time when crops are already struggling would be devastating."

Sin rested his hands on the top of a window and stared into the fading afternoon. From this room, he could see the corner of Loch Munro, the heather-strewn hill where Winnifred had sat and watched him in his kilt. Mountains rose in the distance, purpling in the approaching night, blunt and beautiful. Just like Scotland.

"You think the rebels intend to destroy Scotland's supply of currency, not merely steal it?" Rothchild asked.

"I'm sure a couple of them will try to sneak a few bills into their pockets." Montague scratched his jaw. "They'd be saints not to. But Summerset indicates the intent of the attack is to destroy, and the number of explosives he discovered was purchased would seem to confirm that."

"If his information is accurate."

"When have you known Summerset to be wrong?" Sin

clenched the stone sill, the chill of the rock doing nothing to cool his ire. Scotland was a strong country with strong people. But this would ruin them, right along with the English economy. "No, the attack is planned. The only question is for when. We need to leave for Edinburgh right away."

"You have a house full of guests." Montague arched a golden eyebrow. "A ball tonight. And a man who needs questioning. Have you forgotten the other part of Summerset's letter?"

No. Sin dug his fingers into the stone until they ached. He hadn't forgotten. "Abercairn is now Liverpool's business. Enough information has been gathered against him to warrant his detention until he answers some questions."

"Still." Rothchild rolled stiffly from the bed and paced over to Sin. "It will be days until he could be taken to London. Days we might not have. He might be able to tell us when the attack is planned. Montague and I will ride ahead to warn the treasury. Your place is here."

Sin pounded the side of his fist against the wall. Damn it, they were right. But simpering through a ball and attempting to flatter intelligence out of Abercairn didn't sit right, not when a fight was brewing in the capital.

"Summerset and Sutton are probably riding here now," Montague said. "Wait and the three of you can join us after your guests have departed. Besides, as you said, there is now enough evidence against Abercairn where you no longer need to use kid gloves when you question him."

Sin brightened. "That's true." Of course, he couldn't just bloody the man in front of all his guests. Some proprieties would need to be observed. He rubbed his hands together. But other than that, the bastard was fair game for his fists.

"Fine," he said. "I agree. Expect me to join you the night after next, hopefully with Sutton and Summerset." All his guests should leave by mid-afternoon on their day of departure. Any stragglers could be left to Winnifred to get rid of. She would do so with efficiency and courtesy, as she handled all obstacles.

He closed his eyes and exhaled, his body sagging. That included unwanted declarations from husbands.

Rothchild clapped his back and chuckled. "You don't have time to daydream about all the rebels you'll get to beat."

Sin turned, forcing his heartache from his features. He attempted a smile, until his friend's next words.

"You have a ball to get ready for."

Sin couldn't fake cheer for that. He dropped his head back and groaned.

Chapter Twenty-Eight

Sin paused in the doorway to the dressing room, his breath hitching. Winnifred's maid was putting the finishing touches on her hair, inserting small, unopened rose buds into the curls styled about her face. The dress she wore exposed a long expanse of neck and the upper edges of her shoulder blades.

Winnifred caught his gaze in the mirror and smiled, her face lighting up.

A vise wrapped around his chest. They could have a very contented marriage if he accepted it as it was. He and Winnifred enjoyed each other's company, respected each other, and rutted like the sheets were on fire. What more could he ask for?

Love.

He needed her love. Her friendship wasn't enough, not for him. But that was a battle he didn't know how to fight. He could control much in life, but not another's emotions.

She thanked her maid and dismissed the girl, leaving them alone. "You look very fine in your evening dress, but I must admit to missing the kilt. You have handsome knees."

A snort of laughter burst past his lips. He went to stand behind her, fingering a lone curl that had been left to dangle enticingly against her shoulder. "That is a compliment I've never heard before, and don't think I need hear again." Needing to touch her, he bent and pressed his mouth against the curve of her neck. "Besides, all the handsomeness is on your part."

She stood and side-stepped around her chair.

Smoothing the end of his cravat under his waistcoat, she quirked an eyebrow. "Who gave you the black eye? Was it in the race?"

He patted the raised skin. It had been such a minor injury he scarce remembered. "No one gave it to me," he said. "I earned it."

She threw her head back and laughed. It wasn't the soft tinkles or melodic titters of so many other women, but a full-throated bark, as honest and straightforward as Winnifred.

And he sank a little deeper into the mire of unreturned love.

Wiping her eyes, she turned to her dressing table and picked up a necklace. "Would you help me with this?" She turned, exposing the back of her neck to him, and held the ruby pendant over her shoulder.

Sin took it and stepped close. He draped the stone over her bosom. The scent rising off her skin muddled his senses. The backs of his fingers brushed the velvety skin of her nape, and his palms went damp.

"Your mother has informed me of all that is expected of a marchioness at this ball, but I offer no guarantees I'll remember the proper order of whom I should dance with or even the dances themselves." She clasped the pendant. "I do hope I don't embarrass you too badly."

"You don't have to worry about that as you won't be dancing with anyone but me." He clasped her shoulders. "To hell with custom."

She turned. "Every dance with you? That hardly seems practicable."

"Well, perhaps one or two with our guests." Why had he ever thought a ball was a good idea? He tugged at the top of her bodice, urging it to cover another inch of skin. "Have you none of those lacey things to go with this?"

She slapped his hand away. "This is a modest gown and doesn't need a fichu. Besides, we both know this ball serves another purpose. Our guests leave the day after tomorrow, and I fear most of them will spend tomorrow abed resting. This might be our last chance to uncover any information about the rebels." She looked down at her bosom. "Perhaps I should change into a lower cut gown to encourage the men to speak."

That wasn't happening. He gave her bodice another tug to no effect. Giving up, Sin pulled a letter from his inside pocket. "I received this from Summerset. He and Sutton uncovered a connection between the Lady Abercairn and Lucien Bonaparte. Apparently, they became acquainted when he was at Worcestershire, and he has since deposited a great deal of money into the lady's accounts." Sin blew out a breath. "Abercairn isn't even fighting for true Scottish independence. He's a lackey for the French. This Bonaparte loves to sow dissent as much as his brother, might even be under the direction of Napoleon. What I don't know is if Lord Abercairn is a true believer who would take help from whatever quarter it arises, or if he is only in it for the money."

Winnifred unfolded the letter, her gaze darting across the page. "This truly is treason."

"It was always treason."

"But—"

"I know." Sin raked a hand through his hair and stalked from one end of the room to the other. "This brings it to a whole other level. Not only the intended attack on the mint in Edinburgh, but the collusion with France."

Winnifred pursed her mouth. "France and Scotland have been allies in the past."

"It is different now. Too many Scotsmen have died in the fields of that country during the war." Sin clenched his fist. He'd known many men, boys really, both Scottish and English who'd spent their blood fighting Napoleon. Too many mothers and wives who would never see their loved ones again. He fought against the rising rage that threatened to swallow him. Hanging was too good for Abercairn.

Sin locked eyes with his wife. "It's different now," he

said quietly.

She refolded the letter and handed it to him. "Are you certain it is Lord Abercairn that you're after? The money did go into his wife's account."

Sin paused. "You think she is the instigator of this madness?" He hadn't considered that, and he should have. He had personal experience with just how clever women could be.

Winnifred shrugged. "Or it is a joint affair. All I know is the countess doesn't seem the type of woman to be either unaware of her husband's activities, or be acquiescent in something she didn't approve of."

The faint strains of music drifted up to them. The ballroom opened up onto the lawn, and Sin knew that even though the double doors were thrown wide, Scottish society would remain safely in the ballroom and his tenants would stay outside. Sin knew where he'd rather be, but he obviously wasn't meant to get what he wanted. His shoulders sagged. "I suppose we should be getting down there." He should just drag the traitor and his wife to his dungeon and force the truth from them. Instead he had to smile and nod and play the host until he could find himself alone with Abercairn.

He cocked his elbow towards his wife. "Shall we get this over with?"

Slipping her hand into the crook of his arm, Winnifred nodded. "We shall. And I daresay our concerns over the evening are overrated. Music, food, and dance. Truly, how bad could it be?"

* * *

Winnifred cursed her words. *How bad could it be?* Had she been trying to taunt the fates? She wasn't one to believe in superstition, but truly, even she knew better than to say something so ill-advised.

She stumbled with a grimace. "I'm most sorry," she said to her dance partner.

Dr. Masson winced before cupping her elbow and leading her down the line with a small limp. "Are ye all right, Lady Dunkeld? Ye seem most distracted this evening."

Winnifred forced her smile even wider, her cheeks aching. "Quite well." The lady to her left began an intricate skipping step around her partner, and Winnifred hurried to catch up. "I must confess that dancing isn't my forte." If only Sin had been her partner. They would have laughed when she trod on his feet. Sin would hold her closer than proper until nothing mattered but the animal heat between their bodies.

But the doctor had asked for her hand in the reel and she couldn't say no. Not to him. Such a refusal at a ball could only appear perverse.

Dr. Masson glanced at her from the corner of his eye, and Winnifred's stomach tilted sideways. She'd thought she'd behaved with all due propriety at the house party, but the doctor's looks were increasing curious. She knew Lady Abercairn was whispering sly innuendos in his ear with her forked tongue.

The last strands of the song faded, and she curtsied to Dr. Masson. She was in no danger; rationally she knew this. She was a married woman, under Sin's protection, and it didn't matter how many physicians thought her mad.

But ever since her mother had been dragged away, that small ball of fear deep within her breast eschewed rationality.

Lord Brandon approached and bowed.

Winnifred swallowed. Was it a conspiracy in this family? Would every male member demand a dance in order to examine her?

"Lady Dunkeld," he said. "If this waltz isnae previously spoken for—"

"It is." A lavender gloved-hand took hers. "The marchioness has promised me this dance. Isn't that right?" Lord Summerset asked, one of his eyebrows raised in a mocking fashion as he faced her.

"Lord Summerset, I did not know you had arrived." She blinked. Not only did the earl's gloves match his silk waistcoat, but his cream cravat was dotted with what appeared to be miniature crops of the same color. She hadn't realized he was such an avid horseman. His jacket and pantaloons were cut from the same satin fabric, a pale primrose. He looked as bright and showy as a peacock. She ran her gaze up and down his outfit several times before remembering her manners. "Welcome back to Kenmore."

"I've only just arrived." The earl clicked his heels together and bowed, kissing the back of her hand. "Your husband is settling Sutton into his room, but I wanted to join the festivities immediately. Shall we?" And without waiting for her answer, he tugged her back onto the dance floor.

Winnifred stared at the swirling couples about her. "As I told Dr. Masson, dancing is not one of my accomplishments."

"Nonsense." Summerset wrapped an arm around her waist and pulled her in closer than was decent. Clasping her right hand, he glided about the floor, his feet in perfect harmony with the rhythm of the music.

With their joined hands, he chucked her chin, drawing her gaze from her feet. "Follow where I lead. You need do nothing more for a successful dance."

The muscles in her back went rigid, and she forced another inch of space between their bodies. "You do think highly of yourself, don't you, my lord?" She had hoped after Glasgow that the man might be a bit less insufferable. Either he still didn't trust her or else insolence was his natural state. "Even being good friends with my husband, I would take care of our distance. That is if you wish to retain use of all your limbs."

The left side of his lips curled up in a lazy smile. "It isn't your husband who concerns me."

He swept her outside the throng of dancers, into an

empty alcove next to the doors to the lawn. A perfect position to remain unheard.

"Meaning I do." Winnifred chewed the inside of her cheek. It was a strange feeling, being a person of concern. "You still believe I entrapped Dunkeld?"

Summerset pushed her hip, twirling her out into a dizzying spin before reeling her back in. "That is no longer relevant. You are married. Sin hopes to make the best of it." Another spin. Another moment where Winnifred tried to gather her bearings. Summerset lowered his head to whisper in her ear. "Do you?"

She slammed her eyebrows together. "I don't understand. Of course, I wish for a successful marriage. Who wouldn't?"

His gaze probed her features, tracing from her eyes to her mouth and back again, as though trying to see beneath her skin into her very brain. "Hosting a successful fête and giving Sin an heir isn't what I understand as success. Beyond that, I would see my friend happy."

She worried the seam of his jacket and stared at his throat. "I want that, too," she said quietly. She raised her gaze to his. "I will do everything in my power to make it so." Everything she was capable of. Her heart she might not be able to control, but her deeds and actions would all be to that purpose.

Summerset pursed his full lips and nodded. "Then I welcome you into our brotherhood, as I should have done upon your marriage."

"Fiend seize it, I turn my back on you for one moment and you're off making advances on my wife." Sin stomped up to them and peeled her hand off his friend's shoulder.

"Better me than Lord Brandon." Summerset flicked a small rose petal from his sleeve. "Besides, I was just telling your wife the secret of how to manage your querulous nature."

Sin proved his friend's accusation correct and growled.

Winnifred grinned, until she caught sight of Dr. Masson

watching her across the room. Her humor died, and she shifted until Sin stood between her and the physician.

"What is it?" Sin looked down at her, his forehead creasing.

"Nothing." She peeked around his chest. Dr. Masson was now joined with his sister, both staring in their direction.

Sin followed her gaze. "Brandon's son?" His body tensed. "Was he improper with you?" Sin pushed her at Summerset then turned for battle. "I swear, I will—"

"Do absolutely nothing." Winnifred stepped in front of him. She shook her head. "You appear to be eager for a fight, but the man did nothing. It is only his occupation that unsettles me."

"Hmm." Sin's body slowly relaxed. He took her hand and squeezed. "You have nothing to fear from him or any man. You should know that by now."

Summerset shifted his weight, and a blush heated her cheeks. Of course, he'd been at that dreadful dinner in Glasgow. He already knew her history, but that didn't stop the wave of shame. She forced her voice into a lightness she didn't feel. "Nothing to fear but traitors and revolution and the future of the United Kingdom."

Summerset snorted. "I'm beginning to quite like your wife, Dunkeld. She might soon become my favorite of the interlopers."

"Interlopers?" she asked.

"Montague's, Rothchild's, and Sutton's wives." Sin rolled his eyes. "Summerset hasn't taken well to our marriages."

The earl opened his mouth to object, but Sin cut him off. "Even though said in jest, Winnifred isn't wrong. Your latest intelligence has underscored our need for haste. I need to confront Abercairn. Tonight. Sutton has agreed to join me in the interrogation. We plan to speak with him after the midnight meal."

Summerset waved over a servant and plucked a glass of

champagne from his tray before shooing the boy away. "Must it be you and Sutton? The two of you aren't noted for your skills in that arena. Why don't you allow me the pleasure?"

"Abercairn has intimated he knows of our activities for the Crown." Sin shook his head. "Sutton has taken himself out of this business; he's only here because I'm involved. It won't matter that he reveals himself. But you wish to continue working for the government. No, if you want to remain a spy, it is best if you keep as low a presence as possible."

Running a hand up the back of his curls, Summerset sighed. "All right, I agree. But if your and Sutton's blunt instrument methods don't work, call me in. I'll be close."

Sin nodded. He looked around the room and frowned. "I only wish your letter had arrived in a timelier manner."

A muscle ticked in the earl's jaw. "The delay was unavoidable."

"I believe you," Sin said. "But it doesn't leave us much time. Montague and Rothchild had to ride hell for leather to Edinburgh to warn of the attack." He snorted. "Poor Rothchild. He could barely climb on his horse. I don't envy him the thirty miles of pain. He was rather banged-up after the games."

"Reeeally." Summerset smirked. "Do tell. I'd like to hear in detail how badly our friend failed so I can mock him later."

Shaking her head, Winnifred tugged Sin away. "We have hosting duties to attend," she said to him. And to Summerset: "And I'm certain there are other games Rothchild excels at."

"Just not vigorous Scottish ones." Sin looked as delighted as a child who'd stolen a pudding.

"He's also never practiced throwing a log before, I'm sure." A pair of young women sat with their backs to the wall, looking hopefully at the dance floor. Winnifred snaked her hand out and grabbed Summerset by the sleeve, pulling him in their wake.

"Caber toss," Sin muttered.

Winnifred ignored that. "Now, gentlemen, before you save the country, there are more pressing matters waiting for your attention. Namely, those two lovely girls haven't danced yet tonight. Go, do something useful."

"I hardly think so," Summerset said.

Her husband whined, "I didn't dance when I was a bachelor. Surely now that I'm married I don't have to submit to such—"

"Stop your nonsense, the both of you." She shoved their backs. "You'll give them a bit of merriment, and that is something Scotland holds in short supply right now." She gave them a stern look. "Go on. Dance now, save the world later."

Summerset tossed back his drink and handed her the empty glass. "I've changed my mind about your wife." But he squared his shoulders and marched into the fray, offering one of the girls his hand. Her face lit up, and she bounced to her feet.

Winnifred nudged her husband. "You too."

Sin inhaled sharply. "You do know I will make you pay for this later."

Her stomach fluttered. "I look forward to it." As far as she was concerned, this night couldn't end soon enough. The stresses of the ball, the investigation, it was all too much. One more day and their guests would be leaving. She could hardly wait.

Making sure no one was watching, she gave Sin a swat on the rear. "Off with you. And good luck." She gripped his wrist. "With everything."

He kissed her cheek. "Like I said, you have nothing to worry about. After tonight, all this will be over, and we can move on with our lives."

He walked away, off to make another wallflower's night, and Winnifred dug a knuckle into her breastbone. She wanted to believe him. She should believe him. When Sin put his mind to something, he didn't let anything get in his way.

But a chill settled in her bones, one that her logical side couldn't reason away.

Chapter Twenty-Nine

Sin threw open another door. It hit the wall and bounced back, but not before he caught sight of what the two occupants inside the east drawing room were doing on the settee.

"Apologies." He grabbed the handle and pulled the door shut. "You might want to lock the door," he shouted through the wood.

"Abercairn isn't in there, I take it." Sutton padded after him as they searched the castle for the elusive earl.

"No," Sin said shortly. That was every drawing room in Kenmore. Where the bloody blazes could Abercairn have gone after dinner? He hadn't joined the other gentlemen for cigars and whisky after the ball. Had he retired already?

The glow from Summerset's candle followed them around the corner, some thirty paces behind. True to his word, his friend was staying close, although the caution was unnecessary. Abercairn would either go quietly, or he'd go unconscious, but after he confessed, he would be leaving for London and Liverpool's retribution. Sin couldn't wait until the man was someone else's problem.

He rounded yet another corner and eased open the next door, not wanting to catch any other couple in a compromising position. He peered inside his private study, and his shoulders hardened. The Earl of Abercairn, Earl of Brandon, and the Viscount Eirlie sat in his leather chairs, drams of whisky in each of their hands. Abercairn lounged with his feet kicked up on Sin's desk.

Son of a— Only Sutton's hand clamped tightly to his

shoulder prevented Sin from tossing the shit sack from his chair.

"Manners are a bit different in the north it would seem." Sutton leaned back against a cabinet, perching his arse on the top edge. "Annexing a man's private study as though it were your own isn't quite the thing."

Brandon had the grace to look embarrassed. He set his glass down and stood. "I believe I'll call it a night. Good evening, gentlemen."

"Come, come, Brandon." Abercairn lifted a cigar from the desk and blew a neat ring of smoke into the air. "We're invited guests. We should be welcome everywhere. Nae need to turn tail and run."

Brandon gave them a tight smile and slipped out the door.

Sutton toed it shut behind him.

Abercairn sighed. "Brandon has always been a wee bit of a disappointment."

Sin gritted his teeth. "I must speak with you, Abercairn. In private."

The man spread his hands. "Eirlie is one of my closest friends. Nothing is private between us."

Was that right? Sin stalked forward and knocked the earl's legs to the floor. "Fine. Have it your way. I frankly don't care about preserving your reputation."

Abercairn arched an eyebrow. "This sounds serious." He leaned back in the chair and laced his fingers together over his stomach, his cigar bobbing in his grip. He grinned at the viscount. "Whatever do ye think the Marquess of Dunkeld could think to impeach me by?"

Sin's temper spiked. "How about twenty thousand pounds deposited into your wife's account from Lucien Bonaparte."

The room stilled. Abercairn raised his cigar and drew deeply.

"Not such a laughing matter, is it?" Sin found the top to his best damn bottle of whisky and shoved it into the bottle.

"Seems rather a paltry sum to turn traitor for the French."

"This isnae true, is it, Ab?" Eirlie scooted to the edge of his seat. "Dunkeld has overindulged, is that it?"

Sin turned his glare on the viscount. "Do I look as though I'm in my cups? This man, who has pretended fidelity to the union of England and Scotland, has been behind the riots, and the assassination attempt on Beaumont, if I'm not mistaken." He turned back to Abercairn. "Well? Have you nothing to say for yourself?"

Abercairn crossed one ankle over his knee and ground the end of his cigar into the sole of his boot. "It sounds as though your mind is already made. What use is there in words?"

Sutton leaned forward. "Unless you have some explanation for the deposits, you'll be arrested. I assure you words can be useful when trying to defend oneself."

Eirlie widened his eyes. "Ab, tell him it's not true." He glared at Sin. "You cannae just threaten an earl with nae facts. Ab, tell him."

Sin turned his back to the viscount and stood over Abercairn. "I can understand your desire for a free Scotland. But ruining our economy along with England's won't lead to independence. You might weaken the union enough to break it, but nothing would remain of Scotland, either." Nothing but mass starvation and societal collapse. Ideal circumstances for a foreign invader. "Joining with the French in order to do so is unconscionable."

The man merely smiled.

"Dear God." Eirlie jerked to his feet. "My brother was killed at Waterloo. How can ye work with those bastards?"

Abercairn gave no response.

Eirlie shook his head. "I have nae love for the French, or anyone who would take orders from them." He set his glass down on the desk, the soft clack echoing through the room, and turned on his heel.

Sutton drew his legs back so the man could pass and gave him a sympathetic nod. He turned back to Sin and

Abercairn, crossing his arms.

A sudden movement, a hiss of fabric, and the sickening sound of metal meeting flesh and bone. Sutton slumped forward onto the carpet, landing heavily on his side.

Sin whirled, only to feel the barrel-end of a pistol press into the back of his head.

Eirlie slapped a short iron rod into the palm of his hand. "Of course, my brother wouldnae have been fighting the French if it wasnae for the filthy English."

Sin flexed his hands, the urge to thrash and beat overwhelming.

Eirlie slipped his weapon into a pocket and pulled out his own pistol. He pointed it at Sutton's prone body.

Abercairn pressed the muzzle into Sin's head. "As ye see, I am not the one without friends here. Perhaps we should have that talk. I need to know what ye do. And who ye've told." He nodded at Eirlie, and the man threw the lock on the door.

The click echoed hollowly in Sin's ears, the metallic ping holding a dread sense of finality.

Sin ground his back teeth. He'd been a fool thinking his size and home-castle advantage would suffice in a confrontation with Abercairn. Or that the man wouldn't have accomplices.

He looked down at his prone friend, relieved to see Sutton's back rise and fall in a steady rhythm. He was alive. But for how long?

Sin's insufferable arrogance might have pounded the nails into both their coffins.

Chapter Thirty

Winnifred paced her bed chambers. Her night rail tangled at her ankles when she spun, and she kicked at the hem. Where was he? The last log in the fireplace popped, and Winnifred glared at it. Sin should have been back hours ago, following through on his promise to make her pay for the dance she'd forced upon him. She'd waited, first curious at his delay, then impatient, and now distracted beyond reason.

Something must be wrong. It shouldn't take this long to present a man with evidence against him and hear his defense.

She clutched the thick bedpost. Unless he'd put up some sort of fight. Abercairn had brought seven servants with him, plus his friends among the guests. Enough men to be able to cause trouble.

She strode to her dressing room and pulled a thick coat from the closet, pulling it on over her night dress and wrapper. She grabbed a lamp and marched out of her room and down the steps to the main floor.

The castle was eerie this time of night. All of the lights were turned down. No servants cheerily bustled about. Perhaps she should rouse Horatio and Banquo from their sleeping spot in the kitchen. She would feel better with their large presences by her side, even if they were cowards at heart.

And once she woke them there would be no need for them, she reminded herself. Because they'd rouse half the castle with their noise, and she wouldn't be wandering the halls alone.

Lengthening the wick on her lamp, Winnifred squared her shoulders and started searching rooms. Everything in the south wing was quiet, and she turned for the east one. Drawing room, empty. Library, empty. Her parlor, as quiet as the grave. She should—

Winnifred paused, squinting. Was that a candle glowing down the next corridor? She set the lamp down on a hall table and crept to the hallway corner. She waited for her eyes to adjust to the darkness before peering around the edge of the wall.

A figure knelt in front of the door to her husband's study, probing at the lock. A figure wearing a primrose coat.

Winnifred tiptoed up behind him. She reached out to tap the earl's shoulder.

Summerset whirled, knocking her hand away. He slid his palm to her throat, squeezing so tight neither sound nor air could pass.

She had a moment of panic, but as quickly as he struck, Summerset released her and stepped back. "I apologize," he said in a low voice. "You are unharmed?"

Winnifred rubbed her neck, her heart beat slowing from a gallop to a trot. She nodded. "Is my husband in there?" she whispered.

"Yes, he and Sutton." Kneeling again, he pushed the candle into her hand. "Hold this and be silent." The earl pressed his ear to the keyhole, listening intently. He tried the latch, but the door didn't budge. Pressing his lips together, Summerset shook his head. "I hear nothing. I hadn't expected Dunkeld and Sutton to be so quiet in their interrogation, nor for it to take this long." A wrinkle creased between his eyebrows.

Winnifred looked over her shoulder but saw only black. "Are you certain he is within? He should have been abed an hour ago."

"Questioning a suspect can take time," he murmured. "It's delicate work, best not rushed." Rising, he eyed the door as though it were a puzzle.

Sweat gathered at the small of her back. "Yes, but my husband isn't delicate. Nor patient."

She and Summerset shared a look, her worry mirrored in his eyes.

"Blast it all." He squared off against the door. "Stand back," he warned a second before he launched a front kick, the heel of his boot splintering the wood near the handle. He kicked again, the crack as startling as a gunshot, and the door bounced inward.

Into complete darkness.

No, not complete. Winnifred followed Summerset in. The candles had all either burned out or been snuffed out, but a faint, silvery light came in through the open window.

"This isn't possible." Summerset stalked around the room, examining each nook and corner. "I watched Dunkeld and Sutton enter this room, and they never left." He pressed against the bookcase. "Any servants' passages?"

Winnifred shook her head before realizing he couldn't see her. "No, at least none that I've been told about." A book lay face down on the rug, its pages bending, and Winnifred knelt to retrieve it. The light from her candle caught on a dark stain on the cream rug. "Summerset! Is this blood?" She brought the light as close as possible.

He squatted down and ran his finger over the blotch. He nodded, grim. "How in the blazes did they get out of here without my seeing?"

"The window." Winnifred hurried over. "There's no other option."

"Look at the size of that window and think on the size of your husband's shoulders." Summerset fisted his hips. "Not likely."

"Likely or no, it's the only option. See!" A bit of fabric clung to the raised head of a nail in the window's frame. "Someone went through here."

Summerset pulled it free and held it to her light. His nostrils flared. "Your husband and Sutton would have to be willing to squeeze through this space. Or unconscious. They damn sure couldn't have been forced through if they put up a fight." He stared out the window, his features hardening, his gaze sharpening like a hawk's on a hare.

A shiver ran down her spine, and she didn't know if it was fear for her husband, or for whoever would have to face the Earl of Summerset.

"Go back to your room," he told her. "I'll take care of this."

"You think you can search the entire grounds of Kenmore by yourself?" Her mind whirled, thinking where two large, angry men could be held captive.

Or where their bodies might be stored.

Bile rose up her throat, choking her. She forced away the panic. "Let's consider this logically. We're agreed Abercairn has them?"

"Lady Dunkeld." Summerset gripped her elbow. "Winnifred. Go upstairs."

She jerked free. "Why? Because a woman couldn't be of any assistance in this situation?"

"No, because your husband will murder me if any harm comes to you."

Her temples throbbed, and she rubbed them with her fingers. "Let's worry about that when we find him." She wouldn't contemplate the alternative. That they might not find him, at least not alive.

She dug her nails into her palm. "Are we agreed we focus on Lord Abercairn?"

Summerset's gaze on her was long, too long for the urgency of the situation, but at the end of his assessment, he nodded. "We're agreed."

She paced to the cold fireplace and strode back. "And he must have had assistance to subdue Sin and Sutton?"

"Absolutely."

She made the march to and fro again. "Abercairn would need to hide their... their bodies until he had taken his leave of Kenmore. He wouldn't want to be stuck here for any investigation."

Summerset took his candle from her and lit another. "I'm disappointed. For such an analytical mind, you've not considered all the options."

His sneery tone made her skin flush with anger. A feeling much more pleasant than the desperation that jockeyed to claim her in its grip. Which was probably his intent with his insult. Even knowing that, Winnifred couldn't keep the pique from her voice. "What's that?"

"That Abercairn would want the information your husband and Sutton hold, as much as we wanted his intelligence." Summerset prowled into the hallway. "He'll keep him alive. At least until he gets the answers he wants."

Winnifred hurried after him. "Until then?" They stopped at an exit that led outside.

"Until then we search." He nodded towards the door. "I'll follow what tracks I can. Rouse the servants. Tell them their master has gone missing. We'll need every set of eyes we can get."

Chapter Thirty-One

The household was in an uproar. Trousers were pulled on beneath banyans. Maids in their wrappers hurriedly lit every lamp and candle in Kenmore. Guests gathered in confused huddles outside their bedroom doors.

Deirdre held a tight grip on Winnifred's hand as she and Tavish organized a search party.

Winnifred stared at the door to Abercairn's bedchambers. The earl stood in front of it, his arm around his wife, looking as sleepy as everyone else.

Winnifred didn't believe it. Was Sin even now hidden in that room? Injured? Unable to call for help?

"I want a count of every guest and servant in the castle," she interrupted her mother-in-law. Someone had to be standing guard over her husband and Sutton. "If anyone is missing, I want to know." She stared at Abercairn as she said it, but he didn't flinch. Merely gave her a sympathetic smile.

"Aren't we searching for your missing husband?" Lady Abercairn asked. "Just how many people do you think have disappeared?"

"Aren't two missing men enough?" Winnifred stepped towards the woman, her fingers curled into claws, but Deirdre pulled her back.

"Your husband and his friend are probably stumbling around outside in a drunken revel." Lady Abercairn pulled her wrapper tighter about her. "I don't see why we have to indulge your delusions at the expense of our sleep. Dr Masson, can't you do something?"

A chill started in Winnifred's stomach, expanding like ice over a pond, until her whole body shook from the cold. So many looks of concern. Of pity and suspicion. All directed at her. The walls tilted closer, and her heartbeat thrummed in her ears. Was this how her mother had felt? In the moments when she'd been rational but everyone treated her as though still mad?

She should sit with Deirdre, wait for Tavish to conduct his search. Wait for news of Sin. It was the logical response, the one a marchioness would take. One more pair of eyes wouldn't be of any great benefit in the search, and she'd be safe from censure.

She stiffened. With Sin as her husband, the censure of others was of no concern. No matter how far outside the bounds of society she danced, he would protect her.

And if your husband is dead? Who keeps you from Bedlam then?

"Those of ye who wish to join the search," Deirdre called out, "your aid will be most appreciated. The rest of ye, go back to bed. There's nae use in everyone losing sleep." She patted Winnifred's hand. "Come along, daughter. We'll help cook brew coffee for the men who are searching."

The voice she always listened to, the sensible one, the safe one, agreed with her mother-in-law's words. Urged her to take heed. She'd survived this long by obeying that voice.

Lady Abercairn rolled her eyes and turned for her door.

And Winnifred told that voice to go to hell.

She pulled free from Deirdre, stumbling forward, her legs carrying her faster and faster down the hall until she was sprinting. She smacked her hand against Lord Abercairn's door before it could swing shut. He turned, his eyes widening in surprise as she pushed her way in.

"I will search your chambers, proprieties be damned." Ignoring his bleats of protest, Winnifred tore through the room, opening every closet and cupboard. Falling to her stomach to peer under the bed.

"Really, this is too much," the earl said. Winnifred didn't bother to see to whom he spoke. "The marchioness has gone mad."

She clawed a loose hank of hair off her face and spun, looking for any possible hiding place.

"Dr. Masson, do something," Lady Abercairn whined.

"Lady Dunkeld." The physician laid a gentle hand on her arm. "Ye are unwell. Let me get a glass of wine to settle your nerves."

She shook him off and hurried to the window. She knew her husband couldn't be hidden behind the curtains. The drapes hung too straight and Sin would surely leave a bulge. But she pushed the fabric aside nonetheless, determined to leave no stone unturned.

Chest heaving, she scanned the room. Nothing. Nothing else large enough to contain a man. "Your friends' rooms."

"Now, Lady Dunkeld," Dr, Masson said, reaching for her, "ye are becoming quite excited. Let's—"

Winnifred dipped her chin and, with her glower, dared him to touch her.

The doctor took a quick step back.

Her chest heaved. She didn't care that each second only convinced those around her that she truly was cracked. She gave barely a moment's consideration to the fact that if she didn't find Sin, alive and well, her behavior could lead her to be committed.

Just like your mother.

She didn't care. Her husband was missing and she would do whatever it took to find him. Risk anything because....

Her feet stumbled over each other as she pushed past Deirdre to the next room to search.

Because she loved the foolish, stubborn, passionate man?

She tossed clothes aside, having zero patience in keeping Lord Brandon's wardrobe ordered.

Was it love that she felt? This panicking, sick feeling

deep in her gut? Did love create a vise around her chest which squeezed more and more air from her each moment that passed with his whereabouts unknown?

She ran to the next room. She had no experience in the emotion, but through a process of elimination she deduced the feeling swamping her must be it. She understood friendship and admiration, had felt those emotions many times before and this wasn't either of those.

Love wasn't pleasant, though she knew once she had her arms wrapped around Sin every twist of her guts would transform into bliss. Knew that there was no other man who could make her a fraction as happy as he did. Why had it taken her so long to understand this?

Slender but strong arms wrapped around her waist from behind. "Child," Deirdre said softly. The sympathy in her voice was almost Winnifred's undoing.

"He doesn't know." Winnifred gulped down air. "He doesn't know that I love him."

"He kens." Deirdre tucked her chin on Winnifred's shoulder and squeezed her waist.

They were the words of someone intent on comforting, but there was no truth behind them. Sin didn't know. Because until moments ago, Winnifred hadn't known. Until faced with the prospect of having everything she loved torn away from her, she hadn't allowed herself to feel the emotion deeply enough to understand.

She drew her hands into fists. Raising her chin, she ignored the pitying and disgusted looks and pulled away from Deirdre. "Every room in this castle will be searched," she said loudly, making sure Tavish and the servants heard. "And I am going to help," she told her mother-in-law. She was the marchioness, damn it. In Sin's absence, she controlled the household. Her orders would be followed.

Deirdre's deep blue eyes, so like her son's, flicked back and forth between her own. Finally, she nodded. "And I will help ye."

The back of Winnifred's throat burned. Such a small

show of support, yet it was enough. Taking Deirdre's hand, Winnifred loosed a tremulous breath and nodded.

She gathered all her raging emotions together, stifling them, snapping locks down on the parts that threatened to undo her, make her useless for the hours ahead. She wrapped her logic back around herself, holding onto it like a warm blanket on a cold winter's night. It was her mind, not her heart, that would help find Sin.

She faced the next bedchamber door. "Let's get to work."

Chapter Thirty-Two

Winnifred slouched on the parlor's armchair, one leg tossed over the armrest, and tapped the blade of a dirk onto her palm. She'd picked up the dagger when she'd searched Kenmore's dungeon. She turned the antique weapon over, a bit of rust on the handle scratching her palm. The weight of it was soothing when nothing else that night had been.

Summerset brought her a steaming cup of dark brown liquid.

Winnifred looked up at him, her eyes taking too long to focus. "I don't drink coffee."

"You do this morn."

Winnifred took the cup. The brew smelled heavenly but tasted as bitter as hellfire. She drank it regardless.

"They must have had horses standing by and removed Dunkeld and Sutton from the estate." Summerset paced to the fireplace and stirred the logs into higher flames. The weak morning sunlight caught his profile, exposing deep fatigue lines around his eyes and mouth.

"What horses?" Winnifred took another sip, no longer noticing the taste. "We spoke to the stablemaster. Two of the grooms were awake all night playing cards. No one snuck any of their horses past them."

"Then they rented the animals from Inver." Summerset picked up a small glass vase from the mantel, one of Deirdre's treasures, and glared at it.

"Tavish sent men to the village, too. No horses are unaccounted for." They had to still be on Dunkeld property. She rubbed her forehead and set her cup on an end table. She knew she would have to give the order to her steward to drag the loch, but she couldn't. Not yet. Not until no further hope remained.

Summerset twisted, hurling the vase against the far wall. The crash of glass exploding sounded behind her, but Winnifred didn't turn. She kept her gaze on the earl.

"Whatever happened isn't your fault." She should rise and go to him but her legs didn't want to move.

Summerset shot her a disgusted look and raked a hand through his hair.

She dropped her head on the seatback. "What would any of them have done differently than you? No one would have expected both Sin and Sutton to be overwhelmed and taken through a window. It is only the fault of those who took them."

His only answer was to pick up another vase, this one full of flowers, and throw it against the wall, too.

"*When* we find Sin, he won't appreciate your having destroyed his home." But she understood the earl, even found some temporary solace in his acts of destruction. The violence perfectly mirrored her feelings, as well.

"I dunnae appreciate it, either." Deirdre strode into the room, the skirts of her gown swishing. "I took a lot of care in growing those flowers. It doesnae do any good to throw a fit like a child."

"Yes, my lady." Summerset turned his back on them, crossing his arms as he faced out the window.

"Now," Deirdre said, rubbing her hands together, "ye need to go up and get dressed, my dear. The guests are starting to leave and it's important that ye bid them farewell." *Like a sane person* went unsaid.

"Leaving a day early? All because their hostess accused them of kidnapping? How banal." Winnifred pushed to unsteady feet. She gripped the handle of the dirk. "I fear that no amount of proper fare-thee-wells will alter anyone's opinion of me now. The die has been cast." And she felt nothing. One of their guests could petition for her incarceration, and it wouldn't matter. Not at this moment. The logical part of her brain knew this was nonsense. That even if she lost Sin, she wouldn't wish to be trapped in Bedlam when the grief eased. But she told that part of herself to stuff it.

"I don't know if I can handle Lord and Lady Abercairn's smug faces." She pressed her free hand to her belly. "They did something to my Sin, and they won't be brought to account."

"No." Summerset jerked his chin over his shoulder to look at her. "Once Liverpool receives my communiqué, he will have them picked up and held until the prime minister decides what to do with them. Whatever has happened, they will not come out of this unscathed. I promise you this."

"Ye should rest." Deirdre's smile wobbled but didn't fall. "I'll stand in your stead and see our guests off."

Yes, that would be the easy thing to do. Avoid the curious and triumphant stares. But something perverse in herself balked. She'd take every cut. Every sneer. Because those insults were somehow still a connection to Sin. If she went to her room and closed the door, there would be... nothing.

"I'll do my duty." She shuffled from the room, with Deirdre and Summerset following only a step behind. Probably worried she'd collapse at any moment and need to be caught.

When she turned for the front doors instead of the staircase, Deirdre squeaked. "But ye must change."

"My night rail covers more than some of those ladies' gowns." She nodded as the footman opened the door for her. His lips twitched. At least her behavior brightened one person's day.

Lady Margaret stood by the door, waiting for her party's luggage to be loaded onto their carriage. Lady Eirlie was beside her. They both gasped when Winnifred marched down the front steps, her wrapper billowing out about her.

Lady Abercairn snickered and raised her fan to cover her mouth. She waited in front of her carriage in a traveling gown. Her husband stood next to her, berating the footmen for not properly securing their trunks to the coach behind them.

He turned at his wife's laughter, his face darkening when he caught sight of Winnifred. "I take no leave of ye or your husband, madam. Ye deserve no such attentions after the abominable treatment we've received. Whenever he sobers up, tell Dunkeld to expect words from me."

Her heart lurched. She wanted to believe him, desperately so, that her husband lay somewhere sleeping off too much drink.

But she didn't.

"I will find my husband," she told him. "And you will pay for what you have done." She could only pray it would be Sin doling out the punishment.

Abercairn snorted and turned for the carriage's door. He moved to hand his wife in, but paused when a hatbox tumbled to the ground from the rear coach. A footman reached for it, his grip slipping from the end of the trunk he held. Forgoing the hatbox, he readjusted his grip on the trunk and tried to lift it up to the servant kneeling on the luggage rails on the coach's roof.

"Take care!" Abercairn glared. Another footman rushed over to help, and they managed to heft the trunk to the top of the vehicle.

The cheerful yellow-and-pink-striped paper lining the trunk turned Winnifred's stomach. She recognized the feminine luggage from Lady Abercairn's arrival. Everything about the woman was outwardly lovely, but her insides didn't match.

Winnifred frowned. Something about that trunk.... She reached for the memory but it slipped through her grasp.

Lady Abercairn disappeared inside her carriage, and her husband climbed in after her. Their driver pulled up the steps and shut the door.

Winnifred dragged her gaze back to the top of the coach. A footman strapped everything down and patted Lady Abercairn's trunk before hopping to the ground. Winnifred tapped the dirk against her thigh. It was merely an obnoxious trunk. She needed to stop thinking about it and find her husband, damn it.

But her gaze turned inexorably back to the yellow-and-pink behemoth, as though drawn with a magnet.

And then it clicked.

What her brain had been trying to tell her.

The trunk was a cheery monstrosity, one that a person could never miss.

And one that hadn't been in the lord and lady's chamber when Winnifred had searched it.

"Stop!" She threw up her hand, and the Abercairn's driver jumped back from the waving blade.

Lord Abercairn lowered the window and poked his red face through. "What now?"

Winnifred raced to the rear of the coach. "Summerset! Help me."

The earl hurried to her side, his eyebrows drawn together. "What is it?"

"The trunks." She stabbed the dirk into the side of the carriage and tried to pull herself up with it. "I never checked any of their trunks. Did you?"

"Son of a—" Without another word, Summerset grabbed her hips and lifted her to the roof, scrambling up behind her.

"Get off my carriage!" Abercairn opened the carriage door and climbed out. "You cannae—"

"Watch us." Summerset pulled a knife from his boot and cut through the leather straps holding the luggage.

Winnifred wedged the blade of the dirk under the lid of the pink-and-yellow trunk and forced it open. A black superfine man's coat met her gaze, one replete with a body. Sutton's face was turned away, but his dark hair and bushy beard identified him.

Summerset pressed his fingers to the baron's neck. "He lives."

She covered her mouth with her hand. It wasn't Sin, but relief crashed through her nonetheless. If Sutton was here, so was her husband.

"Sutton." Summerset cut through the ropes around the baron's wrists and ankles and tugged out the gag. He shook the man's shoulder. "Can you hear me?"

No response.

Summerset turned. "Tavish, arrest Lord Abercairn. Hold him until we can bring the authorities."

Winnifred turned to the next trunk, prying it open. She threw the gowns and corsets onto the ground. "Sin!" She scrambled to the edge of the carriage, and Summerset grabbed her wrist, lowering her down. "Sin!"

A large brown trunk on Lord Eirlie's carriage jolted. One of Kenmore's footmen darted forward, and the viscount pulled a pistol from his coat. The footman froze.

"Eirlie, what is the meaning of this?" his wife asked. Lady Eirlie stepped off the stairs, a deep vee creasing her forehead.

Her husband ignored her. Lady Margaret took the woman's hand and tugged her back, huddling by her side.

Lord Abercairn drew his own pistol, aiming it at Summerset. Abercairn's and Eirlie's servants shifted uneasily before forming a barrier around their masters.

"Come now, Abercairn." Lord Brandon stepped in front of his daughter. "You're frightening the women. Lay doon your weapons."

The brown trunk bounced, shifted to the edge of the carriage's roof.

Winnifred stifled a moan. She stepped towards Eirlie's carriage, and the report of a gun cracked through the air, pulling her up short.

"Dunnae tempt me, Lady Dunkeld." Two points of color rode high on Abercairn's cheeks. "Ye think your clever, don't ye?"

She looked from the pistol to the trunk and back again. "Yes, of course, but my cleverness has nothing to do with your downfall. Listen to Brandon and lay down your weapons before you make matters worse for yourself." A flash of white hair caught her attention as Tavish slunk into the castle. "You've lost, and all that remains is how deep a grave you wish to dig for yourself."

Lady Abercairn hovered in the open door of the carriage. "Abby, we should leave immediately."

Abercairn strode forward and jerked Winnifred's arm. The dirk fell from her grip, a puff of dust billowing in the air where it hit the dirt. "Aye, and you're coming with us."

"In my night rail?" A high-pitched giggle slipped out of Winnifred's mouth. She clapped a hand over her lips. Her blood pulsed sluggishly through her veins, making her limbs heavy, and she giggled again. Confound it, now was not the time to succumb to a case of nerves. She felt like she had when she'd drunk the wine she'd stolen from Lord Stamworth's cellar.

The night she'd met Sin.

The night her life had begun.

Her gaze flew to Eirlie's coach, and she tugged on her arm to no avail.

"Release her, *Abby.*" Summerset jumped to the ground, his lips pulled back, baring his teeth.

Abercairn leveled the pistol on Summerset. "If ye try to stop my carriage, Lady Dunkeld will die. Is that understood?"

The brown trunk rattled, bounced.

Winnifred twisted her wrist back and forth, but Abercairn's grip held fast. Could Sin breathe in there? Was he losing the use of his limbs from being folded into such a small space?

The trunk lurched, hopped, and plummeted from its perch onto the ground. The wood splintered, the lid popped open, and her husband rolled onto the dirt.

His blackeye was now swollen closed, and dried blood

crusted half his face from a cut on his forehead. His auburn hair hung in disarray around his shoulders and his cravat was bunched under his chin. His one good eye found her, locking on her with an expression so intense it stole her breath.

He kicked free from the cloth binding his ankles and drew himself up, a titan rising. His gaze shifted to the pistol in Abercairn's hand. The tendons in Sin's neck bulged, and with a roar, he yanked his hands apart, his bonds splitting in two.

Lord Eirlie stepped forward and pointed his gun at Sin. "Calm yourself. We—"

Without turning his head, Sin threw his fist to the side and punched the viscount in the jaw. The man crumpled. Sin staggered forward, his left leg buckling under his weight. He caught himself, straightened, and took another step, dragging his leg behind him. His movement forward was slow and deliberate, his rage a living thing.

"Get in here!" Lady Abercairn yelped.

Abercairn shifted, placing Winnifred's body between him and her husband. "Unless ye want more blood to be shed, I'd suggest ye stop right there, Dunkeld."

Stagger forward, straighten, drag his useless leg. Sin took another limping step towards them, inexorable. He looked a man possessed, and each foot he gained appeared hard-fought and painful. Stagger, straighten, drag.

Abercairn nodded at one of his servants, and the young man bounded over to intercept her husband.

Winnifred winced at the crack of bone, the crumple of the young man's body.

Stagger, straighten, drag. Her husband kept coming.

Abercairn aimed the barrel of the pistol over her shoulder, taking aim at her husband, and something nameless clawed through her body. Something feral.

Her mind went white. Twisting, she bared her teeth and sank them into his wrist, biting down until she tasted blood.

Abercairn screamed and dropped the pistol.

She brought her knee up, right into the center of his falls, and the blackguard's eyes and mouth rounded in identical circles. His face drained of blood. With a pathetic squeak, he clutched his ballocks and tilted sideways, crumpling to the ground. Winnifred stomped on his chest, his thighs, his shoulder, wishing she wore something deadlier than slippers. All of her fury, her despair, she unleashed onto his curled body. Every blow she landed exorcised some of the terror that had choked her since Sin had disappeared.

Gentle hands encircled her shoulders, pulling her back, away from Abercairn and into a firm, warm, and breathing body. Sin turned her, folding her into his arms and holding her until her body stopped shaking. Leaning back, he examined her from head to toe.

He loosed a jagged sigh and tucked her into his side. Lips pressed into a white slash, he glared down at the whimpering heap at their feet.

Summerset joined them. "I never thought I'd see the day. The mighty Marquess of Dunkeld, saved by a woman."

Sin growled.

"Abercairn fell without you even landing a finger on him." Summerset smirked. "You must be taking this very ill."

"You!" Lady Abercairn pointed to one of her servants. "Bring Abercairn inside here." She glared at Sin. "Do not think you can stop us. With all our servants, we outnumber you."

"Count again, milady." Tavish marched through the front door, an antique breastplate over his livery, a rifle notched against his shoulder. Every male servant of Kenmore who hadn't been in attendance spilled out of the castle behind him. They fell into formation around the steward, each one bearing a weapon from the armory. Rifles were leveled, swords pointed. Even a mace was raised in defiance. Kenmore's own army had arrived.

Lady Abercairn paled, and drew back into her carriage,

slamming the door shut. Those in service to Eirlie and Abercairn raised their hands in surrender.

"And now saved by your servants." Summerset planted his foot on a carriage wheel spoke and slid his blade back into his boot. "Truly, what use are you?"

Sin bent and grabbed the front of Abercairn's jacket. He raised him with one hand and pounded him in the face with the other. He threw him back to the ground with a grumble. "Enough. I will pound the living hell out of my enemies later, and that might include you if you don't watch your tongue."

Summerset grinned.

Sin held Winnifred's face between his palms. "Tell me you're all right."

She nodded and wrapped her hands around his wrists, afraid to let him go. "You?"

"Irritated beyond measure that I was incapacitated and stuffed into a trunk."

Summerset hopped back on the coach. "Sutton needs a physician."

Dr. Masson pushed through the Kenmore footmen and rushed forward. "Let's get him oot of there and bring him inside."

Several men worked together to carry Sutton down. Deirdre led the way into Kenmore, calling for bandages and water to be boiled.

It was over.

Winnifred's knees went weak, and she tightened her grip on her husband's wrists. Sin was bruised and bloodied, but he was whole. Safe.

Hers.

She pressed her lips into his palm and whispered, "I love you."

Sin's good eye swiveled back to her face, flaring wide. His chest heaved. "Repeat that."

A grin stretched her face. Repeat it? She wanted to shout it to the uppermost turret.

"I love you." She stepped close, leaning into him. "I'm sorry it took me so long to recognize it. That I ever believed that what I felt for you was merely friendship. When I thought I might never see you again, or have the chance to tell you...." She swallowed, her throat burning. "Don't ever disappear on me again. I cannot survive another night like—mmff!"

Sin cut her off with a kiss. His mouth crashed down upon hers. Their teeth knocked together, and she tasted the tang of blood on her husband's lips. She didn't care. The kiss was hungry, one meant for the bedroom and not for broad daylight in front of God and servants and shocked guests. It mattered not.

Threading her fingers into his hair, she kissed him back with all she was worth. Gave him every moment of fear, every hope she held for their future. Every drop of love in every molecule in her body she revealed to him in that kiss.

Her husband was returned. They'd married as strangers, but against all odds she loved him and he loved her.

She must be as mad as her mother because life didn't get any crazier than that.

Chapter Thirty-Three

Winnifred curled closer into his side, her hand tucked tight between the buttons of his waistcoat. The scent of oranges teased his nose, and Sin breathed deep. A stone under the blanket they lay on dug into his side, but he disregarded the ache. He never wanted to move, not with the woman he loved lying next to him.

The woman who loved him.

Sighing, he reread the last paragraph in the letter. His eyes had moved over the words, but he hadn't comprehended a one of them.

His wife's presence tended to have that effect.

He set aside the designer's note. A seal with Winnifred's very own coat of arms was on its way, and Sin couldn't wait to surprise her with it. A badger, with its teeth bared, sitting in front of the letter *D* seemed appropriate. Winnifred stood guard over the Dunkeld name, and its men, as ferociously as their badger did the tunnel.

For the service the badger had performed in chasing away MacConnell when he'd threatened Winnifred, Sin had decided to allow the beast to remain.

That, and the fact he still hadn't been able to catch the slippery devil. Sin sniffed, and picked up the letter from Sutton.

Winnifred finger-walked her hand up his abdomen, slipping under his cravat and finding its way to bare skin.

"When you dragged me outside for this picnic, you did say I could read my correspondence," he reminded her. Not that his complaint had any teeth. Any time Winnifred wanted to express her affection, he would revel in it. The intimate gazes, the whispered *I love you's*, all were coming more frequently, but each gesture was precious to him. His wife could declare her love morning, noon, and night, and he would still be greedy to hear it.

Sliding her leg over his, Winnifred protested. "I haven't said a word while you've read your letters." She rocked her hips into his thigh, the heat between her legs felt even through their clothes. "Has everyone involved in the plot been apprehended? And has Lady Eirlie made it safely back to Spain? I am sorry for her. She had no idea her husband was such a scoundrel."

The sly minx. Sin knew her game. And she played it well, trying to seduce him while pretending innocence to the effects of her actions.

Well, he could play, too.

"Shall I read you the letter?" he asked as he dropped his free hand to her knee. He inched the material of her gown up as he read her the high points. "Lady Eirlie is back in Spain and seeking a divorce, which I believe she will have little trouble obtaining. The three men who were to attack the mint are facing charges in Edinburgh. Abercairn and his associates have been removed to London, however, for trial." Including that bastard MacConnell. Sin still owed him a debt of honor. Although he had to admit, each blissful day that passed at Kenmore with Winnifred by his side, the urge to exact his revenge lessened. And besides, killing the man might anger Winnifred. One thing he'd learned in his short marriage was that if his wife was happy, so was he.

Perhaps just a healthy beating if the man ever stepped foot outside of prison.

Sin finally found silky skin. He dragged the pads of his fingers up her leg to dip in the crease where thigh met cunny.

She sucked in a breath.

Sin bit back a smile, pleased with his triumph. Until her hand began exploring, too. She stroked him through his trousers until his cock hardened.

Sin cleared his throat and forced himself to focus. "This bit of intelligence won't please you. Lady Abercairn has foresworn her husband, declaring no knowledge of his subversive activities. As the earl has yet to speak against her, Liverpool feels he has no choice but to release her from custody."

"What?" She removed her devilish hand and rolled onto her side to glare down upon him. "She was just as involved as her husband, if not more so. I believe she was the one who reigned in that marriage."

Sin took her hand and put it back where it belonged. "I don't doubt it, *mo chridhe*. Lord knows I would do anything for you. But we are a nation of laws, and if there is no evidence, there can be no conviction."

"Hmph." But she settled back against his side and resumed her tantalizing strokes. "You wouldn't betray your people and your country for a woman."

No, but Winnifred would never ask him to, either. For something she truly wanted, there was no limit to what he wouldn't do to give it to her.

"Ah, here's a bit of good news." A breeze ruffled the page, and Sin snapped it straight. "Sutton requests three copies of your planting guide when you've finished writing it. He and two other landowners he knows would like to implement your findings."

She huffed. "My research isn't completed. It is still too soon for there to be any findings in my experiment at the Fraser's farm. You give me too much credit to your friends."

That hardly seemed possible. "But you will send him the guides when you've finished?"

She kissed his jaw. "Yes, I'll send him the copies."

A groan escaped him as a cool breeze met his hot skin. Winnifred released the last button on his falls and took him in hand. She gripped his base, squeezing snuggly, and twisted her wrist as she fisted his length up and down.

Sin's eyes rolled back in his head. Sweet Saint Mungo. The woman was going to be the death of him.

But not before he returned the favor. Grabbing her hips, he pulled her on top of him so she straddled his stomach, his letter buried under her skirts. "Enough nonsense, woman. Ride me."

She widened her eyes innocently. "But I wish to hear the rest of the letter."

Grumbling, Sin crumpled the missive into a ball and tossed it away. He lifted her until her center hovered over his cock. His crown dipped between her lips, but she held herself away.

"I have a bit of good news myself," she said.

He groaned. Now was not the time for conversation. Unless her news involved an invitation for him to—

"I am increasing."

Sin's mouth dropped open. He blinked. "Are you certain?"

Her eyes twinkled. "Fairly so."

Sin shouted in triumph. He rolled, holding himself between her splayed legs. "I'm going to be a da." He crawled backwards and rested his face against her abdomen.

"And a very good one, too." Winnifred widened her legs. "But you're still a husband. My husband. Don't forget your duties to me."

Sin chuckled. Warmth radiated through his body, his thoughts a scattered mess. Except for two.

He was going to be a father.

And his wife hungered for his attention.

Both of these things thrilled him.

He eased back and buried his face in her heat. He licked and nipped, loving the taste of her. The scent. The moans spilling from her mouth as readily as the honey from her core.

He raised his head. "Say it again," he ground out. He'd demanded she say the words every day. Sometimes they came easily; other times she made him work for it.

Winnifred sucked one finger into her mouth then lowered it to circle her nub. "Say what?"

Sin knocked her hand away. He would be the one to give his wife pleasure. It was his duty after all. His duty and his obsession. He flattened his tongue and slowly swiped from her opening to her clit. "I can do this all damn day. Never allowing you to tip over the edge." He couldn't. He would go mad if he didn't bury himself ballocks deep within her soon. "Say the words I need to hear."

Taking his hand, she placed it at the base of her throat, holding it in place with both of her own.

He squeezed lightly.

"I love you, Sin." He felt as much as he heard the words, the vibrations from her throat tickling his palm. "You mean more to me than you can ever know."

The animal within roared in triumph. He crawled up her body and pushed inside.

She had given him everything. Her body. Her trust. Her love. And now a bairn.

He had worried that they were too opposite to ever suit. She was everything intelligent and deliberate, rational and composed. He was decidedly not.

But he could make her come undone when it counted. Match him scratch for scratch, bite for bite. Their differences out of the bedroom were what made them strong as a couple; their similarities under the sheets what brought passion to their marriage.

She was perfect for him, and he would strive every day to be her equal.

He dropped his forehead to hers.

Her arms, her scent, her heat surrounded him, muddling his mind even as his senses thrilled.

He said the only words his awe-struck brain could conjure. The only thing he knew with certainty to be true. "You are my heart, Winnifred. My love without end.

"You are mine."

* * * *

About the Author

Like almost one-third of all romance writers, Alyson Chase is a former attorney. (Seriously, what is with all of us disillusioned lawyers?) She happily ditched those suits and now works in her pajamas writing about men's briefs instead of legal briefs. When she's not writing, she's probably engaged in one of her favorite hobbies: napping, eating, or martial arts. (That last one almost makes up for the first two, right?) She also writes humorous, small-town, contemporary romance novels under the name Allyson Charles.

Connect with Alyson at:

www.alysonchase.com
www.facebook.com/AlysonChaseAuthor
Twitter: @1alysonchase
Email: alysonchaseauthor@gmail.com

Printed in Great Britain
by Amazon

55362774R00187